STORM WATER

Set on the Isle of Dogs during the Blitz, Storm Water is the final volume of Peter Ling's Docklands saga. Marcus Judge, head of the Brotherhood, is succeeded by his nephews Jimmy and Bertie, whose lack of scruples ensure that the family business—and the Brotherhood—continue to thrive. A newcomer, Tony Jasper, displays an uncanny knowledge of the Judges' secret past. Another stranger, a US army colonel, throws light on an ancient and horrific tragedy. As the war ends, the final strands of the Judge family saga are woven together. The Brotherhood is dissolved, but new alliances are already being formed...

For Yvette Goulden
with grateful thanks for her help and encouragement

STORM WATER

by
Peter Ling

Magna Large Print Books
Long Preston, North Yorkshire,
England.

British Library Cataloguing in Publication Data.

Ling, Peter
  Storm water.

  A catalogue record for this book is
  available from the British Library

  ISBN 0-7505-0756-X

First published in Great Britain by Random House UK Ltd., 1993

Copyright © 1993 by Peter Ling

Cover illustration by arrangement with Random House UK Ltd.

The right of Peter Ling to be identified as the author of this
work has been asserted by him in accordance with the Copyright,
Designs and Patents Act, 1988.

Published in Large Print December, 1995 by arrangement with
Random House UK Ltd.

Magna Large Print is an imprint of
Library Magna Books Ltd.
Printed and bound in Great Britain by
T.J. Press (Padstow) Ltd., Cornwall, PL28 8RW.

Acknowledgements

Once again, I owe a great debt to Christopher Lloyd and the Local History collection at the Bancroft Library. I would also like to thank the Island History Trust and Eve Hostettler, editor of *The Island at War,* and all those Islanders who contributed to it.

Other invaluable reference books were: *How We Lived Then* by Norman Longmate (Arrow Books); *Under Fire* (London Fire Brigade Headquarters); *The London Blitz: A Fireman's Tale* by Cyril Demarne (Newham Parents' Centre Publications); *Cockney Campaign* by Frank R Lewey (Stanley Paul & Co); *London at War* by Joanna Mack and Steve Humphries (Sidgwick and Jackson); *The Blitz* by Constantine Fitzgibbon (Macdonald) and *A People's War* by Peter Lewis (Methuen).

THE JUDGE FAMILY

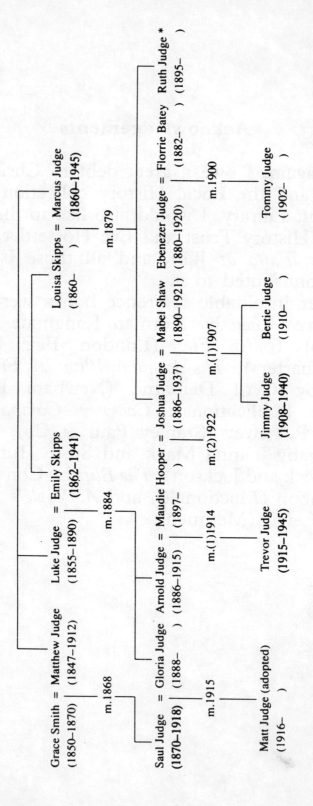

Grace Smith = Matthew Judge
(1850–1870)   (1847–1912)
        m.1868

Luke Judge = Emily Skipps
(1855–1890)   (1862–1941)
        m.1884

Louisa Skipps = Marcus Judge
(1860–)   (1860–1945)
        m.1879

Ebenezer Judge = Florrie Batey   Ruth Judge *
(1880–1920)   (1882–)   (1895–)
        m.1900

Tommy Judge
(1902–)

Saul Judge = Gloria Judge
(1870–1918)   (1888–)
        m.1915

Arnold Judge = Maudie Hooper
(1886–1915)   (1897–)
        m.(1)1914

Joshua Judge = Mabel Shaw
(1886–1937)   (1890–1921)
        m.(2)1922

Jimmy Judge
(1908–1940)

Bertie Judge
(1910–)

Trevor Judge
(1915–1945)

Matt Judge (adopted)
(1916–)

*see O'Dell family tree

THE O'DELL FAMILY   THE KLEIBER FAMILY

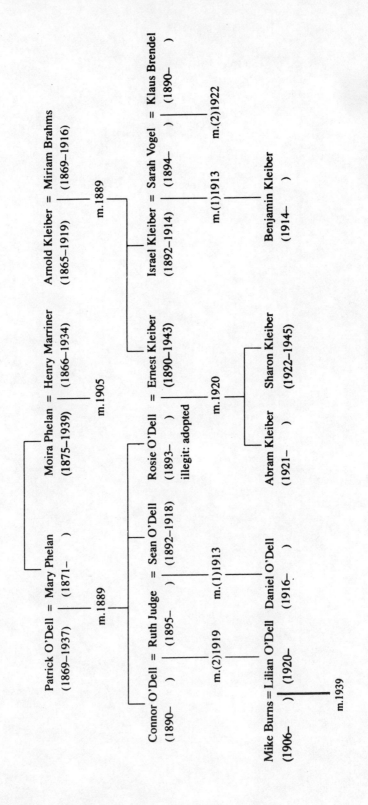

Prologue

Soon it would be dark; a clammy mist was seeping in off the river. It was not the kind of evening for a stroll through the Isle of Dogs—that was why he had chosen it. There wouldn't be many people about on a night like this.

The pale young man's eyes were hidden behind dark glasses, but he walked swiftly and silently, purposeful and sure-footed as a cat. The soft brim of his hat was turned down, and his coat-collar turned up against the moisture in the air. The smell of sea-salt and tar and soot and poverty was in his nostrils, sickening him.

Lighted windows in a saloon bar were mirrored in puddles on the roadway; oily patches glittered like rainbows. Picking his way carefully between them, the pale young man crossed the street. He had no desire to visit the Three Jolly Watermen; he wanted to see, without being seen.

He took a side turning, then another, until he came to a narrow street—so dark, he could not read the numbers above the doors, but he would have found his way blindfold, he had been there so many times.

He knocked once, then waited; he did not need to knock twice. The door opened and a grey-haired old man with a straggling beard stood back to let him in. They went through to a back room, lit by one reeking oil-lamp.

The young man came straight to the point. 'Well? What have you got for me?'

The old man, who was in his seventies, sat down slowly and painfully in a sagging armchair.

'Not much,' he said, sniffing, and wiped his nose on the back of his hand. 'Things don't change a great deal... The O'Dells are still at the pub—Marcus Judge is still living at the Rope Walk, though I ain't seen him meself. He don't go out nowadays, excepting to Chapel of a Sunday. They say the old devil's off his rocker... There's nothing else happened.'

'Not good enough.' The young man shook his head impatiently: 'I don't pay you to tell me nothing's happened.'

'It ain't my fault there's no news,' whined the old man. 'I never asked for your money, did I? And never asked you to come badgering me, neither. All I want is to be left alone, see? So go away, and don't come back!'

'*Don't say that...*' The young man's hand shot out, gripping his greasy, collarless shirt, half-choking him. 'Don't you ever tell me what to do. It's your job to find out what goes on round here, and let me know—let me know *everything*—understand? Because I'll keep coming back, make no mistake about that.'

The old man struggled to get free, gasping, 'D'you mean—some day—you might come back for good?'

The pale young man smiled. 'For good—or for bad. Both, probably.'

10

1

For Ruth, the war began when the pillar-box exploded.

Officially, war was declared on 3 September, 1939, but when she looked back on it afterwards, Ruth always remembered the sunny Sunday afternoon in June when the bomb went off, and her world changed completely.

It was such a pleasant day, too. As they climbed the slope of Greenwich Park, watching some children flying kites on the crest of the hill, she turned to her husband and smiled, 'Now are you glad I made you come with me?'

'If I'd known we were walking so far, I'd have worn my other boots.'

'You old misery! Admit it, this is better than frowsting upstairs in the bedroom with the *News of the World*. A nice peaceful walk in the Park will do you a power of good.'

'Peaceful, is it?' After a lifetime in London, Connor's Irish brogue was still as strong as ever. 'Would you call that a peaceful sight now?'

He wasn't looking at the bright paper kites floating on the breeze, but further down the hill, where scores of men—some in shirtsleeves, some stripped to the waist—were busy digging trenches; deep and long, with mounds of newly-turned earth on either side, cutting raw scars across the grass.

'They have to take precautions, just in case,' said Ruth. 'But we must hope for the best. Maybe there won't be a war after all.'

'Don't be fooling yourself,' said Connor. 'Haven't you noticed? People don't say *if* there's a war any more—now they say *when* instead.'

Ruth bit her lip. She did not tell him that when she had gone to early mass that morning, she had lit a candle and prayed for peace, as she had done regularly ever since the Germans marched into Czechoslovakia, three months before.

They stood beneath a chestnut tree that still had a few pink-and-white flowering candles clinging to it, and looked at one another in silence. Impulsively, she put her hand on his arm.

'It will be all right, won't it?' she asked, 'Nothing terrible's going to happen to us—or the children?'

'There's going to be a war,' he told her quietly. 'But we'll get through it somehow, I'm sure of that.'

They stared deep into each other's eyes, and she tried to smile. 'Then I'm sure too,' she said.

Strangers passing by glanced at them curiously; for they made a striking couple. At forty-four, Ruth O'Dell was still a beautiful woman; tall and slim, she had kept her figure, and her chestnut hair was hardly touched with grey.

Connor's dark hair was pepper-and-salt by now, and receding from the temples; his weather-beaten face seamed with deep furrows, and in the past few years he had put on some weight—but his shoulders were still broad and strong, his muscular arms as powerful as ever. Something in his bearing indicated that he had once earned his living as a prize-fighter, before he gave up the ring and took over the management of the family pub—the Three Jolly Watermen, on the Isle of Dogs. Five years older than Ruth, Connor O'Dell was a fine figure of a man.

He gripped Ruth's hand. 'Aunt Moira may be awake by now—let's go.' They turned and began to retrace their steps, strolling down the hill.

The night before, there had been a telephone message at the pub; Con's mother took the call, and reported caustically afterwards: 'That was Moira's maid. Seemingly, Madam's too high and mighty to come to the telephone herself these days. Well, she says she's got a touch of summer 'flu, and she's taken to her bed. She was wondering if we'd be kind enough to go over and visit her tomorrow. Trust Moira to ring up on a Saturday night, when we're full to bursting with customers!'

Mary O'Dell was fond of her sister, but she could never quite get over the fact that Moira had married a wealthy man. By now both sisters had been widowed, but while Mary, at sixty-eight, was still doing her bit in the pub, serving behind the bar or helping Ruth in the kitchen, Moira Marriner lived alone with two servants to look after her, at a fine house in Greenwich, just off Crooms Hill.

Next day, at breakfast-time, Mary was still brooding over it. 'Well, I can't go to see

13

her, that's for sure,' she concluded. 'I've four members of the Blessed Rosary Guild coming round for tea. But maybe the children would enjoy the outing? You'll have to make my excuses, Danny-boy, and tell your great-aunt I hope she'll soon be feeling brighter.'

'I can't go either,' said her grandson. 'I've promised to meet a friend—we're going to the flicks.'

'Would that be a *lady*-friend, by any chance?' Lil's eyes twinkled as she teased her brother. 'What's her name—or can't you remember? They come and go so quick, I'm surprised you keep track of them all!'

Daniel and Lilian—aged twenty-three and nineteen respectively—had long since given up trying to convince the rest of the family that they were no longer 'children'; but Daniel drew the line at a nickname which dated back to his babyhood.

'It's Dan, Grandma, not Danny-boy,' he reminded her automatically, but without any hope of convincing her.

Ruth looked across the breakfast-table and marvelled that her two babies could have grown up into a young man and woman; it seemed to have happened when she wasn't looking, taking her completely by surprise.

'That leaves you, Lil. Will you come to Greenwich with me?' she asked. 'Shall we take Auntie Moira some flowers?'

'Sorry, Mum, you'll have to count me out. It's Sunday,' said Lil.

Every Sunday afternoon, provided he wasn't

14

on weekend duty, Lil went out with Mike Burns, of the River Police. Come rain or shine, they spent the rest of the day together—sometimes going for a walk in the Island Gardens, or to Poplar recreation ground. If the weather was unpromising, they would take a bus-ride instead, or travel 'up West' on the Underground, for some window-shopping or a trip to the museums at South Kensington.

Ruth smiled at her daughter, and suppressed an inward sigh. 'I was forgetting,' she said. 'Give him my love, won't you?'

She was very aware of the contrast between her son and her daughter. Lil was right about Dan; he had a wide circle of girl-friends, and although he was always making new conquests, he seemed unable to settle for one regular partner. Lil, on the other hand, had been going steady with Mike Burns for over two years, and though she had never so much as looked at another man, they were still no more than 'good friends'. Of course Mike was a lot older than Lil, but they were obviously devoted to one another—and yet Ruth sometimes wondered if they would ever get married.

Shaking her head as if to throw aside these doubts and fears, she addressed her husband: 'That settles it, Con. You'll have to give up your precious Sunday afternoon for once, and come to Greenwich with me.'

'I'll do no such thing!' he retorted. 'Me? Give up my one bit of free time in the whole week?'

'My heart bleeds for you; I'm sure it must be

15

a terrible burden, running a public-house...but Moira's asked us to go, and she *is* your aunt and I'm not going all that way on my own, so that's that!'

In the end Connor had been forced to don his Sunday-best suit and, still objecting furiously, he accompanied his wife through the pedestrian tunnel that led from the southern tip of the Island, under the Thames, emerging on the Surrey side.

They continued up Crooms Hill, to the neat detached house with its trim front garden where lilac blossom was beginning to turn brown at the edges, making way for the first pink buds on the rose-bushes.

The parlourmaid who opened the front door apologised in a whisper. 'Madam's taking an afternoon nap. She had rather a bad night... Would you care to wait in the parlour until she wakes up?'

Connor took a deep breath, but Ruth forestalled him. 'We'll take a walk in the Park and come back in half an hour. May I leave these with you?'

She handed over the bunch of wallflowers which they had brought for the invalid, and steered Connor away before he could express his feelings, thankful that they were safely out of earshot before he roared: 'How d'you like that? She drags us all this way, and then can't be bothered to stay awake long enough to say hello!'

But the half-hour had passed soon enough, and now they were on their way back to Mrs

Marriner. As they passed the men digging air-raid trenches, Connor muttered, 'That's no way to prepare for a war. If the Germans decide to attack this country, a few slit-trenches in the parks and some homemade air-raid shelters in the backyards aren't going to stop them. Anyhow, we shouldn't be defending ourselves at all. That's the golden rule in boxing—take the other feller by surprise. We should go in quick, and go in fighting! If there's going to be air-raids, what's the good of sitting around, waiting for the first bomb to fall?'

The words were scarcely out of his mouth when the bomb exploded.

They felt the rush of air as the blast hit them, and the earth shook beneath their feet; a second later, the detonation made their ears ring. Instinctively, Connor threw his arms round Ruth, dragging her to the ground and throwing himself on top of her.

For an instant, nothing happened at all, then the stillness was broken by a shrill twittering and a flurry of wings as a flock of birds rose from all the trees in the neighbourhood, followed immediately by confused shouts and screams, and the sound of running feet.

Ruth held Connor tightly, gasping, 'It's the war—it's begun.'

They soon found out that it hadn't. A noisy crowd gathered at the end of Mrs Marriner's road; only a few minutes after the explosion, a policeman was already putting up a barrier. Beyond it, smoke poured from a pillar-box with a sharp metallic split in the iron casing, and the

17

scarlet paintwork black and blistered.

'What is it? What's happened?' Everyone was talking at once. 'Is it the Germans?'

The policeman's hands were shaking as he put up a No Entry sign, but he made an effort to keep his voice calm and steady. 'Not much chance of that. By the looks of it, this is the IRA.'

Since the beginning of the year, terrorists from the Irish Republic had been keeping up an intermittent campaign against Britain. Bombs had created havoc in Southwark, in the tube stations at Tottenham Court Road and Leicester Square. Now they had begun a new type of attack; within the last few days, nearly thirty bombs had gone off in pillar-boxes throughout the United Kingdom. As the policeman cordoned off the road, he remarked wearily, 'Seems like our Irish friends have been making a ruddy nuisance of themselves again.' Then he broke off, saying sharply, 'Hello! Where do you think you're going, sir?'

Connor, who had been trying to guide Ruth past the barrier, replied, 'We're visiting a relative of mine, an elderly lady at number fifteen.'

'Don't you see the notice, sir? No Entry—there's always the danger of a second explosion. It's for your own protection.'

'But I must go to my aunt; she's not well. She'll have been disturbed by the explosion—'

'I'm sorry, sir, but orders are orders. Nobody's allowed into this road till the experts have examined the damage. You'll just have to be patient.'

18

But 'Connor's patience was already wearing thin. 'For God's sake, man, I have to make sure the old lady's all right—'

He was interrupted by a voice from the crowd: 'D'you hear the way he talks? He's one of the Micks himself. I bet you a quid he's the one what done it—and he's come back to gloat...'

An angry murmur broke out. Ruth grabbed Connor's arm as he shouted back, 'Come here and repeat that, whoever you are. We'll see if you're man enough to accuse me to my face!'

The policeman took out his notebook, and cleared his throat. 'If I might have your name and address, sir...'

Before Connor could tell him to go to hell, Ruth intervened quickly: 'We're Mr and Mrs O'Dell, from the Three Jolly Watermen—that's a public-house on the Isle of Dogs, just off the Manchester Road.'

'Isle of Dogs, is it? Emerald Isle, more like!' jeered the voice from the crowd, and Connor lowered his head, about to charge into the mob. It took the combined efforts of Ruth, the policeman and three able-bodied bystanders, to hold him back, and by the time they released him, the unknown accuser had taken to his heels.

On the way home, Connor was very silent, and Ruth knew better than to try and make polite conversation. When they finally reached the Watermen, Con said grimly, 'My own countrymen—setting off bombs, behaving like hooligans. The English running round like a flock of geese, hissing and squawking...and all the while, the Germans are getting themselves ready to move in and take over the world—and nobody's doing a blind thing to stop them.'

'Somebody's got to stop them,' said Dan O'Dell.

It was Monday morning and he was on his way to work at the Royal Victoria Dock, but he had made a short detour to call in at an Army Recruiting Office.

The khaki-clad Sergeant behind the desk looked up and gave Dan an appraising grin. 'That's the spirit, lad,' he said. 'All right, then—take a seat, and let's be having your particulars. Name, address, present place of employment...'

Dan gave him the information, explaining, 'I'm an apprentice Dock Engineer at the Royal Vic, but I've already told my gaffer I'm thinking of signing on as a Reservist. That means I can carry on at work as usual, and go for Army training in my spare time, doesn't it?'

'Yes—more or less. Reservists have to put in a few weeks of full-time training every year.'

'But the way things are now, I might be called into active service sooner than that?'

The Sergeant looked him over thoughtfully, 'That's right, son. As and when war is declared, you'll be wanted right away...OK?'

Dan nodded. 'OK,' he said.

The Sergeant filled out the rest of the form, then rubberstamped it, and handed Dan a printed card.

'See this address? You'll have to go there

for your medical before this can go through. Take the card with you when you report for the examination. And—good luck.'

Dan was given some time off from work to go for his medical. By three o'clock that afternoon he was sitting in a draughty drill-hall, stark naked and shivering in a screened-off cubicle.

'Next!' bawled a voice, and he stood up, shuffling gingerly over a dusty plank floor, hoping he would not get splinters in his bare feet.

The Medical Officer gave him a cursory check-up, pulling and pushing him, slapping and probing various parts of his anatomy, and scribbling some cryptic notes on a clipboard. When he was satisfied, he told Dan, 'Very well—go and put your clothes on. Next!'

As Dan walked back to the cubicle, he passed another naked man of about his own age, on his way to the Medical Officer. They gave one another sidelong glances, at first in embarrassment, then in sudden amazement.

'Dan O'Dell! What are you doing here?'

'Matt Judge! Same as you, I should imagine.'

'I said *next!*' snapped the MO, impatiently.

'Better not keep him waiting. I'll see you afterwards,' said Dan, and hurried away to get dressed.

A few minutes later, as he was tying his shoelaces, he heard Matt return to the next cubicle. He called over the partition: 'They finished with you as well?'

'Seems like it.' Matt's reply was muffled, and Dan guessed that he was tugging his vest over

21

his head. 'You going back to the Island now?'

'Yes, I've got the afternoon off.' Dan pushed aside the screen and joined Matt, adding tentatively, 'If you're going that way, we might as well walk back together.'

Still in his underwear, Matt turned away, flexing his muscles as he shrugged into his shirt, and mumbling, 'Don't mind if I do.'

The two young men were very different in appearance. Dan O'Dell was tall and rangy with long limbs and alert eyes, his face open and lively, whereas Matt Judge was rugged and heavily-built, his large, impassive face concealing his thoughts.

Though their mothers were cousins, there was no actual blood-tie between them, for Matt was the adopted son of Gloria and the late Saul Judge. As children, the boys had been friends and schoolmates, but as they grew up their paths diverged. Dan was a staunch left-winger, while Matt had joined the British Union of Fascists under Oswald Mosley's leadership; they had not met or spoken since the time of the Cable Street Riots, three years earlier.

As he watched Matt pull on a pair of grubby canvas trousers and an oily woollen sweater, Dan asked, 'What are you doing these days? Still working on the river?'

'Yeah—following in me dad's footsteps, like. I've got me own wherry now, taking passengers over the water, but I s'pose I'll have to lay the boat up for a while, now I've joined this lark.'

Dan smiled. 'You and me both.' Matt's face cracked into an answering grin. Dan remembered that they had been on good terms once, long ago, and he said impulsively, 'Come on back to the pub, and I'll stand you a drink.'

'It ain't opening-time yet,' objected Matt.

'That's all right,' said Dan cheerfully. 'It'll be on the house.'

They entered the Watermen through the side door; in the saloon bar, Huw Pritchard was mopping the floor.

'You're back early,' began Huw, with the Welsh lilt in his words, but then he recognised Matt and his expression changed.

'Yes, I ran across an old mate,' said Dan. 'You remember Matt?'

'I know Mr Judge,' said Huw, unsmiling. 'I'll leave you to pour your own beers, Dan. I have work to do.'

Using his mop as a walking-stick, he limped out of the bar. For many years, Huw had been a stevedore and a member of the Brotherhood at Jubilee Wharf, until he was seriously injured when a load of timber slipped and fell on him. After that, he would have known hard times if Connor had not offered him a job at the pub, where he soon learned a new trade. By and large, he got on well with the customers, though he nursed a deep loathing for Mosley's fascist bullies. If Dan chose to bring Matt Judge back to the pub, that was his look-out, but Huw would not stay and be civil to the man.

In his absence, Dan pulled two pints of beer with practised skill, and passed one over the counter to his guest, saying, 'Your good health.'

23

Matt lifted his glass and sampled it. 'Ah—that's a drop of good stuff,' he said, before taking a second, longer swig.

An appreciative silence was broken by the sound of the side door opening again, and footsteps hurrying down the passage. Lil put her head into the saloon, 'Anyone at home? Hello, Dan—back already?' She glanced at Matt. 'Hello. Fancy seeing you.' She too had known Matt since childhood, and like her brother she had fallen out with him when he joined the Blackshirts, but she still saw him from time to time, for since leaving school she had worked as an assistant at Gloria Judge's hairdressing salon in Millwall Road.

'You're home early as well,' said Dan. 'I thought you didn't knock off till half-past five?'

'Things were quiet this afternoon, so Glory said I might as well go home. What's your excuse?'

'The gaffer let me have the afternoon off, on account of I'm serving my King and Country!' Dan explained. 'I went and signed on, then I had to go for a medical, to make sure I've got the usual number of arms and legs...and that's where I ran into Matt. Talk about a small world, we've both enlisted on the same day.'

'Congratulations. Have you told Mum and Dad yet?'

'Not yet.'

'Better break it gently; they're not going to be best pleased.'

She turned to go, and Dan called after her: 'Stay and have a drink to wish us luck!'

'You know very well I don't drink.'

'You could propose a toast to a couple of gallant lads in fizzy lemon, couldn't you?'

'No thanks, I've got better things to do,' she retorted, and left the bar without another word or look in Matt's direction.

He shifted uncomfortably. 'Maybe I'd better be pushing off, seeing as I don't seem to be too popular round here.'

'Oh, don't be daft—take no notice of Lil. She's remembering the bad old days—but we're on the same side now, aren't we?'

'Reckon so.' Matt buried his face in the beer-mug again, then looked up, saying artfully, 'If you'n me's mates again, what if I was to ask you a favour, eh?'

'Depends what it is.'

'Well, Mum's been and got one of them air-raid shelters delivered, and she wants me to dig a hole in the yard and get it fixed up. It'll take a month of Sundays on me own, but if you was to help me, we could get it done in no time—so how about it?'

Dan sighed, but agreed to go to Millwall Road the following evening and lend a hand. Matt finished up his beer and left, and then it was time for supper, since the O'Dell family always had an early 'high tea' before the pub opened for business.

They sat together round the kitchen table and Connor's mother said grace; they all repeated 'Amen' after her, except for Huw, who bowed his head but—as an avowed Communist and a lapsed Welsh Baptist—elected to remain silent.

As they dug into slices of home-baked gammon and salad, Lil kicked Dan under the table, and he yelped: 'Ouch! What was that for?'

'Weren't you going to tell us some news?' she prompted him.

'Oh, yes.' Dan squared his shoulders and admitted that he had signed on as a Reservist, together with Matt. 'So, if there should be a war—'

He left the sentence hanging in mid-air, and Connor broke in gruffly: 'There's no if about it. It's only a matter of time now.'

Mary O'Dell crossed herself. 'Holy mother of God, I pray it won't come to that.' She rounded on her grandson. 'Why did you have to go and do such a thing? Isn't it bad enough for them as gets called up whether they want to or not, without you volunteering?'

Connor defended his son. 'The boy's only doing his duty. In any case, they'll be calling all the men up before long... I've half a mind to sign on myself.'

'Don't say such things, even in jest,' Mary scolded him. 'Have some consideration for your poor wife's feelings, can't you?'

Connor frowned, and looked along the table. Facing him, at the far end, Ruth managed a convincing smile, while in her heart she was beseeching God: *'Don't let there be a war—don't let Danny go— Don't let anyone be hurt...'* But all she said was, 'If Dan feels he should go, I wouldn't stand in his way. We'll all be proud of him.'

'And I promise you, I wasn't joking,' Connor told his mother. 'I tell you, I'd give my eye-teeth to join up again. It's a lot of stupid red-tape nonsense, so it is, putting an age limit on volunteers. Didn't I fight in the last war? And aren't I as much of a man today as I was then?'

'You're also twenty years older,' Ruth pointed out, trying to keep her tone light. 'After all, you're nearly fifty.'

'Not a bit of it!' Con's clenched fist struck the table-top, making the cutlery shiver. 'I'm barely a day over forty-nine!' When they all burst out laughing, his face darkened, and he grumbled, 'Will you hold your row and listen to me? If they won't let me into the Army, I'll go into Civil Defence—Heavy Rescue duty, that's the job for me... How about it, Huw? Are you going to sign on as well, to keep me company?'

Huw had been silent; now he pushed back his chair and rose to his feet. 'Somehow I doubt if I'd be much use,' he said, hobbling out of the room on his gammy leg. 'If you'll excuse me, it's nearly opening-time.'

They all looked at one another, and Ruth said softly, 'Oh, Con, couldn't you have been more tactful?'

'Damn and blast it—I never think of him being crippled.' Connor was about to stand up. 'I'd better go and have a word with him.'

But Ruth stopped him. 'No, you'll only make it worse. And anyway, you were talking

27

nonsense. If you two were to leave the pub, who would be left? You're not expecting Mam and me to run the place on our own, I hope?'

'No, I suppose not.' Unhappily, he sank back into his chair. 'All the same, I'd like to feel I'm doing my bit.'

'There'll be plenty of work for all of us, I'm sure of that,' Ruth told him. 'Civil Defence are crying out for help. If you and Huw want to sign on as part-time ARP wardens, they'll welcome you with open arms.'

Con wrinkled his nose without enthusiasm. 'Well, we'll see about that. I'll make some enquiries tomorrow.'

And in her heart, Ruth continued to repeat the same desperate plea: *'Dear God, don't let there be a war. Don't let anyone be hurt...'*

Dan was as good as his word, and on Tuesday evening he turned up at Millwall Road, ready to help Matt build the air-raid shelter.

When he knocked at the door of the hairdressing salon, Glory came to let him in then took him through to the back of the kitchen, where her mother, Emily Judge, was peering short-sightedly at a printed page of directions and looking extremely flustered.

'Here's Danny come to help us, Ma—isn't that nice of him?' said Glory. 'Would you like a cup of tea before you start, Dan? Or something stronger to wet your whistle?'

Glory Judge was one of those indomitable women who never let anybody or anything get the better of them; not even time itself.

At fifty-one, she no longer had the deliciously curving shape of the pretty blonde she used to be, but her figure, discreetly corseted, bulged in all the right places, her face was a masterpiece of make-up, and she had used all her professional skill on a glorious creation of bright golden curls, piled high on her head.

'Nothing for me, thanks,' said Dan. 'Where's Matt?'

'Out in the yard, hoping he's got all the pieces,' grinned Glory. 'It's going to be a regular jigsaw, putting them together. We can't make head or tail of the instructions, can we, Ma?'

Unlike her confident, cheery daughter, Aunt Emily had always been a martyr to nervous anxiety. Her bony fingers fluttered constantly to her face, plucking at her lips, dabbing wisps of snow-white hair back into place, and turning the printed paper over and over, trying to make sense of it.

'I'm very much afraid they've sent us the wrong shelter,' she explained in her breathless, quavery voice. 'It says here that this one belongs to somebody called Anderson...'

Glory threw a despairing glance at Dan, and took the paper from her mother's trembling fingers, 'No, Ma—that's its name. It's called an Anderson shelter after some big pot in the Government. Come on, Dan—let's go and see how Matt's getting on.'

Behind the shop there was a small patch of trodden earth. Some of the other people in the terrace had struggled to turn their yards into gardens, wrestling with poor soil, brickbats and

29

broken glass in an attempt to produce a row of runner beans here, a few gallant geraniums there—and now, with their hearts breaking, the gardeners were destroying their little havens of greenery to dig holes and plant chunks of corrugated steel.

Glory had never bothered to make a garden; to her, the yard was a storage area for old packing-cases and empty bottles. Today there were curved steel sheets propped against the wall; Matt had marked out an area with string, stretched between pegs, and was making a small preliminary excavation at one corner.

He looked up, saying hopefully, 'All we've got to do is dig out some earth and shove these into the ground, bolt the pieces together, cover it all up with the dirt what we've dug out—and Bob's yer uncle!'

'Are you sure that's the right size?' Glory compared the marked-out area with the instructions. 'Seven foot six long by six foot wide, to a depth of four feet... It doesn't look very big, does it?'

'It'll seem big enough by the time we've dug it out,' said Dan, taking off his jacket and rolling up his sleeves.

'Well, I've been down the street, borrowing spades. We've got three altogether, so I can give you a hand,' said Glory. 'I've done a good many things in my time, though I never worked as a navvy before...but I know they always spit on their hands before they start!'

She soon discovered that spit and determination were not enough; it was very hard work. After twenty minutes, she straightened up, saying, 'I think I'll just slip indoors and make sure Ma's all right. And I'll put the kettle on while I'm there. We could all do with a nice hot cuppa.'

Left alone, the two men carried on doggedly, each determined not to be outdone by the other. After a few more minutes Dan grunted, 'It's a funny thing. When I was a kid, I sometimes thought it must be wonderful to work on a farm—living in the country, out in the fresh air, digging potatoes. I'm beginning to realise now, it must be a dog's life.'

'Bloody murder,' agreed Matt, resting on his spade. 'I never wanted to be a farmer—never wanted to go away from London neither, come to that.'

'And here we are, the two of us—about to go off and join the perishing Army.' Dan wiped the sweat off his forehead with the back of his hand. 'We need our brains tested!'

'Still, I'm glad we're both going,' said Matt. 'I didn't fancy setting off with a load of strangers.'

Dan agreed. 'Let's hope they send us to the same regiment.'

When Glory reappeared with mugs of tea, they decided to take a breather for five minutes, and sat on a mound of earth with their backs against the wall. Stirring his tea, Dan said awkwardly, 'If you don't mind me asking—do you still go to those Mosley meetings? I haven't heard much about the BUF lately.'

'Nah.' Matt shook his head gloomily. 'There's been a lot of trouble this past year. That Unity What's-her-name turned up at one of them

31

socialist rallies wearing a swastika armband—she nearly got lynched. She's gone over to Germany now—and our Leader's thick as thieves with Hitler and that lot. I reckon it's got a bit warm for 'em over here, the way things have turned out.'

'Very likely. What about Jimmy and Bertie? Still loyal Party members?'

'Shouldn't think so. They're too busy at Jubilee Wharf, running their Brotherhood. It wouldn't do for people to start calling them Nazis, would it? I dare say they've put their black shirts away for a while, and all.'

'I'm glad to hear it.' Dan smiled. 'Like I said—we're both on the same side now.'

'Yeah, I s'pose so. Though mind you...' Matt hesitated. 'I still think there's a lot of sense in what Mosley had to say. If you ask me, old Hitler's got the right idea.' He leaned closer. 'It's them bloody Jews what started all the trouble in the first place...'

Before Dan could argue, Glory reappeared with a teapot, saying, 'Ready for second cups? Here—you're supposed to be digging, not chin-wagging! It'll be dark before you've finished, at this rate!'

Dan sighed, and picked up his spade. Even if they were on the same side now, they were still fighting different battles.

Digging the hole took longer than they had expected, and it wasn't until Thursday evening that they managed to get the steel walls into position.

Lil watched from the back door, taking off the lilac overall she wore in the salon, and called to Dan: 'I'm getting ready to go home. How much longer are you going to be?'

'Another hour at least, maybe more,' he answered wearily.

'Can't rush a job like this,' said Matt. 'It's got to be done proper.'

'In that case I won't wait,' she decided.

As she turned to go, Gloria yelled from inside the house: 'Lil! Come here, will you? You've got a visitor!'

The blinds had been pulled down in the shop, and in the half-light Lil could only see the outline of a man silhouetted against the windows—but she knew him immediately.

'Mike...' she said, going to meet him.

Gloria watched them fondly; she had had a soft spot for Mike Burns ever since he was a police constable on the neighbourhood beat. She would never forget the night he had rescued Lil; Glory was glad he'd had the sense to bring her back to the salon, instead of taking her home to her parents.

'I'll leave you two together, then.' She smiled to herself, and went off to the kitchen.

'I didn't expect to see you,' said Lil, going towards him with her hands outstretched. He took both hands in his, but they remained at arms-length; they never embraced or kissed—this was their only physical contact. 'I thought you were on night-duty this week?'

'So I am, but not tonight. I only got a couple of hours' kip this morning. It's been a busy old

33

day...I had to come and tell you about it.'

'Why? What's happened?' She knew at once that something had changed. She could feel the excitement tingling through his fingertips, and it scared her a little.

'Are you going home to the pub?' he asked. 'All right if I walk back with you?'

'Of course. Hang on while I get my bag and put my things on.' She threw a scarf over her head, and he helped her into her light summer coat; accidentally, his body brushed hers, and she tensed slightly. He felt it too, but neither of them referred to it.

'I'm off now, Glory!' called Lil. 'Good night!' Out in the street, Mike offered his arm, and they set off together. 'Well, go on—tell me,' she said. 'This is my last week in the district,' he began. 'I'm leaving the River Police.'

'You've not been transferred again?' she asked in dismay. 'Where are they sending you this time?'

'I don't know yet, I've got to wait for orders. But it's not in the Police—I've signed on for the Navy, as a regular.'

She stopped dead, swinging round to face him. 'No! You can't—you mustn't do that!'

'I can't stay in this job while all the others are going off to fight. The Navy's a good life—best of the Services by a mile. And with all the training I've had already on motor-launches, they say I'll stand a good chance of promotion.'

'But that means you'll have to go away, doesn't it?'

'That's the general idea.' He forced a grin. 'They don't keep His Majesty's fleet in dry-dock all the time, you know.'

'How will I manage without you?' she asked.

The sound of an aircraft engine made them glance up. Gleaming in the evening sunlight, a small bi-plane was flying along the river, towing a pennant bearing the message: JOIN THE AFS.

'What is the AFS?' she asked.

'Auxiliary Fire Service,' said Mike. 'They're looking for volunteers.'

It seemed to be a sign from heaven. On the spur of the moment, Lil exclaimed: 'That's what I'll do—I'll join up as well! If I keep busy, I shan't have time to miss you so much.'

His hand tightened upon her arm as he said, 'I'll get leave every now and then, and we can write to each other, can't we? That's how we started—writing letters.'

Three years before, when Mike was a constable on the Island, he had been pounding the beat one night when he came across Lil, huddled up on the pavement near the gates of the Jubilee Wharf. She was sixteen then. She had been to a party given by her uncle Joshua Judge, the Chairman of the dockers' Brotherhood, and at the party, his son Jimmy had amused himself by getting Lil drunk, and then raping her. When Mike found her, she was bruised and bleeding, still fuddled with wine; too frightened and too ashamed to go home to her family.

Glory had cared for her and lied for her and spun a story to explain her absence from home

35

until the following day; she had also urged PC Burns to arrest Jimmy Judge and charge him. Mike had to explain that they'd never get him into court. The assault had taken place in the dark, Lil had been drunk at the time, and Jimmy had armed himself with friends who would swear he had never left them all the evening.

Mike could hold out no hope of justice for Lil. All he had to offer her was good advice, and—more important—tender and loving friendship.

She had grown to rely on Constable Burns, and they had been seeing one another regularly ever since. When he applied for a transfer to the River Police, and was sent away for training, they began to write to one another, conducting a kind of courtship on paper. By now Mike and Lil knew a great deal about each other; he loved her very much, and she...

Lil did not know what she felt for Mike. She only knew that she hated the prospect of being parted from him.

As they approached the Watermen he asked, 'Are you doing anything special tonight? Or can we go out for a meal?'

'Nowhere grand, I'm afraid, just fish and chips. If you'd fancy it?'

'Yes—I'd like that.'

The pub hadn't long been open when they walked in. Lil found her father serving in the saloon; Connor acknowledged Mike with a friendly nod and said, 'Seeing you're not in uniform, will you take a drink with me?'

'No thanks, Mr O'Dell. I've asked Lil out for

a bite of supper, if that's OK?'

'Why not? This place is at sixes and sevens tonight.' Con told his daughter, 'Your Mum and your Grandma are off out any minute, so it looks like Huw and me will be running the pub by ourselves.'

Lil stared, puzzled. 'Off out? What do you mean?'

Another customer walked up to the bar and Con said, 'They'll explain. You'll find them in the back—and your Aunt Rosie with them.'

In the pub kitchen, the table was laid for supper, but the meal remained half-eaten. Mary O'Dell was putting on her hat and coat, and Ruth was searching through her purse, saying, 'I'll need some change in case we take a taxi coming back.'

'Don't you go throwing good money away!' Mary scolded, eyeing her reflection in the glass. 'Dear God, don't I look a sight?'

Sitting in the armchair, Connor's sister Rosie was also in her outdoor clothes; when Lil came into the room, she stood up and kissed her. 'Lil, dear—how are you? Prettier than ever!'

Rosie had been a beauty in her younger days. At one time she was a fashion model with her picture in the papers; in middle-age, the sparkle in her eyes had dimmed a little, and her glossy black curls were sprinkled with silver, but her fine Irish complexion was as fresh as ever.

Looking from one to another, Lil asked, 'Where are you all going?'

'I'm on my way home. Ernest will be wondering what's become of me,' answered

Rosie. 'I thought I should call in and tell Mam, I've been over at Greenwich all afternoon, and I'm sorry to say the news isn't good.'

Ruth continued the story. 'Aunt Moira's taken a turn for the worse. That summer 'flu has developed into pneumonia. They're taking her into hospital tomorrow, but Rosie suggested we ought to go and visit her this evening.'

'Pneumonia...I hate the sound of that word,' said Mary O'Dell darkly. 'None of the doctors seem to know what it really means. All I know is, that's what carried my old feller off. Maybe we should stop by at St Anthony's on our way and light a candle for poor Moira.'

'I wish I'd seen her when we went over last Sunday,' Ruth told Rosie, 'but there was all that trouble with the bomb going off.'

'She told me about that. She asked me to thank you for the flowers you left at the house, and I know she'll be pleased to see you this evening.'

'Will you come with us, Lil?' asked Ruth.

'Oh, Mum—I'm sorry, but Mike's waiting for me in the saloon; he's taking me out for some fish and chips. Give Aunt Moira my love and tell her I'll see her soon.'

When the three older women left the pub, they set off down Manchester Road, then Rosie turned off along Silmour Street, where she and her husband ran a small photographic shop. Mary and Ruth walked on until they reached the slipway at the end of the Island; Mary preferred to cross the river by boat, for she had an instinctive dislike of the deep pedestrian tunnel.

At the foot of the slipway, two or three wherries were moored, waiting for passengers; one of the boatmen raised a finger to the peak of his cap.

'Evening, Aunt Ruth...Mrs O'Dell. Where d'you want to go?'

It was Matt Judge. They stepped into the boat and he bent over the oars, propelling them through the waves with long, steady strokes.

'We're going to visit Mrs O'Dell's sister; she's not been very well,' said Ruth, making conversation. She held on to the brim of her hat, for there was a frisky breeze coming up from the estuary. 'Dan told me he met you when he went for his medical.'

'S'right. We'll both be in uniform any day now, I reckon.'

'Don't say that!' Mary crossed herself rapidly. 'God willing, there'll be no war at all.'

'D'you think so?' Matt shook his head, 'I said to Ma last night—I've been rowing people over the water long enough; it'll make a change to do a bit of travelling myself. So I hope as how there will be a war.' After that the conversation flagged; the women had nothing more to say.

When they reached the Surrey bank, Matt asked if they wanted him to wait and take them back, but Ruth said, 'No, thanks. We don't know how long we'll be.'

He helped them out on to the jetty. Ruth paid the fare and they started the long climb up Crooms Hill. When they turned into Mrs Marriner's street, Mary was too preoccupied to notice the wrecked pillar-box, and Ruth decided not to draw her attention to it.

They walked up the garden path and rang the bell. As they waited, Mary asked suddenly: 'Why are the curtains drawn? It's not time to light the lamps yet.'

Then the door opened, and the parlourmaid greeted them with a scared, tear-stained face. 'Oh, dear. Oh, madam, such a dreadful thing...' She stepped back to let them into the hall, adding in a hushed whisper, 'The doctor's with her now. Cook and me sent for him right away, as soon as she collapsed, and he was ever so good, he got here in five minutes. But it was too late...she'd slipped away already.'

After the fish and chips, Mike and Lil went for a walk. Soon it would be getting dark, but there was just time for a stroll through the Island Gardens before the park-keeper turned them out. As they wandered arm in arm beneath the trees, Lil said, 'What are those white flowers? I can smell them from here.'

'Night-scented stock. They're at their best after the sun goes down.'

She sniffed the air. 'Lovely...but it seems to make everything worse, somehow. It's been such a good summer—so many flowers, and so peaceful—I can't believe there's going to be a war.'

'I know what you mean.' Mike paused for a moment, then added cautiously, 'A little while ago, you said you'd miss me when I went away. Did you really mean it?'

40

'Of course I did. It's going to be horrible without you.'

'I'll miss you—very much.' He felt as if he were walking a tightrope; one false step, and he'd come crashing to the ground. 'You—you've become the most important thing in my life. Did you know that?'

'I suppose I did.' Although it was very quiet in the Gardens, she was speaking so softly, he could hardly hear her. 'It's the same for me... You're the best thing that ever happened to me.'

'I'm glad. But what I'm trying to say is—when two people feel about each other the way we do, they generally get married.'

She said nothing, and he thought: 'God, now I've done it—I've ruined everything.'

At last she blurted out, 'Oh, Mike, I wish—I do wish we could. But you know how I am. I do love you, I really do, but I don't think I could ever...' She swallowed, and began again. 'Perhaps, one day, it'll be different. I don't know.'

Ahead of them, the park-keeper waited at the gate, jingling a ring of keys and calling, 'Everybody out! Closing time!'

Mike cursed under his breath and muttered, 'We'll have to go.'

They went through the gate, and it clanged shut behind them. As they walked on, Lil looked up into Mike's face, 'You do understand, don't you? If you'll just wait a bit longer, if you'll be patient—'

'Yes, but the thing is, when the war begins

41

and I'm sent away to sea, it might be a long time before I see you again, I—I want to make things right between us. I want us to belong to each other—legally.'

'That's 'cos you're a policeman—everything has to be legal!' She tried to make a joke out of it, but her voice faltered. 'I'm sorry, Mike. I've let you down, haven't I?'

'Just a wedding—a ring—our names on a certificate, saying *Mr and Mrs Burns*—that's all I want. I promise you I'll be patient. The rest of it can wait until—as long as you like. That doesn't matter. It's us—being together—that's all I care about.'

By now they had reached the slipway down to the river, and through the gathering dusk a voice hailed them from one of the boats drawn up on the cobbles. 'Hello, Lil. I just bin talking to your Ma and your Gran. Took 'em across the water, I did. Are you two going over and all?'

Lil shook her head. 'No, Matt,' she said. 'Not tonight.' For a moment she was swept by a wave of nausea. Once, when she was still a schoolgirl, long before Jimmy Judge attacked her, Matt had kissed her, clumsily trying to make love to her. At the time she had found it quite exciting, but now the thought sickened her. Now the idea of physical contact with any man was repulsive.

'We ought to be getting back,' she told Mike. 'Dad and Huw are running the pub on their own tonight—we should go and give them a hand.'

She threw Matt a good-night, and as they walked away from the river, the darkness closed in around them. She hung on to Mike's arm, realising suddenly how much she loved him, and how much she trusted him.

'If you think it'll be all right, if you're prepared to put up with me being silly, if you're really sure...then—all right, Mike. Let's get married.'

2

'Mum, will you come to Lil's wedding? Please?'

In the little scullery of her old home in the Rope Walk, Ruth felt like a child again, pleading with her mother.

Louisa Judge had been busy at the sink, peeling potatoes. For a moment she stood quite still, the vegetable-knife motionless in her hands, then she turned, looking over her shoulder at her daughter. Nearly eighty years old, Louisa's hair was white, her skin creased with tiny lines, and her cheeks rosy and wrinkled like an old apple—but her smile was as full of wistful longing as a young girl's.

'I'd like to, you know I would, but...'

A shadow fell across the red-tiled floor. Florrie, Louisa's daughter-in-law, was standing in the kitchen doorway.

'You couldn't possibly go to a Roman church!' she broke in sharply. 'Whatever would people say?' She jerked her head, indicating the old man who sat dozing by the kitchen range in the other room. 'What would *he* say?'

Ruth's father, Marcus Judge, was no longer a powerful and terrifying figure; for many years now he had been sick in mind and body. After an attack of pleurisy and a subsequent stroke, he had become a chronic invalid, rarely setting foot outside the house. Yet even now, his presence brooded over the household, and his wishes—his prejudices—could not be ignored.

Suddenly determined, Louisa left the potatoes and wiped her hands on the scullery towel. 'I can ask him, can't I?' she said. Brushing past Florrie, she went into the kitchen and approached her husband.

Roused from sleep, he lifted his head sideways, squinting at her under bushy eyebrows. His square-cut beard had all shades of colour in it, from black, brindled with brown streaks, to patches of silver and tufts of white; his scalp gleamed through his straggling grey locks. He had lost most of his teeth, so the prominent eagle-beak nose seemed as if it would meet his jutting chin, like the portraits of Mr Punch. Physically he was a wreck of a man, but his penetrating eyes, red-rimmed and glittering, hinted at the fires which still smouldered at the heart of Marcus Judge.

'What is it, Louisa!' he growled. 'What do you want?'

'I want to go to a wedding, Marcus,' she told him calmly. 'Lilian is to be married on the twelfth of August, and I've been invited.'

'Lilian? Who's she?' he demanded. 'Do I know her?'

44

'Of course you do—our Lilian, Ruth's daughter. Our granddaughter.'

'Ruth... Is she here?'

'Yes, Father.' Ruth followed her mother into the kitchen. 'I'm here.' She steeled herself to meet his accusing glare—his eyes grey and dangerous as a gathering storm—and reminded herself that she was a grown woman; she did not have to be afraid of him any longer.

'You are not welcome here. You are no daughter of mine,' he told her, as he had done so many times before. 'You left this house to take up with sinners and idolaters. You cut yourself off from us, and you have no place in our family. How dare you creep into this house behind my back?'

'She didn't do anything of the sort, dear. She came through the front door in the proper way, only you didn't see her because you were having forty winks,' said Louisa placidly. 'You mustn't say such dreadful things. Of course she's our daughter, and she always will be. And I should like to go to Lilian's wedding on Saturday week, and wish her happiness.'

'I don't know this Lilian. I've never seen her,' he grumbled.

'Yes you have, lots of times. You forget things nowadays, that's the trouble.'

Suddenly the old man turned on Ruth. 'Is the girl of your persuasion? Brought her up a Roman, have you?'

'Yes Father, but her husband's Church of England. It's what they call a mixed marriage.'

'Mixed!' Marcus spat out the word. 'And

45

they're to be married according to the Papist rites?' He closed his eyes as if he were in pain, swaying from side to side in his armchair.

Then he threw back his head and began to declaim in a loud, harsh voice: 'Woe unto those who have turned from the way of the Lord. Woe to the children of Satan, who have lusted after false gods. For behold, a darkness shall fall upon all the land, and there shall be no moon by night, nor any sun by day—and the keepers of the house shall tremble. Strong men shall bow down, and those that look out of windows shall be darkened, and the mourners will go about the streets, for thus it shall come to pass at the ending of the world. *Behold, the Day of Judgment is at hand!*' Flecks of spittle appeared on his lips, dribbling down to his beard; he was growing breathless, and his entire body was shaking violently, exhausted by the passion of his own eloquence.

Louisa sighed, and put her arms round her husband, helping him to his feet. 'There now, you've gone and tired yourself out with so much talking,' she said. 'Let's go up to the bedroom, then you can have a nice lie down.'

She was not a big woman, and it took all her strength to get him to the stairs. Ruth moved forward, offering to help, but Louisa shook her head. 'It's all right, dear, I can manage. He'll be better with me... Don't worry, I'll be down in a minute.'

Slowly, the old couple mounted the stairs. Ruth turned to her sister-in-law, who had resumed her place at the table and was sewing brass rings on to a length of thick black cloth, 'Is he often like this?' she asked.

'Only when something sets him off,' said Florrie, trying to re-thread a needle. 'Here, you'd better do this, your eyes are younger than mine.' She continued, 'I must say I think your Mum was silly to bring up the wedding like that. Still, I suppose it's none of my business.'

Ruth refrained from saying, 'You're quite right—it isn't,' and changed the subject. 'What are you making?' she asked. 'Are they curtains?'

'Yes, for the black-out. I got the material in Wickhams' summer sale. I thought it'd come in handy—well, people have been saying for a long time now that when the war starts, we'll have to black-out all the windows. I got plenty of material to be on the safe side, so when I'd finished the curtains at home, I said your Mum could have what was left.'

Ruth noticed that she now called Joshua's house in Denmark Place her home. Florrie had been married to Ruth's eldest brother, Ebenezer, who was wounded in the Great War and died soon after the Armistice; when their son Tommy left home and ran away to America, she became a lonely, embittered woman.

'How are Jimmy and Bertie?' Ruth asked politely.

Eb's brother Joshua had survived the war, becoming Chairman of the Brotherhood, but when he lost his wife, Florrie offered her services as his housekeeper. Now Josh too was dead, but Florrie continued to live at Denmark

47

Place, running the house for James and Albert, his two sons.

'The boys are well enough. I don't see much of them, as they're out a good deal. Organising the Brotherhood keeps them both very busy, you know.'

'I suppose it does. What will happen if they get called up for the Army?'

Florrie threw her a reproachful look. 'Oh, they won't do that. Jimmy's over thirty, and Bertie's heart isn't strong enough to get him through the medical. Besides, people in important positions don't go into the Army, and they're in what's called "reserved occupations". Keeping the docks going is essential work, they said so on the wireless.' Then she added pointedly: 'How about your Daniel? I suppose he'll be joining up soon?'

'Yes, Dan's enlisted,' said Ruth. 'And Lil's training for the AFS.'

Florrie nearly dropped the curtain she was working on. 'In the Fire Brigade? How could you let her do such a thing? I think it's shocking, the idea of young women fighting fires.'

'The women don't do any fire-fighting; they work on the telephone switchboard, or run messages. Some of them learn to drive cars or motorbikes.'

'It shouldn't be allowed.' Florrie's pinched lips were tightly set in disapproval. 'Whatever is her fiancé thinking of, letting her do it?'

'Mike's joined the Navy. That's why she wants to do something useful, while he's away at sea.'

'On board ship, is he? I thought you said they were getting married soon.'

'He's not at sea yet—he's doing his basic training at Portsmouth. And they're letting him come home for the wedding, on a weekend leave.'

Louisa came down at that point and rejoined them. She was looking very tired, but managed to smile as she said, 'He'll be better when he's had a little rest.'

'I've never seen him quite like that before,' said Ruth. 'He seemed to be, well—almost raving.'

'It takes hold of him sometimes—he can't help himself. It used to frighten me too, at first. Some of it are bits he remembers out of the Bible, but it's all muddled up.'

'Some of it sounded more like prophecies.' Ruth fingered the edge of the black-out material and quoted softly: *"Those that look out of windows shall be darkened..."* You don't really think it's going to be the end of the world, do you?'

'I shouldn't take any notice,' said Louisa soothingly. 'Half the time he doesn't know what he's saying, and when he wakes up he'll have forgotten all about it. Anyway, thanks for asking me to the wedding, dear, but you see how he is. I'd better not risk upsetting him again.'

It was very quiet in the darkroom. The only sound was a faint ripple when Abram tilted the tray of developer; the only light was the glow of the red lamp as he and his father worked

49

together on another batch of prints.

'Careful now—you can never hurry it,' said Ernest. 'It must take its own time.'

'Yes, Papa,' said Abram dutifully.

A stranger seeing them together would have known at once that they were father and son; they looked almost identical, for the red glow blotted out the differences in complexion and hair colour. They were both tall, a little round-shouldered, with the same long nose and intense expression on each thin, angular face.

Out in the shop, Rosie Kleiber called to her husband: 'Ernest! The post's come!'

'Thank you, we'll be out presently,' he answered.

Abram raised his voice. 'Anything for me?'

'No, not today,' said his mother, moving away from the door.

Abram gave a small sigh—whether of disappointment or relief, Ernest could not tell. 'Were you expecting a letter?' he asked.

'Not really. But you never know, one of these days perhaps they will send me my call-up papers.'

'Don't be foolish. You're only just eighteen. They don't call up anyone under twenty.'

'Not yet, Papa, but soon perhaps—when the war begins...' Abram broke off, pointing out: 'Look—the pictures are coming through.'

As the two men watched, the photographs emerged slowly in the developer; half a dozen shots of a wedding party, posed in various groups. Ernest leaned closer, examining them critically.

'Not bad,' he said at last. 'Not bad at all. I was afraid this fast film would not give enough definition, but the contrast is surprisingly good—you see?'

'Yes, I see.'

Abram tried to sound enthusiastic, but his father was not deceived. 'You're not really interested, are you?'

'I am interested, Papa, but photography is your life. For me it's different—I have to find something else, I'm sure of that. I'm sorry if I've disappointed you.'

Ernest put his hand on the boy's shoulder. 'How many more times must I tell you? It would have been very convenient if you had wished to take up photography as a career, but the important thing is that you should find the work that is right for you. Until then, I am happy to have you here, helping in the shop.'

When the prints had been hung up to dry, they emerged from the darkroom. Rosie was at the counter, packing some glossy pictures into sturdy envelopes, reinforced with cardboard. She looked up and said, 'These are ready to go off. Do you want me to post them?'

'I could deliver them for you,' suggested Abram quickly. 'They're all local, aren't they?'

'Yes, why don't you do that?' agreed his father. 'A good idea.'

Abram took the envelopes and glanced at the addresses, 'It won't take me long. I'll be back by eleven at the latest.'

When he had gone, Rosie said, 'I thought you wanted Abram to help you clear out the stockroom this morning?'

'That can wait till this afternoon, there's no hurry. The boy looks restless—the fresh air will do him good. And a long walk might give him a chance to decide what it is he wants to do.'

Rosie smiled reminiscently. 'You're two of a kind, sure enough. It's funny, I was just thinking how you used to go off on long walks by yourself, when you were sorting things out in your mind. Those were hard times, before we opened the shop. Sometimes we didn't know where our next meal was coming from.'

Ernest picked up the mail that lay on the counter; there was a brightly-coloured seaside postcard on top of the pile, and he turned it over eagerly. 'Sharon's written to us again—she's a good girl.'

'Yes, she was at Scarborough last week. This week it's Sheffield—after that she's not sure.'

Ernest read the rest of the scrawled message aloud: *'There's a lot of talk in the dressing-room about the tour coming off sooner than expected—business has been terrible everywhere. They say it's the war keeping audiences away, but I think it's the show. Who wants to see* No, No, Nanette *after all these years? I shan't be sorry if we close. I look forward to coming home and seeing you both—and I shall have a thing or two to say to my agent. It's time he got me a featured role; I'm sick of chorus work. Love to all—Sally.'*

Ernest frowned. 'Why must she call herself Sally? She knows I don't like it.'

'It's only her stage name. Now she's a

52

professional, "Sally King" looks better on the posters.'

'Her name isn't *on* the posters! She's only one of the dancers.'

'Ah, but she's going to be a star soon, you wait and see.' Rosie took the next letter from the pile and gave it to him. 'This one's addressed to both of us, but you can open it.'

'What's the matter? You don't know what it is.'

'It's printed on the back. That's what reminded me of the bad old days.' On the flap of the envelope were the words *Horner & Hardiman, Solicitors*. 'I hate those lawyers,' Rosie said uncomfortably. 'They only stir up trouble.'

'How can you say that? They were very helpful when your mother lent us the money to set ourselves up in business.' He tore the letter open; it was brief and to the point. Mr Hardiman presented his compliments to Mr and Mrs Kleiber and asked if they would oblige him by calling at his office in Stepney on Tuesday afternoon between three and five o'clock.

'That's today!' exclaimed Rosie. 'I call that a damn cheek!'

'He says if we can't manage it, we can ring up to make another appointment, but he hopes to see us as soon as possible as he has a certain matter to discuss which will be to our advantage.'

They exchanged glances. 'My mother's will...' said Rosie.

'After three o'clock,' mused Ernest. 'Abram

53

can stay here and mind the shop. Clearing out the stockroom can wait till tomorrow.'

At precisely three, Mr Hardiman rose from behind his desk and extended his hand. 'Mr Kleiber, Mrs Kleiber—this is indeed a pleasure. It's been some time since we last met.'

'Yes, just before our daughter was born,' agreed Ernest. 'And that was seventeen years ago. I'd just managed to sell my father's house in Poplar, and from the proceeds we were able to pay off the money Mrs Marriner had lent us, to open the shop.'

'Just so.' A little vexed, Mr Hardiman settled back into his chair. 'It's good of you to remind me of the circumstances, but I do assure you that I have all the details at my fingertips. I keep everything on file, Mr Kleiber—facts, figures, dates—they're all in my files. Nothing is ever left to chance.' He gazed round the cluttered office, indicating the box files stacked upon his desk and built up into precarious towers all around him. 'Pray be seated.'

The Kleibers managed to find two chairs that were not covered in files, books or documents, and sat down facing the desk.

Rosie wondered how old Mr Hardiman must be; he had always been a big man, with a large florid face and an imperious manner. Over the years he had lost the frill of hair which used to frame his bald pate, and now his head was a shining pink dome from his double chins to the top of his shining skull. Apart from that, he had hardly altered. To Rosie, seventeen years ago, he had seemed to be an elderly man, and

54

she decided he must be one of those mysterious people who pass straight from youth to age, and remain unchanged ever after.

Now he removed his gold-rimmed spectacles and began to polish them upon a white silk handkerchief. 'The first time you visited this office would have been even earlier still, I fancy,' he said.

'Yes, it would have been a year or two before we—'

'Thank you, Mr Kleiber!' snapped Mr Hardiman. 'Do not trouble yourself to try and recall the date. I have it here in black and white—9 October, 1920, to be precise. And I believe I was able to give you some welcome news upon that day?'

'You told us about the loan.' The words died on Rosie's lips as the solicitor fixed her with a basilisk glare.

'I *know* what I told you, Mrs Kleiber. And if you will be kind enough to allow me to continue, I am about to give you some information which I trust will be similarly welcome. I am speaking, you understand, in my capacity as the solicitor of your natural mother, the late Mrs Marriner—and as an executor of her estate. Naturally, I shall go through the exact provisions of the will in due course, but that need not detain us long, since they were not numerous, nor are they of any great consequence—small presents of money and clothes to her domestic staff—some other personal possessions, gowns and jewellery to her sister, Mary O'Dell, and

55

some silver tableware to Mr and Mrs Connor O'Dell. Apart from these bequests, the bulk of the estate—the house in Greenwich and the contents thereof, together with such money as shall be remaining after the deduction of death-duties, legal fees, et cetera, are to pass entirely to you, Mrs Kleiber, as the only child of the deceased, for your use and enjoyment—and that of your husband Ernest, together with your two children—Sharon and—um—er...'

He hesitated and began to search through the papers on his desk as Ernest said helpfully, 'Abram. Our son's name is Abram.'

'Abram, to be sure. That is quite correct, I have it here... I trust you find this entirely satisfactory, Mrs Kleiber?'

Rosie shook her head, hardly able to utter a word, but she managed to say at last, 'Satisfactory? Oh, yes, it's all very satisfactory.'

It was on the way home that the argument began. To begin with, she had been so happy. She had held Ernest's hand as they walked along, feeling as if she were in a dream.

'That beautiful house—I fell in love with it the minute I saw it. And the garden, too...we've never even had a window-box of our own. It's going to be like paradise for us.'

'I don't know what you mean,' said Ernest. 'You speak as if we were going to live there.'

'Well, of course we are!' She let go of his hand, staring at him. 'You like the house, don't you? You told me you did—I remember you saying so.'

'I may have done. It's a pretty enough place, but we couldn't live there. What would happen to the shop?'

'Don't you understand?' She laughed. 'We shan't have to stay in that poky little flat over the shop, not any more. We'll live at Greenwich. You and Abram can walk to Silmour Street every day, through the tunnel. So can I, when I'm not too busy with the housework, and the garden...'

He stared at her, equally mystified. 'We should leave the shop empty at night? For burglars to break in and make off with the stock—all our cameras and equipment?'

'The shop's insured, isn't it? And the contents? We'll have a burglar alarm fitted, if that's what you're worried about. You don't seem to realise, we'll be rich now!'

'Not so rich. You heard what Mr Hardiman said—since Henry Marriner died, your mother had been living off capital. There is not much money left—the house was her only real asset.'

'But there's *some* money, there must be... I don't know why you're being so miserable about it. Anyone'd think you didn't *want* me to have the house. I tell you what! We can let Abram stay in the flat, to keep an eye on things—will that satisfy you?'

'No, no, it's out of the question. You know very well I've been elected Chief Warden for the district. If there are air-raids, I must be there in case of emergencies.'

She interrupted him fiercely. 'Now you're being ridiculous! Who says there will be any

57

air-raids? There may not even be a war! You're just being awkward on purpose, because I've inherited a house—that's the truth of it. What am I supposed to do? Leave it standing empty with all her furniture in it, like a museum?'

'You could put the house up for sale and invest the money.'

'I'll do no such thing! It's not only for me—she left it to all of us, you and me and the children, for our use and enjoyment—that's what she said. I wouldn't dream of selling it. We're going to live there!'

They walked the rest of the way home in an angry silence.

The following morning Rosie called in at the hairdressing salon in Millwall Road, 'I know it's not my usual day for a shampoo and set,' she said, 'and I haven't got an appointment, but can you fit me in?'

Glory took a long, careful look round the empty salon, then replied solemnly, 'You can see I'm rushed off my feet this morning, but seeing as it's you, moddom, I'll try and squeeze you in somehow.'

'Oh, dear. Business a bit slack, is it?'

'That's one way of putting it. I haven't bothered taking on a new assistant since Lil left me to go and join the Fire Brigade. The way things are now, I may as well manage on my own and save the wages.' She settled Rosie into a chair and threw a lilac cotton wrapper round her shoulders. 'But I suppose you can't really wonder at it. People are saying to themselves, "Why should I bother to have my hair done

58

when we might all be blown to Kingdom Come by a German bomb tomorrow?"'

'Don't say that,' shuddered Rosie. 'I've had enough of that kind of talk from Ernest. He's forever telling me the war's going to break out any minute. The shop's full of leaflets about *What to Do with Your Gas-Mask*—or *How to Protect Your Windows in Case of Blast*—that's why I came here this morning. If I'd stayed listening to him another minute, I swear to God I'd have thrown a saucepan at his head!'

Glory laughed. 'That's not like you, Rosie! I always thought you and Ernest were the Darby and Joan of Cubitt Town.'

'So we were—once. The trouble is, it'll take wild horses to drag him away from Cubitt Town!' And she poured out her bottled-up grievances, telling Glory about the legacy, and Ernest's stubborn refusal to move across the river to Greenwich.

'It's not fair on the children, either!' she concluded. 'My mother said in her will, she left the house for all of us to enjoy it.'

'And would Sharon and Abram be happy to move?' Glory tested the temperature of the water as she filled the wash-basin. 'I hope that's warm enough for you.'

With her eyes shut tight and the lather running down her face, Rosie replied in muffled tones, 'Sharon doesn't know about it yet, she's still off on tour, but I'm sure she'll love the house. And I think Abram will like it too, once we've moved in. We did talk about it over breakfast, but he didn't say much. Well, you

59

know what he's like—he lives in a little world of his own.'

'Anyway, I can see you're dead set on making the move. I suppose that'll be the last we see of you,' said Glory, pouring rinsing water over Rosie's head. 'You'll be going to some smart hairdresser over on the Surrey side, and living like Lady Muck!'

'Don't be silly, I'll be popping to and fro all the time,' spluttered Rosie. 'Quick, give me a towel, it's gone in my eyes. After all, I'll be working in the shop sometimes—that's if Ernest and me are still speaking! And you don't imagine I'm going to stop visiting my own family, do you?'

'Oh, that's nice. So we can expect to catch a glimpse of you now and then at weddings and funerals?' Too late, Glory realised that her little joke might have been tactless, and she added, 'Sorry, I shouldn't have said that.'

Wiping her eyes, Rosie met Glory's apologetic gaze in the mirror. 'You mean because of my mother? Oh, that's all right. It was a shock when she went, especially happening so sudden like that, but I've got over it now. I can't pretend we were all that close, really.'

There was a short silence. For years, Rosie had been completely estranged from her natural mother; it was a long time before she could forgive Moira for giving her away at birth, to be adopted by the O'Dells.

She dabbed her eyes once more with the towel, and said quietly, 'Ah well, she did her best to make it up to me—and we finished up friends in the end. But I never expected her to leave me the house—I was very touched. I wish I could make Ernest see that it wouldn't be right for us to sell it now; it's not what she wanted.'

As Glory began to put the curlers into Rosie's hair, she asked, 'Speaking of weddings, have you talked to Lil lately? It won't be long till her big day, will it? Is she getting excited?'

'I couldn't tell you—she's never been at the pub when I've looked in. Ruth says she's working all the hours God sends on that fire-training course. And her young man still away—it's a funny sort of engagement, isn't it? Them hardly seeing one another...'

Half an hour later, when Rosie emerged from under the drier, she looked at herself in the glass again and said, 'Yes—very nice. Thanks, Glory. Let's see, how much do I owe you? I'm sorry, I've got no silver—can you change a note?'

At that moment the shop door opened, and Matt Judge came in, demanding breathlessly: 'Ma, can I have a bit of bread and cheese for me dinner?'

Glory scolded him, 'Where's your manners? Don't you see I've got a customer? Say good morning to Mrs Kleiber.'

'Morning, Mrs Kleiber. Sorry, I didn't see it was you.' In his canvas trousers and jersey he looked out of place against the feminine background of the salon; he stood uncomfortably in the doorway, shifting from one foot to the other.

Rosie smiled. 'That's not surprising, as we

haven't seen each other for quite a long while, have we, Matt? You're not usually here when I come to have my hair done.'

'No, I s'pose not. Ma, can I go through and help meself out the larder? I'm in a hurry, see.'

'No, you can't. Just look at your hands, black all over. I'll go and see to it presently. What's the rush?'

'I got a big job on, taking some geezers from Customs and Excise out to inspect the cargo on board a ship in the deep water, and wait till they're ready to come back. I said I'd pick 'em up down the slipway at midday. If I keep 'em waiting, they'll take another boat.'

Glory looked at the clock on the wall. 'It's ten to twelve now—you're the limit, you are! I've got to find some change for Mrs Kleiber; there's none in the cashbox.'

'That's all right,' said Rosie. 'You see to Matt's dinner first. I can wait.'

'Well, if you're sure. Thanks, Rosie.'

Gloria disappeared into the back room behind the shop, and Rosie said to Matt, 'You'll have to keep me company while I'm waiting. I can't remember the last time I saw you, it was so long ago, but you hadn't long left school—and now you're a grown man.'

He scratched his head, restless under her appraising scrutiny. 'Did Ma tell you I'll be leaving soon—going into the Army?'

'Yes, I hear you and Dan are both enlisting together.'

'Yeah... I'm really looking forward to it.'

'Well, I wish you all the luck in the world, but I expect your mother will be sorry to see you go.'

'Maybe. Still, it's not like as if I was married, leaving a wife and kids, is it?'

'Perhaps not. Though I imagine there must be some young lady who's going to miss you when you're gone?'

Sheepishly, he looked down at his feet. 'No—not really.'

'No regular girl-friend? You do surprise me.'

'Nobody in particular.' He managed an awkward grin. 'I mean, there's no one—special.'

'Ah, I understand. Of course, a handsome lad like you, you must have hundreds of girls eating their hearts out.'

When she came back into the shop, Gloria saw them together: Matt red-faced and laughing, Rosie looking him up and down, flattering him. Sharply, she cut in on them, saying: 'Here's your bread and cheese. You'd better hurry if you don't want to be late.'

'Thanks, Ma!' Matt grabbed the paper bag and shot out of the door, calling over his shoulder, 'So long, Mrs Kleiber!'

Rosie watched him through the plate-glass as he ran up the street. 'He's grown into a fine young man. You must be proud of him.'

'I am,' said Glory abruptly. 'I think you wanted to change a note?'

Something in her voice made Rosie turn and look at her. 'Yes. Do you mind?'

'Of course not. I've got some silver in my handbag.' She would not admit that she was shocked. It was understandable in a way. Rosie had fallen out with her husband—privately, Glory had always thought Ernest was rather a dull, unattractive man—so to restore her self-confidence she amused herself by flirting with Matt. No doubt it was harmless enough, but Glory didn't like it. Matt had obviously been embarrassed—and Rosie was twice his age, at least.

'I've just got to find my bag,' she said, moving away. 'Sorry to keep you hanging about.'

Lil had never been afraid of anything in her life, yet now she felt afraid all the time.

The worst part was, she couldn't tell anybody. How could she admit to her mother and father that she was afraid of getting married? She had made half-joking references to her feelings once or twice, but they had only smiled and said, 'Everyone gets nervous before the wedding—it's natural.'

But this wasn't natural at all, and she knew it.

Since the night Jimmy Judge threw himself on top of her, on the floor of a darkened room in the Brotherhood offices, holding her down, forcing her legs apart, taking his satisfaction and using her as if she were a mindless object, Lil had never been able to think about sex without horror. Her fear was going to ruin everything; it was killing her love for Mike—a pure, uncomplicated love. He had promised that he would be patient with her, that he would never make any demands upon her, yet day by day, the wedding drew nearer and she could think of nothing but the time when they would be alone at last—when she would have to undress—to get into bed with him... She was even starting to be afraid of Mike; she wasn't sure she loved him any more—she thought she might easily hate him.

She spent most of her waking hours at the Fire Station, on the AFS training course, and that helped a lot because there was so much to learn and it kept her so busy, she didn't have time to think about Mike or the wedding. And when she came home to the Watermen each night, she was so tired she fell asleep the minute her head touched the pillow.

But today was different. Today there was a special conference of Senior Fire Officers, making emergency plans for organisation in the event of enemy action; all the instructors had been called to attend the meeting in central London. The trainees had been given a 'rest day', and most of them were very happy about that.

But Lil wasn't happy. She roamed around the pub, trying to make herself useful, trying to find something to do, but everywhere she went, the others were occupied with their own problems and no one had much time for her.

Her father was down in the cellars with Huw. They had spent a lot of time converting the rambling underground vaults into a clean, safe air-raid shelter that could accommodate thirty or forty people at a pinch, throwing out the rubbish that had accumulated there, clearing space to erect camp beds, putting in additional lights and stocking a cupboard with medicines and bandages—for this was to be an ARP casualty station as well as a refuge.

She found her father grumbling to Huw. 'Why the hell should Ernest Kleiber be elected Chief Warden for the area? All I get is a tuppenny-ha'penny armband and a tin hat—and whenever I offer to help him, he says: "Don't worry, everything's under control. I will let you know when you're needed". All the other wardens have plenty to keep them busy—testing gas-masks, filling sandbags, taking First Aid classes. How come I'm given nothing to do?'

Huw tried to pacify him. 'Most of the training classes are in the evenings, when the pub's open. I'm sure that's why they don't want to trouble you. They know that you've got your hands full, after opening-time.' Seeing Lil, he broke off to ask: 'Were you looking for something?'

'No, I just wondered if I could do anything to help.'

'It's a family failing, so it is,' said Connor bitterly. 'You'd best go round to Silmour Street and ask your Uncle Ernest if he has any little jobs to be done. But I dare say he'll tell you to stand by and wait for further orders. That's what he generally says...'

So Lil gave up and went back to the saloon, where she found the daily cleaner on her hands and knees, scrubbing the lino.

'Can I give you a hand, Mrs Hobbs?' she offered.

Nora Hobbs, a mousey little woman in

her forties, looked up and uttered a shrill, meaningless laugh. 'Ooh, no, dear. Ta ever so, but we're managing nicely, ain't we, Kaff? I have to bring her with me, you see, what with it being the school holidays, so she helps me polish the tables and that...don't you, Kaff?'

'Kaff'—whose full name was Katharine Doris Hobbs—didn't even bother to glance in Lil's direction, but merely nodded half-heartedly. She was eleven years old, and small for her age; her face rarely showed any emotion but apathy. Although she had a duster in her hand, she was not making much attempt to polish the table in front of her. She perched on one of the bar settles with her skinny legs drawn up under her, crouching like a little animal, and giving the table a perfunctory wipe with the duster. The only remarkable thing about Kaff was her complexion, for it was a delicate shade of milk-chocolate—and her eyes, when they were not hidden beneath heavy, drooping lids, were a dark velvety brown.

Everyone called her mother 'Mrs Hobbs', but it was a courtesy title for she had never been married, and though she never spoke of Kaff's father, it was generally supposed that he had been a sailor off a cargo ship from Africa—literally, a ship that passed in the night.

To keep the conversation going, Mrs Hobbs was chattering on in her high, squeaky voice. 'Kaff's going away for a lovely holiday soon, ain't you, Kaff?'

Kaff did not bother to reply, so Lil said, 'Oh,

67

that's nice. Where are you going?'

Her mother answered for her. 'We don't know yet. Somewhere in the country, that's all they said—and we don't know when, neither. But I put her name down at the Town Hall, see, for the 'vacuation. So she might be going any day now. Won't that be lovely, eh?'

Kaff went on listlessly rubbing the same small area of table-top; for all the interest she showed, she might have been on another planet.

Thwarted once more, Lil went into the kitchen, where her grandmother pounced upon her immediately. 'The very person I was looking for! I need your help, my girl.'

'I'm glad someone does. What do you want me to do—washing-up?'

'No, no, nothing like that,' said Mary O'Dell. 'Sit yourself down there and help me make out a list. I need to know the exact number of people that's coming to the wedding—and you must tell me what I'll be giving them to eat, apart from cake, I mean.'

'Do I have to?' Lil felt the familiar panic rising within her. 'We don't need to decide anything yet, do we? It's still a long way off.'

'It's nothing of the kind! Today's Thursday, tomorrow's Friday and the next day's Saturday—and aren't you getting married one week after that? Let's see, that's one, two and seven—I make it just nine days from now till you walk down the aisle. Sure, that's no time at all! Come along now, dotey. Put on your thinking-cap and let's make that list.'

'Nine days? Is it really...' Lil was afraid she

would be sick. She backed away, saying, 'I can't stop now. Some other time, Gran. I have to go upstairs. I just remembered something.' She fled from the kitchen, leaving her grandmother staring after her, and ran upstairs to her bedroom. Throwing herself on the bed, she buried her face in the pillow.

The sound of footsteps approaching the bed roused her, and her mother's voice, soft and gentle, asking: 'What is it, Lil? Aren't you feeling well?'

She forced herself to speak calmly. With an effort she sat up, hoping her mother would not notice that she was still trembling. 'I'm fine. Just a bit tired—it's nothing at all.'

'You look quite washed out. It's not right, they work you too hard on that old training course.' Ruth sat on the edge of the bed and took Lil's hands. 'And you're cold as ice! I hope you're not getting a chill—so near the wedding, too.'

'Oh, Mum, *don't!*' The words burst from her, but she tried to make light of it. 'You're as bad as Gran! She's just been on at me about the guests and the reception—how many people, what are they going to eat, all that stuff... I couldn't stand it another minute!'

'But what's wrong? I don't understand.'

'I—I just wish I wasn't—' She broke off, unable to continue.

'You wish you weren't getting married?' Ruth stroked her daughter's hands. 'You're not having second thoughts about Mike, are you?'

Now—now was the moment to tell her mother

everything—but she could not. Her mouth was dry. She moistened her lips, then said: 'No, of course not. I love Mike—I do want to marry him. It's...' She hesitated again, then plunged suddenly. 'It's the flat, where he lives. Where we're going to live.'

Mike's father had died when he was still a boy; five years ago his mother had been taken off to the infirmary after a bad haemorrhage, from which she never recovered. Since then he had lived alone in their small, top-floor flat in a tall Victorian house just off Coldharbour, on the north-east side of the Island. It had small windows under low sloping ceilings, and consisted of two tiny rooms, a cramped kitchen not much bigger than a broom-cupboard, and a shared toilet and wash-basin on the landing. There was no bathroom.

'I thought you said it's got a nice view of the river?'

'The view's the best thing about it. It's cold and dark—and when Mike's away, I'll be so lonely all on my own.'

'When he's away, you can come back and stay with us. It won't be as bad as you think. Some people start married life in worse places—a lot worse.'

Married life... Lil shivered, and at once Ruth took her in her arms and held her tight.

'I know what it is,' she said. 'It's last-minute nerves, that's all. I felt exactly the same—everybody does. But there's nothing to worry about. Once you're married, it'll be fine. You wait and see.'

70

Lil nodded slowly, wishing it were true. Perhaps if she waited a little longer—long enough to get used to the idea...

But there was no time at all. The nine days flew past—seven—four—two—and suddenly it was Saturday, the twelfth of August, and her mother was helping her into a white dress, pinning a bandeau of white rosebuds to her hair, and straightening her veil... Then she was walking up the aisle at St Anthony's on her father's arm—and Mike, looking unfamiliar in his uniform, was standing at the foot of the altar steps, smiling at her. Everyone had told her this would be the happiest day of her life, and she wished she were dead.

Somehow she smiled, too—and when the ceremony was over and they all went back to the reception at the Watermen, she managed to go on smiling.

The saloon was packed; she and Mike stood side by side, greeting the guests, remembering to thank them all for their wedding presents. Most of them were Lil's friends or family—Mike had no one to support him, except a few old colleagues from the River Police, one of whom acted as Best Man. Lil realised he must be feeling rather overwhelmed by so many introductions to unknown relatives, and squeezed his arm sympathetically. He threw her a swift, grateful look, and for the only time that day she felt suddenly close to him and wished the party was over, so they could be alone together.

Then she remembered that they would be

alone together all too soon, and the fear began again.

Since that night—the worst night of her life—she had never touched alcohol, and when the champagne corks started popping she shook her head each time someone offered her a glass. After the cutting of the cake, the Best Man shouted: 'Come on, lad, do your duty—kiss the bride!'—and she had to turn her face to her husband.

He guessed something of her mental turmoil, and whispered softly, 'It's all right... Everything's going to be all right.'

Then he put his hands on her shoulders, drawing her gently to him. His face came down towards her, and she shut her eyes as if she were flinching from a blow. His lips touched hers for a long moment, then he let her go; and though she felt relieved, there was a surge of revulsion too—for he had just taken a glass of champagne and now the taste of it was on her lips—a taste that brought back all the worst memories of the night when she had tasted too much sparkling wine, when she was too drunk to defend herself...

The memory was so vivid, she felt as if she were drunk again; the room seemed to swim around her, the chatter and laughter were unbearably loud. Faces loomed up out of the crowd like distorted reflections in a Hall of Mirrors—her friends, her family, all saying meaningless things.

'You look lovely, my duck—Mike's a lucky man—but I say, isn't it a scorcher? I must go and powder my nose, I'm starting to melt...'

That was Glory, her face bright pink and glistening; she had Matt with her, and their white carnations were already wilting. Lil noticed a line of froth on Matt's upper lip, and she smelled the beer on his breath as he leaned closer and winked at her. 'Don't I get to kiss the bride, an' all?'

She pretended he had made a joke, and turned away with a light, unconvincing laugh... And there were the Kleibers—Ernest in his best suit and Rosie in a white dress with black stripes, kissing her on the cheek and murmuring: 'I shouldn't really be here, so soon after Mother's funeral, but I couldn't let this day go by. Specially now Sally's come home too.'

For a second, Lil was completely blank. 'Sally?'

Then she understood, as Sharon put her arms around her, enveloping her in a wave of expensive perfume, saying, 'The tour folded last weekend, so here I am—and you're looking simply gorgeous, darling, don't you think so, Abram?'

Abram shook hands shyly and wished Lil every happiness, then the Kleiber family resumed what seemed to be a long-running argument. Rosie was saying to her daughter, 'But she wanted us to live there—and you'd love the house, I know you would.'

Sally tossed her blonde curls and giggled, 'Quite honestly, I don't give a hoot one way or the other. If my agent gets me into the new Cochran revue, I'll have to take a flat up West anyhow, to be near the theatre. So maybe you ought to sell the house—it must be worth pots of money.'

Ernest Kleiber interrupted gloomily, 'In the present situation, it's impossible to sell it at a reasonable price. As long as there is the prospect of war, nobody is buying property.'

Rosie said triumphantly, 'There, now—every cloud has a silver lining! And when this stupid crisis is over, you'll be very glad we've still got that beautiful house.' Then she added in a different tone, 'Oh, look, there's Gloria—and Matt. Excuse me, I must go and say hello.'

They all drifted off, and Lil found herself face to face with Huw, who was pouring more champagne.

'Where's your glass, Lil?' he began. 'Oh sorry, I was forgetting—you don't—Mrs Hobbs, how about you?'

Nora Hobbs was almost unrecognisable in her wedding finery, with an improbably red rose pinned to her straw hat. At her side little Kaff asked without hope: 'Can I have some as well?'

Dan appeared from nowhere, 'I shouldn't if I were you,' he told her, 'it's not as nice as it looks. Here, you come with me, and we'll find a bottle of Tizer!' Kaff cheered up immediately, and allowed Dan to steer her away through the crowd.

Lil watched them go, and felt a sudden pang of loss. She had hardly seen Dan today; soon he would be going into the Army—and she was leaving home too. Their lives were carrying them off in different directions, and she wondered if they would ever see one another again.

This sense of loneliness was sharpened when she saw her mother and father coming towards her. When they hugged her, she clung to them as if she could never bear to let them go.

'Hey, what's this?' asked Connor. 'It's supposed to be a celebration, and you look like it's the end of the world!'

'It is—the end of my world,' she blurted out, looking from one to the other. 'I'm going away from you.'

'You'll never do that,' Ruth said firmly. 'I told you—while Mike's off at sea, you can have your old room again. Now cheer up—and look who's come to see you!' She stepped aside, and Louisa Judge held out her arms to the young bride.

Tears started up in Lil's eyes. 'Oh grandma, I thought you weren't coming today. I didn't know—'

'I didn't know myself till half an hour ago.' Louisa kissed her, and explained, 'I've been thinking of you so much, and praying for you—and then after dinner, when your grandfather was having his afternoon nap, I suddenly thought—well, why not? So I left Florrie looking after the house, and put on my hat and coat, and here I am... I mustn't stop, but I had to come and wish you well, didn't I? My only granddaughter...'

When Huw offered her a glass of champagne,

75

she said politely, 'I won't, thank you all the same.'

Mary O'Dell appeared at her shoulder, taking her arm and saying, 'I know what you will have, though. Come away now and I'll make you a decent cup of tea—how about that?' and the two ladies disappeared into the kitchen like old friends.

The blur of the noise and the press of people gradually dwindled down; at last the party dragged to an end, and it was time for the happy couple to leave the pub. For Lil, the day had come and gone like a dream—or like a nightmare—but now dream-time was over, and she had to face reality.

They climbed the stairs to the top-floor flat near Coldharbour, and Mike held the door open for her.

'Welcome to your new home, Mrs Burns,' he said.

She tried to smile, but when she walked in she could not speak. Looking round the little room, there was only one thought in her mind: *'I must get away... It's a trap— I must escape...'*

She moved over to the window; looking across the bend of the river, through the dusk, she could see the masts and funnels in the East India Dock.

'It looks better in the morning.' Close behind her, Mike's voice sounded strained and awkward. 'You'll see the sun rising over there.'

'Yes, of course—better in the morning,' she repeated.

They talked of this and that; she unpacked her suitcase, and he made some coffee, and for a while they sat facing one another across the empty grate—but time and again she found herself drawn back to the window, gazing out at the darkening sky as if she were hypnotised, until the shadows thickened and there was nothing to be seen but a few bobbing lights in the distance... And then it was time for bed.

Mike let her go into the bedroom first, while he pottered about in the sitting-room, laying cups and saucers and plates on the table, ready for tomorrow's breakfast.

Lil undressed slowly, and put on the new nightdress her mother had given her. It was the first time she had worn it, and when she caught sight of her reflection in the mirror above the chest of drawers, a stranger looked back at her. Then she climbed into bed and lay on her back, and waited.

A few minutes later, Mike tapped at the door. 'Can I come in now?'

'Yes—come in.'

When he entered the room, he had already changed into pyjamas. 'Hello,' he said.

'Hello.'

He switched off the light, and at once her body was rigid with fear. The bed creaked and lurched as he climbed in beside her.

'Well—here we are,' he said.

'Yes.' She could scarcely breathe; she kept yawning, taking in great gulps of air. 'I expect you must be tired,' he said.

'I suppose I am, rather. It's been a long day.'

Even before they touched, he could feel the tension within her like an electric shock. After a long silence, he managed to say: 'You know I love you, don't you?'

'Yes... I love you, too.' Then she added quickly, 'But I can't—I mean I really couldn't.'

'I know. Is it OK if I kiss you good night?'

She made a small, inarticulate noise which could have meant anything, and turned her face towards him. In the darkness, he put his mouth against hers, then drew away again. 'There—that's all,' he said. 'Don't worry about anything else. It's all right.'

'Oh, Mike.' Guiltily, gratefully, she made an impulsive movement towards him, trying to offer some kind of loving gesture. As their bodies touched, she felt the strength of his passion, hard as a clenched fist against her, and she realised the intolerable strain he was under. But there was something else, something she had forgotten until this instant—the strong, musky smell of male sexuality—and she pulled away from him.

'I'm sorry,' she gasped. 'I'm so sorry...'

'Don't be sorry. Just as long as we still love one another, that's all that matters.' Then he rolled over, and the bedsprings protested as he turned his back on her.

'Good night, Lil,' he said. 'Sleep well.'

'Yes, you too. Good night.'

But it was a very long time before either of them fell asleep.

3

'No more merchant ships?'

Stupidly, Jimmy Judge repeated the words, unable to believe what he was hearing.

'The Admiralty has announced that as from today, the Baltic and the Mediterranean are to be closed to all merchant shipping from Great Britain, for security reasons. I take it you understand the significance of this order, Mr Judge?'

'Yes—I—I suppose I do. It's just come as a surprise, that's all.'

'To you, perhaps. We have been expecting some such move, haven't we, gentlemen?'

The Wharfmaster glanced round the table at his fellow directors; they nodded gloomily, and one lugubrious voice added: 'This is only the first step. The news gets worse every day. What will they do next? Close the North Sea—the Atlantic Ocean?'

The Wharfmaster resumed smoothly, 'So, taking this in conjunction with the imminent possibility of conscripted men being called-up, you will appreciate that the Jubilee Wharf is facing a very serious crisis. Our regular traffic schedule in and out of the docks is likely to be thrown into chaos, and we can expect a sharp drop in available manpower. Is your Guild ready to deal with problems on this scale?'

Jimmy swallowed, then replied with more confidence than he felt, 'The Brotherhood won't let you down, sir. You can depend on that.'

'You are an optimist, Mr Judge. I can only hope your optimism is well-founded... Do you know how many of your membership are likely to be joining the armed forces?'

'Well, no, not exactly—but I'm sure a good many of them will want to stay on. I mean, as long as it's a reserved occupation, they're doing Government work here, aren't they? The docks have to keep going, isn't that right?'

'Nevertheless, some of them may prefer to get into uniform and go off to fight. For all I know, you may be entertaining some such patriotic ambitions yourself, Mr Judge?'

'No, sir—not me. The way I see it, it's my duty to stay here and keep the flag flying, as you might say.'

'I'm glad to hear it. But I must warn you—if the Brotherhood should find itself unable to function at full strength, for whatever reason, the directors of this Wharf might be forced to make other arrangements—to look elsewhere for an adequate labour force.'

'You mean—bring in outsiders? Throw our jobs open to non-members? But we've got an agreement—'

Jimmy's protests were cut short as the Wharfmaster raised a restraining hand. 'Believe me, we should not take such a drastic step without the deepest possible regret. However, in the event of a national crisis, it might become inevitable—I trust you appreciate that? Have you anything further to contribute to this discussion before we close?'

There was a short silence; someone shuffled his feet, someone else blew his nose. Jimmy could sense their general impatience to wind up the meeting, and he muttered uncomfortably, 'No, sir. Except, like I said, the Brotherhood won't let you down.'

'Very well—let us shake hands on that. I don't think we need detain you any longer. Good day, Mr Judge.'

When Jimmy got back to the Guild offices, his face was dark and resentful. His brother Bertie looked up from his desk, 'Well? What did they have to say?'

'Bloody twisters, the lot of 'em—trying to wriggle out of our agreement!' Rapidly, Jimmy sketched in the main details—the restrictions on the movement of merchant ships, the likely drop in manpower, the threat to bring in outside labour and break the Guild's monopoly. He concluded bitterly: 'Do you know what he had the nerve to say to me after all that? He wanted to know if I had any "patriotic ambitions". He as good as hinted it was my duty to sign on for the forces myself! How about that?'

Bertie pursed his lips judicially, and his plump cheeks quivered. 'Well, I suppose from his point of view it was a possibility—you might have wanted to do your bit for your country. A lot of the chaps have volunteered already.'

'Sod that for a game of soldiers!' snorted Jimmy. 'Anyhow, you're a fine one to talk. I don't notice you in any great hurry to dash off to the recruiting centre and do your bit.'

'It's not the same for me, is it?' retorted Bertie, trying to look sorry for himself. 'The doctor told me the Army would never accept me with my weak heart, you know that. But it's different for you—you're physically Al.'

'And I intend to stay that way,' said his brother grimly. 'Strikes me we'll have our work cut out here as it is, keeping the Brotherhood going.'

'Shall you say anything about it at tonight's meeting?' Bertie enquired. 'Warning them there might have to be some changes made?'

'No bloody fear—the less said, the better. By the way, you'll be in the chair this evening. I've got other fish to fry.'

'Oh, but I think you should be there. It could be a difficult meeting—the men are bound to ask a lot of questions.'

'I'm sure you'll handle it very well, Bertie. Just make my apologies, and explain to them. I've got a previous engagement.'

'Oh, Sharon, there you are. Wherever have you been?' Rosie Kleiber greeted her daughter with a mixture of relief and reproach. 'I expected you home hours ago! I had dinner ready for you at one o'clock—I've been really worried.'

'Don't make such a fuss, Mums, and for goodness sake don't call me Sharon! How many more times? You're as bad as Poppa.'

'Sorry, dear—force of habit. I do call you Sally mostly, but sometimes Sharon just slips out. I thought you were seeing your agent at eleven o'clock?'

'Yes, I did—and a fat lot of good that was! You know he promised he'd get me an audition for the new Cochran revue?'

'Yes—what happened? Did they like you?'

'They didn't even see me—there *wasn't* any audition. Owing to the international situation, the show's been postponed indefinitely. I ask you! This rotten Government ruins everything nowadays.'

'Oh, I am sorry—how disappointing for you. But if you didn't have to go and audition, what took you so long?'

'Well, you can imagine, I was really down in the dumps after that, so I nipped round to the Limelight Club in Wardour Street for a drink, and I met a few old chums. I had to try and cheer myself up, didn't I?'

'The Limelight Club? I didn't know you belonged to any club.'

'I don't, but one of my pals signed me in as a guest. It's a good meeting-place—just for pros—that's how you get to hear about any new jobs going.'

'And are there any? Jobs, I mean.'

'Nothing. Nobody's working—the business is totally dead.' Sally perched on the counter and looked round the shop, adding, 'You don't look as if you've been exactly rushed off your feet today, either. Where's Poppa?'

'He had to go to a meeting at the Wardens' Centre. It's just as well we haven't been very busy. Being Chief Warden for the district, he has to be on call at all times.'

'Well, never mind that.' Sally dismissed the subject, and went on airing her own grievances. 'You know, what really gets me down is that if I don't get a part in a new show, I'll never be able to rent a flat in town.'

Rosie tried to look on the bright side. 'But if you're not working in the West End, you won't need to live there, will you? It'll save you money to stay at home with us—and I wouldn't have had a minute's peace, worrying about you all by yourself, up there.'

'Oh Mums, you don't understand. I've got to have a place of my own—I'm not a kid any more,' said Sally, who would not be seventeen until the beginning of October. 'Besides, I want a smart address. You need to be right in the middle of things, so you can keep in touch with everything that's going on. You've got to meet people—get yourself known!'

'Well, you'll just have to hope for better luck next time. I'm sure your turn will come, one of these fine days. You never know—perhaps Adolf Hitler will change his mind and stay out of Poland, so there won't be any war—and then Mr Cochran can put on his new show, and you'll get a wonderful job after all!'

Rosie glanced at the clock by the darkroom door and continued, 'I mustn't stop here talking. I ought to go and start getting the tea ready. We're having lamb chops—that'll be nice, won't it? And I got some lovely runners in the market. Would you be a dear and give me a hand stringing the beans?'

'Sorry, I've got some letters to write. I made up my mind on the way home that what I really need is a new agent, so I'm going to write round all the top ones and ask for an interview. And you needn't bother about making any tea for me. I'll just grab a bit of bread and cheese and an apple—I'm going out this evening.'

'Oh? You never said. Where are you off to this time?'

'I thought I ought to drop in at the Grosvenor to say hello to the old girls. I haven't seen them since I got back from that awful tour, and they always want to hear how I'm getting on.'

Not all the girls who trained at the Grosvenor Academy of Dance were lucky enough to take up the stage as a career, but then very few of the young hopefuls were as talented as Sally. The principal, Miss Ethel Grosvenor, always described her as 'our star pupil', and her occasional visits were red letter days at the old school.

When she walked into the main rehearsal-room, Sally unbuttoned her loose summer jacket and slipped it over the back of a chair, for the place was uncomfortably warm and stuffy under its glass roof.

Once, long ago, this had been the workshop of a small tailoring business, where a little group of seamstresses sat at their benches day after day, hand-sewing seams and edging lapels with minute stitches. One of those girls was young Rosie O'Dell, for this old house in Poplar had been the home of the Kleiber family; and this was where Rosie first met and fell in love with

Ernest, their eldest son. Years later, after Ernest had moved out to set up his own photographic shop in Cubitt Town, he sold the property to the Grosvenor sisters, when they were seeking suitable premises for their new dancing-school.

The seamstresses who used to ply their needles and thread under the high glass roof had long since departed, and their places had been taken by three rows of red-faced, perspiring children—seventeen little girls and three small boys, struggling to learn how to tap-dance.

Miss Ethel Grosvenor tutted irritably as the door opened—she disliked any interruption when she was taking a class—but as soon as she recognised the newcomer her expression changed, and she clapped her hands. Her sister, Miss Hilda, stopped playing the piano in the middle of a bar and looked over her shoulder in surprise.

'Silence, please. Gather round, children, this is a great occasion!' announced Miss Ethel dramatically. 'Look who's here, Hilda—our own dear Sally! Miss Sally King, children—who was once a pupil like you, in this very room, and is now a bright star, shining in the theatrical heavens!'

She clapped her hands again, indicating that a round of applause was called for, and the children dutifully followed her lead. Sally smiled, making a modest, deprecating gesture and saying, 'Oh no, please. You're too kind...'

Then she kissed Miss Ethel on the cheek, and shook hands with Miss Hilda, who exclaimed 'How lovely to see you, Sally dear—we thought you were away on tour! I know you sent us that beautiful postcard from somewhere exciting. Let me see, where was it?'

'Sheffield,' said Sally briefly, adding, 'That was the last week of the tour. Of course, *Nanette* was a huge success—we played to packed houses everywhere—but all good things have to come to an end, don't they?'

'So what are you doing now?' asked Miss Ethel. 'Having a little rest before your next engagement?'

'A few days at home, to see the family and catch up with old friends.'

'How delightful... But I expect you'll be off again very soon, going on tour with another musical comedy, perhaps?'

'Actually, it might be a bit nearer to home than that, next time. My agent's negotiating with a West End management. They're after me for a featured role in a new revue, but no, I mustn't—not another word! I never talk about things like that until they're signed, sealed and settled. I expect it's very silly and superstitious of me, but I can't help it.'

'Very wise, I should say. Well, whatever it is, I'm sure you're going to be a big, big star—and we all wish you every success, don't we, children? Perhaps you'd like to sit and watch the rest of our rehearsal, dear? We've still got ten minutes to go before the end of the class.'

Sally obeyed, and sat through *The Wedding of the Painted Doll* with a fixed, polite smile—how *could* the old dears go on trotting out the same old fashioned numbers year after year?—but at the end she applauded enthusiastically, and watched as Miss Ethel dismissed the class.

'Run along now, children. Off with your tap-shoes, and get dressed to go home—hippety-hop!'

The boys raced off to change in the Gents Cloakroom, while the girls retreated to the back of the room, where they had left their street-clothes and sandals; chattering like sparrows, they began to undress.

Almost immediately the door opened again, and another visitor entered the room. Sally looked at him—a long look. She knew him at once; there was a time when she had known him very well indeed, though they had not seen or spoken to one another for more than two years.

'Oh, Mr James—how nice!' Ethel Grosvenor greeted him effusively. 'What a shame you're just too late to see the rehearsal.'

'I know. I'm very sorry, but I was held up at my office. We're very busy at the Wharf these days,' said Jimmy Judge.

He hardly looked at the elderly spinster; his eyes were on the group of little girls who were tugging off their practice-dresses, pulling on blouses and skirts over white vests and knickers and ankle-socks.

'It's very good of you to spare the time to look in at all,' Miss Ethel assured him. 'But then you've always been such a great friend and supporter of our little efforts.'

'I like to encourage the youngsters, you know that,' he told her. 'So who's the lucky winner this week?'

'Another girl, I'm afraid. Isn't it a pity our boys never seem to be quite up to the mark? But little Patsy Pollinger has collected the most gold stars—isn't that right, Hilda?'

'Quite right, dear. Patsy has four gold stars,' her sister chimed in. 'For punctuality, grace of movement, musical interpretation and cartwheels.'

'In that case it will be my privilege to take Miss Pollinger home in my motor, stopping on the way for a Knickerbocker Glory at the Ice-cream Parlour,' said Jimmy Judge. 'If that's all right by you?'

'Oh, yes. I know she's looking forward to it—she'll be ready in two shakes of a lamb's tail!' Miss Ethel slipped her arm through his. 'And while you're waiting, come and meet our other celebrated visitor. I'm sure you must have heard me speak of Sally King? One of our old pupils, and almost certainly the most brilliant. Sally, this is Mr James Judge.'

Jimmy's face never moved a muscle, but he bowed rather stiffly as Sally rose to shake hands with him.

'Mr Judge and me are old friends,' she said sweetly. 'I remember you very well, though I don't expect you to remember me. I believe I was one of the very first girls lucky enough to be rewarded with an ice-cream sundae.'

'Sally King, of course. This is a great pleasure,' he said.

At the far end of the room, shrill voices were suddenly raised because someone had taken somebody else's shoe-bag by mistake—and the

Grosvenor sisters both scurried off to settle the argument.

'So you do remember, that's nice,' murmured Sally. 'I wasn't sure if you would. After all, I was so much younger then.'

'Yes, of course.' Jimmy cleared his throat. 'Keeping well, are you? That's good. And what are you up to these days? Still doing the old song-and-dance stuff, eh?'

'Oh yes, though at the moment I'm between engagements—"resting", you know. Spending a few weeks at home with my family.'

'Good, good.' Clearly he was not particularly interested; his eyes slid away to those little girls who were still getting dressed.

Slightly piqued, Sally moved closer and stood directly in front of him, straightening his necktie and saying quietly, 'While I'm in the neighbourhood, perhaps we could have a drink together some time, for auld lang syne? How about that?'

He shifted his focus back to her, and a spark of excitement gleamed in his eyes. 'Yeah, why not? Still at the same address, eh—the photographer's shop? Righty-ho, I'll look you up in a day or two.' Then, as Miss Ethel returned, hand in hand with an impish little girl with bright blonde ringlets, he turned away, adding, 'You'll have to excuse me. Got to go now—be seeing you.'

And he walked off with an avuncular smile, to be introduced to little Patsy Pollinger. At the same time Miss Hilda returned to the piano to collect her sheet-music, and she remarked fondly to Sally, 'I'm not surprised you remember him. Such a wonderful man—and always so kind to the children. He doesn't change, does he?'

'No,' said Sally. 'He doesn't change.'

'So the great day's here at last,' said Connor. 'Well, we can't say we weren't expecting it.'

It was the last day of August, and everything seemed to be happening at once. At the Watermen public-house, the most important event was the arrival of Dan's call-up papers. He took them out of the buff envelope, scanned them quickly then passed them along the breakfast-table to his father.

Lil asked, in a small voice: 'When?'

'This morning,' Dan told her. 'I'm to report to the Recruiting Centre. There'll be an Army lorry there to take us off to barracks, for kitting-out and primary training. I'm very glad; I was getting fed up with waiting.'

Ruth said nothing. She nodded, and made herself smile, but she could not speak. Mary O'Dell did not even try to look cheerful. Her eyes shone with tears as she said, 'May God go with you. Your Grandda would have been proud of you this day.'

As soon as breakfast was over, Dan went upstairs to pack his suitcase and Ruth began to make some sandwiches, for the new recruits were advised to bring a packed lunch for the journey.

Lil, hanging round the scullery, offered to help, but her mother said: 'No thanks, love—I can manage. Hadn't you better be getting off to work? You don't want to be late on duty at the Fire Station.'

'I know, but I must say goodbye to Dan before he goes. We don't know when he'll be home again, do we?'

Seeing the look in her daughter's eyes, Ruth put down the bread-knife and wiped her hands on her apron, then she put her arms round Lil and said, 'I know how you feel—and it's worse for you than the rest of us, because you've had to say goodbye to your husband already.'

Lil nodded, tight-lipped. She didn't talk about Mike very often and it still seemed unreal to hear him referred to as her husband. Even after their honeymoon weekend, she knew in her heart that they were not yet husband and wife, and she wondered if they would ever be. Yet she still loved him, in her own way, and missed his company now he was back in Portsmouth—and worried about him—and prayed for his safe return.

'Yes,' she said. 'Dan going away—it's like saying goodbye to Mike all over again.'

Then Huw arrived, ready to begin his day's work, and they had to explain to him about Dan's call-up. For a few seconds he said nothing, then he turned aside, throwing a few words casually over his shoulder. 'Right then—I'll be in the office if I'm wanted. Give me a shout before the boy goes. I'd like to wish him all the best.'

As quickly as he could, he hobbled out of the room. Ruth and Lil looked at one another:

there would never be any call-up papers for Huw Pritchard.

Soon afterwards, they were interrupted yet again by the arrival of Mrs Hobbs, who had Kaff with her as usual, and Ruth greeted them with surprise. 'Hello, you're very bright and early. I wasn't expecting you so soon.'

'No, well, that's why I called in, see—to tell you I won't be coming this morning,' said Nora Hobbs, looking hot and bothered. 'I'm ever so sorry, but it's because of the girl, see? I got to take her to the Town Hall.' The little woman gave Ruth a meaningful nod and wink. 'For the outing, you know... They said as how the coaches will be leaving at ten.'

Then Ruth noticed that Kaff was carrying a large, shapeless bundle wrapped up in brown paper, and she had her gas-mask in its cardboard box dangling round her neck on a string. A label, with her name and address scrawled on it was fastened to her jumper with a safety-pin.

'It ain't an outing!' the eleven-year-old girl burst out sulkily. 'It's a 'vacuation, that's what it is—and I don't know where I'm going—and—and—I don't want to!' Whereupon she burst into tears and clung to her mother, wailing 'Don't send me away, Mum. I don't want to go to the country. I ain't never been there, and I don't like it!'

Nora looked as if she might be about to cry herself as she patted her daughter helplessly on the head, saying, 'Oh, do give over. Don't carry on so, Kaff—you'll enjoy it when you get there, you know you will. You was just the same when

93

you went to the Zoo with the school party.'

Sniffing back her tears, Kaff asked hopefully, 'Will there be monkeys? And elephants?'

'I shouldn't think so, but you might see some cows—and horses.'

At this the tears welled up in Kaff's huge dark eyes again, and streamed down her brown cheeks as she sobbed, 'I don't want to see no rotten old cows and horses. I hate cows and horses. I don't want to go!'

Ruth produced a handkerchief and helped her dry her eyes and blow her nose, while Nora made ineffectual dabs at her offspring, alternately petting and slapping, scolding and consoling her.

'Come along now, stop that crying, there's a good girl. I dare say you won't be there long. It'll be over soon and then you'll be coming home again—and—and—oh, do shut up, Kaff, for goodness sake!'

Order was eventually restored by the return of Dan, his suitcase packed and his raincoat slung over his shoulder, ready to depart. Quickly summing up the situation, he took charge.

'Going to the Town Hall, eh? Now isn't that funny? I'm going that way myself, to join the Army. I tell you what, how about us going together, eh, then we'll be company for each other, Kaff. You see me off, and I'll see you off—that's fair enough, isn't it?'

She brightened up at this prospect, and in the end Dan's leave-taking was swift and cheerful. He kissed his mother and grandmother, slapped his father on the back, shook hands with Huw, told his sister to behave herself, and left the pub with Mrs Hobbs on one side and Kaff on the other, skipping along and swinging on his hand.

After that, Lil took herself off to work, and Mary O'Dell went upstairs; she said she was going to make her bed, but her eyes were still suspiciously moist. Left alone, Connor and Ruth looked at one another. Suddenly, the big kitchen seemed horribly empty.

About half an hour later, Rosie Kleiber walked into the hairdressing salon in Millwall Road. To her relief, there were no customers in the shop, and Gloria appeared from the back room almost immediately.

'Hello, what are you doing here on a Thursday? Don't tell me you want another shampoo-and-set already?'

'No, nothing like that.' Rosie laughed—a shade too loudly, because she was feeling a little nervous. 'As a matter of fact, it wasn't really you I came to see. Is Matt at home, by any chance?'

Gloria's smile faded. 'Matt? No, he's not. What did you want him for?'

'Nothing special, only... I heard on the wireless this morning, they're calling up the Reservists today. So I thought it would be nice to say goodbye before he goes, and—you know—wish him luck.'

Stone-faced, Gloria regarded her for a long moment, before saying, 'Then you've had a wasted journey. You've missed him by about ten minutes.'

'Oh, no!' Rosie's face fell; she could not hide her disappointment. 'He's gone already? I hadn't realised...'

'He wanted to make an early start, 'cos he's got to join the rest of 'em at the Recruiting Centre.' A sudden thought crossed Glory's mind, and she added pointedly: 'I dare say your nephew Daniel will have been going off today as well. Did you call in and wish him good luck too, on your way here?'

'No—no, I didn't. Perhaps I should have...' Ridiculously, Rosie found she was blushing, and she turned away—only to come face to face with her reflection in one of the wall-mirrors above the wash-basins, and with Gloria's hostile, accusing gaze. Defensively, she tried to explain. 'Well, Dan's got so many people to see him off and wish him well—and Matt's only got you.'

'No, he hasn't—he's got his Grandma as well. She knitted him a khaki muffler, and she got up specially this morning to give it him before he went off... Very good of her, I thought, at her age.'

'Oh yes—Aunt Emily. I was forgetting... As it happens, I brought him a little present myself.' Rosie pulled a package from her shopping-bag. 'Two hundred cigarettes. I believe these are the kind he likes... What a shame I missed him.'

'Yes, isn't it?' Coolly, Glory continued to stare at her. 'I'm sure it's very good of you, but I can't think why you should go to so much trouble on Matt's account.'

'Oh well, you know how it is. You being Ruth's cousin, I feel we're all part of the same family. Besides, I've always been very fond of Matt.'

'Have you? Funny, I wouldn't have thought you'd ever taken that much notice of him, till recently. Not till he grew up to be a young man, in fact.'

'Really? Well, I must be off, I've got a thousand things to do today.' Rosie shrugged her shoulders and moved away, adding casually, 'Oh, by the by, could you give me Matt's address? These barracks they're sending him to—where are they, exactly?'

'Couldn't tell you, I'm sure. I don't suppose he'll know himself till he gets there. Why, you're not thinking of writing to him, are you?'

At the doorway, Rosie turned to face her, wide-eyed. 'I just want to send him the cigarettes, that's all. It would be a pity to waste them.'

In the early hours of the following morning, Poland was invaded by the German Army. The news broke too late for the daily press, but was announced on radio bulletins during the day, and made headlines in the evening papers.

In Silmour Street, at the end of the afternoon, Ernest Kleiber studied the front page of the *Star,* then turned to his wife. 'Now there is no possibility of peace. This country must go to war.'

Rosie gasped, and held on to the edge of the shop counter to steady herself.

'What is wrong? Are you ill? Come and sit down.' Ernest was immediately solicitous, and called up the stairs, 'Sharon—fetch your mother a glass of water!'

'I'm all right—just a bit dizzy for a moment.' Rosie closed her eyes. 'It was the idea of—all those young men-going off to fight... I can't bear to think of it.'

For many years now she had been a good wife, accompanying her husband to the synagogue every week, but at this moment she found the old familiar words returning to her mind: *'Holy Mary, mother of God, pray for us sinners, now and at the hour of our death...'*

'We must be thankful Abram is still too young to be called-up.' Ernest put his hand on Rosie's shoulder. 'That is a mercy, at least.'

She tried to smile. 'Yes—thank God for that.' But she had not been thinking of Abram.

When Sally came downstairs with a glass of water, Rosie apologised. 'Poppa shouldn't have bothered you. I was just being silly... He says now Hitler's gone into Poland, there must be a war. It could happen any day.'

'Damn!' exclaimed Sally, and Ernest frowned. He did not like to hear his daughter swearing. She put the glass down on the counter so hard, some of the water slopped over the edge, 'Well, that's really put the tin lid on it! I suppose they'll close all the theatres—goodness knows when I'll get another job.'

'It's going to be hard for everyone,' Rosie reminded her. 'Anyway, I shall go on praying for peace. You never know, there could still be a last minute miracle.'

'It'll take more than a miracle to get me into

the West End now! And I got so near, that's the infuriating part.' She ran her hands through her short, fair curls and paced up and down; then an idea struck her, and she said suddenly, 'I'm going out. There's somebody I've got to see.'

'But you haven't had your tea,' began Rosie, and Ernest broke in, 'And look at the time—have you forgotten what day it is?' It was a Friday. At sunset, the Sabbath would begin, and Ernest had never abandoned the ancient family ritual. 'Today of all days, we must surely light the candles and ask a blessing.'

'Oh, Poppa—I'm sorry, but you know I don't really go in for all that stuff—it's so old fashioned. Besides, there's this friend I've got to see—it could be important. Say a prayer for me, will you? You never know, it might change my luck.'

They tried to argue with her, but once she had made up her mind there was no stopping her; she raced up to get her hat and her bag, then ran downstairs once more, and out of the shop. They heard her high heels clatter away along the pavement, and Ernest said quietly, 'We are losing our daughter.'

'Of course we aren't—what a thing to say! She's young, that's all. Give her time—she'll settle down in a year or two.'

'You think so?' Ernest looked very tired, and though he was not yet fifty, when he walked over to the street door, he moved like an old man. He turned round the Closed sign, then pulled down the blinds. 'We may as well shut up shop early;

I don't expect any more customers today.'

Outside, Sally walked briskly through the narrow streets, crossing the Island; several men turned their heads to watch her go by. In her sky-blue summer dress and pillbox hat with its matching blue bow, she looked a cut above all the other girls in Cubitt Town, not just because she was smart and pretty, but there was something in the way she walked—the way she swung her hips, the way she carried herself—which created a kind of electricity. Sally herself was fully aware of this, and it gave her a feeling of confidence. 'I'll get what I want—I know I shall,' she told herself 'Nothing's going to stop me.'

She walked the length of West Ferry Road, making her way to Denmark Place. When she reached the home of the Judge brothers, she rapped the knocker and waited impatiently.

The door was opened by Florrie Judge; on seeing Sally, she drew back her head suspiciously, like an old crow confronted by a bird of paradise.

'Good evening,' said Sally. 'Is Jimmy Judge at home?'

'What d'you want with him?' asked Florrie.

'I'm a friend of his, and I've come to see him on business.'

'Oh, yes?' Florrie narrowed her eyes, as if she were dazzled by Sally and her vivid colours. 'Well, you can't see Mr Judge 'cos he ain't here. He's working late at his office, but his brother's here, having his tea. You can talk to him if you like.'

'No, thanks. This is a private matter, between myself and Jimmy—no one else. Never mind, I'll probably catch him at the office.'

'You can't do that. He's a very busy man, he's not to be disturbed.'

'Don't worry about that.' Sally threw her a brilliant smile before she turned to go. 'I'm quite sure he'll see *me*.'

She was equally determined when she reached the locked gates of the Jubilee Wharf, and managed to persuade the old gate-keeper to let her in, explaining that she was a close personal friend of Mr Judge, and that she had to see him immediately.

Minutes later, she tapped on the door of the Guild Office, and walked in without waiting for a reply.

Seated at his desk, surrounded by various lists, ledgers and closely printed Government forms, Jimmy Judge stared at her, open-mouthed.

'What the hell are you doing here?' he asked. 'Who let you in?'

'The old man at the gate. I explained I had to see you on urgent business, and he was absolutely sweet.' She took off her hat, shaking out her blonde curls, then perched on the corner of the desk. 'You did promise you'd take me out for a drink—remember?'

He eyed her speculatively for a moment, then gestured at the piles of paperwork which surrounded him. 'You haven't picked a very good time,' he said. 'I'm up to my eyes here with this blasted Whitehall red tape. For two pins I'd chuck the blooming lot in the bin, but it's no use—I've got to stay here and sort it out. You can see how it is.'

She moved a little closer, leaning towards him, then stretched out her hand and stroked his chin. 'Poor old you,' she said. 'I'm sure if we went for a nice quiet drink somewhere, I could take your mind off your worries... You can come back and finish your work later, can't you?'

He smiled reminiscently. 'You always were a cheeky little devil. I'll admit it's very tempting, but I've got to say no. Some other time, perhaps.'

'We might not have another chance. And this isn't just a social call, Jimmy—I meant what I said about talking business. I want to make you an offer.'

In spite of himself, he felt a stirring of interest. 'What are you on about? What sort of offer?'

On her way to see him, she had been rehearsing what she would say, and now she set out the facts quickly and concisely; her success on the stage, her speedy rise from the chorus to cameo roles—and above all, her lost opportunity to get into the West End.

'I could have had my name up in lights by now. It's only because of this damn war that I'm not being featured in the new Cochran show—but the minute things get back to normal, there's no doubt I'm going to be a star—everybody says so. The trouble is, I must have something to tide me over. What I really need is a little flat in the West End, so I can mix with the right sort of people...'

The penny dropped at last. 'You want to

borrow some money?' he asked.

'Of course not!' She looked very shocked. 'As if I would... I don't sponge on my friends! No, what I am looking for is someone to invest in me—well, in my future, really. You see, I'm going a long way, but I do need some backing to get me started. What I thought was—if you could invest some money in my career, I could sign a contract with you, making over a share of all my earnings—fifteen per cent, for instance? You'd be doing yourself a favour, and helping me at the same time.'

Jimmy chewed his lip thoughtfully. 'How much money?' he asked.

'Well, enough to live on, to pay my expenses—food and clothes and that sort of thing—and enough to rent a nice little flat in Mayfair.' She glanced round the office. 'You've obviously got a good job here, I bet you're rolling in it—you could spare a thousand pounds, couldn't you?'

He shook his head in wonder. 'You're a caution, you are really... You're not asking for a loan—you're expecting me to fork out a thousand quid as a gift! And all I get in return is a little share of your earnings—*if* you ever earn anything...'

'That's not a very nice thing to say, is it?' She bridled a little. 'Here I am, offering you a golden opportunity. Anyway, the flat can be in your name, if you'd rather... Don't you think it would be nice—a little nest where you could come and stay overnight sometimes?'

'You've got a bloody nerve!' He threw back

his head and laughed; it was not a cheerful sound. 'Catch me throwing money away, setting you up like a West End tart. You must think I came down with the last shower of rain... Look—just push off and let me get on with my work, do you mind?'

She slid off the desk and moved closer still, trying to fondle him, saying, 'Don't be like that. We used to have some fun, didn't we? We could still have a good time together. I've learned one or two things I didn't know in those days.'

He stood up, pushing her away roughly. 'Times have changed since then, my girl—and you're not my type any longer. Now get out, before I lose my temper.'

She took a step back, and her face changed. 'Oh, no,' she said. 'I'm not your type now—but that's because I've grown up... I saw you at the Grosvenor the other day; still up to the same old tricks—taking the little dears out for an ice-cream, touching them up under the table, taking them for a ride in your lovely car and pulling down their knickers... It's about time somebody put a stop to you and your little games.'

It was very odd; although his expression did not alter, something behind his eyes told her he was afraid—and she knew she had won.

'You're talking rubbish,' he began.

'Think so? How would it be if I was to tell Miss Ethel what sort of man you really are? The kind of things we used to get up to? I wasn't quite fifteen years old then—remember? I think the police might be interested as well, not to mention the Mums and Dads of all those dear little kiddies you've taken out for a lovely treat... By the time I'm done with you, you won't be able to show your face around here any more.'

'Don't you threaten me! You wouldn't dare!'

'Wouldn't I? What have I got to lose?' Now she was smiling again, 'But it needn't come to that, Jimmy. Look—I've made you a very good offer, and now I'm going to leave you to think it over for a day or two. When you've made up your mind, we can go and call on some estate agents in Mayfair, and find ourselves a cosy little flat—won't that be fun?'

The next day was Saturday; Lil had done an early shift at the Fire Station, but by midday she was free to go back to the pub.

Her mother was pulling pints in the saloon, and as Lil came through the swing doors, Ruth called to her across the bar. 'Come here a minute—I've got a message for you!'

'Oh no, don't tell me, let me guess. The Duty Officer rang up to say somebody's gone sick, and can I work the whole weekend?'

Ruth shook her head, her eyes twinkling. 'Not exactly, though you won't be staying here tonight, either.' She passed the drinks to her customers, and rang up the cash register, then moved back to Lil. 'You've got to go upstairs and pack your nightie and your toothbrush, and then go home to Coldharbour. There's a gentleman there who's expecting you.'

'Mike? He's home? Why didn't he let me know?'

'He said everything happened so quickly, he didn't know himself till first thing this morning. Now run along—don't keep your husband waiting!'

As she hurried back to the flat, Lil's thoughts tumbled over one another. How long would Mike be staying? Had she left the place clean and tidy when she moved out? Of course there would be no food there—she must do some shopping at the market on the way, and she'd have to air the sheets and blankets before she made up the bed...

Suddenly the confused feelings twisted together into one sharp knot of anxiety: would Mike be less patient with her this time? She couldn't expect him to lie beside her, without touching her. He had been kind and forbearing on their wedding night, but sooner or later he would expect something more. Her joy at the prospect of seeing him again became overshadowed by guilt and fear. She loved him—she trusted him—yet she could not control the freezing paralysis that gripped her, at the thought of consummating their marriage.

Laden with shopping, she climbed up to the top-floor flat. Mike heard her footsteps on the stair, and flung open the door. He had brought flowers for her, and the room was full of the scent of carnations. Letting parcels and paper-bags spill on to the kitchen table, she held out her arms to him.

He hesitated for an instant, searching her face

as if to ask whether she really meant him to embrace her; she smiled and moved towards him, and when he kissed her on the cheek, she thought for one wonderful moment: *'It's all right. Thank God, it's going to be all right...'*

Then he kissed her on the mouth, and the male smell of sweat and shaving soap and his rough serge uniform blotted out the perfume of the carnations; she felt her gorge rise, and her stomach turned to ice.

But he must not know that. She had to convince him that she was happy, and show how much she loved him. Desperately, she pulled him still closer, as if the pressure of his body against hers might bury her fears.

'I love you,' she said. 'Oh, Mike—I love you so much.'

Later on, when she had unpacked the shopping and started to fry bacon and eggs for their supper, she asked, 'Why did they give you weekend leave at such short notice?'

He sighed. 'It isn't the whole weekend—just the one night. I'm off at crack of dawn—first train from Charing Cross.'

'Why? Where are you going?'

He tried to make a joke of it. 'We're not allowed to say, but how many Naval Dockyards do you know in Kent?'

She thought quickly. 'Chatham?' And then she understood the full meaning of his words. 'You've finished training at Portsmouth? You're being sent to join your ship?'

So it was to be his last night ashore; by this time tomorrow he would be on the high seas—and at any moment, Britain and Germany would be at war.

They didn't talk very much during the evening; there didn't seem to be anything to say. The same thought was in both their minds—all too soon he might find himself in the thick of a naval battle. There was no knowing when Lil would see him again—it might be a long time before Mike came home on his next leave—and there was the possibility that he might never come home at all... But they could not talk about things like that.

Finally, when they had washed the dishes and put them away, Mike set the alarm clock for six am, then said tentatively: 'I don't know whether you're feeling sleepy yet, but I suppose I really should have an early night.'

'Yes, of course. I'm quite ready for bed myself.'

'Right. Well, you go ahead,' he suggested awkwardly. 'I'll just stay here and get myself undressed.'

At first it was like their wedding night all over again. Lil put on her best nightdress and got into bed, and waited for him. Presently Mike came into the room, wearing pyjamas, and switched out the light.

But this was not—*must* not—be a repetition of the wedding night. It might be the last time they would ever sleep together; Lil could not let him go without some proof of her love for him.

The bed creaked as Mike slipped between the sheets. He was careful not to get too close, and although she could feel the warmth from his body, he left a gap between them. For a little while, neither of them spoke, and then: 'Well, we'd better say good night, I suppose.' Mike's voice sounded unexpectedly close. 'Sleep well.'

'I'm not—all that sleepy—not yet,' she whispered. 'Aren't you going to kiss me?'

'If that's all right?' he asked doubtfully.

Unable to see one another, their faces met in the darkness and her nose collided with his jaw; she laughed, and then they found each other's lips, and he kissed her. It was a gentle kiss, but it seemed to last for ever...

Fear rose within her, but she would not give way to it. She put her arms round him, and the feel of his strong body against her sickened her, yet at the same time it was somehow reassuring.

He was a man—yes, but he was a human being too, and though she was afraid, she sensed that he had fears and inhibitions of his own. She was not alone in her nightmare; she was with Mike, the man she loved more than anyone else in the world—she had to go on trusting him.

Slowly, with clumsy, trembling fingers, she began to unbutton his pyjama jacket. She felt him tense at once, and she knew she had taken him by surprise. He wasn't sure what was happening.

'Lil, should we be—I mean, do you really want to?' he blurted out.

'Yes, I want to,' she said. 'Please let me.'

'Well, if you're certain. Only I don't want you to be frightened,' he said, and as she went on, he added hoarsely, 'I won't do anything unless you want me to.'

'I know...' She slipped his jacket off, and ran her fingertips over his body; his skin was surprisingly soft and smooth. She felt reassured, and began to relax slightly, then she reached the rough, wiry hair on his chest, and faltered—but she made herself go on. Her hands moved down to his waist, and she fumbled with his pyjama-cord, 'I'm sorry. I'm not very good at this,' she apologised.

'You don't have to. You mustn't do anything you don't want to.'

'I didn't mean that. I only meant, the knot's rather tight...'

When it loosened, she eased down the pyjama-bottoms, and at once the terror came rushing back, stronger than ever before—but she couldn't give in to it. Steeling herself, she began to explore the secret parts of his body, trying to tell herself that this was Mike—the man she loved—though all her instincts denied it, and an insistent voice within her screamed that he was Jimmy Judge, come back to avenge himself upon her again... His masculinity was hard and burning, shocking and scorching her. She longed to retreat from him, to confess this had all been a horrible mistake, and run away—but she knew she could not draw back now.

He was breathing faster, and as she rolled on her back, pulling him to her, he asked: 'Are you sure you want me to?'

'Yes. Yes, I want you—now,' she gasped, and

opened herself to him as if she were tearing the heart from her breast. *'Now!'*

Then the fear was overtaken by pain, and the pain too was hideously familiar. She gave herself up to it, clenching her jaw tightly, and when at last she could speak, she panted: 'I love you, Mike. I love you—I love you...'

The alarm went off at six, and she got up to make his breakfast. Half an hour later, he set off for Charing Cross, looking very smart in his uniform. His face was radiant, and as he kissed her goodbye, he said, 'I'll write. I'll send a letter as often as I can... I want you to know—last night was so beautiful. I mean, I never expected it, but you've made me so happy... I just hope you're happy too.'

'Oh, yes!' She kissed him again, telling him, 'Of course, I am—very happy.'

As he walked away down the street, she watched him from the little window; he looked up once and waved—and she waved back, still smiling until he had turned the corner and was out of sight.

Then she tore off her nightdress and poured hot water from the kettle into the washing-up basin, and soaped herself all over, trying to scrub away the memory of last night. When she had dried herself and dressed herself, she went out to the first mass at St Anthony's and prayed for God's forgiveness, because she had lied to her husband.

Afterwards, she did not go back to the flat, but went to the Watermen instead, where she found her mother polishing the brass fittings on the bar.

'Hello, stranger! I didn't expect to see you yet—is Mike with you?'

'No, he's gone. He only had the one night—he's joining his ship today. So I've come back to stay here, if that's all right with you?'

'You know it is.' Ruth dabbed some metal-polish on the duster, then asked, 'And how is he?'

'Mike's fine. He's looking forward to going to sea.'

'That's good.' Ruth gave Lil a sidelong glance, guessing there were things she preferred not to say. 'And how are you?'

'I'm fine too. Everything's fine.'

'I'm glad to hear it. Now you'll be able to come to church with me and your Gran, at ten o'clock.'

'Oh, I went to the eight o'clock... I'll stay here and make myself useful. Shall I peel some potatoes for dinner?'

In the middle of the morning, Lil was slicing carrots in the kitchen when her father came in with Huw, saying, 'Would you turn the wireless on? Seemingly the Prime Minister's going to make some sort of announcement.'

At eleven-fifteen, the voice of Neville Chamberlain came from the loudspeaker—solid, catarrhal, and seventy years old: *'I am speaking to you from the Cabinet Room at 10, Downing Street. This morning the British Ambassador in Berlin handed the German Government a final note...'*

The door opened again and Con turned, raising a warning hand to silence Ruth and Mary O'Dell, who had just returned from church; but his gesture was unnecessary—they were already startled into silence. Mary's lips moved, and the rosary beads ran through her fingers, while the Prime Minister's words rolled on: *'I have to tell you now that no such undertaking has been received, and that consequently this country is at war with Germany.'*

In one way, it was an end to uncertainty; the thing was settled, and the long wait was over. But Dan had gone, and Mike had gone, and the future was even more uncertain than before. To make matters worse, not ten minutes after Connor had switched the wireless off, the air-raid sirens began to wail.

'Mother of God, it's like a banshee!' exclaimed Mary, with the colour draining from her cheeks. 'What must we do? Go down to the cellar?'

'That'd be the best thing,' said Connor. 'Huw, take Mam downstairs, would you? I'm going to the Wardens' Centre—I might be needed. Ruth, Lil—you'd better go with Mam.'

'I can't,' said Ruth. 'I'm sorry, Mam, but I must go to my mother. You do understand, don't you? I can't stay here—I have to make sure she's all right.'

'You're not going on your own,' said Lil. 'I'll come with you.'

Con tried to argue, but Ruth wouldn't listen to him. She repeated, 'I must go, Con. I'm quite sure the air-raid won't start yet, and we

113

can be at the Rope Walk in ten minutes if we're quick. Lil, if you're coming, don't forget your gas-mask.'

As it turned out, there were no air-raids at all that day. Long afterwards, they heard that a civilian airplane from France had crossed the English coast without first seeking permission, and as a result the alarm was sounded; but in recent months, the effects of poison gas had been so well publicised, everyone was prepared for the worst.

As they hurried through the deserted streets, Ruth and Lil overtook a solitary figure going in the same direction. It was Sally—half walking, half running. Bewildered, but relieved to have their company, she asked breathlessly, 'What's going on? Is it some sort of ARP rehearsal? Where is everybody?'

She had left Silmour Street before the Prime Minister's broadcast, and did not know that war had been declared. When they told her, she exclaimed crossly: 'Damn and blast! This would have to happen now—I'm on my way to see a friend at Denmark Place... What do you think we ought to do?'

Then she broke off, as a whistle shrilled and a policeman came round the corner on his bike. He had a whistle between his lips, a tin hat on his head, and a cardboard notice round his neck with the words: *Alert in progress. Take cover.*

Ruth knew him slightly—he sometimes called in for a pint when he was off-duty—and she explained: 'We're on our way to my parents' house. My mother's quite elderly, and my father's an invalid. There's nobody else to look after them.'

As they were only a dozen yards away from the Rope Walk, he let them go on, but advised them to take shelter as soon as possible.

'You'd better come as well, Sally,' said Ruth. 'We'll be safer indoors.' But when they reached Number 26, there was no one at home. Ruth knocked, and Lil called through the letterbox, but they got no response.

'Where on earth can they be?' Ruth asked.

The answer was very simple; together with some of their neighbours, Louisa and Marcus Judge had taken refuge in the brick surface shelter that had been erected at the end of the street. Ruth discovered them there, sitting side by side on a slatted wooden bench, their backs against the wall.

'Oh, Mum—thank goodness!' Ruth hugged her. 'I couldn't think what had happened. Are you all right?'

'Of course I am—why shouldn't I be?' Louisa patted her hand. 'Your father and me were just coming home from Chapel when that nasty hooter went off, so I thought we ought to come in here till it's over.'

Ruth looked at her father; his head was lolling, and his eyes were shut.

'How is he?' she asked. 'Shouldn't he be in bed?'

Without opening his eyes, Marcus growled, 'I'm resting from my labours. The sins of the world weigh heavy on my shoulders, and I must renew my strength.' Then he snored once, and fell asleep.

'Take no notice, dear.' Louisa lowered her voice. 'He gets like this sometimes after he's been to Chapel. He'll be better when he's had his forty winks. Aren't you going to sit down? I'm afraid it isn't very comfy, but let's hope we shan't have to stay here for long.'

The three newcomers settled themselves next to the old couple; Lil had a sudden ridiculous memory of sitting in a row on a hard bench just like this, to have a school photograph taken—but this was no laughing matter.

There was no electricity in the shelter; the only light came in from the open entrances at either end, and she could see patches of damp on the walls which trickled down to make puddles on the cement floor. The place smelled disgusting, of foul air, rubbish, dogs' mess and urine—and the little band of shelterers talked to one another in anxious undertones, miserably confused, while they waited for something unimaginably frightening that might happen at any minute.

'Well, I suppose it could be worse.' Ruth tried to sound cheerful. 'At least we're all together, that's some consolation.' Suddenly, she remembered Sally. 'Oh Mum, I'm sorry, I haven't introduced you—or did you meet on Lil's wedding day? This is Connor's niece Sharon, I mean Sally.'

'How do you do?'

With professional charm and poise, Sally stood up and presented herself to the old lady, holding out her hand, while Ruth continued: 'We were on our way here when we ran into Sally, quite accidentally, so we brought her with us.'

'I'm very pleased to meet you,' said Louisa as they shook hands. 'But I'm sorry it has to be like this. Perhaps later on, when it's all over, you'll come in for a cup of tea?'

'That's ever so kind, but I'm afraid I can't stop. I was going to meet a friend when all this happened... It's very inconvenient—I don't really know what to do.'

'There's nothing any of us can do,' Louisa told her. 'We're in God's hands. All we can do is pray, and leave it to Him.'

Lil nodded. 'That's what I thought too, Grandma. I lit a candle for Dan—and one for Mike.'

Ruth reminded her mother, 'Mike's in the Navy, Dan went off to join the Army a couple of days ago and Matt went as well—Gloria's son.'

'So many of them. So many fine young men.' Louisa sighed. 'And this morning, at Chapel, Florrie told me I've another grandson gone to serve his King and country. She says James came home from the office on Friday night and said he'd made up his mind to enlist. So he went and signed on first thing yesterday morning, and last night he came back to say goodbye. So now he's gone as well, and there's nobody in charge of the Brotherhood except poor Bertie. Your father's really very worried about that, because—'

Sally, who had been about to sit down, swung

117

round suddenly and asked sharply: *'James?* You don't mean Jimmy, Jimmy Judge?'

'That's right, dear. It's really very patriotic of him, because he didn't have to go. He volunteered—isn't that splendid?'

Lil was next to Sally; even in the half-light she could see the anger blazing in her face, and she was the only one close enough to hear her furious whisper: *'The lousy, rotten bastard...'*

Five minutes later, the sirens sounded the All Clear. The first alert was over, but the war had only just begun.

4

Saturday, Feb. 10th, 1940.

Dearest Mike,
I love you, and I miss you every day

At her desk in the Fire Station Duty Office, Lil looked up from her writing-pad, then decided to complete the sentence, knowing it would make him happy:

and every night. I wonder where you are now, and what you are doing. Things here are as quiet as ever. I've been in since six am and spent the first couple of hours making breakfast for the crew, spring-cleaning the office, checking the stores, and now I've got nothing to do but sit and wait for the phone to ring, and pass on any messages to

118

the Chief—so I'm taking this opportunity to write to you.

February has always been the month I hate most, and this year it's worse than ever. January was bad enough. First of all they started food-rationing—it's perfectly fair, and we all get enough to eat, but it does make life difficult. Then there was the weather. It was so icy cold last month, the Thames froze over—not here, of course, but higher upriver, where it's not so wide and the tide's not as fast—and then one night we had the most awful storm; they say the worst this century. I hope your ship was somewhere far away, in a warmer climate, and that you were well out of it.

But if January was terrible, February's even worse. Everybody's fed up. War-time isn't a bit like we expected—it's not even exciting. It's dark and drab and dreary, and there's nothing to cheer us up.

Since that false alarm the first day, we haven't had any air-raids at all, which means that most of the time we do nothing but Stand By and now people are saying behind our backs that us AFS girls have a cushy job, getting paid for doing nothing! It's just as bad for the poor old wardens. Even though most of them are only part-time, and they don't even get paid for it, they're still pretty unpopular...

A mile and a half away, in the saloon bar, Ruth was arguing with Mrs Hobbs on the same subject.

'I can't help it, I don't like them ARP wardens!' Nora Hobbs was on her hands and

119

knees, scrubbing the floor. Her voice, shrill at the best of times, now rose to an indignant squeak. 'I had one come round last night just before I went to bed, shouting at me 'cos me curtains wasn't fitting properly. "Put that light out!" he yelled at me. "If you don't do it this minute, I'll report you and have you up in court for breaking regulations!" Trouble is, they ain't got nothing to keep them busy, so they go round taking it out on the rest of us... I tell you, I hate blooming wardens.'

Ruth was about to defend her husband, but broke off at the sound of the side door slamming and two pairs of boots thudding along the passage. She heard Connor exclaiming indignantly, 'D'you know what them young devils had painted on the wall? *Adolf Lives Here!*—in great red letters a mile high! Took me half an hour to get it off with turps, so it did.'

The two part-timers came into the bar, taking off their tin hats and hanging up their respirators. Both men were in navy-blue boiler-suits, and had just returned from the Warden Centre, where they checked in every morning to report for duty.

Huw was trying to placate Connor. 'They didn't mean anything. It was only a couple of kids playing silly buggers.' Too late, he saw Ruth and Nora, and broke off in confusion. 'Oh, beg your pardon.'

'I was just telling Huw what they'd painted outside the Chief Warden's office,' Connor explained.

'Yes, we heard you,' said Ruth, adding anxiously, 'You don't suppose it was on account of Ernest being a German, do you?'

'Not a bit of it. Besides, he became naturalised British long ago... No, it's the same for all of us in the ARP—Public Enemy Number One, that's what they call us nowadays!'

'Yes, Mrs Hobbs was saying much the same.' Ruth turned to the little woman. 'But I hope you make an exception for present company?'

'Oh, of course I didn't mean you, Mr O'Dell—we all know what a lovely gentleman you are... But some of them others really get on my wick. Reporting us to the police for one little chink of light—it's not right, is it? Throwing their weight about, telling us to put sticky paper on our windows, nagging us about not leaving our gas-masks at home—like a lot of little Hitlers, they are!'

Connor scratched his head judicially. 'I know what you mean. To tell you the truth, our friend Ernest's inclined to get a bit above himself now and then. He gets very pernickety over things nobody in their right minds would bother about. I mean, what does it matter if a pail of water's full or only three-quarters full?'

Huw turned to Ruth, with the ghost of a smile. 'There was a difference of opinion this morning about filling the fire-buckets. Mr Kleiber says we must be prepared at all times.'

'Prepared for what, I'd like to know?' retorted Ruth. 'No wonder the papers call this the Phoney War—we've got no air-raids, our boys are over in France somewhere behind the Maginot Line, waiting for something to happen—and nothing ever does! Why can't they come home, that's what I'd like to know?'

Then the telephone rang, and Huw said: 'There you are—something's happened, hasn't it? I'll see who it is.'

He went behind the bar, into the office, as Ruth continued, 'And no jobs for you at the Centre today either, I suppose Con?'

'That's where your wrong,' he said. 'I've got to report at the Baths in Glengall Road at three o'clock, for work of national importance, My dear brother-in-law thought it would make a nice change for me to test a lot of gas-masks.'

Ruth tried not to laugh. 'Well, I suppose somebody's got to do it.'

'Would you come along with me?' Connor suggested. 'We might as well test yours while we're about it.'

'I can't,' she said. 'To be perfectly honest, I don't exactly know where it is at the moment. I must have left it somewhere—but don't worry, it'll soon turn up. It's either in the Church Hall, or else it's at the grocers. I might have put it down while I was getting my ration-book out, one or the other.'

At this point Huw returned, saying, 'Mrs Hobbs—it's for you.'

Terrified, she scrambled to her feet. 'For me? Oh, whatever can it be? It's not bad news, is it? Is it something about Kaff?'

Huw reassured her. 'It's Kaff on the line. And you'd better hurry, 'cos she's ringing from

Saffron Walden, and she'll be running out of pennies soon.'

White-faced and shaking, Nora Hobbs hurried into the office, and shut the door.

Ruth and Connor looked enquiringly at Huw, who said, 'The kid's in tears, begging to come home.'

'Poor little soul.' Ruth sighed. 'I've been hoping she'd settle down, but she keeps getting homesick.'

Ever since she was evacuated six months earlier, Kaff had been pleading with her mother to bring her back, sending her tear-stained letters, saying how much she hated living in the country. At Christmas Nora had gone to stay for a few days in a nearby village, to be with her daughter, and she had returned, saying unhappily, 'They're not bad people, but they don't understand my girl, and they never will. She says they make her work on the farm, cleaning out the cowshed and shovelling—well, they call it manure—and they tried to teach her how to milk, but one of the cows kicked her and now she's scared to go near 'em... She has to get up early every morning while it's dark, and she's so tired all day long, she keeps nodding off during lessons at the village school, so the teacher thinks she's backward—but what can I do about it? The Government says we got to send our kids away for safety's sake.'

Now the office door opened again, and Nora Hobbs emerged slowly. She was still trembling, but she seemed a little calmer. 'Well, that's it,' she said. 'Kaff's coming home.'

'You mean, they're sending her back to London?'

'Oh no, not them. It's her—she's run away. She rung up to say she's had enough. This morning she packed her things and nipped off after breakfast, when nobody was looking. She got as far as the railway station at Saffron Whatsit, but she hasn't got enough money for a ticket. She said that if I don't go and fetch her, she'll get on the train when nobody's looking, and hide under a seat. So I told her not to be so daft—she'll end up in the police station if she carries on like that. I told her to buy a bun and a cup of cocoa and stay in the buffet till I come.'

Ruth said firmly, 'Of course—and I'll come with you. We'll have to go to the farm and explain, or they'll be sending out search parties. Cheer up, Mrs Hobbs, it's not the end of the world.'

The little woman nodded. 'That's right. I think I'm glad about it, really. Maybe it's all for the best, eh? I'd been missing her, and all. It'll be good to have her home again.'

At the Glengall Road Baths, Con was explaining the situation to Ernest.

'I tried to talk the silly creature out of it, but there was no shifting her. I told her she'd do better to go and stay in the country and look after the kid herself, but she wouldn't hear of it. She says she's lived in London all her life, and she's not moving out for Hitler or anybody else.'

124

Gravely, Ernest looked over the top of his spectacles. 'This has been happening a lot recently. As long as there are no air-raids, the parents think they may as well bring their children home. Of course it's a great mistake, but people can be very stubborn.' He glanced at his watch; the gas-mask testing had been going on since three, and during the past hour only a handful of people had been in. 'This is another example,' he continued. 'When the war began, everyone was afraid of poison gas. People carried their masks everywhere they went, but now most of them don't bother. I tell the customers who come into my shop that they should have their masks with them at all times, but they don't care. The Lost Property offices are full of gas-masks which have been left in trains and buses—can you imagine such a thing?'

Con was saved from having to answer, for at this point a middle-aged lady came in, saying that she'd had a leaflet through her door, and had she come to the right place?

The two men sprang into action; Ernest examined her mask, while Connor put on his own respirator and went into the 'gas-chamber'—a converted shed out in the yard. When Ernest had made sure that the mica eye-piece had not cracked, or the rubber parts perished, he helped the lady put her mask on, adjusting the straps to ensure that it fitted tightly.

'There now,' he said. 'Is that quite comfortable?'

Her voice was muffled as she replied in quavering tones, 'I s'pose so, only it always makes me feel I'm going to choke.'

'You'll be all right, have no fear. Now I'm going to take you into the testing room. This way, please.'

Inside the shed, Connor put a match to a white, cone-shaped pellet; it looked like an indoor firework, as if a sparkling volcano might erupt from it at any moment—but there was nothing to be seen except some wisps of pale smoke.

Ernest, also masked, ushered the lady in and offered her a chair. 'Please sit down—this won't take long,' he said.

'What's going to happen?' she asked nervously.

Through the masks, their voices sounded hollow and distorted, as Ernest tried to reassure her. 'There's nothing to worry about. We just have to make sure you can't smell anything.'

Eyeing the hazy smoke, she whispered, 'Is that—poison gas?'

'No, no, nothing so terrible—though it would make your eyes sting if you weren't wearing a mask. You're not feeling any ill-effects, I hope?'

It was very eerie in the shed. Lit by one small square of greenish glass, they might have been underwater; the only sound was the faint hiss of the burning pellet.

After a few moments Ernest asked kindly, 'All right, are you?'

'Yes, I think so. Does that mean my gas-mask's working properly?'

'I'm sure it is, but perhaps we should wait a little longer,' Ernest told her.

126

Encouraged, she rattled on, 'My hubby thinks gas-masks are rubbish. He says the Government only sent them round to keep people quiet, and they don't really do any good at all.'

'Now you'll be able to tell him he's mistaken,' suggested Ernest.

'Oh no, I won't do that!' She sounded rather shocked. 'He wouldn't like it. He says those brick shelters are no good either—that's why he built an Anderson in our back garden, 'cos he doesn't trust the one in the street.'

A deep rumble emerged from behind Connor's respirator, as he joined the conversation. 'Your husband's right there, ma'am, and no mistake—surface shelters are a waste of time and money. One bomb in the vicinity, and they'd tumble down like a pack of cards. A direct hit would knock 'em out altogether!'

'Oh, do you think so?' she began, but Ernest cut in sharply.

'Thank you, Mr O'Dell. I believe we've detained this good lady long enough. You can extinguish the fumes now.'

He escorted the visitor off the premises, telling her that her gas-mask was in perfect working order. Crossing the yard once more, he met Connor coming out of the shed, and said coolly: 'I'd be grateful if you'd keep your opinions to yourself in future. There's no point in frightening members of the public.'

'Ah, she'll be fine. You heard her, she's got an Anderson—'

'That won't stop her telling her neighbours that one of the wardens said surface shelters are useless. Don't you realise, if that gets about, it could start a panic?'

Uncomfortably aware he had said too much, Connor defended himself. 'Have some sense, man—isn't everyone saying the same thing? Them brick bunny-hutches are death-traps. The Government should have built deep underground shelters years ago, only they're too stingy. They won't lay out money to protect the public, and you know that as well as I do!'

'Please, Mr O'Dell, you could be overheard!' Ernest looked over his shoulder at the entrance to the Baths; they had been converted into a Medical Aid Centre, and he wasn't sure who might be listening.

'Sure, them in there know better than anyone that it's God's truth I'm telling you! They've not enough medical supplies or blankets, or food and clothing for emergencies—it's a public scandal, so it is.' Warming to his theme, Connor went on, 'One of our regulars at the pub works for West Ham Council, and they applied for funds to build deep shelters—they said it'd be cheaper in the long run than paying for funerals—and do you know what the Government told them?'

'No, I don't know, and I don't want to.' Ernest tried to shut him up, but Connor had got into his stride now, stabbing his forefinger into Ernest's chest to underline his point.

'They sent a whole lorry-load of shrouds and cardboard coffins, and advised 'em to make their wills!'

Ernest steered away from the open doorway, saying quietly but fiercely: 'That will be enough of that! I'm sorry to have to remind you that I am the Chief Warden for this district, and I cannot allow you to spread defeatist rumours. You can think yourself lucky I don't report you for creating alarm and despondency!'

Clenching his fist, Connor made a great effort to control himself. 'Ah, go and take a running jump at yourself, why don't you?' he retorted.

Ernest drew himself up, saying stiffly, 'Yes, I shall go now, Mr O'Dell. I have family business to attend to, and since it seems we're unlikely to be overwhelmed with callers, I shall leave you in charge. But if you should have to deal with any more visitors, I strongly advise you to guard your tongue. Good afternoon.' With that, he turned on his heel and walked away, leaving Connor for once in his life at a loss for words.

The family business did not take long. At Silmour Street, Ernest was just in time to wish his daughter 'bon voyage' before she left home. Sally was in the shop, saying goodbye to her mother; Abram stood waiting in the doorway with her luggage, while Rosie held Sally in her arms, saying, 'You will ring up tomorrow to say you've arrived safely, won't you? I wish you weren't travelling overnight. Why does it have to be such a long journey?'

'It's all right, Mums. I'm meeting the rest of the company at Euston, and we're changing trains at Crewe. That means a four-hour wait at least, but I might be able to have a snooze in the station waiting-room. Then tomorrow we catch the first train to Liverpool, and when we get there I'll have to start hunting for digs—*and* there's an early band-call to look forward to, first thing Monday! No peace for the wicked, as the saying goes.'

Rosie tried to smile. 'Of course I'm glad you're working—if only it wasn't quite so far away. You will send us postcards as often as you can, won't you? And I'll write you every week—oh!' Suddenly she remembered an important detail. 'You still haven't told me the name of the show! Wait while I find a pencil.'

Sally laughed. 'Don't bother, Mums. I've written down all the dates for you, and the theatres we're playing—the name's not important... Last time I asked, they still hadn't decided what to call the show. You know how it is with these touring revues; they change the name every five minutes, to keep it topical. Honestly, I must dash, or I'll miss my train.'

She hugged her father. 'Goodbye, Poppa—wish me luck!'

'God bless you, my dear girl. Would you like me to come with you to the station?'

'That's all right, Abram's offered to carry my big case. You stay and look after Mums. 'Bye now!'

She set off at last in a flurry of goodbyes and blown kisses, carrying her handbag and a little vanity-case; at her side, Abram lugged the heavy suitcase. When they turned the corner of Silmour Street and headed north up Manchester Road, he asked her: 'Why did you tell them that

130

tale about the name of the show?'

'I don't know what you mean. Like I said, it's not fixed yet.'

'Yes, it is. I found your copy of *The Stage* in the kitchen; I looked it up under next week's touring dates.'

'Damn. Well then, you know why I said it! I couldn't tell them the show's called *Strip, Strip, Hooray*, could I? They'd go through the roof!'

'So that's it? You have to take your clothes off?'

'Of course I don't—the idea!' She tossed her curls indignantly. 'Catch me doing anything like that. I've got my own spesh dance routines, one in each half... Some of the chorus may be doing artistic poses, but not me. I wouldn't dream of it.'

'Glad to hear it.' He shifted the big case from one hand to the other. 'This weighs a ton—how are you going to manage it on your own?'

'Oh, don't worry about that. There's bound to be somebody in the company to carry it for me,' she said confidently. 'There always is. Promise you won't say anything to Poppa about it being a nude show? It'd upset him.'

'I won't say a word. The way he looked when he came home—I think he was a bit upset already.'

Connor was still brooding about Ernest when he returned to the pub. As he climbed out of his boiler-suit, he told Ruth what had happened at the Baths, finishing: 'Honest to God, I could have clouted him!'

'Oh, Con!' Ruth exclaimed in dismay. 'You

131

didn't, did you? Ernest's not strong—nothing but skin and bone and besides, he wears glasses!'

'I never laid a finger on him.' Con grinned momentarily. 'Though I was sorely tempted... I'm telling you, he'd better not lay down the law to me again. Another time, I might lose my temper!' Then he remembered Ruth's expedition to Saffron Walden. 'How did you get on today? Did you find the kid all right?'

'Yes. Kaff's back home with her mum, safe and sound.'

'I still say Nora Hobbs was wrong to bring her back.' Connor rolled up his shirtsleeves, ready to go and serve behind the bar. 'But I'll try and keep my opinions to myself in future. I suppose if Kaff's happy, that's the main thing.'

'Oh, she's happy all right. Do you know what she hated most about living in the country? The food! She said they never gave her fish and chips once, all the time she was there!'

The long winter dragged on, but when spring 1940 came at last, the news was no better. By April, Hitler had moved into Denmark and invaded Norway. In May, his army swept across the Low Countries; Holland and Belgium fell, and it seemed clear that France would be his next target.

Late one night, after the Watermen had closed its doors, Huw Pritchard was on his way home to bed; as he turned into Millwall Road, he saw a gleam of light inside the hairdressing salon. Looking through the window, he saw that the door into the back room was ajar, and that a light had been left burning in the kitchen. He banged on the street door several times; at first there was no response, then the inner door swung open, the beam of light broadened, and he shouted: 'Put that light out, can't you?'

Immediately, it was switched off. He heard someone coming towards him through the darkened shop, and the street door was unlocked. Gloria began apologetically, 'I'm sorry, I didn't realise—' Then she recognised Huw, and said in a different tone, 'Oh, it's you. I thought it was the warden.'

'I am a warden, Mrs Judge—part-time,' Huw told her. 'Though I'm not on duty tonight.'

'Thank Gawd for that. You're not going to report me, are you?'

'By rights I should do, but seeing it's you... Just be a bit more careful another time, eh?'

As he was about to move away, she asked, 'Will you come in for a minute? D'you fancy a cup of tea?'

'I'm just on my way home, thanks all the same.'

'Please, Mr Pritchard.' She held the door wide open. 'Quite honestly, I'd be glad of your company.'

So he went in, and she led the way to the kitchen.

'I was just going to have a cup myself—sorry I can't offer you anything stronger.' Shutting the inner door firmly, she switched the light on again. 'Between you and me and the gatepost, it's a blessing to have somebody else to talk

133

to—my mother's driving me barmy! That's why I forgot the blackout. She's had me up and down those stairs ever since eight o'clock... Take your coat off—hang your tin hat on the back of the door.'

He obeyed, watching as she filled the kettle and put it on the stove. 'This is very good of you,' he said. 'But I mustn't stop long.'

From the floor above, a thin, anxious voice called down: 'Glory—who are you talking to? Who was that at the door? It's not the Germans, is it?'

Gloria rolled her eyes to heaven, and shouted up the stairs, 'No, Ma. Don't be so daft—of course it isn't!' In an undertone, she explained to Huw: 'She's been listening to the wireless, and now she thinks the Germans are coming to murder us all in our beds. I've tried to reason with her, but it's like talking to that wall.' Raising her voice, she continued, 'It's Mr Pritchard, Ma—from the pub!'

'What? I can't hear you. Who did you say?'

'*Mr Pritchard—from the Watermen!* I suppose you wouldn't be a dear and nip up to say hello, would you? Once she sees you, she might calm down again, with any luck.'

Feeling rather foolish, Huw climbed the stairs and tapped on the old lady's door; he found Emily Judge sitting up in bed, with a nightlight burning beside her and a slumber-cap askew on her head. As soon as she recognised him, she became quite coquettish, smoothing down her woolly bed-jacket and asking him to excuse her attire. She hoped he was keeping well, and asked

134

after her niece and that nice Mr O'Dell. Ruth was fortunate, she said, to have her husband living at home.

'I haven't felt really safe here since poor Matthew went off to be a soldier. Glory does her best, but it's not the same, is it? Two women on their own, without a man about the house...'

Huw eventually managed to say good night, and was able to report to Glory that the old lady seemed to be settling down peacefully at last.

'Thanks—you're a pal.' Glory passed him a cup of tea. 'I suppose I ought to count my blessings—can you imagine what she'd be like if there was an air-raid, and I had to take her down into the Anderson?'

They went on talking about this and that for some time, and eventually Huw looked at his watch. 'Good lord! I'm keeping you up—I must be on my way.'

'Well, if you must. Where is it you live? I've forgotten.'

'Over the Welsh Dairy in Three Colt Street. I've always stayed there, ever since I first came to London. They're from Treorchy, like me.'

'Oh, that's nice. Old friends of the family, are they?'

'In a way, though I don't know how much longer I'll be living there, because the old dears are getting on now, and hankering after moving back to Wales. Not that I blame them, but it's going to be a problem, finding somewhere else to live.'

'Wouldn't the O'Dells give you a room at the pub?'

'They might—but I wouldn't like to ask them. Lil's moved back into her old room now, and they keep the other one ready for Dan, whenever he comes home on leave.'

'Seems a bit silly, if the room's standing empty most of the time. I'm sure if it was Matt, he wouldn't mind me letting his room while he's away. In fact...' She stopped and looked at Huw thoughtfully, then said: 'Did Ma tell you she feels nervous without a man in the house?'

'Well, yes, she did mention something—'

'P'raps it's not such a bad idea, come to think of it. How would you like to move in, and be our lodger?'

He stared at her. 'Are you serious?'

'Why not? When Matt's on leave, you'd have to bunk down on that sofa, but if you wouldn't object to that... I know Ma would feel a lot happier, and so would I. How about it, Mr Pritchard?'

On 10 May, Neville Chamberlain bowed to public opinion and resigned, ostensibly on the grounds of ill-health. Churchill replaced him as Prime Minister, and under his leadership the people of Britain took new hope—but across the Channel, the Nazi Blitzkrieg destroyed the Maginot Line by the simple expedient of encircling it, and the British Expeditionary Force, which had been backing the French defences, had to retreat to the Channel coast.

136

On the last Sunday in May, at the Emmanuel Chapel, the Minister called upon the Almighty to intervene in this terrible conflict.

Standing before the congregation, his eyes closed, he prayed: 'Today let all men of goodwill unite in Thy name, O God. Let our friends and allies, wherever they may be, join us in one faith. Just as we welcome the unhappy refugees from Europe, let us as Christians put aside our differences, recognising Thee as Our Saviour, embracing all true believers in one universal creed—Baptists and Anglicans alike, Catholics and Methodists, church or chapel, high or low, let us unite.'

'Silence!'

The Minister opened his eyes, and the words died upon his lips. In the middle of the aisle, an old man had struggled out of the pews and was shaking his fist and shouting hoarsely.

'I denounce thee! How dare you preach the word of Satan in the house of God? There is but one truth—all other creeds are naught but a snare and a delusion. I denounce thee as the tool of the Anti-Christ—and I—I...' He began to pant for breath. His face was leaden, and there were white flecks of foam upon his beard.

'I...denounce...thee...' Then he clawed at his throat, and fell headlong.

The congregation seemed stunned, frozen with embarrassment, except for one little woman, white-haired and pink-cheeked, who hurried to the old man, dropping to her knees, and saying, 'It's all right, Marcus, I'm here. Will somebody help me to get him home? Florrie, can you give me a hand?'

But Florrie Judge, sobbing with humiliation, shrank away, retreating down the aisle and hiding under the shadows of the porch, whimpering, 'I've never been so ashamed in all my life. How *could* he? Showing us up like that...'

Two men in black Sunday suits picked Marcus Judge up from the floor and carried him out into the fresh air. The Minister followed helplessly, asking, 'Is there anything I can do?'

'We can manage, thank you.' Louisa apologised. 'I'm sorry about the disturbance. Sometimes he doesn't know what he's saying—he's not been well, lately. He'll be better when I get him home. I'm so sorry.'

The colour began to creep into Marcus's face; his lips moved, his eyelids fluttered and he groaned, 'Where am I? What happened?'

'Nothing's happened, dear,' Louisa told him. 'You're quite safe now. We're going home.'

The dressing-rooms at the Grand Theatre, Byker, were not palatial. This week, to her intense annoyance, Sally was sharing again with Greta Hayward, the conjuror's assistant. It wasn't even as if Greta was a proper artiste. She didn't sing or dance, she only stood about, waving coloured handkerchiefs, looking after the white rabbit and having swords stuck through her inside the magic cabinet... According to Sally, Greta didn't qualify as a speciality performer at all, and she resented having to share a dressing-room with her.

To add insult to injury, Greta finished work every night a good ten minutes before the finale, and didn't have to wait for the line-up and the curtain-calls, so by the time Sally ran back up the narrow stone staircase to the Number Five dressing-room, Greta had got her make-up off and used up all the hot water. Hot water was strictly rationed on this tour; the management maintained this was to save fuel and help the war effort, but Sally knew better—it was just another example of their penny-pinching meanness.

Greta was already wriggling into her skirt and jumper, and grabbing her coat, saying, 'Ta-ta, ducky—see you tomorrow. Sleep tight—hope the bugs don't bite!'

Then she ran noisily down the stone steps, leaving Sally glaring at her own reflection, and wiping the greasepaint off her face with cold cream. God, what a dump! And what a bloody awful show... For two pins, she'd tear up her contract and tell them to get stuffed, and take the next train back to London.

She had just put on her street-clothes, and was powdering her nose, when there was a knock at the door. Guessing it would be the Company Manager—though it was funny she hadn't heard him on the stairs, because he was a big man and heavy on his feet—she called out: 'OK, Joe. If it's about the change in the running-order tomorrow night, I've already been told!'

The door opened, and a pleasant voice said, 'It's not about the running-order—and it's not Joe.'

Sally turned, and saw a pale young man in the doorway. He was very good-looking, and had dark, wavy hair, a polo-necked sweater and an expensive sports jacket; he also had a playful smile.

She smiled back. 'Hello,' she said. 'And who might you be?'

'My name's Tony Jasper—how do you do?'

'How do you do?' Surprised but pleased, she shook hands, adding, 'I know who you are.'

'Do you?' He seemed rather taken aback. 'We've never met, have we?'

'Oh, no—but I've heard about you. You're in the business, aren't you? In management.' Sally picked up her lipstick, 'You won't mind if I carry on? They like to get us out as quick as possible, so they can lock up.'

'Of course. But I'd like a word with you, if you've got a moment. May I sit down?'

'Not on the sofa; it's had Mystero's rabbit on it, so it might not be very clean. Have the other chair... You were in front tonight, to see Bertha, weren't you? She's been going on and on about you, coming all this way to catch her act.'

Bertha Brick—'Big Bertha' on the bills—was the show's comedienne; her Cockney charwoman had been a favourite with audiences for years.

'Yes, I've just been talking to her. She's still very popular; I hope to have something to offer her later on... But I thought—since I'm here—I'd like to have a chat with you as well, Miss King.'

'Call me Sally,' she said, putting the finishing touches to her make-up. She was determined not to let him see she was thrilled—a West End manager, coming to see her! This was the chance she'd been waiting for. 'I'm afraid we shan't have long. Like I said, they'll be turning the lights off soon.'

'Just tell me one thing. You're represented by an agent—Harry Packer, is that right?'

'Yes, how did you know?'

'Oh, I've done my homework. Are you signed up with him on a long-term contract? Exclusively?'

'No, nothing like that. Actually, it's funny you should mention it, 'cos I've been thinking it's about time I made a change.'

'Yes, I heard that too.' He smiled again, and her heart beat a little faster. 'I wonder, would you be free to have supper with me tonight?'

'Oh, I'd love to, only...' She grimaced. 'There's nowhere round here to eat—nothing but caffs and pie-shops, and they all shut by nine o'clock. I'd ask you back to my digs, but the landlady goes to bed early. She leaves me a couple of sandwiches under a plate... You'd be welcome to share them, but I warn you they're not up to much!'

'By the time you get there, the crusts have curled up round the edges, eh?' His eyes twinkled. 'I think we can do better than that. I'm staying at the Grand tonight, and they promised me the Grill Room will stay open till I get back, so if you're ready?'

'The Grand?' Her face fell; Byker was some way from the centre of Newcastle. 'It'll be rather a long walk.'

'We're not walking; I've got a taxi waiting outside.'

They were there in ten minutes, and the Grill Room was still open, though they were the only people in it. Afterwards, she could never remember what they had eaten, yet the occasion was unforgettable.

He ordered a bottle of red wine, topping her glass up several times; it was the kind of evening she'd always dreamed about, and he couldn't have been nicer. Not only because he was handsome and charming and funny—he seemed to have taken to her right away, and he was so interested in everything she told him, asking heaps of questions about her career and her ambitions. He hardly talked about himself at all, except to say: 'I've been travelling round the north of England, and I decided to come and take a look at dear old Bertha. I'm very glad I did.'

'Yes, she told everybody. She says you're putting on a new show—is that right?'

'Absolutely. Not in Byker though! Number One dates—no rubbish. And if it really takes off, a West End opening in September or October.'

'Lovely...and Bertha's going to be starring, is she?'

'Well, no—I'm afraid not.' For a moment he looked sad. 'I wouldn't say this to anyone else, but I'm sure I can trust you not to let it go any further.'

'Of course not!' She put on a serious, concerned face. 'Go on.'

'I'm afraid poor old Bertha's a bit past it. She had to fight for every laugh tonight—they didn't warm to her.'

Sally sighed. 'I know, it's a shame...but they do say cockney humour never goes down north of Coventry, don't they?'

'That's very true, but even so, Bertha's not quite what I'm looking for. She's not Shaftesbury Avenue... Still, I told her I may be able to use her in panto, next Christmas. I'm thinking of having a female Dame, it might be a novelty. She seemed to be quite thrilled about it.'

'I'm so glad.' Sally took another sip of wine, and he continued.

'I must admit, earlier tonight I was afraid I'd had a wasted journey, but then you stepped out on that stage and all the lights seemed to go up.' He put down his knife and fork and leaned forward, saying earnestly, 'You're too good for this sort of thing. The rest of the show, quite frankly, is a load of old tat, but you made it all worthwhile. You've got real quality, Sally—and I do know what I'm talking about.'

Breathlessly, she managed to say, 'I'm sure you do.'

'Of course I'm not an agent, I have my own company—we put on shows. I go round talent-spotting and when I find someone exciting, we sign her up. If you put yourself in my hands, I could shape your career...does the idea appeal to you at all?'

'Yes, it does,' she whispered. 'Oh yes, it really does.'

'Believe me, this could be a real Cinderella

story—the little girl from the East End who became a shining star!'

Disconcerted, she said: 'How d'you know I'm from the East End?'

'I told you, I've been doing my homework.' There was that playful smile again. 'If I'm not mistaken, you come from the Isle of Dogs, and you used to be Sharon Kleiber—am I right?'

'Well, yes. I changed my name for professional reasons.'

'Good idea. And since we're both being so frank with each other, I'll let you into a secret. Strangely enough, I come from that part of the world myself.' He refilled his glass, then raised it in a toast. 'Here's to our long and happy association, Sally—here's to us!'

They clinked glasses. As he was about to drink, he paused and added casually, 'And that's another thing we have in common... I changed my name too, a long time ago—for professional reasons.'

On 31 May, there was a special bulletin on the six o'clock news.

The BBC announcer said: *'Men of the undefeated British Expeditionary Force have been coming home from France. Their morale is as high as ever; they are only anxious to get back soon "to have another crack at Jerry" as they put it.'* Ruth and Mary O'Dell were in the pub kitchen, clearing away the tea things. They looked at each other in dismay.

'So it is true,' said Ruth.

Over the past few days rumours had been

flying about. People reported that troop-trains were coming into London from the south coast, packed with soldiers—most of them alseep, many of them wounded, all exhausted.

'Danny will be coming home then.' Mary crossed herself. 'Please God.'

The door into the backyard was open; little Kaff Hobbs was sitting out on the step with a magic colouring book, a paintbrush and a glass of water. Her mother still came in every morning to clean the pub, but now she had an afternoon job as well, to make ends meet, and Ruth had agreed to keep an eye on Kaff till Nora collected her.

Hearing Dan's name, Kaff looked round. 'Is he really coming home?' she asked eagerly. 'When? Will he be here tomorrow?'

Ruth tried to sound cheerful. 'We don't know when, exactly. Soon, I hope.'

'Why's he been gone so long?' Kaff persisted. 'Where is he now?'

Ruth turned away and began to fold up the tablecloth. 'We don't know that either,' she said. 'I wish we did.'

It had been another brilliant summer day on the French beaches, and now the sun was going down in a riot of orange and gold.

'Red sky at night, shepherd's delight,' quoted Dan. 'Another fine day tomorrow.'

'It'll be a red sky all bleeding night, by the looks of it,' said Matt, glancing back over his shoulder.

They were sprawled amongst the marram grass

of the dunes, on an endless beach that stretched in both directions as far as the eye could see: eastward to Belgium, which had capitulated to the German invaders, and westward, where the last remnants of the British Army kept up a desperate rearguard action, caught in a pincer movement as the Nazis swept across France.

They were trapped in a tiny patch of territory which grew smaller every day. Behind them lay Dunkirk—the little seaport that had been battered by repeated artillery attacks and wave upon wave of bombers; the sky was soiled with black smoke, and reddened by fires below that seemed as if they would go on burning for ever.

And—facing them—there was the sea; the only possible way of escape. Dan lifted his head and sniffed the breeze blowing across the Channel.

'Wind's from the north-east,' he said. 'Funny to think of England, just a few miles away. So near, you can almost smell it.'

Matt hawked and spat into the sand. 'You're lucky,' he said. 'I can't.'

'I said almost...' Dan shivered a little; the salty tang in the air could not wipe out the smell of burning from the ruined town, or the stench of death that hung over the area like a funeral pall.

'What's up? Not catching cold, are you?' asked Matt.

'No, but it's getting parky now the sun's gone down. And I still haven't dried out from our last dip!'

Dan's tunic was spread over a clump of reeds; it was almost dry, but his khaki trousers still clung wetly to his legs. A few hours earlier, it had seemed as if they were about to get away; a small flotilla of private boats—launches, motor-yachts, cabin-cruisers—kept coming over from England, picking the troops up from the shallows and ferrying them to the destroyer *Ivanhoe* which lay off-shore, at anchor.

They had been among the men who waded out, waist-deep; but there were so many thousands of them, and only a handful of boats—and then the enemy planes had come back, raking the beaches with machine-gun fire, throwing up bursts of white spray where the bullets tore through the water... Many men were killed outright, others badly injured—and the rest had turned and run for cover, trying to find some hiding-place among the barren dunes. By the time the hit-and-run raiders had gone, the destroyer had moved off as well, nobody knew where—perhaps under orders to try another rescue operation further along the coast... And the men could do nothing but stay where they were—and wait.

Matt and Dan had been waiting there for days; tonight would be their third night on the beach. When their platoon was cut off from the rest of B Company, somewhere near St Omer, they lost touch with HQ Division and had to make their own way back to the coast, hiding out as the enemy advanced, lying low by day in copses or under haystacks, and making slow progress across the flat open farmlands by night.

They had had several narrow escapes, so when they reached Dunkirk they thought their troubles were over—only to discover that the rest of B Company had disappeared. Wiped out, some said; others thought they might have been taken prisoner—either way, there was only a small band of stragglers left. They attached themselves to C Company and waited for orders—only there were no orders. No one knew what was happening; the whole Army seemed to be in a state of chaos. All they could do was stay on the beach, and hope to be rescued—and try to stay alive.

As soon as the sun had gone down into the sea, the sky began to darken although, as Matt had predicted, it never became totally dark. The glare of the burning buildings, less than a mile away, was reflected back from the clouds, lighting up the seashore in a lurid glow.

Suddenly a voice yelled, 'On your feet, men—look sharp! Platoon will form in threes to take up places on the mole. Jump to it, can't you?'

'If that's Sergeant sodding Judge, he can get knotted!' grunted Matt.

When they rejoined what was left of their regiment, they had been startled to find their cousin there, in a position of authority—Sergeant James Judge, of C Company. Though he had enlisted later, he had already been given promotion; while Matt and Dan were still in the junior ranks, Jimmy now had three stripes on his arm.

They made themselves known to him, expecting he would give them some assistance, but found him cool and unfriendly. Matt was indignant—'The rotten bugger, him and me used to be mates in the old days!'—but Dan said: 'Perhaps he doesn't approve of your choice of friends. Jimmy Judge and me fell out a long time ago.'

'Ah, that's all over and done with. We're the same family, ain't we?' But Sergeant Judge had not shown much in the way of family feeling.

Now they scrambled to their feet, and Dan pulled on his tunic as they formed up into an untidy platoon and set off along the sands. A few hundred yards away was the 'mole'—a long wooden pier that stretched out into deep water, and acted as a landing-stage for small fishing-boats in happier times.

As they drew near, an excited shout went up, for there, at the end of the mole, was a small steamer; the engine was chugging, churning up white water beneath her stern.

'Blimey, d'you see what I see?' exclaimed Matt. 'It's *Tudor Rose!*'

She was one of the river-steamers that used to ply between Tower Bridge and Southend, taking day-trippers down the Thames; like her sister-ships, the paddle-boats, she had been pressed into service in this emergency, and was now standing by to take off another load of troops.

They crowded out along the jetty, while officers and NCOs barked at them to keep moving. 'No pushing there. Keep three abreast, and wait your turn!'

Dan and Matt were halfway along the pier when they heard the sound of approaching aircraft. Looking up, they saw the Messerschmidts returning, and there was a sudden hush—the planes dived towards them—they heard the rattle of machine-gun fire, and the bullets ripped through the waiting ranks. Then they uttered a great howl—a howl that had notes of fear in it, and of pain—above all, of anger.

'Murdering bastards!' yelled Matt, turning his face up to the night sky, as the plane roared off into the distance. 'They don't give us a chance!'

Three or four men near the head of the jetty had been wounded, and Sergeant Judge elbowed his way along the line, shouting: 'Stand back—make way for stretcher-bearers!'

The injured men were lifted on to stretchers and carried ashore to the First Aid station. Sergeant Judge remained where he was, at the bottom of the gangplank, to supervise the embarkation, and the line of men shuffled forward once more.

Just as Matt and Dan reached the head of the queue, someone high on the ship's bridge called down, 'Two more only. Next two men get aboard quickly—then cast off!'

Dan and Matt could hardly believe their luck. They moved forward eagerly, but a brawny arm barred their way. Dan found himself looking into Jimmy Judge's eyes, and saw the hatred there.

'Stand clear!' ordered Jimmy, and pushed them back.

Dan staggered, nearly losing his balance; he clutched at Matt to save himself from falling into the sea. Instantly, Jimmy Judge vaulted aboard the steamer, then turned and pulled in the gangplank. There was a splash as the mooring-rope dropped away, and the beat of the ship's engine increased. The propellers turned and the steamer drew slowly away.

It was so quick, hardly anyone except Dan and Matt realised what had happened, but when they saw the rescue-ship departing, the waiting men roared with frustration. But there was nothing to be done; someone rapped out fresh orders, and they began to make their way to the beach.

That was when another plane came over, not a Messerschmidt this time but a Stuka—and it was not aiming for the mole. Looking back, Dan saw the bomb fall; it hit the *Tudor Rose* amidships with a shattering explosion and a blazing sheet of flame as the fuel-tanks blew up.

The ship seemed to shudder from stem to stern, then she keeled over and slipped sideways; the watchers saw her break apart, and the sea engulfed her. Within two minutes, *Tudor Rose* had gone, and there were no survivors.

Some hours later, just before midnight, Dan and Matt went out on to the mole for the last time. The *Ivanhoe* had been ordered to return to Dunkirk, and had put out a launch to pick up the next contingent of men.

As they went aboard, Dan turned to Matt and said, 'You know what? It just struck me; he may not have meant to do it—but Jimmy Judge saved our bloody lives...'

5

Walking home through the black-out was always an ordeal; at the end of a late duty at the Fire Station, when she was tired, Lil found it worse than usual.

Her pocket torch had been dimmed, according to official regulations, with two thicknesses of tissue paper and a rubber band, so it only emitted a faint glow; she suspected that the batteries had started to wear out as well. That was going to be a problem, for number nine batteries were like gold dust these days... By its glow-worm light, she could just make out the edge of the kerb, which was painted white; people said that so far most of the civilian casualties had been caused by pedestrians tripping over in the dark, colliding with lamp-posts or falling down unseen flights of steps.

But there were more sinister tales as well, of night-time prowlers who haunted the empty streets, ready to snatch a handbag and run—and sometimes there were stories of worse assaults... That was why Lil hated walking back to the pub late at night, but when she was on the last evening shift, she had no choice.

She turned the corner, and was glad to recognise the familiar outline of the Watermen, its rooftops and chimney-pots silhouetted against a starry sky. Then she caught her breath. She saw a darker shadow move in the alley that led to the side door, and heard the scrape of a heavy boot on the stone step. The man, whoever he was, seemed to be lying in wait... She stopped dead and switched off her torch, but he had already seen her...

Dan's voice said, 'Lil? Is that you?'

With a sob of relief, she flung herself upon him. In that split second, terror turned to joy. Her brother was no longer missing somewhere in France. He was safe. And so was she.

'You great ape!' she laughed. 'You scared the living daylights out of me!'

'It's a good job you came along,' he told her. 'I've been trying to unlock the door, but I'm all fingers and thumbs tonight. I didn't want to wake the whole house.'

She used her own key to let him in, taking him through to the kitchen and turning on the light. His appearance shocked her; his uniform was filthy, he was unshaven and grey with tiredness.

'You look awful,' she said. 'Sit down, for goodness sake. Have you had any supper? I'll cut you some bread and cheese—there's plenty, Mum only got our rations today.'

'Don't bother, I'm not hungry. But I'd give a week's pay for a cup of tea.'

As she filled the kettle, he went on, 'These last few days have been a bit of a slog. I haven't had much sleep. I dare say I don't smell too good, either—I can't remember the last time I had a wash. You heard about it, did you, what happened at Dunkirk? I suppose it was a miracle any of us got away. God knows how many blokes copped it... I was one of the lucky ones—and so was Matt.'

'Where is Matt? Didn't you bring him with you?'

'He's gone straight home. We got into Waterloo about half-past eleven and caught the last underground as far as Mile End. We had to walk the rest of the way.'

'You're safe and sound, that's the main thing.'

'Yes, we're still alive but...' He rubbed his eyes, struggling to stay awake. 'Some aren't. Jimmy isn't.'

'Jimmy Judge?' She swung round. 'Are you sure?'

He nodded. 'I saw it happen. There was another boat before ours—he just managed to get on board, then it was dive-bombed. She went down so fast—nobody got off alive.'

Lil and Dan exchanged glances; there was no need to say anything more. They both had cause to hate their cousin, but this was not the time to drag up old, bitter memories. Lil crossed herself, saying quietly, 'May he rest in peace.'

Then they heard hurrying footsteps on the stair, and the kitchen door opened again as their mother and father came in, tousle-haired and in their night-clothes.

'Danny—I *knew* it!' Ruth was laughing and crying at the same time, hugging her son. 'Didn't I say so?'

Connor tried to get a word in edgeways. 'We hadn't gone to sleep, we were still talking—then we heard voices and your Mam said "That's Dan," and I said: "Get away with you, how can it be Dan?"—but of course she had to be in the right, didn't she? How are you, son?'

When the kettle had boiled, Connor scorned the thought of tea and insisted on opening a good bottle of wine, saying, 'It's not every day the whole family get together. This calls for a celebration!'

Lil said nothing, but turned away. Seeing her expression, Ruth reminded Con gently, 'Not quite the whole family.'

Lil cut in quickly, 'I expect Mike will get leave very soon.'

'Of course he will; that will be something to look forward to,' said Ruth, and they raised their glasses to a complete family reunion.

Lil drank to that—but in tea. She thought of Mike's homecoming with mixed feelings, for the longing to see him was still coloured with secret dread. She loved him so much, and she wanted to be a good wife to him. She told herself that now she had done it once, it would be easier the next time—yet her body still rebelled at the thought of his lovemaking... But whatever happened, she was determined that Mike should never know how she felt.

Next day, Dan went to the Jubilee Wharf

and sent in his name, asking to see Mr Albert Judge.

It was the first time he had set foot in the Guild offices since he resigned from the Brotherhood nearly three years ago. Bertie welcomed him with some surprise, and wary politeness; there had never been any love lost between them.

'What brings you here, Daniel?' he asked. 'Home on leave, eh? I'm sorry I can't spare much time for a chat—there's a great deal to be done. I'm in sole charge here, you know, since Jimmy joined up—and I've had my work cut out, keeping the business going...' Noticing Dan's shoulder-flashes, he added, 'Of course, you and him are in the same regiment. Have you seen him lately? Did he send me any messages? You can tell him with my compliments, the sooner he wins this damn war and comes back to do his share in the office, the happier I'll be!'

Dan moistened his lips, then said: 'I wasn't sure if you knew. I thought you might have heard by this time... I'm sorry, Bertie—I'm afraid I have some bad news for you.'

Bertie's face went completely blank. 'Bad news?'

As simply as possible, Dan told him Jimmy was dead. He described the lone bomber, and the speed with which the ship went down; he did not mention his last encounter with Jimmy at the foot of the gangplank.

When he had finished, Bertie put his head in his hands, 'I can't believe it. I never dreamed—I never expected... I've been waiting for him to come home and take on some of this work. How am I going to manage?'

He pulled open a filing cabinet and took out a half-bottle of whisky. Unscrewing the cap, he put it to his lips and swallowed greedily. Then he remembered Dan; shamefaced, he held it out to him. Dan said it was a bit early in the day for him. Bertie took a second swig, then asked abruptly: 'How long have you got? How long are you going to be at home? D'you think you could come in and give me a hand, getting the paperwork up to date? I'm snowed under at present, and it's getting worse. You were always a bright lad, and you know how the Guild operates. Could you help me sort things out? I'd pay you well.'

Dan interrupted, 'Sorry—I've only got a weekend pass. I'm due to report back on Monday morning.'

'Oh. Oh, well...' Bertie sank back into his chair, staring at the untidy piles of paper that littered his desk, muttering resentfully, 'I don't know how I'm going to manage without him. I can't get over it. Jimmy, of all people, going like that. It doesn't seem fair, does it?'

'Isn't it wonderful to have our lads home again?' said Ruth. 'Even if it is only for a few days.'

Gloria agreed. 'Just to see them, safe and well—it makes all the difference.'

While Gloria was doing Ruth's hair, they compared notes about the homecoming. Ruth explained how Lil had let Dan in quietly, hoping

157

not to disturb them, but she had heard his voice downstairs—too far away to pick out the words, yet she had known him instantly.

'Matt wasn't that considerate!' said Glory. 'He couldn't find his key, so he just kept hammering on the door till I woke up and came down. I thought I must have left a light on somewhere, so when I saw Matt standing there on the step, I nearly passed out!'

'They didn't all come home,' added Ruth, in a different tone. 'Did Matt tell you about Jimmy?'

'Yes, he did.' Glory lowered her eyes. 'Of course it's very sad, and I'm very sorry, but—' She stopped, then burst out suddenly: 'That's not true! Why should I bother to lie about it? I've hated Jimmy Judge for years. He was a cruel, selfish bully—and I'm not shedding any tears over him!'

Ruth stared at her. 'I know he could be a bit rough, but what had he ever done to upset you?'

'He never did anything to *me*. It was what he did to other people...' She set her lips. 'Never mind, he's gone now. We'll say no more about it.' Just in time, she had remembered that Ruth never knew what had happened to Lil, all those years ago. Instead, she changed the subject. 'I still think it's rotten, making the boys report to barracks first thing Monday morning. I suppose it's the same for Dan as for Matt?'

'What's all this, then? Talking about me again, eh?' Matt came through from the back room, and greeted Ruth cheerily. 'Hello, Mrs

158

O'Dell—and how's Dan feeling today? All the better for being home, I dare say?'

'Oh, yes—and how are you?' said Ruth. 'You're looking very smart.'

'You should have seen him last night.' said Glory. 'More like something the cat dragged in!'

'Don't be so cheeky!' As he passed by, Matt slapped his mother's bottom, then stopped to admire himself in the glass, smoothing down his hair and knotting his tie a little tighter. 'Yeah—it feels good to be in civvies for a change,' he said. 'And a good night's sleep, in my own bed... I just hope Mr Pritchard didn't mind being turned out at short notice!'

Grinning, he crossed to the street door, saying over his shoulder, 'I'm not sure when I'll be back, Ma. I thought I'd drop in on some of me pals. Be seeing you!' They heard him whistling as he strolled off down the street.

'What was that about Mr Pritchard?' Ruth asked. 'Did he mean Huw?'

'Yes. We felt bad about waking the poor chap last night, but Matt was practically dead on his feet. He needed a long lie-in—and Mr Pritchard was very good about it. I made up a bed on the sofa. He says he doesn't mind—it's only for a couple of nights, after all.'

Ruth was still mystified. 'Are you saying Huw's been staying here—in Matt's room?'

'That's right. He's our lodger now. He had to move out of Three Colt Street—didn't you know?'

A long time ago, Huw had fallen hopelessly in love with Ruth; it was when she and Connor were going through a bad patch, and she had been strongly attracted to the young Welshman. Nothing had come of it, and she remained faithful to her husband yet now, although she knew it was absurd, she couldn't help feeling a little hurt, as Glory chattered on.

'Well, why shouldn't I take in a lodger? It suits him, and I'm glad of the extra money.'

'Yes, I see. I'm glad it's worked out so well for you both, only...I can't imagine why he never told me he was living here.'

'P'rhaps it slipped his mind.' Glory thought for a moment, then smiled. 'Or p'rhaps he didn't want you to start getting any wrong ideas!'

'Wrong ideas?' Ruth looked at her. 'You don't mean, I might have thought that you and he... Oh, honestly—that's ridiculous!'

Glory's smiled faded. 'What's ridiculous about it?'

'Well, because... It just is, that's all.'

'You mean because I'm a few years older?' Her face hardened. 'There's not much difference in age between him and me.'

'Twelve years,' said Ruth, who had been working it out. 'I'm five years older than Huw, and you're seven years older than me.'

'What if I am? There's no need to make me sound like Methuselah!' Glory was beginning to get indignant. 'Twelve years isn't that much, is it? There's plenty of women older than me, throwing themselves at younger men, I can tell

160

you. Look at your precious sister-in-law, for a start!'

'Rosie?' Now Ruth was completely at sea. 'What's Rosie got to do with it?'

'Nothing at all—except that for the past six months or more, she's had her eye on my son, that's all! Sending him presents, writing to him—and her a married woman! Of course he takes no notice—he just thinks she's making a fool of herself.' She made a last, irritable dab at Ruth's hair and said, 'Anyhow, that's you done. I hope it's satisfactory?'

With an effort, Ruth managed to focus upon her reflection, replying in a daze: 'What? Oh yes, thank you. That looks very nice...'

'I'm sorry, not this afternoon. Could you come back tomorrow?' Rosie opened the shop diary, and picked up a pencil. 'I can make an appointment for you, if you like?'

The young man in RAF uniform and the girl in a summer dress looked at one another sadly, then he said: 'I won't be here. My leave finishes tomorrow. We were hoping to get a photo of the two of us before I go.'

The girl held out her hand, showing off the new ring on her finger. 'We just got engaged, you see. Couldn't you fit us in some time this afternoon?'

Rosie began, 'I really am sorry. I'd like to help, but my husband's the photographer, and he'll be out until—'

The shop door opened again, and another young man came in. Rosie glanced at him,

161

and her face lit up. She stopped in mid-sentence, unable to remember what she was going to say.

'Hello there,' said Matt, shyly.

'Hello, Matt...' She was afraid that she might blush. 'Will you excuse me a minute, while I deal with this lady and gentleman?' She turned back to the customers. 'I'm so sorry—what was I saying?'

'You said your husband's out,' the Aircraftsman reminded her.

'Yes, that's right—all afternoon. He won't be home till the shop's shut.'

'Isn't there anyone else who could do it?'

'Not really. My son helps in the shop, and he sometimes takes photos too, but he's not here either. They're both working at Mudchute this afternoon, on the allotments—digging ditches and knocking stakes in, so the enemy planes won't be able to land there.'

'Oh dear, do you think they might try?' The girl held her fiancé's hand tightly. 'Oh, Neville!'

'I'm sure it'll never happen,' Rosie hastened to assure her. 'It's only a precaution, that's all.'

The young man saw the girl's frightened expression, and squeezed her hand, pleading more urgently: 'Isn't there any way we could get a photo today? It would mean such a lot to us.'

Rosie made up her mind. 'Come back about seven o'clock, he'll be home by then. The shop will be shut, but I'll make sure you get your picture.'

'Thanks—thanks a lot. We'll be here bang on seven, then.' He tucked his arm round the girl's waist, and they went out.

As soon as the door had shut, Rosie turned to Matt, her eyes shining. 'It's so good to see you. Ruth rang this morning and told me Dan was home on leave—and you as well. I was hoping I might see something of you, this weekend. How are you?'

She held out both hands to him. Awkwardly, he grabbed her right hand, and shook it. 'I'm OK, ta,' he said. 'How are you keeping?'

'I'm very well indeed.' She tried to pull herself together. 'What can I do for you?'

'Nothing. I didn't come to have me picture took,' he grinned. 'I only come to say thanks.'

'Oh, you don't have to do that,' she told him. 'It was nothing.'

'Nothing? All them cigarettes and books, and the bars of chocolate? And them letters—I s'pose I should've wrote back, only I ain't much of a hand at letter-writing.'

'I didn't expect you to. I just wanted to let you know we were all thinking of you.'

'All? The whole family, like? You told 'em you was writing to me in France, did you?'

'No. I don't believe I—I don't think I mentioned it.'

'How about your husband? Did you tell him?'

'No, I didn't. He—he might not have understood. As a matter of fact, I believe your mother thought it was rather strange, me asking for your address. You didn't mind, did

163

you?' she asked anxiously.

'Course I didn't. Always glad to get news from home. Ma don't write me often—if it weren't for you, I wouldn't get many letters at all. And as for sending me presents—the other blokes are pretty jealous, believe me!' He grinned again, adding: 'You will go on writing, won't you? If you was to stop now, I'd never hear the last of it. They'd pull my leg something rotten!'

'I won't stop,' she promised.

Then the door opened yet again, and in a cloud of perfume, Sally King swept into the shop, exclaiming: 'Mumsie! Surprise, surprise!'

She leaned across the counter, kicking up one leg in an arabesque, and kissed her mother on both cheeks in the fashionable continental style. She was fashionable in every way; her hair swept up on top in a row of bright golden curls, and her bottle-green linen suit with square padded shoulders.

'But—where did you spring from? I thought you were in Yorkshire!'

'Palace Theatre, Attercliffe? That was last week—and I swear I'll never go there again, as long as I live. Next week it's the Theatre Royal, Wednesbury, but in between times we had a few days off, so here I am... Aren't you pleased to see me?'

'You know I am, but today's Saturday. What have you been doing this week? Where were you?'

'Oh, I've been in town. They had to replace half the company, so we've been having endless

164

rehearsals. It's been sheer bloody murder.'

'Language!' Rosie corrected her from force of habit. 'Don't you see we've got a visitor? You remember Matt, don't you? Matthew Judge?'

Sally flashed a brief, insincere smile. 'Of course. How are you?'

'How do?' They shook hands, but she withdrew hers immediately. She had summed him up at a glance, and he was of no possible interest to her. Perhaps she didn't recognise him? He tried to jog her memory. 'I ain't seen you since that time we was hop-picking down in Kent,' he said with a wink. 'We had some fun then, didn't we, eh?'

'Did we? It was donkeys years ago; I'm afraid I've forgotten,' she told him, and went on talking to her mother.

'Stuck-up bitch,' he thought. 'All right—you're a hot little piece, right enough, but your Ma's worth two of you! And she thinks the world of me, even if you don't...'

He waited sulkily, resenting the interruption, while Sally went on. 'And of course I had to go and call on Tony Jasper at his office in Charing Cross Road; he's been simply wonderful—I told you last time I wrote, didn't I? As soon as this god-awful tour packs up, he's going to put me in his next revue.'

'But where have you been staying in London?' asked Rosie. 'Why didn't you come home?'

'Darling, I've been working from morn to night, I haven't had a minute to breathe. I couldn't possibly have trailed in and out on buses and tube-trains every day. Some friends

165

in the company very kindly put me up—nobody you know... I did think I might have stayed here tonight, but I've got a train-call tomorrow, terribly early as per usual, so it wouldn't be worth it...' She looked round. 'Where's Poppa? Where's Abram?'

'They're out—and I'm not letting you go until they come home, so that's that!' Rosie went and put the Closed sign on the door. 'The shop can look after itself for ten minutes. Come upstairs, both of you, and I'll make some tea.'

When Sally got back to Charing Cross Road, it was nearly eight o'clock. Tony Jasper's office, at the top of a ramshackle building near the Phoenix Theatre, was also his flat. She took the creaky Victorian lift to the top floor, and rang the bell.

After a moment, she heard him call out: 'Who is it?'

'Tallulah Bankhead,' she said. 'Who else were you expecting, this time of night?'

He opened the door to her, with one towel round his waist, drying his hair on another; trickles of water ran off his spare, pale body—he moved easily, like a dancer.

'You're dripping all over the carpet,' she said.

'So what? It's my carpet,' he said, shutting the door. 'What took you so long? I thought you'd deserted me and signed up with Cochran instead.'

'He did offer—but he's not my type,' she replied. He was about to take her in his arms, but she held him off. 'What are you trying to do? Ruin my new suit?'

'You know what I'm trying to do,' he said, loosening the towel at his waist, which fell to the floor. 'In case you hadn't noticed, you have a very strange effect on me, Sally King.'

'I noticed,' she said. 'I thought I was being taken out to supper?'

'Later,' he said.

Afterwards, they lay side by side on the big bed; he lit two cigarettes, and put one between her lips. 'All right?' he asked.

'Highly enjoyable,' she told him. 'As always.'

'So glad I came up to expectations,' he said, then asked, 'How were the family?'

'They're fine. Poppa's looking a lot older—he works too hard. Mumsie's fine, and I think Abram's OK—he didn't say much, but then he never does. He's the quiet type... And there was somebody else there—Matthew Judge. He's a sort of relation on Mumsie's side of the family, home on leave. He was at Dunkirk—so was my cousin Dan. They were lucky to get away... There was another cousin who didn't.'

'Oh? Who was that?'

'He was called James Judge. Matt said he'd just got on the rescue ship when the bloody Germans dropped a bomb on it—he actually saw it happen. I felt rather sad about it; as I used to know him quite well at one time. Poor old Jimmy Judge—what a way to go.'

She felt the bed shake, and looked round. To her astonishment, Tony was rocking with silent laughter. 'What's so funny?' she asked.

'*Poor old Jimmy,*' he repeated the words, then

convulsed with giggles.

'That's not very nice, is it? You oughtn't to laugh about people being killed, even if you don't know them.'

He tried to control himself. 'But that's the point of the joke,' he said, when he could get the words out. 'I do know him... I used to live in the same house for a while, with him and his slimy brother Bertie. Their dad was my stepfather, Joshua Judge. He wasn't a bad old stick, in his way.'

Sally sat up, leaning on one elbow, staring into his face. 'What are you talking about?' she asked. 'Who are you?'

'I told you I'd changed my name, didn't I? I used to be called Trevor Judge, but that was a whole lifetime ago—someone else's life... I don't often think about it now.'

'I've heard of you.' She gazed at him, wondering. 'You ran away from home. You used to work at Jubilee Wharf—there was some trouble...'

'Oh, you heard that, did you? Yes, I was a proper little devil in those days. I borrowed some money from the till, and did a disappearing act—the Great Mystero had nothing on me! Of course, I've seen the error of my ways since then, and I'm dreadfully sorry for being such a bad boy, but it did get me off to a good start.'

'And—all this time—you've never been back?'

'I used to pass through from time to time—I like to keep up with all the news. I had an old friend who used to tell me the latest developments, so I heard how my dear little Ma followed my example and ran off to the States with her fancy man... And I heard how poor old Josh kicked the bucket—caught up in a nasty fire at the warehouse... But the pick of the bunch was Jimmy Judge—I really hated his guts—and now he's gone as well.'

He rolled over, taking her in his arms again. 'That's the best news I've heard for a long time—thanks a lot.'

'Hey!' Aware of his growing excitement she said, 'What's all this, then? I thought we were going out to supper?'

'All in good time,' he told her. 'You've just given me a new lease of life.'

It was a perfect summer; the days followed one another in unbroken sunshine and it would have been ideal holiday weather, if anyone could have taken a holiday.

Upon cloudless blue skies, white vapour-trails scrawled sinister hieroglyphics, as German planes flew across the south of England, and RAF Spitfires went up to meet them. At Dunkirk, the war had begun at last; yet even now people found it hard to believe. They watched the life and death struggles being played out high above their heads, as if they were a new kind of sporting contest. Even the news vendors, selling evening papers, chalked the latest scores on the placards: *Germany 103, England 12* or *Germany All Out—185 for 26.*

At the same time, they shared one unspoken thought, and one evening in July, Churchill broadcast to the nation and put that thought into words. He admitted Hitler was planning to invade Britain, and made no bones about it.

'Perhaps it will come tonight—perhaps it will come next week—perhaps it will never come.'

And the people remembered Holland, and Belgium and France; they dug deeper trenches, and filled more sandbags and they waited.

When Connor switched off the wireless in the saloon bar, he said to Huw: 'We'll be ready for Adolf if he does come—bet your life on that.'

Huw looked at the clock. 'It'll be getting dark soon. Shall I start putting up the shutters?'

The windows in the bar were blacked-out with wooden frames covered in tarred paper; they fitted more securely than curtains and could not be brushed aside by a careless elbow.

'Hang on, I'll give you a hand,' Connor told him. 'It's easier with the two of us.'

As they were manoeuvring the first shutter into place, the door banged open and Bertie Judge came in.

'Give me a scotch—neat!' he snapped. 'Make it a double.'

Connor began, 'Singles only, I'm sorry to say. We have to be fair to all our customers,' but Bertie interrupted him.

'For God's sake, man, this is medicinal! I've got a dicky heart—I need something to keep me going!' He certainly looked ill. He was shaking uncontrollably and his face was a sickly greenish-white, with beads of perspiration on his forehead.

'Very well,' said Connor. 'Sit yourself down, and I'll bring it you.'

As he served Bertie he remarked, 'We don't often see you in here, Mr Judge. The Watermen isn't one of your usual ports of call, is it?' Connor had no reason to feel friendly towards the Judge family; he would be civil to Bertie since he was Ruth's nephew, but no more than that.

Bertie swallowed half the whisky in one gulp. 'I'm not often in this neighbourhood,' he excused himself. 'I wouldn't be here now, only I've just left the police station, and this was the first pub I came to.' He polished off the rest of the drink, then said, 'Christ, I needed that.'

'The police station?' Con cocked an eye at Huw, who was still busy with the shutters, but following the conversation closely. 'You're not in any trouble, I hope?'

'Of course not.' Bertie pulled out a handkerchief and mopped his face. 'Bunch of loonies—they took me in for questioning... Me! I've never been in trouble with the law in my life! All a mistake, obviously.'

'What sort of mistake was that?' Con asked.

'They'd got it into their thick heads that I was one of Oswald Mosley's henchmen. You know he's been locked up, him and his cronies?'

This was the time of the great spy-hunt. On all sides, it was rumoured that Nazi sympathisers were preparing to pave the way for the German invaders, as they had in so many other countries. Mosley had recently been

171

arrested and imprisoned, along with hundreds of his supporters.

'Can you imagine it?' Bertie exclaimed indignantly. 'They accused me of being a fascist!'

Huw put up the last shutter, and turned to face him. 'And so you were,' he said. 'I remember you, in your black shirt and your swastika arm-band—you and your brother. Ask anybody who was at the Whitechapel riots. We all saw you, breaking the Jewish shop-windows!'

Bertie stuttered in his haste to explain. 'That was Jimmy's idea. He was a member of the Blackshirts, and he took me along with him. I didn't want to, but he made me... I was never a fully paid-up member of the BUF.'

'Well, well—you do surprise me,' said Huw dryly.

'I expect you surprised the police, too,' said Connor. 'But did they believe you, that's the question?'

'Of course. I've always been a law-abiding citizen. I'm engaged in important work for the Government, keeping the Docks running. They soon realised they'd picked the wrong man!' He brushed himself down, still very aggrieved. 'I said, if they want to go hunting for Nazis, they should start by rounding up all the Germans over here. There's enough of them around these parts, heaven knows!' He turned to Connor accusingly. 'Like that brother-in-law of yours. I told them, he's the one they should question, not me.'

172

Connor growled, 'You told them *what?*'

'Well, it's true, isn't it? He can't even speak proper English—and the Inspector agreed with me. In fact, they'd already got his name on the list. They're pulling him in tonight!'

'Are they so? Huw—take over in here, would you? Tell Ruth I'll be home later,' said Connor, and left the pub without another word.

It was nearly dark when he got to Silmour Street. When he entered the photographic shop, the light streamed out and Ernest said immediately, 'Shut the door!'

Connor obeyed, then asked, 'What's going on here?'

Ernest was standing in the middle of the shop, facing two plain-clothes policemen in raincoats. Rosie was on the stairs, looking as if she might faint, and Abram was supporting her.

'These gentlemen wish to take me to the police station,' said Ernest. 'I have tried to tell them I am a naturalised British citizen, but all they seem to care about is that I was born in Germany.'

'We have our instructions, sir,' said the senior of the two men. 'And you'll be given every opportunity to defend yourself in due course.'

'Connor, can't you explain to them?' gasped Rosie.

'Certainly I shall,' said Connor. In two strides, he crossed the floor. Putting his hand on the senior man's arm, he steered him firmly away from Ernest, saying, 'You're going to be very grateful to me, officer. It's lucky I arrived in time, for I'm about to stop you making the

173

biggest mistake of your life.'

'Now look here, I don't know who you are, but you'll kindly take your hands off me,' the police officer began to bluster. He tried to release himself from Connor's grasp, but for some reason found he could not do so.

'With pleasure—when you've heard what I have to say,' Connor continued in a friendly manner. 'My name's Connor O'Dell, and I'm the landlord of the Watermen public-house—and I've an unblemished record, as you'll see if you look it up. I'm also a part-time ARP warden, and I'm here to tell you that Ernest Kleiber is the Chief Warden of the area, and there isn't one man or woman on our team who wouldn't stand up in court and swear on a stack of Bibles that he is the most patriotic citizen of Great Britain you could ever wish to meet.'

The man opened his mouth to interrupt, but Connor was unstoppable.

'And I'll tell you another thing. In case you're not aware of it, in the East End of London, our Chief Wardens aren't appointed, like they are in other places. We believe in democracy round here—we like to elect our own leaders, and I'm happy to tell you that Ernest Kleiber got more votes than yours truly when it came to the election. This man is the people's choice, my friend—and if you try to take him in, you might very likely wind up getting yourselves lynched! I just thought I'd mention it.'

The senior policeman looked into Connor's eyes, and something he saw there gave him pause for thought.

He cleared his throat. 'It seems we've been misinformed,' he murmured at last, then signalled to his colleague. 'All right, let's go. Sorry to have troubled you, Mr Kleiber—good night to you.'

As the two men left the shop, Ernest and Connor said with one voice: *'Shut that door!'*

Then Ernest flung his arms round his brother-in-law, 'My dear Connor, I have never heard such eloquence! You should be in Parliament! How did you manage it?'

'They say it's on account of the blarney stone,' said Connor—and then Rosie was hugging him too, and Abram was shaking his hand.

'Thank you—thank you very much. And oh, thanks for my card as well,' the lad said.

'Card?' Connor was confused. 'Which card would that be, Abram?'

'My birthday card, from you and Aunt Ruth. I believe she signed it for both of you.'

'Ah, I dare say she did. Anyhow, many happy returns, lad! Let's see—how old are you now?'

'Nineteen.'

After a brief pause, Rosie said quietly, 'He'll be getting his call-up papers any day.'

'Well, good luck to you.' Connor slapped Abram on the back. 'Which have you chosen? Army, Navy or Air Force?'

There was a slightly longer pause, then Abram replied, 'None of them. I am going to register as a Conscientious Objector.'

Connor, who had had so much to say a few minutes ago, found himself at a loss for words. It was Ernest who came to his rescue, saying gently, 'I hope you are not shocked... Rosie and I are very proud of him.'

It was while Violetta was writing her farewell note to Alfredo that they heard the explosions. On stage, the soprano only faltered for an instant; glancing at the conductor, she picked up the tempo again and continued the aria as if nothing had happened.

In the audience, Gloria turned to Huw and whispered, 'Was that gunfire?'

He shook his head, mouthing his reply. 'I don't think so.'

At the end of August, there was a performance of La Traviata at the People's Palace. A true Welshman, Huw loved good singing, and he had persuaded Connor to give him a night off from the pub. On the spur of the moment he had bought two tickets instead of one, and asked his landlady if she would care to accompany him.

Glory was surprised and flattered. She had never been to an opera in her life, and wasn't at all sure she would like it—but she was so pleased to be asked that she accepted gratefully. A neighbour agreed to sit with Emily and see that the old lady got to bed at her usual time, so they were able to set off together for an unaccustomed evening out.

Although the air-raid sirens were wailing when they entered the theatre, they were not going to let that bother them. There had been a good many warnings this summer, since the Battle of Britain started, and they often heard bursts of ack-ack gunfire in the distance, keeping the raiders at bay—but nothing worse than that.

During Act Two, Scene One, the explosions had sounded rather different, and a great deal nearer; and when Alfredo had read the farewell letter and gone chasing off to Paris after Violetta, and the curtain came down, the manager appeared on stage, blinking in the spotlight and announcing that there had been some activity from hostile aircraft in the district, but that the opera would continue. However, patrons were advised that if they wished to leave, they should do so now, in the break between scenes, in order not to disturb the rest of the audience.

Huw asked Gloria, 'Do you want to go?'

She brushed the tears from her eyes, and sniffed, 'I don't *want* to—I'm really enjoying it—but I think p'haps I ought to. Ma will be having forty fits if I'm not there. But you must stay; I can get home all right on my own.'

Huw wouldn't hear of it. 'Come on, we'll go together,' he said.

Outside in the Mile End Road, the night sky was broken by swinging searchlights beams, and they heard distant rumbles of gunfire.

'So that must have been bombs we heard, mustn't it?' said Glory.

'Yes. Let's go this way; we might find a taxi outside the dance-hall.'

Cruising taxi-cabs were few and far between in the East End, but young men sometimes showed off to their girl-friends by taking them out in a cab, and Huw was lucky enough to grab one setting down its fares at the entrance to The Blue Lagoon.

As they drove through Poplar, Glory said, 'I feel awful, spoiling your night out, Mr Pritchard. And wasting your money on a cab, as well. We could easily have walked.'

'Not if there's going to be any more bombs,' said Huw. 'The sooner we get home the better. Your mother will be very anxious.'

'Well, yes—I suppose so. But it's a real shame. My first opera, and I've missed half of it! You'll have to tell me what happens in the end.'

'Violetta dies of consumption,' explained Huw. 'But by then she and Alfredo have got together again, so she's in his arms when she pops off.'

'Oh!' Glory felt quite choked up. 'I wish it ended up a bit more cheerful... Still, the music's lovely. Thanks ever so much for taking me.'

'Glad you enjoyed it,' he said. 'We must do it again, another time.'

When they got to Millwall Road, the neighbour who had been sitting with Emily told them the old lady had gone to bed early. Glory tiptoed upstairs and found her mother sound asleep. She slept right through the bombs, and never knew anything about them.

When the neighbour went home, Glory made cups of cocoa for herself and Huw, saying, 'Now I feel a proper fool. We could have stayed till the end, and Ma would have been none the wiser!'

'You weren't to know that. I'm sure we did

the right thing,' comforted Huw. 'Anything could have happened.'

It was still quite early, and they sat in the back room, sipping cocoa and talking about the opera. Gloria said it was very romantic, even if it was sad—she liked a nice love story. Then she looked at him for a moment and asked, 'You don't have a young lady, do you, Mr Pritchard? Nobody special?'

'No, I don't,' he answered.

'I thought not. I've never seen you out with anybody... Haven't you ever had a regular girl-friend—if you don't mind me asking?'

He shrugged. 'There have been girls—in the old days, when I was young. Before—' he thumped his lame leg, 'this happened.'

'What's that got to do with it?' she asked, genuinely puzzled.

'Oh, come now, Mrs Judge. You must admit it makes a difference! Girls don't exactly flock around chaps who are dot-and-carry-one!'

'That's rubbish! If a girl loved you, she wouldn't think twice about it—and by the by, do you suppose you could bring yourself to call me Glory? Every time you say "Mrs Judge", I think you're talking to my mother!'

He laughed. 'All right, then—Glory! I've always thought that's a very good name. It suits you, somehow.'

'Thank you very much—Huw.' She smiled at him. 'You can be quite a charmer when you try. It beats me why you never got married. Haven't you ever been in love?'

'Well...' He took a breath, then said, 'Since

we're being so honest, yes, I was in love—for quite a long time. The problem is, she's married to someone else.'

Suddenly it all fell into place for Glory. 'You're talking about Ruth, aren't you?'

He was going to deny it, but she was being so kind and understanding, he could not lie to her. 'Yes,' he said. 'I suppose I'll always love her—and she'll always love Connor—so that's the end of that.'

'And of course she knows how you feel about her,' Glory continued. 'Which is why you never told her you'd moved in here—I wondered about that.'

'I was afraid she—I didn't want her to think...'

'I know... My God, what a lot of time we waste, worrying about what other people might think,' she added sadly. 'As if it mattered a damn.'

'So now you know,' he said, and they both fell silent. Presently he ventured, 'I'm afraid I never knew your husband.'

'Well, it's over twenty years since he died. And if you had known him, you might not have liked him—lots of people didn't.'

'As long as *you* did, what does it matter what other people think?'

She smiled at that. 'I didn't like him much either at first! It was only later, when he was so good to me—when I got to know him better, that I really loved him... I still think about him sometimes. I still miss him.'

Slowly, Huw stood up, with a strange look

on his face; she wondered what he was going to say. Stiffly, he shook her hand. 'I think I'll be going up now. Thank you very much for a most enjoyable evening. Good night, Glory.'

Then he went upstairs, undressed and got into bed. A quarter of an hour later, he heard a faint tapping on his door.

'Are you awake?' asked Glory, in a low voice. 'Can I come in?'

'Yes, all right—only don't switch on the light. I didn't bother to draw the curtains.'

She entered the room quietly, closing the door carefully behind her. The night was clear, with a touch of moonlight, and he saw that she was in her nightdress.

'What's the matter?' he asked. 'Is it the old lady?'

'No—she's sleeping like a log. I just want to tell you something.'

'Oh? What's that?' He propped himself up; as she sat on the edge of the bed, she could see the faint moon-glow on his naked shoulders.

'Just because you love Ruth, that doesn't stop you feeling lonely, does it? I've been on my own for a long while... I get lonely too, sometimes.'

She began to draw back the bedclothes but he stopped her, holding on to the top sheet and saying—so quietly, she could hardly catch the words: 'I've got nothing on. I wouldn't want you to see—my leg's ugly and twisted...'

She interrupted him, whispering, 'Don't be so daft.'

Then she kissed him, and he let go of the

sheet—surrendering himself altogether to the softness and the sweetness and the warmth of her love.

The raid that night had been a sheer accident. A German pilot lost his way, and unloaded his bombs on the City before making his escape; but Churchill assumed this was the start of a deliberate attack on London, and ordered immediate reprisals. The next night, the RAF were sent to Berlin—and they continued to raid it for a week.

On Wednesday, 4 September, Hitler announced that London was to be his next target, and during the days that followed, the full strength of the German Air Force was massed upon the French coast.

On the Saturday afternoon, Lil was working at the Fire Station, on the corner where East and West Ferry Roads met. She was in the little kitchen, waiting for the kettle to boil, measuring enough tea into the big brown teapot to serve all the firemen and auxiliaries who were on duty.

As the kettle boiled, the air-raid sirens went off, but she carried on making the tea. She gave it a good stir, then poured half a dozen cups, which she set out on a tin tray to take up to the Recreation Room on the top floor. Climbing the stairs, she sang out: 'Tea up!'

Expecting the usual cat-calls and cheerful insults, she entered the room and found the snooker table and the ping-pong had been abandoned. The men were crowded round the open windows, looking out over the river.

'What's up?' she asked.

'Planes—lots of 'em,' muttered someone.

She heard it then; the rumble of approaching aircraft. Putting down the tray, she craned to see over their shoulders. 'Ours? Or theirs?'

'Theirs... My God, look at them.' They seemed to be coming straight for the building—sinister black objects, moving closer, slowly and steadily.

'Better go down, in case we're needed,' said one man.

'In a minute—might as well have our cuppa first!' said another.

She left them to it, and set off downstairs with the empty tray. The noise of the planes was getting louder and louder, until it was blotted out completely by a series of massive explosions. On the half-landing, Lil shrank back against the wall, and felt the building rocking beneath her feet. Dust floated down from the ceiling; the whole place had been shaken to its foundations.

When she reached the ground floor, the Control Room was in darkness. In the wavering beam of a torch she saw Sub-Officer Patterson—a taciturn, gloomy man as a rule—striding up and down, rubbing his hands and shouting: 'Lights out, first bomb! Didn't I say the electricity would be the first thing to go? First bomb—every light in the place goes out!'

Lil rushed to the store-cupboard to find candles, and began putting them in glass jam-jars at strategic places round the room.

Sub-Officer Patterson snapped his fingers impatiently at her. 'Never mind that. Get on

183

the switchboard, can't you?'

The telephones had already begun to ring, and from that moment, they went on ringing. Calls were coming in from all over the Island, and further afield; calls for assistance from brigades at West Ham and Barking, from Dagenham, and from over the river.

Lil scribbled down messages as fast as she could and passed them on; the first bombs had fallen on the Ford motor-works at Dagenham, followed by high explosives and incendiaries on the gas-works at Beckton.

By now the planes were directly overhead; the great loop of the Thames with its U-shaped curve round the Isle of Dogs, was an unmistakable landmark, shining like liquid gold in the setting sun. And the docks lay spread out all round it—a sitting target.

Still the bombs rained down—too many to count—and still the telephones rang and the messages came pouring in; hoarse voices demanding assistance—asking for extra men, for more engines, for auxiliary pumps...

One after another, the engines roared out along West Ferry Road, until there were no more machines and no more appliances to send.

Patterson barked out new orders to Lil and the other girls. 'Pass all messages back to District Control—explain we've no one left. Relay full details—time and location—tell them we're stretched to the limit!'

Lil tried to concentrate on the task in hand, forcing herself to ignore the thunder of the planes overhead, the whine of falling bombs, the ear-splitting explosions—and then, one by one, the telephones stopped ringing, and they realised that the lines were down, the cables broken; they were cut off from the outside world.

'Send out the messengers—where are our despatch riders?'

Adolescent boys in tin hats jumped on their bikes and rode off into the night...only this was no ordinary night. The sun had gone down, but the sky was not dark; it was as bright as day out there—a glaring orange glow, as if the sun had set, not in the west, but at every point of the compass, turning the entire horizon into a ring of fire.

And even now, the requests for help kept coming in. Messengers returned with tales of different crises all round the Island—water supplies running low, hoses not functioning at full pressure—then Lil saw a grim-faced warden in the doorway, muttering to one of the other firewomen. She turned and looked at Lil, then went quickly to Sub-Officer Patterson and said, 'Excuse me, sir, but can I take over from Lil? There's a landmine in the street where her parents live... The Warden says they need extra help—couldn't you let her go?'

6

At first sight, the Watermen public-house looked like a complete wreck. Lil's heart turned over as she approached it. Large areas of tiles had come off the roof, all the front windows were gone, leaving the frames hanging drunkenly askew, and one of the doors, blown from its hinges, was lying on the pavement.

She saw all this quite clearly, because the blazing fires all around made the sky as bright as day; a day in a nightmare. Steeling herself, she walked in, prepared for the worst.

The air was thick with dust, and she could hardly see across the saloon. Tables and chairs were overturned, and there was broken glass everywhere. Making her way through the dust-clouds, she was thankful to see her mother and Huw, trying to clear the shelves behind the bar, stacking into crates any bottles that were still unbroken, and sweeping up the rest.

'Mum,' she began.

Ruth swung round; her face was smudged with grime, but it relaxed as soon as she saw Lil.

'Thank God you're safe.' She took her daughter in her arms, holding her tightly. 'It's not as bad as it looks. We were very lucky—nobody got hurt.'

'Where's Dad?' asked Lil.

'Where d'you think? Out with the rescue party, helping to get people out of the ruins. They say there was a land-mine at the other end of the street.'

'I know, I came that way. There's half a dozen houses gone, and the bombs are still coming down. I could feel the road move under my feet, going up and down like a switchback.'

'You shouldn't have come through all that—you might have been killed.'

'I had to get home, didn't I? I had to make sure you were all right.'

'We're all right now, but it took everyone by surprise. When the first planes started coming over, people were all rushing out into the street to have a look. We thought they must be ours, there were so many of them. But when the first bombs landed, we knew better...Dad got everybody inside, down into the cellar, then he grabbed his tin hat and set off.'

Lil looked round the shattered bar-room and said, 'Is there another broom? I'll help you sweep up.'

'No, don't bother with that. If you want to help, go and see if you can do anything for the ones down below. It's worse for them, not knowing what's going on.'

In the cellar, the shelterers were in a state of shock. Some of them sat silently hunched up, staring into space, while others were becoming hysterical. Nora Hobbs was in tears, exclaiming shrilly, 'I can't stand it, I can't stand it! We're all going to die. I want to get out of here!'

Kaff was tugging at her mother's sleeve,

'Don't cry, Mum. We'll be all right—please don't cry.'

Lil tried to calm the frantic little woman, assuring her she was much safer where she was and adding: 'It's lucky you were here and not at home, as there's a lot of houses damaged at your end of the road. Just stay put, and I'll see if I can rustle up a pot of tea—then you'll feel better.'

The front of the building had taken the full force of the blast, so the back kitchen was more or less undamaged, but when Lil filled the kettle, she found she could not light the stove, and guessed that the gas-main had been fractured.

Instead, she fetched a bottle of orange squash from the larder and made up a jugful, taking that down to the shelter and explaining they would have to wait a little longer for a hot drink... And then she realised that Mrs Hobbs and her daughter were nowhere to be seen.

'It was what you said about them houses round where she lives being hit—that set her off again,' explained an old man. 'She made up her mind to go and see if her place was all right, and she took the kid with her. I tried to stop them, but she wouldn't listen. Off they went, and she ain't been back since.'

Lil ran up to the saloon, asking her mother and Huw: 'Have you seen Mrs Hobbs? They say she went home, with Kaff.'

They looked at her blankly and Ruth said, 'They didn't come through here, but she could have gone out by the side door—the whole place is wide open.'

As if to prove the point, an elderly warden came trudging along the side passage at that moment, taking off his helmet and wiping his sweaty face.

'Give us a drink, eh?' he said hoarsely. 'I don't care what it is. Water will do—anything to wet me whistle. I got that much brick-dust in me tubes, I can't hardly breathe.'

Huw knocked the cap off a bottle of light ale and handed it to the man; when he started to fumble in his pockets, Huw added with a weary smile, 'No charge. It's open house here tonight.'

The warden put the bottle to his lips, took a long pull, then said, 'Ah, that's better. It's hot work out there...but it's worse over West Ferry way. They've had a whole storm of fire-bombs round there. They say Millwall Road's burning from end to end.'

Ruth turned to Huw. 'Dear God, that's where—' Before she could finish the sentence, Huw had already pulled on his tin hat and was heading for the doorway.

'See you later,' he said—and was gone.

'Of course, he's living at Glory's now,' Lil remembered. 'I suppose he's gone to make sure Aunt Emily's safe.'

'And Gloria,' said Ruth quietly.

As Huw brushed past her, she had seen the look on his face; and now she knew.

Kaff stood on the pile of rubble which had once been the backyard behind their little house. Looking up at it, she thought it seemed to be leaning a bit, sideways. Without doors or windows, and with gaping cracks running through the walls, it didn't look much like a house any more...but then it had never been much of a house—two rooms up, two down, and an outside lav at the back. Still, it had been home to Kaff, ever since she was born.

Now the lav was just a broken bowl; she could see the wooden seat, split in half, under the cistern which lay upside down on the ground. She wondered where she would go when she needed to use it—and suddenly realised that she wanted to, very badly.

'Mum!' she called. 'I want to wee!'

Nora Hobbs' head appeared through a hole that had once been a window, shrieking back crossly, 'Kaff! Be quiet—somebody might hear you!'

'But I want to go, Mum, *now.*'

'You'll just have to wait. I'm getting our stuff out, ain't I? Shan't be a minute...' She popped back inside, and Kaff waited, hopping from one leg to the other.

Altogether, Nora made three trips inside, collecting up what she called 'all me valuables'— odds and ends of cutlery, blankets and cushions, some pieces of a tea-set that were still miraculously intact, a couple of saucepans and a frying-pan.

Each time she reappeared, Kaff pleaded, 'Can we go now, Mum? It's *urgent,*' but her mother told her to hang on just one more minute. She'd thought of something else.

The third time, she gave Kaff a bag full of

cutlery and crockery to carry, saying, 'There, that's the lot.' Lugging their bundles, they hurried down the side alley into the street, and then Nora stopped.

'Blimey, I forgot the clock—our clock off the mantelpiece, and the china dogs. You go on, I'll catch you up. This will be the last time, I promise.' She put down her household treasures, and ran back into the house.

It was the last time. Kaff waited, looking back and calling, 'Mum, do hurry up!' Then her cry changed to a terrified scream as before her eyes, the whole house began to move. The roof-beams gave way and the upper storey fell in upon Mrs Nora Hobbs, with a crash like the end of the world.

For once, Huw forgot about his bad leg. Lame or not, he kept up a turn of speed he would never have believed possible, under the circumstances. Ahead of him, he could see the fires burning; a great column of orange smoke and flame billowing up into the night sky.

A warden darted out of a side street, yelling, 'Get back! You can't go through there—the road's closed!'

Huw touched his tin hat, with the letters ARP stencilled on it, shouting, 'It's OK—I'm on special duty!' and went on without slackening his pace.

He ran down the middle of the road, because walls and masonry were tumbling down on to the pavements at both sides. Then he saw he had reached a dead end; a huge crater stretched

191

right across the road, and a thirty-foot wall had collapsed into it. He stopped for a moment to get his breath, and tried to decide what to do. He had to go on—he had to get to Millwall Road; there was no turning back.

The smoke smelled acrid—no, aromatic—and with a shock, he realised that the spice warehouses along the dock must be on fire. Of course, it was the outer dock wall that had come down; that meant he could get through the gap and take a short cut along the Jubilee Wharf.

There was no one to stop him. He passed some firemen struggling to direct their hoses on to the blazing buildings, but they were too busy to notice him, and he ran on.

There were flames everywhere; telegraph poles, fences, barges—anything made of wood was burning, and so were the warehouses, and the contents of those warehouses.

There were pepper fires, which made the hot air sting; every breath Huw took seared his throat, as if he were swallowing liquid fire... There were rum fires, where the barrels burst into flame, throwing off heady fumes like the memory of a thousand Christmas puddings... There 'was a paint store on fire, shooting out explosive jets of white-hot fire, and ammonia belching black rolls of smoke that made Huw's eyes stream with tears.

But he hobbled on without stopping until he reached the dockgates, which had been opened to let the fire-crews through—and he knew he was approaching his journey's end.

That was when the ground beneath him seemed to give way, and he felt as if a giant hand had picked him up and flung him across the road. The thought came into his mind: 'It's a bomb—I'm going to be killed,' and then he could not think at all, because the blast was so strong, it sucked at him, ripping his shirt, tearing his trousers... Instinctively, he put both hands on his eyeballs, to hold them in place. For a moment he could not breathe at all and when he could, the smoke was like acid in his lungs; everything danced crazily around him, in violent flashes of crimson and yellow.

He picked himself up and ran for his life, as behind him, an entire terrace of houses burst into flame. Now there were fires all around him; he could not go back, even if he had wanted to.

When he reached Millwall Road, the smell of soot and charred wood was overpowering; there were still fires from small incendiaries licking at the roof-tiles, but some of the flames had already burned themselves out. He went into the shop; the hairdressing salon was a shambles. Picking his way through the debris, he found the Anderson shelter in the yard—and there were the two women—shocked, stunned, but unhurt.

He picked Emily up and carried her out to the street; one of the salon chairs was in the gutter, still in one piece, so he sat her in it.

She looked round her, and said in a prim, disapproving voice, 'Well! *That* wasn't very nice, was it?'

He turned to go back for Glory, and found she was following him.

'Look at it...' she said. 'Just look at my poor old shop. That Hitler—he's a real bugger.' Then she burst into tears, and Huw put his arms round her. 'Thank Gawd you found us,' she said. 'Where are we going now?'

Over her shoulder, he looked at the continuous ring of fire surrounding them. 'You'll have to give me a moment or two to think about that,' he said.

St Anthony's Church hall was prepared for emergencies at the beginning of the war; tonight for the first time, it had been pitched headlong into action, and the preparations turned out to be woefully inadequate.

Ruth was still busy at the pub, but when a neighbour hurried in to explain the situation, she asked Lil: 'Can you carry on here till I get back? I'd better go and see if I can do anything to help. It sounds pretty desperate.'

It was desperate indeed. An old priest, together with some nuns from the next-door convent and a handful of parish-workers, was trying to cope with a crowd of bombed-out, homeless people. The lamps were not alight, for the electricity had failed—and in any case there would have been no way to black out the doors which were constantly opening and shutting as more and more refugees flocked in, seeking shelter—but the continual orange glow outside filtered in through broken windows, bathing the hall in an eerie, unnatural light.

194

People sat about where they could, but there were not nearly enough chairs to go round, and many of them were stretched out on the floor. An old nun kept a kettle boiling on a small paraffin-stove, and a young novice did her best to bathe the blood and filth from the faces of those who had been cut by flying glass.

There were no major casualties here—stretcher-cases were being taken to the Medical Aid Post in Glengall Road—but there was an overwhelming feeling of anguish, of mental suffering, of fear and loss.

Ruth remembered that a small store-cupboard had been stocked with emergency supplies, and when she found the key, she made it her business to provide refreshments of a sort. She discovered some packets of tea and dried milk and tins of corned beef, and prevailed upon the nuns to let her have some margarine and loaves of bread from the convent. Within a quarter of an hour, she was distributing sandwiches and hot drinks, which gave the victims of the raid a little comfort, if nothing else. But that was only the beginning; they wanted so much more than that. These were people who had nothing—nothing but the clothes they wore. They were going to need hot meals, a change of clothing and beds to sleep in. Above all, they had to have shelter.

The most heart-breaking were the children; crying babies, and toddlers who clung to their mothers' hands, silent and wide-eyed, unable to understand what was happening... And some of them had no mothers.

The young novice appealed to Ruth: 'Mrs O'Dell, do you think you could get this little one to have something to eat or drink? She has nobody with her. We don't know where she's come from—she just sits in this corner with her head against the wall and her eyes shut. She won't speak.'

Ruth put her hand on the child's head, but she did not move or open her eyes. Her face was black with dirt, her hair matted with grease and dust. And then, to her astonishment, Ruth recognised her. 'Kaff?'

At the sound of her name, Kaff stirred for the first time. Her eyelids opened, and when she saw Ruth she clutched her hand, whispering, 'Is it really you, missus?'

'Yes, lovey, but what's happened to you? Where's your mum?'

Kaff turned her face away. 'She's gone. We was going to get away, see, but she went back—and the house fell on top of her. I saw it.' Then she lifted her head, saying fiercely, 'She went back for the china dogs, and the bloody clock...'

For a moment, Ruth could not speak, then she fell to her knees, hugging the girl and saying, 'It's all right, Kaff, you're safe now. You're coming home with me.'

But Kaff struggled in her arms and began to cry. Deep, agonised sobs shook her thin frame as she confessed: 'I'm sorry, I didn't mean to. I don't know how it happened, but—I wet myself. I couldn't help it.'

'I know I shall be seasick. I'm always sick when I go on the water, even at the boating-lake,' complained Emily.

'I shouldn't worry too much about that, Ma,' Glory said quietly. 'There's worse things than being sick.'

They were crammed into a motor-launch, so tightly, there was hardly room to breathe, let alone move. Huw was aware that the overcrowded vessel was dangerously low in the water, but it was their only hope.

More than a hundred people who were trapped by the fires surrounding Millwall Road had retreated to the river; they had nowhere else to go.

Among the wharves, there was a small sub-station manned by the River Police, and it was to the police that these refugees turned for help. There were only two men on duty, and just one launch, moored at the bottom of a flight of stone steps. The little crowd stood huddled together, too tired and frightened to argue or grumble, waiting their turn to be ferried to safety.

Between them, Huw and Glory somehow managed to get Emily down the steps, then the officer cast off, and they set out on their trip upstream.

Pressed together in the half-dark, Glory groped for Huw's hand and held it. Nobody spoke; they sat in shocked silence, staring at the incredible spectacle before them.

Across the water to their left, Huw calculated that more than half a mile of the Surrey Docks must be on fire—wharves and warehouses, piers and bridges. Against that raging inferno, he could see little groups of firemen—black, antlike figures, doing their utmost to fight the flames.

Glory nudged Huw, pointing at the sky. 'Look up there...'

He lifted his head and saw a flock of pigeons circling helplessly. They seemed lost, no longer knowing where they had come from or where they should go; their feathers shone pink in the unearthly glow.

'It's the middle of the night, and those poor creatures don't know if it's sunrise or sunset,' said Huw. 'They don't understand what's going on.'

'Me neither,' said Glory, and held his hand a little more tightly. 'It looks like the whole of the Thames is on fire, and we're going smack into the middle of it.'

Immediately ahead, a curtain of smoke and sparks hung over the water; the pilot of the launch had no choice but to steer straight through it.

Inside that pall of suffocating smoke, it was like a river flowing through hell. They could still hear the roar and hiss of the conflagration on shore, but all they could see was an extraordinary panorama of fire. All around them, moving banks of flame floated upon the surface, reflected in crimson water.

There were always huge quantities of timber stored at the docks; barges stacked with cut planks, ready to send up the canals, along Britain's waterways. Tonight the burning barges had been cut adrift, which presented another hazard; as they came swinging upriver on the current, the launch had to manoeuvre from side to side, trying to give them a wide berth.

'Tide's just about on the turn,' muttered Huw. 'In ten minutes it will be running the other way... They'll still be burning when they reach the open sea, I reckon.'

'And where shall we be?' asked Glory, in a whisper.

The police launch carried them on, upriver, until the blitz was left far behind, then put them ashore at Richmond and went back to fetch another party of refugees.

For what was left of the night, they were given shelter at an emergency rest centre; from the top of Richmond Hill, they could still see the mushroom shaped cloud of smoke and flame on the horizon—a gigantic, terrifying beacon.

'Funny thing,' said Huw. 'A good many Londoners never even knew where the Isle of Dogs was... Well, they know now, all right.'

Glory put her hand on his arm. 'If you hadn't come to find us, I don't suppose we'd ever have got away. But what's going to happen now? What'll we do?'

'Do?' he repeated. 'We'll go back home, as soon as it's light. What else can we do?'

When dawn came, the raiders turned tail and departed, and London was left to count the cost of that horrific night, known then and ever afterwards as 'Black Saturday'.

On Sunday morning, Huw took Gloria and her mother back to the Island. It was a long, slow journey, for they had to cover the distance in several stages; by bus, by underground, and then by bus again. When they reached Whitechapel, there seemed to be no hope of any further public transport, and since Emily was much too frail and elderly to walk, Huw hunted round until he discovered a taxi-driver who would take them to Millwall Road.

When they drew up, one glance at the salon was enough. Huw said quietly to the cabbie: 'Stay here and keep an eye on the old lady, while we nip indoors and take a look. We shan't be stopping long.'

Then he and Glory walked in. The salon was just as they had left it. She gazed around and tried to laugh, but her laughter was very close to tears. 'Talk about an invitation to burglars! Anyone could have walked in and helped themselves—not that there's much left worth pinching.'

Huw said, 'Don't worry, I'll come back later and board up the doors and windows, and make a start packing up your belongings. But first we've got to find you somewhere to live.'

'Live? What d'you mean? This is my home!'

'Have some sense, girl. There's no electrics, no gas or water, no heating or lighting. You can't live here, not till I get things straightened out. Think of the old lady—how could you bring her in here?'

Glory sighed. 'No, you're right—it wouldn't do. I suppose we could go round to Auntie Lou at the Rope Walk; she took Ma in once before, after the shop got flooded. I'm sure she'd put us up...but how about you? Where will you go?'

Huw brushed this aside. 'I'll find somewhere. Under the circumstances, I suppose I could ask the O'Dells. They might let me have Dan's room for the time being.'

'Yes, I expect they would.'

He put his hands on her shoulders. 'Don't look so miserable. Things are going to be all right.'

'Are they? I just wish we could be—you know—together.'

'We will. We'll sort something out, I promise.'

'I hope so.' She picked her way through the wrecked shop, making for the staircase. 'Anyhow, I'd better see what I can find upstairs. We're going to need a couple of suitcases and a change of clothes.'

Halfway up the stairs, she stopped on the landing and turned to him. Without a word, they embraced one another, and he could feel her trembling in his arms. At last she said: 'I'm going to miss you so much...' Then she added ruefully, 'I'd just got used to having a man about the house!'

'You'll have your uncle with you at the Rope Walk, won't you?' Huw teased her gently.

'Old Marcus?' Glory groaned. 'Thanks very much. That's all I need, him and his batty sermons! He thinks I'm the Scarlet Woman already!'

'What's wrong with that?' Huw kissed her again. 'It's my favourite colour...'

Later that morning he arrived at the pub, explaining to Ruth what had happened. 'Glory and Emily are settled in pretty well at the Rope

201

Walk. Your mother said she'll be very glad to have them there, for company.'

'Bless her.' Ruth smiled. 'I don't suppose my father was quite so welcoming, was he?'

'He sat in the corner, turning the pages of his Bible and growling to himself. I'm not sure he knew what was going on, exactly.'

'Oh, dear. And are they going to squeeze you in as well?'

'No. I didn't suggest it—that would be too much to expect. As a matter of fact,' Huw cleared his throat, 'I was about to say—would you have any objection if I took over Dan's room? Just while he's away, of course.'

'Oh, Huw,' began Ruth. 'I'm sorry, but I'm afraid that's not possible.'

He met her eye, and was suddenly overcome with embarrassment. 'No, *I'm* sorry. It was wrong of me to ask... Only I didn't think you'd—I mean, you know I'd never do anything to make things awkward for you.'

Now it was her turn to be embarrassed, and her cheeks flamed. Feeling like a schoolgirl, she broke in quickly: 'Of course you wouldn't. I never thought for a moment... What I'm trying to say is, we've got somebody else in Dan's room.' And she told him about Kaff.

'...She's still in a state of shock. I bathed her and put her into one of Lil's old nighties, but it was ages before she calmed down, and even then she couldn't get to sleep. I stayed with her for the rest of the night, down in the cellar, and this morning when the raid was over I made up Dan's bed while Lil gave her some breakfast.

202

Now she's asleep at last, thank goodness.'

'Poor kid. What's going to happen when she wakes up? Where's she going to go?'

'There isn't anywhere for her to go. She's got no other family...I talked it over with Con last night, and we decided that she's going to stay with us—for good.'

'I'm very glad.'

'But it does mean we can't put you up. Of course, you can always sleep downstairs. I know it's not like having a room of your own, Huw, but for the time being?'

'Yes, just till I find somewhere else that will be fine.' Huw looked round. 'Where's Lil this morning?'

'We both went to early Mass, first thing, and now she's gone back to work.'

On Sunday morning, the Fire Station was busier than ever. Men who had been out fighting fires all night were coming off-duty. Some of them had been on the go for twelve hours without a break, most of them were half-dead with exhaustion and all of them had tales to tell.

'I never seen nothing like it in all my born days. We had to report back—the blaze was too big for us to handle. When the tide went out, the water-level dropped below the level of the pumps—not so much as a trickle... We got some fires under control, but there's a hell of a lot still burning. The day boys are going to have their work cut out to get it under before it gets dark.'

In several places, they could not manage it.

When the sun set, the sirens sounded again, and the raiders came back—their flight-path clearly marked at intervals by fires from the previous night which still lit up the sky. For nine hours they kept on coming, in wave after wave, and again the docklands were a principal target.

It was just as well that no one who endured the merciless bombardment that night was able to see into the future. How could they have carried on, if they had known that the raids were to continue, almost every single night, for the next eight months? As it was, they got through each day that dawned, and each night that fell, hoping and praying that it would soon come to an end.

Not everyone carried on. To begin with, the disaster caught the authorities off-guard; bombed-out families found that no provision had been made for them, and the emergency services, totally overwhelmed and badly understaffed, could not cope. A kind of exodus began—an unplanned evacuation of men, women and children, with their belongings piled on top of prams and hand-carts, setting off on foot to go and stay with friends and relations in the suburbs; in Kent or Surrey, or in the rural heart of Essex, where they thought they would be safe.

The others all had their own reasons for staying on. They had their jobs to do, on the river or in the docks; they had businesses that could not be left—their own shops or pubs or offices, or they could not be parted from a dog or a cat, or a favourite goldfish. And perhaps they had the strongest reason of all; this was their home, and they were not going to let Adolf Hitler or anyone else turn them out.

Even so, by day the Island had a deserted air, not only because of the bomb-craters and the empty shells of buildings. The streets seemed strangely empty, like a ghost town.

The Watermen pub stayed open right through the Blitz, and the customers who remained were grateful for it. Perhaps Connor did not obey the licensing laws quite as strictly as before; when someone called in for a drink to keep him going, Con would serve him, no matter what the time was—and the police looked the other way.

Everyone got accustomed to a different routine, as one day followed another in a new pattern. Around five o'clock the sirens would moan, and as it grew dark the first planes would come over. Those who were too old or too young to be involved in Civil Defence picked up rugs and blankets, cut their sandwiches and filled their thermos with tea, then settled into the shelters for the night.

Some time before dawn the All Clear would sound, and they'd emerge, stretching and yawning, to return to the comfort of their own beds until the alarm-clock went off and they had to face another day.

After a day's work at the pub, Connor and Huw reported to the Wardens' Post, to deal with any emergencies that might occur during the night. They rarely got any sleep until the raids were over, then they snatched an hour or two before starting work again.

Ruth, too, was on call every minute of the day. She helped in the pub, as always, and she devoted every spare minute to Kaff, who needed all the support and reassurance she could give her, and in between times she made herself useful at St Anthony's. She had been very shocked to find such a state of confusion in the church hall, and went back time and again, trying to get things organised.

She was not a trained social worker, but she had spent a great many years helping to run the pub, and when she saw something which needed to be done, she went ahead and did it—even if that meant cutting through red tape and by-passing the official channels.

She invaded the local schools (which were closed during this period of emergency) and commandeered all the cutlery and crockery she needed; she begged shamelessly for basic food supplies from all the distribution centres in the district—and she raided charitable institutions, taking away clothes and blankets and babies's nappies without stopping to ask anyone's permission.

At first the nuns were rather scandalised, but then they decided she was doing the Lord's work, and followed her example. Very soon, St Anthony's became a model Rest Centre. Homeless people were provided with hot baths, clean clothes, cooked meals, and there were enough mattresses and pillows for everyone to get a good night's sleep. Many offered to stay on, helping the Sisters in the task of cooking and cleaning for other people in distress.

Afterwards, when she looked back on those days, Ruth said, 'I suppose we never had time to be frightened—there was always too much to do.'

They all felt the same way. Every night, Con preferred to be out and about, patrolling the streets or hurrying to deal with an unexploded landmine, rather than sit in the Wardens' Post, waiting for orders. At the Fire Station, Lil too grew impatient with manning the telephones, passing on messages, or making endless fry-ups for hungry men coming in off-duty. She wanted to be out there, in the thick of it.

Early one morning, after a long night on the switchboard, she came home and told her mother: 'Oh, by the way, could you give me a call at half-past nine? I've promised I'll be back at the Station by ten.'

Ruth protested, 'That's ridiculous! They can't expect you to start work after two hours sleep!'

I won't be working—not my usual work, anyway. I'm going to start taking driving lessons.'

'What?' Ruth stared at her. 'We haven't even got a car!'

'I've put my name down to train as a driver. They're getting twenty thousand old taxis to tow trailer-pumps, and they're screaming for volunteers. There aren't that many girls round here that can drive, so they're offering to give us lessons. Well, I wasn't going to miss a chance like that, was I?'

'Yes, but does that mean you'll be out at night, driving around during the raids?'

'I sincerely hope so. Anything's better than being stuck indoors all the time. I'd rather be out there *doing* something!'

'Why does Sharon never come home to see us now?' asked Ernest.

It was late October; another night had passed, another raid had come and gone. Londoners soon discovered that the heaviest raids took place under a full moon—a 'Bomber's Moon', they called it; 18 September and 15 October had both been particularly bad. But this morning Ernest came home saying it had been a quiet night; the nearest reported incidents were in Romford, so he had not been called out.

While his father was busy with ARP duties, Abram stayed at home, keeping his mother company in their makeshift shelter under the stairs. For many people who could not build an outdoor shelter, the space beneath the staircase was the next best thing. This seemed to be the safest place in any building, and they were able to settle down to sleep there, provided the anti-aircraft guns were not too loud, and the bombs not too near.

They were in the kitchen having breakfast when a postman delivered the morning mail. There was just one letter, in Sally's handwriting—and it was addressed to Abram.

'Now she doesn't even write to her parents any more,' Ernest continued sadly. 'She sends letters only to her brother.'

'Don't be silly, dear. She hasn't written to Abram for a long time either. I expect she wants to wish him luck today.'

About to tear open the envelope, Abram hesitated. 'You told her about the tribunal?'

'Of course, last time I wrote. I always pass on the family news; she likes to keep in touch.'

'So why does she never come and visit us?' Ernest persisted.

'You know very well she's on tour in Scotland now,' Rosie scolded him. 'This week they're in Aberdeen. You should be glad she's safely out of harm's way up there.'

'She's not always in Scotland. She told us she would be passing through London last month, but we never saw her. Why didn't she come home then?'

'Perhaps she didn't have the time—she's always so busy. I know she had to go and see that agent of hers—Mr Jasper.' Rosie smiled. 'Her letters are always full of this Mr Jasper. I get the feeling she's rather keen on him.'

Ernest frowned. 'That worries me also. She's too young for such things.'

'She's eighteen now. At her age, it's only natural for a girl to—'

Their argument was interrupted by Abram, who put down Sally's letter, saying flatly, 'She's not wishing me luck, that's for sure.'

'What do you mean by that?'

He picked out some key phrases and read them aloud: '"*How could you do such a thing? Couldn't you change your mind before it's too late? What will people say if they find out my brother is a conchie? I'd never be able to hold up my head again.*" Reading between the lines, I get

209

the feeling she's not too keen on the idea.'

He tried to smile, but Rosie realised he was hurt. She said quickly, 'Sally doesn't understand. She doesn't mean it.'

'Doesn't she? I expect a lot of people feel the same way. Uncle Connor and Aunt Ruth have never said anything, but I could tell they were shocked.'

Ernest pushed his chair back and walked round the table, putting his hand on Abram's shoulder. 'We must not concern ourselves with other people's opinions. It's a matter for you to decide; a matter for your own conscience. This morning, when you appear before the Tribunal, remember that your mother and I will be giving you all our support, and our love, and our prayers.'

'Thanks, Poppa, that's good to know. Anyway, maybe they'll turn me down, then Sally can go on holding her head up while she's tap-dancing.'

When Abram's call-up papers arrived, he had returned them with a note stating that he wished to be exempted from conscription as a Conscientious Objector. He filled an application form, sent it off, and waited. Six weeks later he received notification that he was required to attend a tribunal to decide upon his case—and the hearing would take place today.

As he sat and waited in a draughty corridor, Abram felt horribly alone. In spite of his parents' reassurance, he knew he was taking a very unpopular step. He could not expect widespread approval if he succeeded in his claim, and if he lost his appeal, he could be sent to prison for his beliefs. Yet he had to do what he felt was right.

A man in a pin-striped suit put his head round the door and said, 'Kleiber? You're next. This way, please.'

The tribunal consisted of three people: two men—a local magistrate and a retired Army officer—and a middle-aged woman with thick spectacles who peered at him as if he were a biological specimen under a microscope.

'You are Mr Abram Kleiber?'

They asked him his age and his address, which school he had attended and what he had done since he left school. The details, as he gave them in nervous, halting phrases, did not sound impressive. They also asked him about his family, and were particularly interested in his father.

'Ernest Kleiber... Mmmm—born in Germany, I understand?'

'Yes, sir, but he's a naturalised British subject now.'

'But not at the time of the last war... According to the information I have here, he and your grandparents were interned as enemy aliens—right?'

'Yes, sir.'

'Tell me, Mr Kleiber—what are your feelings towards the German nation? You must have divided loyalties, no doubt?'

'No, sir. I feel completely British. I was born here and I've lived here all my life.'

'You mean you've never been to Germany at all?'

Caught wrong-footed, Abram stumbled over his reply. 'No. That is, yes—just once. I went with a school party to the Rhineland, in the summer of 1935—that's all.'

'So you had no contact with anyone from the German side of the family while you were there?'

'Well yes, as a matter of fact, I visited my Aunt Sarah and her husband—and my cousin Benjamin.'

'Did you discuss political affairs with them on that occasion?'

He remembered the swastika badge he had brought back—a present from Ben, after the meeting of the Hitler Youth group—and felt irrationally guilty as he replied, 'No, sir. It was only a social call—and I was only fourteen at the time.'

The members of the panel conferred in whispers; after that they seemed to regard him with grave suspicion, and his heart sank. The retired officer addressed him again. 'Have you prepared a short statement of your personal convictions?'

'Yes, sir.' Abram took the sheet of paper from his pocket, and unfolded it. 'Would you like to see it?'

'That won't be necessary. You may read it out to us.'

He hadn't expected this, his throat felt dry, and the words blurred before his eyes, but he tried to breathe deeply and speak calmly as he made his declaration.

'It is my convinced opinion that all war is

wrong. It is a sin against civilisation, and against mankind itself. It is wrong morally and logically.

'The world can only be saved by morality and by logic—by faith and by reason. Without these two qualities, mankind is doomed to self-destruction. When animals disagree, they resort to violence; if we do the same, we are no better than animals. All violence is an offence against the human soul, but the violence of war is especially evil, because the law of the land encourages us to commit murder in the name of patriotism.

'This is what Hitler believes in, and this is why I feel certain it must be wrong. We can never defeat Hitler if we sink to his level, following his example and using his methods. All that a war can prove is that one side is stronger than the other—it has more men, more bullets, more bombs. We won the last war because we were stronger than Germany; and Germany has learned that lesson.

'I respect the laws of my country, but I cannot obey them if they call on me to deny my own conscience. I believe in the sanctity of human life, and I will never deliberately set out to destroy my fellow men, even when they are called my enemies. I am prepared to do all I can to defend my country and protect its people against attack, and I shall be happy to work for the Civil Defence, but I will never learn how to commit murder, and I will never agree to enter the armed services.'

He folded up the paper, and they conferred

again; then they asked to see the declaration and passed it between them, muttering in low tones. For Abram, time stood still.

At last the retired officer spoke. 'Mr Kleiber, we are satisfied there is in this case a conscientious objection within the meaning of the act. We therefore agree that your name shall be added to the register of Objectors, and you will be directed into appropriate duties with Civil Defence. That will be all. You may send in the next applicant.'

Days turned into weeks, weeks into months, and still the nightly bombing continued.

On Christmas Eve 1940, Trevor Judge drove down to the Isle of Dogs in a smart silver roadster; he had bought it for a song from the widow of an RAF pal who had been shot down over the Channel. Beside him, snug in the new fur coat he had given her as an early Christmas present, sat Sally.

'But when are you going to start work on the new show?' She had been badgering him all the way from Charing Cross Road. 'You keep saying you're going to make me a star—but *when?*'

He gazed out at the derelict buildings, the craters, the No Entry signs blocking impassable roads—and whistled in disbelief.

'What a bloody mess,' he said. 'The old place has certainly changed.'

'I think it's disgusting, the way people go on and on about bomb-damage. You're not listening to me, are you? I just wish you'd tell me something definite. I haven't earned anything since that ghastly tour folded, and a girl's got to eat!'

He shot her teasing look. 'I hadn't noticed anything wrong with your appetite lately.'

'No, well—you've been very sweet, and I'm ever so grateful, but I do have my career to think about. So when does the new revue go into rehearsal? Have you booked a theatre?'

He shook his head. 'We can't rush it, baby. The way things are now, it's madness to open a new show in town. Suppose I sank all my capital in it, and the theatre got blown to Kingdom Come on opening night? We've got to sit tight until the bombing's over—then we can start making plans.'

She pouted, but she realised there was sense in what he said.

'So just be patient for a while, eh?' He braked, and drew up at the corner of Silmour Street. 'I'll drop you here—I'm going a bit further. I've got to see someone on business.'

'I thought you were coming in to meet Mumsie and Poppa? I told them I was bringing you.'

'Later, don't worry. I'll be seeing you very soon—if all goes well.'

She was already out of the car before his words sank in, and she asked: 'What do you mean, "if all goes well"? The family are expecting you!'

But the car was already gathering speed. Frustrated and confused, she walked along the street to the photographic shop, wondering how she was going to explain to her parents that her gentleman friend was so unpredictable.

Ten minutes later, Bertie Judge was at his desk when there was a knock at the door and a visitor walked in, saying cheerfully: 'Afternoon, old boy. Nice place you've got here—I must say it's a great improvement on the old offices.'

Bertie glared indignantly. 'Now just a minute! You can't barge in here without an appointment.'

'There's nobody about in the general office. I expect they've all packed up early because it's Christmas, eh? But I guessed I'd find you here—still hard at work as usual!' The pale young man pulled up a chair and sat down, crossing his legs, then offered a silver cigarette-case to Bertie. 'Care for a smoke?'

'No, thank you—I don't. Look here, I don't know who you are, but you've no right to come marching in here out of the blue...'

Bertie's voice trailed off into silence. Something in the stranger's smile was uncomfortably familiar.

'Haven't you heard that bad pennies always turn up, sooner or later?' Trevor chuckled. 'Don't you know your little step-brother?'

'*Trevor?*' Bertie phrased it as a question, yet he had no real doubt about it; this self-possessed chap in the expensive suit could be nobody else. When he had recovered his breath, he gasped, 'You've got a nerve, I must say, after what you did. You robbed Dad, you stole money out of the business. He should have had the law on you.'

'Ah, but he didn't, did he? Dear old Josh hushed it up and repaid it out of his own pocket, and I was truly grateful. Which is why

216

I'm here now—to wish you the compliments of the season and a little bit more. I know I called myself a bad penny, but that was just a joke, really. The fact is, I've come to put things straight between us.'

'What do you mean?'

'That money I took—well, let's say I borrowed it, shall we? Think of it as a loan made to me by the dear old Gov'nor; it's been on my conscience for a long time, Bertie, that's why I've come back to repay you.'

Bertie goggled at him. 'Repay?'

'With interest.' Taking out his wallet, Trevor placed a wad of notes on the desk. 'Four hundred smackers. Count it if you like, it's all there.'

Bertie's piggy eyes narrowed. 'Oh no, that's not right. Dad said you made off with about seven hundred.'

'Nowhere near. He must have made a mistake—it was somewhere between three and five... Of course, you'll have to take my word for it, 'cos when the old warehouse caught on fire and your office went up in smoke, I believe all the account books went with it, eh? By the by, I was sorry to hear about the Guv. It wasn't a nice way to go, and he was always pretty decent to me. I was very upset to hear about Jimmy, too. At Dunkirk, wasn't it?'

'How the hell did you know?'

'A little bird told me. Anyway, you say it was seven hundred quid, and I say it was about three. Shall we split the difference and call it four?'

'I don't know so much about that...' Bertie's fingers were creeping towards the wad of notes. 'Besides, you said you'd repay it with interest.'

'And so I shall. But I didn't mean money; the interest I had in mind was my interest in the old firm. I hear you've been going through a hard time lately, old son. Up to your eyes in work, they tell me, and probably a little bit out of your depth as well. So what I propose is this; I was the best accounts clerk you ever had—I know more about running this office than any man alive, and now you've proof of my good will—so why don't I come back in an advisory capacity, to give you a hand and get the Brotherhood back on the rails, eh?'

Bertie's mind was still on the cash; he picked it up and flicked through it with his thumbnail—it seemed to be all there. Slipping it into the desk drawer, he said slyly, 'That's an interesting suggestion, Trev, and I won't deny I could do with some extra help—we're very short-staffed at the moment. But it's not really up to me. I'd have to put it to the Wharfmaster and the Board, though I dare say I might persuade them to take you on, as my assistant.'

'Not your assistant—your partner. We'd be running the show together.'

Bertie was outraged. 'You must be off your head! It's out of the question. The Board would never agree—'

'Oh, I think they would, if you put it to them nicely. And I really think you should—for your own sake.'

'*My* sake? What are you talking about?'

'I hear there was some unpleasantness with the law recently—questions asked about your politics—being a member of the Fascist Party, and so on... If that got to the ears of the Wharfmaster, you might find yourself in a very awkward position, Bertie.'

'You wouldn't! You wouldn't say anything!'

'Of course not. But it might be helpful, if the subject ever came up again, for me to be able to tell anyone who's interested that your politics before the war were as white as the driven snow. After all, I was there, living in the same house. You couldn't have a better character witness on your side, could you, Bertie?'

Although it was rather chilly in the office, sweat was running down Bertie's cheeks in big, greasy drops. He mopped his face, then muttered: 'All right, then. Partners...'

'That's more like it.' Trevor looked round, smiling. 'Do you still keep a bottle of scotch in the filing cabinet? How about a toast to the new arrangement, eh?'

Bertie poured the drinks with a shaky hand, and Trevor raised his glass. 'Here's to the old firm, and the new partnership. Long live the Brotherhood—and God bless us, every one.'

7

Satisfied with his afternoon's work, Trevor left
the Guild Office, but before he could go back
to Silmour Street and meet Sally's parents, he
had one more call to make.

He parked the car on the edge of a bomb-site
and continued on foot, through a dockland
labyrinth, to a narrow cul-de-sac.

The house was small, dark and cheerless;
when the front door swung open, the smell of
stale food, fetid air, grime and grease sickened
him. He was glad he would never have to come
here again.

'So it's you, is it?' croaked the old man in
the doorway. 'You're quite a stranger—how've
you bin keeping?'

Trevor did not waste time in conventional
greetings, but walked straight down the passage
into the poky back room, lit by a single
oil-lamp.

'Sit yerself down,' said old Mr Otley, shuffling
in after him. 'I got a lot to tell you. There's been
plenty going on lately, and no mistake.'

'Forget it.' Trevor turned away from the
filthy armchair with its stuffing escaping from
torn upholstery. 'And I won't sit down—I'm
not stopping long.'

'Aincher?' Sidney Otley peered at him from
weeping, gummy eyes. 'But your fambly's bin

having all kinds of upsets since you was here last. Glory Judge's hairdressing shop had to pack up, and the Watermen got all its winders blown out. They say since Jimmy Judge got killed, that fat brother of his is having a job to keep the wharf running.'

'I said *forget it!*' Trevor cut in sharply. 'Your news is out of date—I'm not interested.'

'But you always said as how I was to tell you everything!'

'Not any more. I shan't be needing you in future.'

'You what?' The old man's expression changed; shock, disappointment and cunning chased themselves across his seamy features. 'Gone and got yerself another spy, have you?' he sneered.

Trevor allowed himself a half-smile. 'Better than that,' he said. 'I've been taken back into the bosom of the family. Behold, the return of the prodigal son!'

'Is that a fact?' Sidney Otley sniffed. 'How'd you manage that, then?'

'None of your business. But I promise you, the lost sheep has been welcomed into the fold with great rejoicing, so I shan't be dropping in again, old man. The deal's off.'

'That's all very well for you, but what about me?' whined Sidney. 'You promised you'd see me all right.'

'I always paid for information, as long as it was worth my while. And here's your final instalment—a little Christmas box, to wind up our arrangement.' He produced a fiver and put

221

it into the old man's bony claw. 'And by the way, if you should happen to pass me in the street at any time and you feel like saying hello, don't bother.'

'But—you'n me, we've bin friends for a long time!'

'We've known each other for a few years and you've made yourself useful once or twice, that's all. From now on, we're strangers. Merry Christmas, Sidney—and goodbye.'

And Trevor walked out of the house without looking back.

The sitting-room above the photographic shop was decorated with holly and paper-chains, and the table had been set out with the best china, on the best Irish linen tablecloth.

Rosie had made a very special effort for the Christmas Eve tea-party. For months she'd been saving up dried fruit and butter and margarine. Luckily the Ministry of Food, catching the festive spirit, had increased the rations for the holiday: an extra four ounces of sugar and two of tea was a real bonus—and she had managed to make a traditional cake with a pink paper frill, and little plaster robins round a plaster Santa Claus, on top of white icing.

Ernest and Abram kept telling her it looked wonderful, and she mustn't fuss, but when she heard Sally and Mr Jasper coming upstairs she still felt very nervous. After all, he was an important man. This must all seem so cheap and ordinary to him.

Thank goodness, he wasn't a bit like that.

'Mrs Kleiber.' He walked towards her, his hand out-stretched, his eyes dancing. 'I don't believe we've ever met, but Sally's told me so much about you, I feel as if I know you already... And now I see where she gets her good looks.'

He was so charming, nobody could possibly dislike him. Ernest greeted him warmly, and beamed with pleasure when the young man congratulated him on some of the publicity photos he had taken of Sally.

Abram shook hands shyly, half-expecting to be asked if he were home on leave, and which of the armed forces was he in? But instead of that...

'Sally tells me you've joined the Pacifist Service unit. I really admire that—it must take a lot of nerve to stand up for your principles. You're with the Medical Aid Patrols, is that right?'

His smile was so friendly, Abram found himself smiling back. 'Yes, I'm in one of the ambulance units. I don't drive, unfortunately, but I dish out First Aid supplies, and help to carry the stretchers.'

'I think that's terrific. In fact, if I were fit enough, I'd probably be doing the very same thing. Unfortunately, I wouldn't get through the medical.'

Ernest interposed, 'I'm sorry to hear that, Mr Jasper. I thought perhaps you were in a reserved occupation?'

'Good lord, no. Theatrical management can hardly be described as an essential service. No,

223

actually I have a tiresome physical problem, a rather rare blood condition. Not enough red corpuscles, or some such nonsense.'

Rosie was immediately concerned. 'Oh dear, I thought you were looking a little pale. It's nothing too serious, I hope?'

He laughed. 'The awkward part is, the doctors don't seem to be too sure! They say I might sail along happily for years; on the other hand I might pop off at any minute. Still, nobody lives for ever, do they? And I try not to brood about it. But that's why I can't join the forces; I'm living on borrowed time, so to speak.'

Sally slipped her arm through his. 'Don't talk about it any more, Trevor, I can't bear it.'

'Quite right. There's nothing worse than telling people all about your ailments, is there?' Changing the subject, he noticed the tea-table for the first time. 'I say! I haven't seen a cake like that since before the war. It can't be real, it must be a stage prop!'

Extremely pleased, Rosie said, 'Wait till I cut it up, then you'll find out if it's real or not.'

'Come and sit next to me, Trevor.' Sally pulled out a chair for him.

'Excuse me, I thought Mr Jasper's first name was Tony?' said Ernest.

'Tony Jasper is my professional name,' he explained, then smiled at Sally. 'May I tell them?'

'Why not?' Sally faced her family. 'He's got a little surprise for you.'

'I hope you won't mind. Funnily enough, we have a family connection, of a sort. My real

224

name is Trevor Judge.'

Rosie put down the cake-knife and stared at him. 'You mean, you're one of the Judge family?'

'Twice over! Arnold Judge was my father, and after he was killed, my mother Maudie got married again—to Joshua Judge.'

'Of course! Trevor—now I remember. You were the one who...' A blush spread over Rosie's face, and she looked down, busily slicing up Christmas cake.

He chuckled. 'I can see you know the whole story. You're quite right—I was the black sheep of the family when I was a lad, but I hope I've turned over a new leaf since then. I'm sorry if I embarrassed you, Mrs Kleiber, but I've made my peace with my stepbrother. In fact, I'm going into partnership with him at the Jubilee Wharf, to help in the office.'

Now it was Sally's turn to be amazed. 'You never told me that!'

'I didn't know it myself until an hour ago. Bertie and I had a long heart-to-heart talk; I've repaid the debt I owed my family, and now I feel I can make a fresh start.'

'But you've got your own business to think about—the theatre—the revue.' Sally looked at him in dismay. 'You're never going to give it all up?'

'No, no—but show business is a bit risky at present. I'll be dividing my time between my own office and the Jubilee. The docks may not be quite as glamorous as the West End, but they're a darn sight more important now. In a

225

way, you might almost say it's my contribution to the war effort.'

'Well, I think that's wonderful, I really do.' Rosie had been working it out. 'So if your stepfather was Joshua Judge, you must be related to my sister-in-law, Ruth.'

'Indeed I am. I suppose she's my step-aunt, if there is such a thing.'

Rosie laughed. 'Goodness me, it's a small world! We're taking Sally with us to the O'Dells tomorrow, for Christmas dinner. May we tell them your news, or is it a secret?'

'It's not a secret, but...' Trevor hesitated. 'I haven't seen Auntie Ruth for years. Do you think she'd be offended if I came too?'

'I'm sure she'd be thrilled!' exclaimed Rosie, adding apologetically, 'I only wish we could offer to put you up for the night. We do have a spare room as a rule, because now Abram's with the Medical Unit, he's billetted at the hospital —but they let him come home for Christmas. And in any case, if there's a raid tonight—'

'There won't be,' said Abram. 'The Nazis are a sentimental lot; they'll all be at home, singing *O Tannenbaum*—and Trevor's perfectly welcome to share my room, if that's any help?'

'You're very kind,' said Trevor, 'but we really must get back to town.'

Rosie's face fell. 'But surely Sally's staying here tonight?'

'Mumsie, another time I'd love to, but I haven't brought an overnight bag, and they'll be expecting me in town.'

'I still don't know where you are living these

226

days,' said Ernest. 'This flat you share with your friends—where is it exactly?'

Smoothly, Trevor replied for her. 'They're my friends, actually. They live on the floor below me at Charing Cross Road. They were kind enough to let Sally have their spare room—although since the raids started, we all troop down to the basement shelter every night. It's really not too bad down there—two big rooms, the Girls' Dormitory and the Boys' Dormitory—and so far underground, we hardly hear anything that's going on overhead... I promise you, she couldn't be in a safer place.'

'I'm very relieved to hear it,' said Rosie. 'She's a lucky girl, to be so well looked after.'

'Oh, I must take special care of Sally. She's going to be a big star and make us all a fortune!' said Trevor.

After tea, he looked at his watch and said he hated to break up the party, but driving in the black-out was so slow, he thought they should be making a move.

As they went downstairs, Ernest remarked, 'You are fortunate to be able to get enough petrol to run your car.'

'Well, I get a supplementary allowance for business purposes. I've been doing so much travelling round the provincial theatres this year. Mind you, there's no knowing how long that will last!'

'As long as you've got enough in the tank to get us to the Watermen for Christmas dinner, I don't care,' said Sally, as she kissed her parents. 'Night-night, darlings—see you tomorrow. And thanks for the tea. The cake was scrumptious!'

Rosie switched off the lights before opening the street door. A gust of cold night air came in, and she shivered. 'At least you won't catch cold in your new coat, Sally.' She turned to Trevor. 'Fancy her being able to save enough to buy herself that lovely fur!'

'She's a very clever girl,' he agreed seriously.

In the car, on the long drive back to the West End, Sally said, 'I felt awful, telling Mumsie I bought it myself, but you know what parents are like. And to make it worse, I still haven't bought your Christmas present yet. I can't think of anything you need.'

'You know what I need.' He stroked her knee. 'You're my Christmas present; I don't want anything else.'

'Mmm—you're so sweet. And you were lovely with the family. I just hope you weren't too horribly bored.'

'Not at all; I enjoyed meeting them. When the conversation got too domestic I whiled away the time, imagining all the things I'm going to do to you when we get back to the flat.'

'Oh, you are naughty...' She sighed happily, snuggling deeper into her coat. 'So you think Abram's right, about no air-raid? We shan't have to sleep in the shelter tonight?'

'No bloody fear,' he said. 'I'm very traditional; I like to unwrap my Christmas presents on the stroke of midnight.'

Dearest Mike,

*I love you, and I wish you a Merry Christmas
and a Happy New Year, wherever you are at this
moment. No—a happier New Year—for you and
me and everybody caught up in this horrible war.*

*I was late coming home tonight, because we had a
sort of party at the Station; paper hats and crackers
and mince-pies. Not really my cup of tea, but I
didn't want them to think I was being awkward,
so I had to stay on for a while. There were no alerts
tonight, and for an awful moment I caught myself
hoping there would be, when somebody suggested
playing Postman's Knock. Imagine it, wishing for
an air-raid—wasn't that awful? Luckily nobody
else seemed too keen on playing kids' games, so
that was all right.*

*Now I am in my room at the pub, sitting up in
bed with the writing-pad on my lap. In ten minutes
it will be December 25th, but it doesn't feel much
like Christmas. I don't expect it's very Christmassy
where you are, either, but I hope the parcel arrived
in time; I sent it off weeks ago. Mum and me made
the cake together and then I iced it. We put it in
a tin so it shouldn't get stale on the journey. We
crossed our fingers and hoped for the best.*

*It would have been so wonderful if you'd been
able to get leave, even for a few days, but I know
you're still on the Atlantic convoys, so you're
probably halfway round the world at this minute.
When I was walking home tonight, I looked up at
the moon, and imagined you out on deck, under*

that same old moon, and for a little while it felt as if we were close together.

Most nights I'm too busy to stop and think about you that way. Perhaps it's just as well, because it makes me miss you more than ever. In your last letter you said you were worrying about me driving the trailer during the raids, but honestly I'd sooner be out there than shut up indoors on that old telephone switchboard—and they say it's harder to hit a moving target!

I don't think there's any family news. We're all well, though Mum seemed a bit quiet tonight; she didn't say much, but I guessed she was thinking about Dan. Last time he wrote, he said they were going to draw lots for Christmas leave, but that was weeks ago and we haven't heard since, so I suppose he wasn't one of the lucky ones.

Of course Kaff is very quiet too; she's been like that ever since she first came to live here. She seems pretty well in herself She eats and sleeps all right and the doctor said there's nothing physically wrong, but she hardly talks at all. She reads a lot—she's been working her way, through the books I had when I was her age—and she doesn't seem unhappy exactly, only she never smiles.

Oh, I nearly forgot, there is one item of family news. At least, it's about mum's family more than ours.

Did I tell you the Kleibers are coming tomorrow, to have Christmas dinner with us? Well, tonight Aunt Rosie phoned up to ask if they could bring someone else as well. It's Sally's manager or agent or whatever he is, somebody called Tony Jasper. Every time I've spoken to Sally this year she's been going on about how marvellous Tony Jasper is. Well, now it turns out that isn't his proper name; he's really Trevor Judge, and he's the son of Glory's brother Arnold, who died in the last war. I remember Trevor when he used to go to our school, but he's a year older than Dan, and you never get to know people in the classes ahead of you, do you? He was always very high-and-mighty, and we didn't like him at all. Aunt Rosie says he's changed a lot, and he's very nice now, but I have my doubts. In fact, I think I'll leave this letter open and finish it tomorrow, then I can put in a postscript after I've seen him, and let you know what he's really like!'*

Every year on 25 December, the O'Dells had their main meal very late, when the customers had gone and the pub closed its doors. After that they had the rest of the day to themselves; the only day in the year when they did not have to re-open for the evening.

This year the family party was too big to fit into the kitchen, so Connor and Huw put up a long trestle-table in the saloon and brought in enough chairs to go round, then Lil and Ruth spread it with a pair of bedsheets and set out the cutlery.

Ruth counted on her fingers. 'We're still one short. We need an extra chair,' but Connor corrected her.

'No, we don't. Huw says he won't be eating with us today.'

'I've been invited to the Rope Walk.' Huw shifted uncomfortably. 'Glory, I mean, Mr

231

and Mrs Judge and Aunt Emily, they're all expecting me.'

'Of course,' said Ruth. 'I quite understand.'

As Huw went out, he met the Kleiber family coming in, and they exchanged the season's greetings before he hurried away.

'Where's he off to in such a rush?' asked Rosie. 'Doesn't he want any dinner?'

Ruth began to explain that he was on his way to join the Judge family, when a quiet voice broke in. 'Now you're making me feel guilty. I should really have gone with him.' Trevor followed Abram and Sally into the saloon, apologising to Ruth: 'I've no right to gate-crash your party like this. I hope I'm not being too much of a nuisance.'

'Trevor! Of course you're not a nuisance. We're very glad to see you.'

They shook hands, and he smiled. 'You haven't changed at all. I feel as if I were twelve years old again. Do we kiss or don't we?'

'Certainly we do!' Ruth told him, and he saluted her on both cheeks, in the French style.

Sally continued the introductions, and Trevor shook hands with the rest of the party. He was particularly nice to Kaff, saying, 'Sally told me I'd be meeting you today. I've been looking forward to it. Happy Christmas, Kaff!'

He produced a small but expensive box of chocolates and presented it to her. She took it politely, saying, 'Thank you very much. I'd better not open them now or they'll spoil my dinner.' She put the box aside, on the bar counter, and took no further interest in it.

Sally concluded the introductions. 'Trevor, come and say hello to my cousin Lil.'

He stared at Lil in astonishment, then exclaimed, 'I'm sorry, there must be some mistake. You can't be Lil. I remember her very well—she's nine years old, and about *this* high—and not nearly as pretty.'

Everyone laughed, and Sally interposed, 'Take no notice, Lil, don't let him embarrass you.'

Then Mary O'Dell came in from the kitchen, bearing a huge serving-plate with a roast turkey upon it, brown and steaming, and there was a general buzz of admiration.

'Where did you manage to find such a beauty?' Rosie wanted to know. 'And how ever many coupons did it take?'

Mary said firmly, 'We've been dealing with that self-same butcher ever since your Da and me came over from Ireland, long before you were born. I told him we were expecting something special for Christmas, and I think you'll agree he's not let me down.'

As they all took their places, Trevor pulled out a chair for Lil, saying under his breath, 'I didn't mean to embarrass you. The truth is, I was feeling rather embarrassed myself. The little girl doesn't seem to care for chocolates—did I do the wrong thing?'

'Not at all,' Lil assured him. 'It was very good of you to think of her. I'm sure she's very pleased really, but she doesn't show her feelings much.'

Sally called sharply from the far end of the

table, 'Over here, Trevor. You're next to me.' He smiled apologetically at Lil, and obeyed.

Conversation became general; they all congratulated Mary on a splendid meal, and Trevor turned to Ruth, asking, 'Tell me, do you think your parents would mind if I drop in at the Rope Walk this afternoon?'

Overhearing this, Sally protested, 'I thought you were coming to look at the house at Greenwich Park?'

'Yes, I want to, but I should call in and say hello to Auntie Gloria, and my Grandma. It's been such a long time—and today of all days...'

'That's a very nice idea,' Ruth told him. 'I'm quite sure they'll be delighted.'

'All right then, I'll come with you.' Sally was quite determined. 'And we can go to the house afterwards.'

'What's so special about Mrs Marriner's house, all of a sudden?' her father wanted to know.

'It's *our* house now,' Sally reminded him. 'Only it's been standing empty for eighteen months, and I can't go on sponging on Trevor's friends in Charing Cross Road for ever. I thought you'd be pleased if I moved in, to look after the place.'

'One girl on her own, in that big house?' Ernest shook his head. 'It's not very practical.'

'I could take in lodgers,' she suggested. 'That would give me something to live on when I'm out of work. And I'm a grown woman now, Poppa. I should have a place of my own.'

234

'We'll think it over,' said Rosie soothingly. 'Let's talk about it later, shall we?'

While Connor carved second helpings of turkey, and Ruth handed round the vegetable dishes, Rosie said to Ernest quietly, 'It might not be such a bad idea. As she says, she can keep an eye on the house—and we can keep an eye on *her!* I'd rather have her living over the river, than miles away up West, where we never see her at all.'

They were interrupted by a loud hammering at the street door. Connor put down his carving-knife and called out: 'Don't you know we're closed? Who is it?'

'Father Christmas!' replied a voice from the street. 'I've been stuck in my sledge all night with a bunch of reindeer—and I'm starving!'

Before he had finished speaking, Ruth was drawing back the bolts; Dan appeared in the doorway, wearing a red hat with a white woolly tassel instead of his forage-cap, and a bushy white beard hooked over his ears.

'You could have telephoned!' she scolded him, as he hugged her. 'Con, fetch another chair. Come in, son, and for goodness sake take off those silly whiskers!'

'Don't rush me. Santa's still got a few presents to deliver.' Slinging his kitbag down from his shoulder, he opened it, pulling out a ridiculous toy dog with big, mournful eyes.

'For Miss Katharine Hobbs, with Santa's love,' he said, and handed it to Kaff. 'He's a lost dog, and I think he needs looking after.'

As soon as she saw the dog's woebegone

235

expression, she began to laugh, saying, 'I call that a soppy sort of present, but I don't mind looking after him for you...'

And then she threw her arms round Dan's neck and hugged him.

After the cheerful noise and bustle at the pub, the house in the Rope Walk seemed very quiet.

Huw sat on the sofa beside Glory, juggling a cup of tea in one hand and a plate with a slice of Christmas cake in the other. Old Marcus Judge was in his usual place, fast asleep in the armchair nearest the fire; Louisa and Emily faced one another across the table.

Stifling a yawn, Emily said, 'Oh, dearie me, I'm quite drowsy. You gave me too much dinner, Lou. She spoiled us, didn't she, Mr Pritchard?'

'It was first-class, all of it,' he agreed. They all spoke in low tones, anxious not to wake Marcus.

'I'm glad you enjoyed it,' said Louisa. 'I'm afraid Christmas isn't like it used to be in the good old days. These are hard times for everyone.' She was interrupted by the rattle of the door-knocker. She turned to Gloria. 'Whoever can that be? You're not expecting anyone, are you, dear?'

'No. P'rhaps it's carols,' suggested Glory.

'I shouldn't think so. Everyone round here knows your uncle doesn't approve of carol-singers. "Bawling out the name of the Almighty as a way of begging", he calls it. Once he's made his opinions known, people don't usually call twice,' she added wistfully, and began to get up. 'I'd better see who it is.'

'You stay put, Mrs Judge. I'll go.' Huw rose to his feet and went off to open the front door. They heard a murmur of voices, and then he returned, saying, 'It's Ruth's niece, Sally, and—and a friend.'

All smiles, Sally bounced into the room, holding out her hand to Louisa. 'I don't expect you remember me, Mrs Judge, but we did meet, ages ago. I'm Sally King.'

Polite but baffled, Louisa shook hands with Sally, then looked enquiringly at the pale young man beside her.

'Hello, Aunt Louisa, merry Christmas,' he said, then went to the sofa. 'Auntie Glory—it's been a long time. How are you?'

'I'm fine, thanks,' said Glory, putting on a bright, meaningless smile, and Sally laughed.

'Don't you recognise your own nephew? It's Trevor!'

The smile cracked and slipped; Glory stared at him incredulously. 'Arnie's boy? Well, I never! Ma, did you hear that?'

Apprehensively, they all turned to Emily, hoping that the shock would not be too much for the frail old lady...but Emily Judge was wreathed in smiles, holding her arms out and saying, 'I knew it—I knew you'd come back to your old Gangan some day...'

'Gangan.' He knelt down at her feet and she enfolded him in her thin arms. 'Will you forgive your bad boy?'

She clung to him, tears of joy running down her cheeks. 'So naughty, staying away all this time. I was getting quite worried about you.'

Louisa threw a cautious glance at Marcus. 'We mustn't talk too loudly. It's best not to wake him when he's resting,' she said. 'But I hope you'll both stay and have some tea and a piece of cake. I'll just go and boil up the kettle.'

As she busied herself in the scullery, Gloria asked pointedly: 'Have you been round to Denmark Place yet? I dare say Bertie might be interested to see you again, too.'

Trevor acknowledged this with a winning smile. 'I haven't been to see Bertie this afternoon, but we had a long talk yesterday. We straightened everything out, don't worry. I paid my debts, and we're the best of friends again.'

'I'm glad to hear it,' said Glory, and looked away.

'Trevor's offered to give Bertie a helping hand in the office, now he's so busy,' Sally chimed in. She went on to explain that even though Trevor was now a leading figure in the theatrical world, family ties were still so important to him, he was prepared to divide his time between the West End and the Jubilee Wharf. She concluded happily: 'So we'll be seeing a lot more of you from now on, won't we, Trevor?'

'I'm ever so pleased.' Emily wiped her eyes, gazing fondly at her grandson. 'Your Dad would have been very proud of you.'

When Louisa returned with a fresh pot of

tea, Gloria stood up, saying abruptly: 'Don't bother about any more tea for us, Auntie Lou. Huw was saying something about having a stroll before it gets dark, isn't that right, Huw?'

'Oh, yes.' He took his cue promptly. 'A little walk will do us the world of good after that big dinner.'

Gloria went on, 'You won't mind if we leave you for a while, will you, Trevor? I'm sure you and your Gangan must have lots of things to say to one another.' With that, they fetched their hats and coats, said their goodbyes, and went out.

'That was a bit peculiar, wasn't it?' asked Sally. 'What's the matter with Glory?'

'I expect it's all been a little sudden,' said Louisa, busily pouring cups of tea. 'Seeing Trevor again so unexpectedly—it was rather a bolt from the blue.'

'Yes, I know, I've been away much too long. I should have written a letter first—broken it gently.' Trevor kissed his grandmother again. 'But I had to come and wish you a happy Christmas, didn't I?'

A strange, croaking sound startled them. In the fireside armchair, Marcus Judge had roused from sleep at last, hawking and hemming, trying to clear his throat. 'Who,' he gasped, pointing a shaking finger at Trevor, 'who is this?'

Louisa went to him at once. 'Don't upset yourself, dear, it's all right. Here's Emily's grandson come to visit you. Do you remember little Trevor? He's a very important man, now. Come and say hello, Trevor.'

Trevor approached the old man respectfully. 'How do you do, sir?'

As he struggled for breath, Marcus' lungs rattled, but no words emerged. Louisa tried to cover this by saying, 'It's very good of him to come all this way from—'

He waved her away impatiently, fighting to regain his strength. Balding and bearded, with the outline of his skull showing through his parchment skin, Marcus Judge still bore some resemblance to an Old Testament patriarch, but with his craggy beak of a nose he also looked like a giant eagle. And when he could speak, his voice had the harsh, piercing note of a bird of prey.

'You don't have to tell me,' he interrupted, panting. 'I know where he is from—I smell the brimstone and sulphur. He comes from the pit.'

Trevor drew back as the old man fixed him with a glittering eye and began to intone: 'The words of his mouth are smooth as butter, but within his heart is a drawn sword. He hath sown the wind, and he shall reap the whirlwind; he hath ploughed in wickedness, and he shall reap iniquity.'

Retreating, Trevor grabbed Sally's arm and muttered, 'Come on, let's go. He's off his rocker!'

Louisa tried to intervene, but Marcus would not be silenced. Lifting his head, he delivered his final words in a fierce, rasping voice that echoed down the hall and followed them out into the street.

'Vengeance is mine, saith the Lord—for the

wages of sin is death...death...*death!*'

When they left the Rope Walk, Glory and Huw walked in a tense silence for some time, until he could stand it no longer.

'What's troubling you, then?' he asked.

'Nothing at all.' She was tight-lipped, her eyes fixed on some distant point in the road ahead, but her thoughts were seething. 'Nothing,' she repeated curtly.

'Look, I know you better than that by now. Something's upset you, that's plain. Is it your nephew that's got your goat? I noticed you didn't seem very pleased to see him.'

Suddenly her pent-up anger burst from her like a pot boiling over. 'What have I got to be pleased about? Trevor was a nasty little squirt when he was a kid. When he grew up, he wormed his way into the Guild Office, then he cooked the books and scarpered with a small fortune! Nobody's seen hide nor hair of him since—until today, and the moment he comes sailing in, all smiles, with his "Sorry, Gangan—I've been a bad boy"—we're expected to forgive and forget! Honestly, it makes me sick!'

Huw put his arm round her waist. 'Don't let it rattle you. Your mum's an old lady, it's only natural for her to dote on the chap.'

'Ma spoiled him something rotten when he was a baby, and she's still doing it! But Gawd knows how he managed to get round the rest of the family. I'd have thought Bertie would have had more sense...'

241

Drawing her a little closer, Huw nuzzled her ear, whispering, 'It's no concern of ours, is it? Let them get on with it, eh?'

Gloria began to pull away. 'Don't do that, someone might see.'

'What if they do? We don't care, do we?'

She relaxed, smiling despite herself. 'No—the hell with the lot of 'em.' Turning her head, she kissed him briefly and they stood quite still, as he embraced her. Then she said, 'You're right—I shouldn't take on so. The fact is, it's not so much Trevor I was thinking of, it was Tommy.'

He did not understand her immediately. 'Tommy?'

'I told you about Tommy. He was the other runaway in the family; he did a bunk as well.'

Then Huw remembered. At sixteen, young Thomas Judge had quarrelled with Glory's husband. There was a fight, and Tommy had left the older man lying dead, stabbed to the heart.

'That was at Christmas, too—Boxing Day, twenty-two years ago tomorrow. The police never caught Tommy. We heard later he'd run off to America, and I dare say he's done very well for himself out there. But tonight, when I saw the way they welcomed Trevor back into the bosom of the family, fawning on him and slobbering over him, I couldn't help thinking: is that how they'd carry on if Tommy came home again? Let bygones be bygones? Sweep the dirt under the carpet and forget it? That's what really turned my stomach.'

242

Still holding her tightly, Huw said, 'Family feelings run deep. They say blood is thicker than water.'

She cut in harshly: 'And how about my Saul? He was family too—and it was his blood I saw, soaking through his shirt that night...I won't forget that, as long as I live. So now you know.' She kissed him once more, then said, 'Come on—let's have our walk. P'rhaps the fresh air will blow away my bad mood.'

When they got to West Ferry Road, she was about to turn left, but he stopped her, saying, 'Not there—let's go the other way.'

'What for? I wanted to go down to the Gardens—it's nice at Christmas. You see the kids showing off their new rollerskates.'

'Not today.' Huw had made up his mind. 'This way, there's something I want you to see.'

'What is it?'

'You'll find out. It's a surprise.'

'What sort of surprise?'

'Kind of an extra Christmas present. Don't ask so many questions.'

Taking her arm again, he led the way purposefully. A hundred yards further on, she stopped, hanging back. 'You're taking me to Millwall Road, aren't you?'

'That's where the surprise is. Do you mind?'

'I'd rather not... I haven't been back there for—I can't remember, it's so long ago.'

In the first few weeks after Millwall Road was blitzed, Glory hadn't felt like this. It was an emergency then, and she used to go there every day with Huw, seeing how much they could salvage from the wreckage. But it soon became clear they would never get it in a fit state to re-open the salon, so to make ends meet, Glory had gone back to her old routine of visiting clients and doing their hair in their own homes. Since then, she had never been near the shop.

'It all looked so hopeless,' she explained. 'Once I realised the house could never be repaired properly, I couldn't bear it any longer, somehow.'

'Don't say that.' He smiled, urging her gently forward. 'It's going to be all right—you'll see.'

'I know you've been going over on your own, trying to patch things up, and I'm very grateful, but you know as well as I do, it's too far gone for that.'

'Shut your mouth,' he said with a smile, 'or else I'll stop it for you... I tell you, I've got you a present, so will you kindly stop moaning?'

'You're a terrible bully,' she said—but she let herself be persuaded. When they reached Millwall Road, however, and she saw the battered outline of the hairdressing salon at the corner, her heart sank. 'Do we have to?' she asked miserably.

'We have to.'

He took a key from his pocket and opened the front door. She exclaimed in surprise: 'Oh, you've mended the lock! Well, I suppose that's a start.'

Inside, the shop was reasonably clean and tidy. Huw had done his best to clear up the debris, but the basins had gone, and so had the mirrors. There was only one chair left for customers, and that had bricks propping it up on one side, where a leg was missing.

'You shouldn't have bothered,' she began. 'It's no good—'

'I said shut up, will you?'

He took her through to the back room, and she looked around in astonishment, saying: 'You've put up new wallpaper!'

'And new paint, and new curtains at the window. There's running water in the kitchen, and the gas-stove's working.'

'You did all this—for me?'

'I'm not that soft. It was as much for me as for you. Well, I couldn't go on sleeping in the Watermen cellars for ever, now could I?'

Her heart leaped. 'You mean, you've done the bedrooms as well?'

'I've made a start. Come and see for yourself.'

Glory's bedroom was Huw's pride and joy; during the last couple of months he had spent every spare minute on it. There were more new curtains and new wallpaper; he had restored most of the bedroom furniture, supplying new sheets and pillows, and a bright pink eiderdown for the bed.

'It's ready for you to move back whenever you like. How about tonight?' he suggested.

She turned to him eagerly. 'Have you done the others too? Ma's room—and yours?'

'Ah well, now. I'm sorry to say the rest aren't really habitable as yet, though I'm working on them. For the moment there's just the one bedroom but I was thinking, we might be able to manage—for the time being?'

She laughed, and flung her arms round him. 'Huw, you're a genius. You are really!'

'Oh, I wouldn't say that,' he told her modestly. 'I'm afraid you'll have to make do with oil-lamps up here, but I've got the electricity working on the ground floor. Here, let me show you...'

Proudly, he led the way downstairs and pressed the switch. The ceiling lamp shone brightly, and from the shop, a voice yelled: *'Put that light out!'*

They had left the street door open when they came in—and they had been joined by an unexpected visitor. Grinning from ear to ear, Matt Judge chucked his kitbag into a corner and kissed his mother, then slapped Huw on the back.

'A happy Christmas to one and all. I wasn't sure if I'd find you here, after what you said in your letter, but it's not looking too bad.'

'So, you got leave for Christmas?' asked Glory, when she could speak.

'S'right! Me and Dan were both lucky in the draw, and I'm home for the week. I hope you don't mind giving back my bedroom, Huw? Will you be able to make do with the sofa?'

Huw and Glory looked at one another in despair, and Huw said, 'I'm afraid your mother's room is the only one fit to sleep in, at present. The others aren't finished yet.'

'Well, not to worry. I can rough it down here on the sofa.' Then Matt frowned, and asked Huw, 'But where are you going to kip?'

Huw could not look at Glory as he replied, 'Oh, I'm sleeping in the cellars at the pub these days. It's more convenient, really.'

For the second night running, there were no enemy planes over the Island, and although some of the regular shelterers went down to the cellars as usual, along with Huw, the O'Dell family were able to spend the night in their own beds. Dan had his old room back, and they made up a camp bed in Lil's room for Kaff, with a nightlight burning in a saucer of water, so she shouldn't be anxious if she woke up during the night and found herself in a strange place.

On Boxing Day, Lil woke very early; she looked across at the other bed and saw Kaff was fast asleep, clutching her toy dog, Dismal Desmond—still with a smile on her lips.

Lying back, Lil thought over the events of the previous day; it had turned out to be a wonderful Christmas after all. Then she remembered her unfinished letter to Mike. The writing-pad was still on the bedside table, and she had promised to give Mike her impressions of Trevor.

Reading over what she had written, she unscrewed the top of her fountain-pen. She cudgelled her brains, chewing the end of the pen. There was so much she wanted to say—Trevor hadn't been in the least like the hateful, stuck-up schoolboy she remembered. He was so nice, so modest, so funny and so charming, she didn't know where to begin. The more she thought about him, the more difficult it seemed.

After several minutes of indecision, she put pen to paper, and wrote: *P.S. Trevor was quite nice.*

She slipped the letter into the envelope, sealed it, addressed it and put it back on the bedside table; then she pulled the bedclothes up to her chin and settled down again, but for some reason she found it impossible to sleep.

8

The day after Boxing Day, Gloria came round to Silmour Street to do Rosie's hair. In the upstairs flat, she gave her a shampoo and set, putting the finishing touches to it while Rosie sat in front of the kitchen sink, and admired the results in a mirror propped up on the draining-board.

At last Glory put a hand-mirror behind her client's head so she could see the back as well, and said: 'There—is that how you like it?'

'Very nice, thanks. Have you got time for a cup of coffee before you go?'

'Ta, I don't mind if I do.'

Glory began to pack away the tools of her trade, and Rosie put the kettle on, saying: 'I'm afraid it's only coffee essence. We used up the last of the real coffee over Christmas—well, you have to spoil yourself now and then, don't you? But there's still some iced cake left, if you'd like a slice.'

Sitting at the kitchen table, they exchanged family gossip. 'I hear you've got Matt home on leave this week?' said Rosie. 'That must have been a nice surprise.'

'Oh yes, it was, though he's been sleeping on the parlour sofa, 'cos there's only one bedroom fit to use at present,' Gloria told her. 'I offered him my bed, but he wouldn't hear of it. He says it's not worth turning me out just for a few nights; he's got to report back to his unit on Monday.'

'They don't give them long, do they?' said Rosie, then added suddenly, 'As a matter of fact, I've been hoping he might drop in to say hello while he's at home. Why don't you bring him round for supper on Sunday night?'

Gloria stirred her coffee, the spoon rattling irritably against the cup. 'I'm afraid Matt's evenings are all booked up. He's got so many friends to see...girl-friends, mostly. Well, it's only natural he should want to be with people his own age, isn't it?'

'Yes, of course. But you must tell him: if he gets a longer leave next time, Ernest and I will always be very pleased to see him.'

Gloria glanced up, surprised. 'Oh? I didn't know Matt had ever met Ernest.'

'Oh, yes. They had a nice chat, last time Matt dropped into the shop. Ernest was quite impressed with him.'

'I hadn't realised...' Gloria softened slightly. 'Well, like you say, another time, p'rhaps.' She went on to ask after the rest of the family. 'Did you know I saw Sally on Christmas Day, when she brought Trevor to the Rope Walk? She's looking prettier than ever.'

'Isn't she? And you must have been pleased to see your nephew again, after all this time. I'm so glad Sally and Trevor have become such good friends.'

'Yes.' Gloria did not wish to get drawn into a discussion of Trevor, and continued smoothly, 'How's Abram getting on? Still with that Medical Service thing, is he?'

Rosie sighed. 'He's out with the ambulance every night. I'm afraid he's not getting enough sleep. It's a shame they won't let them live at home; at least I could make sure he was properly looked after, and give him a square meal.' Then she brightened up. 'Talking of meals, how about supper on Sunday? Even if Matt's busy, you could come without him, couldn't you?'

For a moment, Glory was at a loss; had she misjudged Rosie after all? 'Well, that's very nice of you.' She stumbled over the words. 'But are you sure? I mean—just me, on my own?'

'Why not? Unless you don't fancy going out at night by yourself? Well, in that case, why don't you bring your lodger as well—if he's not on duty at the Wardens' Post? Ernest and Huw Pritchard always have plenty to talk about.'

Glory shone with pleasure; it was the first time she and Huw had been asked out together.

'If he's free I'm sure he'll be glad to,' she said. 'Let's hope the bombers give us a quiet night.'

In one sense, Sunday was a quiet night—at

least, in the dockland area, though from the moment the sirens sounded, soon after dark, endless waves of planes came in over the estuary, flying westward. But they did not drop a single bomb on the Isle of Dogs that night; they were heading for another target.

At the Fire Station, Lil nursed a mug of cocoa and waited to be called out; it was an odd twist of fate that the auxiliary drivers should be sitting and twiddling their thumbs, for the girls on the switchboard were taking incoming calls so fast they could hardly cope with the messages.

Then Sub-Officer Patterson appeared in the doorway, snapping his fingers at the waiting drivers. 'You, you and you!' They jumped to their feet and hurried over to get their orders. 'Those damn Jerries must know a thing or two. The tide on the river's a lot lower than usual tonight, and that's making it difficult to get pumps down to the water-line. There's been a big concentration of fire-bombs all over the City. As far as I can make out, half the buildings are ablaze, and they're yelling for extra pumps, so jump to it!'

He gave them their directions; Lil had to report as fast as possible to a point between Ludgate Hill and Paternoster Row. His parting words were: 'And mind you put your foot hard down—because every minute counts!'

Like most Islanders, Lil's knowledge of London was fairly sketchy, but she had a rough idea where Paternoster Row was—in the shadow of St Paul's. Obeying orders, she drove at top speed through Limehouse, along

251

Cable Street and round the Tower—but when she reached her destination, it was no longer in the shadow of the Cathedral. Tonight, there were no shadows in these narrow streets; nothing but a dazzle of scorching flame.

She found the fire-crew waiting for her. They did not waste words, but someone shouted above the roar of the conflagration: 'And about time too!' as they sprang into action.

Lil scrambled out of the cab to watch; detaching the trailer pump, they fixed it to a street hydrant and began to run out a line of hose. Feeling useless, she asked the officer in charge of operations, 'Is there anything I can do to help?'

'You can pray for us, if you want,' he said tersely. 'Pray that the bloody mains aren't damaged!'

By this time, water was in very short supply. Many street mains had been fractured, and the fire-boats on the Thames were finding it hard to get more than a trickle from the abnormally low river. And this was the night that the Luftwaffe had chosen to throw a storm of high-explosive bombs and incendiaries at the City of London, showering the close-packed streets, spires and rooftops with flame.

Obediently, Lil prayed—and her prayer was answered. The branch filled—went rigid—and a powerful jet of water hit the nearest blaze, exploding in a gush of scalding steam as it reached the heart of the fire.

She had never felt such intense heat. As the current of hot air rose to the night sky, a great wind came from nowhere, sucked through the narrow alleyways to fill the vacuum, while burning embers and vicious, stinging sparks flew about them like tracer-bullets.

'This is no place for you,' the officer told her. 'You'll have to leave the pump with us and pick it up after we've got this lot under control—if we ever do... You'd better get back to your own HQ while the going's good.'

She didn't argue—she was not sorry to leave this inferno; getting back into the cab, she slammed the engine into gear and backed off from the fire hydrant, then swung round and made for home.

Almost at once, she realised that the return journey was not going to be easy. Emergency calls had been going out all round London, appealing for auxiliary pumps and other relief services, and by now the roads were jammed with vehicles, all heading towards the City: there were taxis and trailers, fire-engines from out of town, ambulances, and hosepipes snaking across every road. Lil tried to take side turnings to left and right in order to avoid the traffic, and soon became hopelessly lost.

All round her, buildings were on fire, and still the bombs kept coming down. Then she turned another corner—only to find the road blocked by an ambulance. It wasn't a regulation vehicle, but a small van that had been painted white, with a red cross daubed on the side. She hooted impatiently, though in such a din it was a waste of time, for the ambulance did not move—or perhaps, she thought, there was nobody in it.

Jumping out, she ran for a closer look. There were two young men inside the van; one of them was wearing an improvised sling, and she could see a dark stain of blood seeping through the shoulder of his jacket. The other young man grinned cheerfully and said, 'Hello, Lil. What are you doing here?'

It was Abram, on duty with the mobile medical unit. She explained as quickly as possible that she was on her way back to the Island, but that the ambulance was blocking the road; she asked him to move it.

'Sorry, I don't drive,' he told her. 'To tell you the truth, we're a bit stuck.'

'But where's your driver gone?' she asked.

The man wearing the sling made a shaky attempt at a laugh. 'I'm the driver,' he said.

Abram chimed in: 'Neville got hit by some shrapnel. I don't suppose you could drive us back to the hospital, could you? Because we're not doing much good like this.'

Lil thought fast. It would mean leaving the cab and picking it up later, along with the trailer, but even that would be better than going round in circles.

'I can try,' she said. 'Where's the hospital?'

'The other side of Liverpool Street Station. Not all that far, really.'

'Right, then. I've never tried driving a van, but I dare say I'll soon get the hang of it.'

Abram made Neville as comfortable as possible on one of the bunks inside the van, then took his place in front, next to Lil, saying: 'There's a nasty hole just ahead of us. You'd better reverse and drive round it.'

Not wanting to admit that she wasn't sure how to get into reverse gear, Lil said confidently, 'It's all right—I can drive straight over it. I'm very good at judging distances.' He was about to argue, but she silenced him by asking, 'Who's driving this van, you or me?'

With great aplomb, she drove on carefully—then managed to stall the engine. They stopped dead, their wheels on either side of the hole. 'Damn...' she said under her breath, and tried to start the motor again.

'Were you thinking of stopping here long?' Abram asked politely.

'I'll be on my way just as fast as I can,' she said between her teeth, as the starter-motor whined.

'That's probably just as well,' Abram told her. 'Because the incendiary in that hole hasn't gone off yet.' At that moment the engine turned over and the van leaped forward, just missing the corner of a building and barely scraping a lamp-post.

'Now which way do we go?' she asked breathlessly.

'Make for Liverpool Street first,' he said. 'I can direct you from there.'

'Yes, but which way is Liverpool Street?'

'Ah...' He scratched his chin thoughtfully. 'I was hoping you might know that—I'm not too good at directions.' He slid back a small panel in the partition behind them and called, 'Neville! Which way to Liverpool Street—left or right?'

A faint voice replied, 'I'm not sure where we

are now. Try going left.'

So Lil turned left, and hoped for the best.

'I'm afraid it wasn't much of a supper,' apologised Rosie.

Huw and Gloria both spoke at once, assuring her that it had been a splendid meal.

'Cold meat and pickles and mashed potato? You're just being kind,' she said. 'But I've a few mince-pies for you, hotting up in the oven. You know what it's like after Christmas, you have to use up the left-overs.'

A series of explosions distracted her. They were some way away, but still near enough to make the windows rattle behind the black-out curtains.

'Oh, dear.' She broke off, uncertainly. 'Do you think we ought to go down to the shelter?'

Ernest stood up. 'There are no bombs in this area,' he said, 'but let me switch off the lights for a moment, so we can look out.'

It was pitch-dark in the room until the curtains were opened, and then they saw the western horizon was a sheet of rose-coloured flame beneath a pall of black smoke.

'Pray God for the poor souls living there, whoever they are,' Rosie murmured.

'There are not very many living in the City, I think,' Ernest pointed out. 'The buildings are nearly all offices; on a Sunday they will be almost deserted... But I think I had better go downstairs and telephone the Wardens' Post, to make sure we are not needed.'

Ernest and Huw had juggled their duty-rosters

in order to get the same night off, but now they felt a strong tug of responsibility. If there were a sudden crisis, they should be there, ready to deal with it.

A few minutes later, Ernest called up from the shop: 'My dear, we are going round to the Post. Apparently there is a large area of fire around St Paul's. We think we should report on stand-by, in case of an emergency.'

'But what about your mince-pies?' Rosie asked.

'We can have them later—for breakfast, perhaps,' he told her, and a moment later she heard the shop door open and shut.

'Well, they can do as they please, but I'm not letting those mince-pies burn to a crisp,' she said firmly. 'We'll have ours now.'

Afterwards, the two women did the washing-up together, and Rosie said: 'I hope the fire doesn't spread any further. I keep thinking of Sally, at Charing Cross. I tell you, I shall feel a lot happier when she moves out of the West End. I don't care what Ernest says; I want her closer to home.'

'Oh, is she moving back here?' asked Glory.

Rosie explained that Sally was going to live at Acacia Grove in Greenwich for the time being, though Ernest wasn't keen on the idea of her taking in lodgers.

'I keep telling him, I can slip over and keep an eye on things. I admit Sally's never been much of a one for housework, but I can easily give her a hand to keep the place tidy. I'm afraid Ernest's a little bit old-fashioned in some respects. He doesn't approve of an unmarried girl sharing a house with strangers—specially if they're men. I tell him, it's different in war-time. Nobody thinks twice about such things nowadays. After all—look at you and Huw Pritchard.'

'What about me and Huw Pritchard?' asked Gloria sharply.

'Well, there weren't any remarks passed when he moved in as your lodger, were there? And now he's getting the place shipshape, I expect he'll move back again soon, won't he? But just because you're living under the same roof, that doesn't mean you're both—well, you know—carrying on, does it?'

'Of course not,' said Gloria, and glanced round the kitchen. 'Could I have another teacloth? This one's getting rather soggy.'

There was another muffled explosion in the distance, and Rosie gasped, 'Oh, I wish those bombers would go away. I can't help thinking about Abram, too, and wondering where he is. I hope he's all right.'

The strangest part of all was that Lil didn't feel frightened.

There was so much going on around her, all the time. On every side, blazing buildings collapsed as the roofs caved in, shooting up great blasts of flame like fountains of fire; and the noise never stopped. One explosion followed another, as gas-mains blew up, bombs fell and ack-ack guns shattered the night. And she had to concentrate so hard, twisting and turning the van, avoiding fresh craters in the road, dodging

258

the burning debris that seemed to fall from nowhere, that she was much too busy to feel afraid.

'Do you know where we are yet?' she asked Abram. 'Can you recognise any of this?'

He shook his head. 'Sorry, I can't say I do—but that means nothing. It's all completely changed, there are no landmarks any more. Let's just hope we're on the right road—and keep going.' He pushed back the sliding panel again, and called: 'Neville? How are you feeling now?'

There was no reply; he tried to peer through the small aperture, but could not see much.

'I think he might have gone to sleep, unless he's passed out. I had a nasty feeling all along that he was trying to make light of that injury. I'm sure it's worse than he's telling us.'

After a moment, Lil asked, 'Is he a Conscientious Objector as well?'

'Oh, yes—a convinced pacifist. He was prepared to go to prison if it came to that, but they directed him into Civil Defence, and he agreed with me: we'd sooner save life than destroy it.'

Lil thought of all the thousands of young men now in the Army—many of them sleeping safely in barracks at this moment, at various places round the British Isles—men who had never heard a bomb fall or seen a building blown up... And some people still branded the conchies as cowards.

She was jerked out of these reflections by the sight of a wooden barrier immediately ahead, and a sign saying No Through Road.

Beyond it, she could see a tangle of hosepipes and a little group of fire-fighters, battling against a huge warehouse, six storeys high, with flames belching from broken windows on every floor. Clearly, there was no hope of getting through that way.

'You'll have to turn round and go back,' said Abram.

She looked in the rear-mirror. 'Can't,' she said. 'There's a whole line of traffic following us, jamming the road.'

'Well, we can't stay here all night,' Abram told her. 'I've got to get Neville to a doctor as soon as possible.'

'I know. Hang on—this could be a bumpy ride!' She swung the steering-wheel over, and put her foot down. On one side of the road there was a barren patch of wasteland, bricks and rubble, the site of an earlier raid. Lil had no idea how far she could get over this unknown territory, which might be full of holes, jagged metal and broken glass—but she had no choice.

The next few minutes were hair-raising, but they skated over the bomb-site somehow, and lurched back on to the open road once more. There, looming up against the sky, silhouetted against the sweeping beams of searchlights, was the outline of a building, huge and impregnable as a fortress.

'D'you think it will be safe to go this way?' Lil asked.

Abram snorted with laughter. 'I should hope

so. That's the Bank of England—you can't get much safer than that. Anyhow, I know the way from here. First left, then first right...'

And behind them, riding the storm, miraculously surviving the horrors of the night, sailed the great dome of St Paul's; gleaming orange, like the morning sun rising through clouds. Though half a square mile of the City around it had been flattened, the Cathedral remained—a symbol of hope—not only to London, but to the nation.

Three days later, Lil had some time off work. The old taxi-cab was rather the worse for wear after its trip to the City, and had to go in for some much-needed repairs, so Lil volunteered to drive it to the garage on her day off. This was not entirely unselfish, since she had arranged to kill two birds with one stone, and do another errand on the way.

When she reached Silmour Street, Abram was already out on the pavement with a pile of luggage and a few sticks of furniture.

'Do you think there'll be room for all this in the back of the cab?' he asked.

'I'm sure we can squeeze it in somehow, though I'm afraid you may have to perch on top of it!' she warned him.

'Oh, I'm going to sit next to you, like we did on Sunday,' he told her.

'Won't Sally want to sit in front?' Lil asked.

'She's not here; she's gone over to Acacia Grove with Trevor, to open up the house and get things ready. They're very grateful to you for volunteering to act as a removal-van.'

'I'll probably get shot if anyone from the Fire Station spots me doing this, but who cares?' Then, more seriously, she asked, 'What's the latest news of Neville? Have you seen him?'

'Yes, he's doing fine. They say he'll be well enough to start work again next week. That's because we got him to a doctor in good time—and that's thanks to you.'

She smiled. 'Do you know, in some ways I almost enjoyed it, though I wouldn't want to try it again in a hurry!'

Then Ernest and Rosie came out of the shop and greeted Lil, and between them they managed to load everything into the taxi.

'Most of Moira's furniture went into store when we shut the house up,' explained Rosie. 'So it seemed easier to let Sally have her own bits and pieces from here—and things like cutlery and crockery and saucepans and so on...'

'I suppose she won't need much, being on her own,' said Lil.

'She will not be on her own,' said Ernest heavily.

'Really? Has she found some lodgers already?'

'Only one,' replied Ernest. 'Trevor Judge is to live there also.'

'Not all the time,' Rosie explained quickly. 'Just the odd night, if he has to work late in the office at Jubilee Wharf—that's all.'

When the furniture was safely packed on board, Lil and Abram climbed in and the cab drove off. Rosie and Ernest stood watching it until it turned the corner. At last he said quietly:

'I wish I could be happy about this, as you appear to be.'

'What do you mean by that?'

'You know very well what I mean. I do not like the idea of our daughter sharing the house with a young man. It is not proper.'

'But she's advertising for some more lodgers, so that will soon make it all right. And besides, Trevor isn't just *any* young man. Sally's very fond of him—and I believe he feels the same way about her.'

'That is exactly what concerns me!' Ernest frowned. 'The two of them—alone together—anything could happen!'

Rosie slipped her arm through his. 'When you first opened this shop and I started work as your assistant, we shared the flat upstairs... Just the two of us. Have you forgotten that?'

'No, of course not, but—'

She drew him into the shop and closed the door; then she put her arms round him and whispered, 'That's how we began, and I don't think we've done too badly, do you? If they finish up as happy as us, I shan't be sorry.'

He relaxed a little, and kissed her. 'You may be right. I hope so.'

Meanwhile Lil drove the cab through the Blackwall Tunnel, turned right into Greenwich, then halfway up Crooms Hill and into Acacia Grove. Sally and Trevor gave them a warm welcome, and Sally hugged Lil.

'You're an angel, you really are. Let's leave the men to unload everything, while I show you round. It doesn't look up to much yet, of course. There's only a few pieces of furniture they didn't put into store, and you can see why! But Trevor's going to bring some of his own stuff down from town, and then it'll look gorgeous. With so many rooms, it'll be like living in a palace!'

'How many lodgers will you have?' asked Lil.

Sally grinned wickedly. 'Between you and me, we haven't even started to advertise yet. Well, we're in no hurry to fill the place with strangers, only don't you dare tell Poppa I said so.'

When the cab was unloaded, Trevor produced a bottle of champagne and insisted they must drink a toast. 'Acacia Grove, and all who sail in her!'

There were only two chairs in the sitting-room, but the men put down cushions and made themselves comfortable on the floor.

'I mustn't stay long,' Lil said. 'I've promised to take the cab to the garage. It got a bit bashed about, the other night.'

'You should have seen her,' Abram told them, 'whizzing through the shrapnel like Queen Boadicea driving her chariot!'

Sally looked wistful. 'I think you're so wonderful, darling, doing your bit for the war—I wish I could. I've just got to sit and wait for the next job to come along, but everything's so uncertain in the theatre at present.'

'You can say that again,' Trevor agreed, stretching out on his cushions. 'In fact, you might find yourself contributing to the war effort after all, sweetheart, whether you like it or not.'

Sally stared at him. 'Whatever do you mean?'

'They say the Government's going to register girls for war-work in the spring. If you're not careful, you could be directed into a factory or a hospital or something equally soul-destroying.'

'You don't mean it! Me—in a factory?' she exclaimed. 'You're teasing me, aren't you? You must be!'

Abram joined in. 'No, he's absolutely right—I heard it myself. Young women who aren't already in work are going to be roped in to keep essential services running.'

'I'd rather die...' Sally dropped on to her knees beside Trevor. 'You must *do* something, Trevor. You must fix me up with a job *fast!*'

'Easier said than done, my love.' Propping himself up on his elbow, he took a thoughtful sip of champagne. 'Come to think of it, there is one possible solution...'

'What's that?'

'ENSA are crying out for artistes; they're sending shows round all the Army camps and airfields and naval bases, and they're desperate for some real talent. Why don't I fix you up an audition with Basil Dean or someone, at Drury Lane? I'm sure they'd be only too pleased to fit you in to one of their shows.'

Sally did not look over-enthusiastic. 'That would mean going on tour again, wouldn't it? I'm sick and tired of touring. I've done my share already... And from what I hear, most of the ENSA shows are awfully tatty. I couldn't possibly get mixed up in anything third-rate.'

'My darling, the top West End names are working for ENSA now—Gracie Fields, Frances Day—the lot! And the main thing is, it counts as war-work, so you wouldn't be called up.' She still looked very dubious, so he urged her: 'They say the troops are marvellous audiences—you'd be treated like royalty. Quite honestly, it could be a real springboard for your career. Build up your reputation with the Forces, and when the war's over you'll take your place on Shaftesbury Avenue as a number one star!' He turned to Lil for support. 'I'm right, aren't I? It could be a very shrewd move—don't you agree?'

Lil laughed. 'Don't ask me! But the way you put it, it does sound like a good idea—and a lot better than working in a factory!'

Sally nodded. 'Yes, I do see that. OK, then—make an appointment for me, and I'll go along and audition.'

'Good girl.' Trevor smiled and patted her hand. 'I'm sure you're doing the right thing. Have some more champagne.'

The first weeks of 1941 were cold and cheerless, but since the New Year the air-raids over London had been much less frequent, and the news from North Africa provided some comfort too. The Italian troops had become a laughing-stock as the Allies chased them further and further back; in January, the British captured Tobruk, and followed this up by taking Benghazi a few weeks later. By the middle of February, the German High Command, determined to stiffen the Italian resistance, threw Rommel's Afrika Korps into Tripoli.

'That won't make no difference,' said Sub-Officer Patterson, who had been listening to the latest news-bulletin on the Fire Station wireless. 'We've got 'em on the run in the desert now.'

'I hope so,' Lil told him. 'My brother's out in North Africa.'

'Lucky beggar,' he grunted. 'All that sand and sea and sunshine—just like being on holiday at Margate.'

Lil wanted to argue, but thought better of it. It wasn't advisable to contradict a senior officer and anyway, it was nearly six o'clock, and she was about to go off-duty.

Slipping into her outdoor coat, she called out, 'See you tomorrow!' and left the building. Working a day shift was a lot easier than being on nights; and today she had spent most of her time on routine maintenance jobs. She looked forward to her evening off, and considered the possibility of going to the pictures.

One of the other AFS girls had been up West last weekend to see *Gone With the Wind,* and reported that it was the most marvellous picture she'd ever seen. She had cried buckets, and Vivien Leigh and Clark Gable were super-duper—but Lil said: 'I don't fancy travelling all that way just to go to the pictures. I'd sooner wait till it comes to Poplar.'

'You'll have a long wait then,' reported her colleague. 'It's been on in Leicester Square for nearly a year, and it seems like it'll stay there for ever!'

267

'Well, I'll think about it,' Lil told her.

The film certainly sounded as if it were something special, and she was rather tempted, but she didn't fancy going by herself. She and Mike always used to go to the pictures together, and she didn't enjoy outings on her own. Perhaps she could persuade one of the other girls to go with her another day.

By the time she reached the Watermen it was nearly dark, and the pub was securely blacked-out, so she didn't see the man coming out of the saloon until they collided in the doorway.

'Oh, sorry!' they exclaimed simultaneously, then he added, 'Hello, I'm in luck after all. I've just been looking for you.'

'Who's that?' she asked, though she knew him at once. Even in the dark, Trevor's voice was unmistakable.

He went back into the saloon with her, saying, 'I just finished work at the Wharf, and I came over on the off-chance I might find you here. Let me get you a drink.'

'No, thanks. I'll be having my tea in a minute, thanks all the same.'

'Are you sure? Well, just for a minute, have you got time to sit down and talk?'

It was still early, and the bar was half-empty; Mary O'Dell was behind the bar and Lil went across to have a quick word with her Gran, then joined Trevor at the table in the alcove.

'What can I do for you?' she asked.

'Keep me company, I hope,' he said. 'Take pity on a lonely man, and rescue him from a miserable birthday party.'

She found herself smiling back at him. 'I haven't the faintest idea what you're talking about,' she said. 'Who's having a birthday party?'

'I am—and all alone, unless you come to my rescue.' He explained, 'I'd arranged to take Sally out to dinner next Saturday, to celebrate. I've booked a table for two at the best night-club in town, and we were both looking forward to it...but that's when disaster struck!'

Lil was concerned. 'Oh dear, Sally's not ill?'

'Worse than that—she's in Aberdeen.' He went on to fill in the details. Sally had been accepted by ENSA some weeks earlier, but at first she had only done a few troop-concerts—single dates, at searchlight batteries and ack-ack stations in the Home Counties, within easy reach of London. Now, quite suddenly, she had been attached to a regular touring unit, and had been sent up to entertain at various secret destinations throughout the Highlands; she would not be coming south again for at least another month.

'So here I am—a lone, lorn bachelor with a birthday party and no guests. Could you be very kind and help me out?'

Lil didn't know what to say. She had only seen Trevor once or twice since he and Sally moved in to Acacia Grove, and she had never spent any time with him on her own. The prospect of an evening at a smart, sophisticated night-club was appealing, but a little daunting too... What could she possibly wear to a place like that?

269

'It's very good of you to ask me, but I don't really think...'

'Don't tell me you're working on Saturday night? At the Fire Station?'

'No, it isn't that. Saturday's my day off, actually, only... I'm sure there must be heaps of other people you could ask. Actresses—singers...'

'Yes, I suppose I could, but I don't think Sally would be too pleased if I did! It'd be different if you came with me. Being her cousin, one of the family, she wouldn't object to that.'

'Oh, I see.' Lil was beginning to weaken. 'The only thing is, I haven't got the right clothes for it.'

'That doesn't matter a damn. Nowadays people wear any old thing.' He indicated Lil's AFS uniform. 'You could wear that if you like. Lots of people will be in uniform. It's you I want to dance with, not your dress.'

'Well, if you're really sure.' She felt it only fair to warn him. 'I'm not a proper dancer like Sally—you mustn't expect too much.'

'Listen, will you kindly stop making excuses for yourself? Are you coming with me or aren't you?'

She looked into his laughing eyes, and felt a strange, inexplicable thrill of excitement. 'Yes, please,' she said. 'I'd love to.'

Later in the evening, when Lil told her mother and her grandmother, Mary O'Dell drew down the corners of her mouth, saying: 'Do you think it's wise?'

'Oh, there haven't been any heavy raids for ages, Gran. I'm sure it'll be all right.'

'I wasn't thinking so much of that. You're a married woman and he's a single man. What would your husband say?'

Rather to Lil's surprise, her mother broke in: 'I'm quite sure Mike would be only too pleased. It's not as if Trevor was a stranger, Mam. He's my nephew, and I think it's time Lil had a night out. She's been working with the Fire Service for so long, she deserves a break. Go on, why don't you? Go out and enjoy yourself.'

Half-convinced, Mary tried to set aside her doubts, and the three women fell into an enthralling discussion about what Lil should wear.

Lil told them: 'Trevor said it wouldn't matter if I went in my uniform, but I certainly won't do that. I don't want everyone staring at me as if I were some sort of freak.'

'Quite right,' said Ruth. 'I know! I've got that long dress—the dark red silk. I bought it for the Licensed Victuallers' dinner dance, before the war, and I've never worn it since. It'll be too big for you, but we can easily take it in at the waist and alter the neckline. We're about the same height, so the length should be all right.'

It was more than all right; by Saturday evening, the dress looked as if it had been made for Lil. Even Connor, who was not altogether happy about his daughter going to some unknown haunt of vice in the West End with a young man—even if he was his nephew by marriage—had to admit that she looked like a princess.

Trevor came to collect her in his car, and the O'Dells saw them off, telling them to have a good time. Trevor warned them it might be quite late before he brought her home, because the dancing always went on into the small hours.

'Don't you dare sit up for me!' Lil scolded her parents. 'I've got my own key, so you can just go to bed and stop fussing!'

As the car drove away, Ruth said to Con, 'I'm really glad she's having a night out. Ever since Mike joined the Navy, she's done nothing but work and sleep. She needs a little fun now and then, or she'll turn into an old woman before her time.'

It was a night out that Lil would never forget.

Even the drive from East London to Piccadilly was an adventure; they followed more or less the same route Lil had taken on the night of the great City fire, but this was very different. For one thing, she wasn't driving; it was a long time since she had been a passenger, and as she sat beside Trevor in the smart two-seater, she found herself noticing things she had never seen when she had to keep her eyes on the road ahead.

And Trevor was a fascinating travelling-companion. He told her anecdotes about the places they passed, including family stories: 'See that shop? I got a whacking when I was a kid, because I chucked half a brick through the window! I couldn't sit down for a week afterwards.' He knew scraps of London's history: 'That church in the middle of the road is St Clement's. Before they stopped bell-ringing, the chimes used to play *Oranges and Lemons* on account of the nursery-rhyme,' and, when they reached Piccadilly Circus: 'That's where the statue of Eros used to be, with his bow and arrow. It's all boarded up now, but judging by the chaps strolling around with their girls, I should imagine he's still shooting off a few arrows, wouldn't you?'

He parked the car, and they made their way through a darkened entrance in Coventry Street, between the Rialto Cinema and Lyons Corner House, down a flight of stairs and into the night-club.

There was a bar in the foyer, but they didn't stop there. Trevor led the way through a pair of swing doors and on to a balcony that ran all the way round the restaurant below. Lil stopped short, dazed by the brilliant lights, the shining chromium and polished mirrors, the glittering coloured glass. She had never seen anything like it, except in Hollywood movies.

'What do you think?' Trevor asked her, with a smile.

'It's like magic,' she said simply.

They walked down one side of the double staircase; between the two curved flights of stairs, a band was playing on a small dais and there was a dance-floor with tables round the edge, lit by pretty shaded lamps.

The head-waiter came up and greeted Trevor like an old friend. 'Good evening, sir. I think this is the table you asked for?'

He took them across to a secluded table at the far side of the dance-floor, behind a pillar, and gave them two menus, enquiring what they would care to drink. Trevor ordered cocktails. Lil was about to say that she didn't drink but as she began to speak, he asked if she would like to dance?

'Why not?' she said bravely.

He put his arm round her waist and she tensed instantly, as she always did when a man touched her, but when they began a slow fox-trot, she found she could relax. He wasn't holding her tightly or possessively; he was partnering her, easing her through a pattern of deft, confident steps which she found herself following automatically.

'I don't know why you were apologising, the other day,' he told her. 'You're an excellent dancer.'

'You make it seem so easy,' she said. 'Besides, the band's very good.'

'Caribbean music,' he told her. 'It has a wonderful beat.' Then he saw that their cocktails were waiting, and they went back to the table. He raised his glass to her. 'Cheers!'

She felt she had to try it, at least. Touching the rim of her glass against his, the way she had seen film-stars do it on the screen, she said: 'Many happy returns of the day.'

'Thank you.' He smiled. 'Many happy returns for both of us... I'm glad you like this place—we must come here again.'

She sipped her drink. She had never tasted anything quite like it—ice-cold and delicious,

274

with a hint of something stronger beneath the sweetness.

Trevor studied her for a moment, then asked, 'When you said this was magic, what did you mean exactly? I'm only asking because I felt there was a touch of magic in the air myself, this evening.'

'You'll think I'm being very childish. When we walked in out of the black-out, it made me think of a transformation scene in a pantomime—the last bit, when they walk down the palace steps and live happy ever after.'

He laughed. 'You're not far wrong! Wait till it gets really crowded. The dear old Café can be quite a pantomime then, right enough.'

'No, I didn't mean that.' She tried to explain. 'Out in the street, there's a war going on, but down here that seems miles away. It's like another world.'

'Absolutely. We're two floors down, underneath the cinema; there can be an air-raid going on up there with all hell breaking loose, and down here you won't hear a thing—it's safe as houses.'

She thought afterwards that it had been a strange thing to say; by now everybody knew that houses weren't safe at all.

On the rostrum, the band was playing the latest popular hit:

Oh Johnny, oh Johnny,
How you can love!
Oh Johnny, oh Johnny,
Heavens above...

Lil gazed around, catching a glimpse of herself and Trevor in one of the mirrors surrounding the dance-floor.

'Mike's never going to believe this when I tell him,' she said.

'Mike?' Trevor raised an eyebrow. 'Who's Mike?'

She was taken aback. 'Mike—my husband! Mike Burns.'

'Ah yes, of course. It's hard to think of you as a married woman, somehow. I suppose it's because I've never met Mr Burns.'

'Next time he comes home on leave, I'll introduce you.'

'I shall look forward to that,' he said politely. 'Where is he now?'

'I never really know; somewhere in the Atlantic, I think. He's just been transferred to another ship, an aircraft carrier called the *Ark Royal.* We write to each other every week; I shall tell him about all this.'

One of the waiters brought the first course of their meal, and another poured a little wine for Trevor to taste. He rolled it round his mouth, then nodded. 'Yes, fine. Go ahead.'

As the waiter filled their glasses, Lil asked, 'What did you say this place is called? The Café something?'

'The Café de Paris,' he told her.

Suddenly there was a very odd noise—a little 'pop', like a cork coming out of a bottle. For a split second Lil thought the waiter must have opened some champagne, because she felt a prickle of ice-cold air striking her face—and

276

then there was a blinding flash of blue light...an intense pressure on top of her head, forcing her down and after that, darkness. Silence.

She found she was lying sprawled upon the floor, and then the sounds came back: people groaning and whimpering. A girl began to scream, and someone tried to quieten her.

Lil wanted to move, but found that the table had fallen on top of her, and she was on top of someone else—there was somebody lying beneath her on the floor. She put out her hand and touched a face in the darkness, close to her own. She thought it must be Trevor, but at that moment she heard his voice; it sounded very far away, and yet he was kneeling beside her, asking: 'Are you all right? Can you move? Let me help you.'

He lifted the table and eased her into a sitting position, propped up against the pillar. She managed to say, 'There's somebody else. Somebody lying on the floor...'

One or two lights were shining, high on the balcony, hardly penetrating the thick cloud of dust that hung over everything, but in the dim glow Lil could see that the man on the floor was the wine-waiter. He was lying flat on his back, with the bottle still in his hand, and an expression of intense anger and amazement in his wide, staring eyes. Without being told, she knew that he was dead.

'Don't look,' said Trevor urgently. 'Are you hurt? Do you think you can stand up?'

'I don't know, I think so. Only, my dress is soaking wet. The wine must have spilled over me. What happened? Was it a bomb?'

There had been two bombs. Even though it was so far below ground-level, the Café de Paris had received two direct hits—straight through the cinema above, through the roof of the night-club, through the balcony, and on to the dance-floor. One had exploded instantly, killing the band-leader, 'Snakehips' Ken Johnson, and another musician, along with thirty-two other people; sixty more were seriously wounded. The second bomb did not go off, but burst into smithereens, making a hole in the parquet floor and spraying a pungent yellow chemical in all directions.

'Thank heaven we were behind the pillar. That saved us from the full force of the blast,' said Trevor.

People were choking and spluttering, because everything was covered with thick grey dust. A man lit a cigarette-lighter in order to see more clearly, and as the flame spurted, a voice shouted: 'Put that out, you bloody fool! If there's gas about, you'll blow us all up!'—and someone else began to laugh hysterically.

An RAF officer was yelling commands at the top of his voice, in an effort to restore order, but by now the dazed and injured customers were beginning to panic. People were frantic to get out, and some of them tried to climb the stairs to the street, until they realised that the balcony was hanging askew, where it had been torn from the wall.

Trevor put his arm round Lil and said, 'Lean on me. Do you think you can walk?'

She tried, but everything seemed to be swimming around her, and she staggered. 'I'm sorry. I don't know what's the matter with me. I'm feeling a bit dizzy.'

'Don't worry—I've got you.' Lifting her into his arms, he began to pick his way through the wreckage of the dance-floor, through the dead and dying, and through a swing door into the kitchens, where he laid her carefully upon one of the serving-tables.

Lil caught a glimpse of some chefs, their faces as pale as their kitchen whites, who stared at her dumbly, too shocked to speak or to move. She shut her eyes and did not resist as Trevor turned her gently on to her side and began to unfasten the back of her dress.

'What are you doing?' she asked vaguely. Everything seemed to be happening far off, at the end of a long tunnel. She could feel his hands upon her body, and an occasional stab of pain in her back—but she did not wince or cry out; it was as if the pain too was far away, and not part of her at all. She heard herself saying in a faint, high voice, quite unlike her own: 'I don't know what Mum will say, when she finds out I've got wine all over her best dress.'

'It isn't wine, it's blood... Those damn mirrors smashed to pieces. Some of the flying glass hit you, but don't worry—the cuts aren't deep.' He called to one of the staring, helpless chefs. 'Fetch me some warm water, man—and a clean cloth.'

Somehow he got all the glass out, using a damp table-napkin as a swab; then he wrapped her in a tablecloth, put her over his shoulder, and carried her out through the back door.

She was aware of a draughty, echoing flight of stone steps, a metal fire-door, and cold night air; after that she knew nothing more until she came to, lying face down upon a soft bed, in a room she had never seen before. She felt cool hands that applied soothing ointment to her back, and heard Trevor's voice murmuring softly: 'Don't move, just lie still. You were very lucky. There are no serious wounds, only superficial cuts and scratches.'

'Where are we?' she asked.

'In my bedroom, at Sally's house in Acacia Grove. You're quite safe.'

'But Mum and Dad! They'll be worried.' She tried to struggle up. 'I must go home.'

'You stay where you are; I'll take you home presently. You'll be as right as rain in the morning. Trust me.'

She drifted off to sleep again, and only woke once during the night.

Her back was smarting a little, but it wasn't too painful. Raising her head from the pillow, she saw Trevor, still fully dressed, sitting in an armchair at the other side of the room; he had been reading a book, but he must have fallen asleep, over it. His eyes were closed, and his head turned to one side. In the soft light of a table-lamp he looked very peaceful and very beautiful.

She realised that he had undressed her, tended her wounds, and put her to bed; she was completely naked, under a sheet and a light

280

blanket. And she knew without any possible shadow of a doubt that she trusted him, and that she loved him.

Contentedly, she nestled down into the pillows once more, and went back to sleep.

9

'She might have been killed.' That was all Connor could think of, and he kept repeating it. 'Our girl might have been killed last night.'

'But she wasn't.' Ruth put her hand on his shoulder, as he sat at the kitchen table that Sunday morning. 'She's alive and well, the scars on her back are beginning to heal already, and in half an hour you and I are going to Mass at St Anthony's, to give thanks to God.'

Frowning, he looked down at the bedraggled dance-dress that lay on the floor, the torn edges of the material caked with dried blood.

It had been a terrible shock to the family; bad enough at first, when Ruth took an early cup of tea to Lil's room and found Kaff alone there, with the other bed not slept in—and even worse when Trevor brought Lil home an hour later, still pale and shaking, incongruously dressed in a jazzy blouse and skirt which she had borrowed from Sally's wardrobe—but worst of all when Trevor and Lil sat down and told them what had happened the previous night.

Instinctively, Con had felt a surge of anger

towards the smooth-talking young man who had taken the girl into such danger and emerged unscathed himself, but before he could speak, Lil forestalled him.

'Trevor's been such a hero. He saved my life—goodness only knows what would have happened if he hadn't been there.'

Quickly, Trevor disclaimed any credit. 'I think that's a bit of an exaggeration. I'm only grateful you weren't more seriously hurt—and sorry that our little outing ended so badly. But you're safe now, that's the main thing.'

After he had gone back to Greenwich, Ruth went upstairs to run a bath for Lil. She came down later with the borrowed clothes, saying, 'I must wash and iron these before we return them.'

Connor nudged the crumpled dance-dress with the toe of his boot. 'And what about this?'

'That's going straight in the dustbin. It's too far gone for mending and anyhow, I don't want to see it again, and I'm sure Lil doesn't either.' Then she glanced at the clock on the mantelpiece. 'You'd better start to get ready for church. We don't want to be late.'

'I suppose Lil won't be coming with us?' he asked.

'Certainly not. I've told her she must go back to bed and try to get some more sleep. The poor girl's still suffering from shock; she needs to rest.'

Upstairs, Lil lay back in the bath, letting the warm water soothe and caress her, feeling strangely happy.

She couldn't stop thinking about Trevor; seeing his face before her when she closed her eyes, recreating the sound of his voice in her ears, and the touch of his hands upon her body. She had never felt like this about any other man.

And it had happened so suddenly, so inexplicably. Nothing in her life had prepared her for it. Of course she still loved Mike—she could not have imagined a better husband—but this was something altogether different.

She tried to examine her conscience: could it be a sin to feel such overwhelming love for another man? It wasn't as if there were any possibility of expressing that love; she would always be a faithful wife to Mike. Nobody would ever know the way she felt about Trevor. It was a secret she would never share with anyone, least of all with Trevor himself. It would be her own private joy and consolation—surely there could be nothing wrong in that?

She remembered that during the evening, Trevor had said something about taking her out dancing another time. At the mere thought of it, an electric thrill swept through her body, but she knew she must resist that temptation. She and Trevor could remain friends—she wanted it to develop into a deep, lasting friendship—but it could never be anything more than that. From time to time, she would meet him socially, on family occasions and when other people were present, and that would be happiness enough.

As it turned out, she did not see Trevor again for some time.

The raid on 8 March proved to be the forerunner of a whole series of night attacks on London; after the two-month respite which had lulled everyone into a false security, the Luftwaffe came back with what the newspapers called 'the spring blitz'.

As a result, Lil was kept busy at the Fire Station, going out night after night, towing the trailer-pump from one scene of devastation to another. Sometimes her path crossed with Abram's, for the Medical Service Units were also in demand, and she was always pleased to see him—but her only contact with Trevor was a phone-call one day, to say that he had theatre tickets for the first night of *No Time for Comedy* with Rex Harrison, and would she like to go with him? She longed to say yes, but she knew she must not; and anyway she was on duty that evening, so that settled it.

Despite everything the German Air Force could do, daffodils were appearing round the Anderson shelters in back gardens, and April flowered into May. As Lil drove her battered old taxi down the long road beside the Jubilee Wharf, the midday sunlight sparkled on the waters of the dock; she knew that somewhere behind the forest of masts and funnels, in that cluster of red-roofed buildings, was the Guild Office; she imagined Trevor sitting there at his desk —and her spirits soared.

A few hours later, London was plunged into the heaviest night raid of the entire war.

The evening began normally enough. Huw was on duty at the Warden Post, but it was

Connor's night off, so he was serving in the saloon. The sirens wailed at the usual time; a few customers went down to shelter in the cellars, and Mary took Kaff down too. Lil, having worked a day-shift at the Station, was helping her mother in the public bar.

As the evening wore on, the raid became very noisy—there were the inevitable arguments among the customers, about whether the loudest bangs were caused by bombs or anti-aircraft guns. One particular explosion sounded very near indeed, and Connor said grimly: *'That* was no gunfire... If they come any closer, I'll be shutting the bars and sending you all down below.'

But the raiders seemed to have passed over, for the sound and fury became more distant. Soon afterwards, the street door opened, and Huw pushed his way through the black-out curtain, with his tin helmet on his head. Going straight to the bar, he asked Connor, 'Can you come and give us a hand? There's been some trouble—I think you might be needed.'

Connor began to object. 'I can't very well leave the pub now,' but something in Huw's expression made him break off, and he asked: 'What sort of trouble? Where is it?'

Huw lowered his voice slightly as he replied, 'The Rope Walk... The Heavy Rescue boys are on their way already.'

'I'll be right with you,' said Connor. 'Wait while I tell Ruth.'

He turned—and found that she was in the archway that led through into the public bar;

285

her face was quite blank. 'You don't have to tell me—I heard,' she said.

Connor was afraid she might try to come with them, and began: 'I think you'd best stay here.'

'Of course. We can't expect Mam and Lil to run the place on their own,' she said flatly. 'Come back as soon as you can, and tell me what's happened.'

He nodded, and went to fetch his helmet. As he followed Huw out of the pub, he looked back. Ruth's lips moved, and he thought she was trying to tell him something—but then he saw she was not even looking at him, and realised that she was praying.

The barricades were up at the Rope Walk, closing the road, but as ARP wardens, Huw and Connor ignored the Keep Out signs and went through. Several houses in the street had been totally demolished; it was hard to tell in the darkness, but Connor thought Number 26 was still standing—at least it hadn't been flattened.

He looked round. 'Where's the surface shelter? I know Ruth says her old folk always go into the shelter, whenever there's a raid on—' Then he choked on the words and concluded hoarsely, 'Oh, my God...'

Huw nodded silently. Where the shelter had been, there was nothing but a gaping crater some ten feet deep, stretching across the road; the shelter had received a direct hit, and collapsed into rubble.

Half a dozen rescue-workers were in the crater, picking through the debris by the light of some shaded hurricane lamps. Seeing the two wardens, the leader of the party called them over and asked them to lend a hand in the search.

'It's going to be a long job,' he said. 'Can't use picks and shovels.'

'Why not?' At first Huw didn't understand.

'Stands to reason! You don't want to put a pick through somebody you're trying to dig out. Find yourself a bit of wood, and use that as a spade. If you're in any doubt, use your hands... Fingers and thumbs are the best.'

Joining the rescue team, they set to work. Nobody knew how many people had been inside the shelter, but they all shared one unspoken thought; they felt certain nobody could be alive under this heap of broken bricks.

The work continued for several hours. Sometimes a smothered gasp or an exclamation of disgust announced that a gruesome discovery had been made—a severed limb, or part of a torso. Then the piece of flesh would be removed and shrouded in sacking, to be taken to the mortuary.

'For identification,' the leader explained. 'That's regulations, that is... Though how they'd ever identify them bits and pieces, God only knows.'

Overcome with nausea, one of the younger men dodged away into the shadows and they heard him retching and vomiting.

Each time a discovery was made, Connor forced himself to look at the remains, dreading what he might see—but they were all unrecognisable. It was hard to believe that such objects could

287

ever have been part of a human being.

They worked on, and eventually the first glimmer of dawn broke through the clouds.

Now Connor was able to take a closer look at Number 26; the front wall had collapsed altogether, and in the grey early-morning light, he saw the Judges' house exposed like a child's dolls-house, with pictures still hanging on the walls, a sideboard with broken ornaments upon it, and pieces of furniture sticking up at unexpected angles.

Suddenly there was an excited shout within the house. 'We've got one here!'

Two men had been digging through the rubble; Connor ran towards them, stumbling over loose stones and tiles, making his way into what had once been the back kitchen.

In the corner, next to the old kitchen range, they had managed to excavate an armchair—and sitting in the chair was an elderly man, fully dressed; the chair and its occupant had been solidly embedded in brickdust and plaster, and both seemed to be undamaged. The man's face was powdered with grey dust and his eagle eyes were closed, but Connor knew him immediately.

'That's the owner of the house,' he said. 'He was Marcus Judge.'

'He still is,' said one of the rescuers, slipping his hand inside the old man's waistcoat. 'He's unconscious, but he's still warm... His heart's beating—very faint, but it's beating.'

Between them, they managed to lift him out. It was as if he had been packed in dust so tightly, it had preserved him from injury—it was amazing that he had been able to breathe.

An ambulance was waiting at the end of the street, and two young men carried Marcus off on a stretcher. As they passed Connor one of them said, 'Hello, Uncle...' By the time he realised it was Abram, they were climbing into the ambulance and driving away.

Then he looked about him, and with renewed hope began to sift through the kitchen rubble. If Ruth's father had survived, surely her mother must be here too?

Slowly, as the sun came up, he had to admit defeat. It seemed that for some reason Marcus had been alone in the house when the bomb fell. Nobody ever knew why. Perhaps he had quarrelled with some of the other inhabitants of the shelter and insisted on returning to sulk in his own home, or perhaps he had answered a call of nature and gone through to visit the outside lavatory. Whatever the reason, it was apparent that neither Louisa nor Emily were with him.

Huw limped through the ruined house and came to find Connor. 'They've found someone else,' he said. 'You'd better take a look.'

Together, they went back to the crater where the shelter had been. The searchers had made another discovery; not a severed limb this time, but a body—complete and unmutilated. Louisa Judge lay on a heap of broken bricks, with a shawl round her shoulders, fastened by a cameo brooch. Her soft white hair, her apple cheeks, her high-necked, old-fashioned dress, were covered in the same grey dust, but her expression was serene—trusting and unafraid.

'She must have been killed instantly,' said Huw. 'She never knew anything about it.'

'Shall I pack up the body for identification, along with the rest?' asked one of the workers.

'There's no need—I can identify her,' said Connor.

He knelt down and took out his handkerchief, moistening it with his lips then, very gently, he wiped the dust from the old lady's face as if he were washing the face of a child; and then he said goodbye to Ruth's mother for the last time.

When he went back to Millwall Road, Huw broke the news to Gloria as gently as he could. She had breakfast ready and waiting for him, but he said he wasn't hungry, and after he had told her what had happened, the breakfast remained on the table, untouched.

He put his arms round her and she clung to him, crying pitifully. Even though he told her that her mother could not have suffered at all, the tears kept flowing.

When at last Glory could speak, she sobbed, 'If it hadn't been for me, me being bloody selfish, this would never have happened.'

'What are you saying? It was nothing to do with you.'

'Oh yes, it was. You've worked so hard to get this house fit to live in. Her room's been ready for over a month—all it needed was new wallpaper and a lick of paint... But we weren't in any hurry to have her back with us, were we? We kept making excuses, putting it off.'

'I'm sure she was quite happy at the Rope Walk. She enjoyed having her sister for company.'

'P'rhaps she did, but this was her *home!* She should have been here.' Gloria turned to him accusingly. 'If it wasn't for you and me, wanting to have the place to ourselves, wanting to live together, she could have moved back weeks ago and then,' her voice broke, and she began to weep again, 'she'd still be alive!'

She calmed down at last; he helped to dry her tears and she told him she couldn't face going to visit her clients and doing their hair. Instead, she would stay at home and have a quiet day.

'And you'd better do the same—go and catch up on some sleep,' she advised him, then added: 'Um, if you don't mind, I think it would be better if you slept in your own room for a while.'

After a moment he nodded. 'Right, if that's what you want. I'll move my stuff out.'

Realising she had hurt him, she tried to explain. 'Oh, I'm not blaming you, and I'm not turning you out for good—I'd never do that. Only for the time being, I'd like to be on my own.'

'I understand.' He began to climb the stairs, then turned back to say, 'But I won't have a sleep this morning as they'll be expecting me at the pub. I dare say I'll snatch forty winks this afternoon, after closing-time.'

'You must be barmy! You've been up all

night, you're in no state to go to work.'

'I'll be fine. I bet Connor will be working already. I can't leave him to do everything on his own.'

He went upstairs and moved his night-attire into the single room. When he came down again, Gloria was waiting for him, with her hat and coat on.

'If you're going to the Watermen, I'm coming with you,' she said. 'I want to see Ruth. There's things we have to say to one another.'

When they arrived at the pub, they found Mary O'Dell and Kaff making themselves useful in the saloon, polishing the brasses and sweeping the floor. There had never been any love lost between Mrs O'Dell and Gloria Judge, but this morning Mary kissed her and said, 'I was so sorry to hear... Your poor mother. I'll have a mass said for her.'

'Thanks.' To her surprise, Glory found some comfort in the old lady's genuine sympathy. 'That's good of you. Where's Ruth?'

'You'll find her in the kitchen. She'll be glad to see you.'

Ruth was at the sink, peeling potatoes. As soon as Glory walked in, she threw down the peeler, wiping her hands on a teacloth, and the cousins embraced without a word, holding one another tightly.

After a time Ruth said, 'Do you mind if I go on peeling the spuds while we talk?'

'Course not. You're very good—I couldn't do a thing this morning, I just went to pieces. When Huw told me, I couldn't stop crying.'

'I expect I shall cry later, but for the moment I'll be better if I've got something to keep me busy. We've still got to cook and wash-up and clean the house. Life's got to go on, hasn't it?'

'I s'pose so... I can't imagine what it's going to be like without Ma,' said Glory. 'Oh, I know she used to drive me potty sometimes, the way she fussed and flustered over things. We were like chalk and cheese, me and her, but even so... She's always been *there*, ever since I can remember. You must feel the same about Auntie Lou.'

'I think Connor was expecting me to break down when he told me, but somehow I knew it already. Last night, when Huw came to collect him—I knew then that she was dead. Suddenly the world seemed quite different, and then I realised—Mum wasn't here any more.'

'Huw told me he saw her—there wasn't a mark on her, he said. Will you go and see her at the mortuary, before...?' Glory's voice trailed off.

'I don't think so. That's not her, lying there. If ever anyone went straight to heaven, Mum did... And I'd sooner remember her the way she was.'

'Yeah.' Gloria sighed. 'It's nice they went together, though I wish I could have seen Ma. I expect Con told you—they never found her.'

'I know.' Ruth tipped the water down the sink and scooped the potato peelings into a bucket under the sink. 'But like you said—they're both together now.' Her voice changed. 'And Father's still here. I'm going over to see him at the Infirmary this afternoon.'

'Seems all wrong, doesn't it? Them going, and him being rescued. It's so unfair—you must feel that.'

'You mean because I loved Mum and I've never got on with Father?' Ruth filled the kettle at the tap. 'Maybe that's why. Maybe God's trying to teach me something... Do you fancy a cup of tea?'

'Yes, ta.' Gloria pondered Ruth's remark briefly, then dismissed it; it made no sense to her. As the kettle began to sing, she went on, 'Would you like me to come with you, to see Uncle Marcus?'

'Yes, if you want to.'

'I've got nothing else to do. Oh, unless Lil's going with you?' She looked round. 'Where is she?'

'Lil's gone out on duty already. Well, her shift starts at midday, but she said she'd got to call in somewhere on the way.'

Lil was standing in the doorway of the Guild offices, feeling frightened and excited at the same time. One of the clerks looked up in surprise. As a rule, women did not enter these premises. He asked aggressively: 'Well? What do you want?'

'I'd like to see Mr Judge, please—Mr Trevor Judge. Is he here?'

'He's in his office, but he's a very busy man, he can't be disturbed.'

'Perhaps you'd tell him I'm here. My name's Burns—Mrs Lilian Burns.'

294

The clerk eyed her speculatively, then said, 'Wait here,' and vanished. He returned almost at once, and his manner had changed. Inclining his head, he said deferentially, 'Mr Judge will be pleased to see you. This way, please.' He led her through to the inner office and left them together.

There were two desks in the room. Smiling, Trevor rose from his swivel chair and came to meet her, his hand outstretched.

'This is a very pleasant surprise. Won't you sit down?'

'Thank you. I won't stay long—I was told you're very busy.'

'Stay as long as you like. I gave orders I wasn't to be disturbed, but when I heard that Mrs Lilian Burns was here—well, that's a very different matter. Can I offer you something? You're welcome to have a nip out of Bertie's private bottle of scotch—or a very indifferent cup of coffee. The choice is yours.'

'I don't want anything, thanks.' She looked at the second desk. 'Is that where Bertie sits? Isn't he here today?'

'He's been on the quayside all the morning. I drove down from town, so I haven't seen him yet, but I gather it's hell's delight out there, after last night's raid. Anyway, he's trying to sort things out while I catch up on the paperwork.'

'I see.' Lil tried to find the right words. 'Then, if you haven't seen him, you might not know...'

'Know? Know what?'

'During last night's raid there was a bomb, very near here.'

'Yes, I heard about that. Somewhere in West Ferry Road, wasn't it?'

'Closer than that. It was in the Rope Walk. There were—some people killed.'

He was not smiling now; she had never seen him look so serious. 'Tell me,' he said.

'My Dad went over with Huw. They saw what was left of the shelter there.' She corrected herself. 'No, that's wrong. There wasn't anything left—just a hole in the road. Nobody inside the shelter was left alive. That's what I came to tell you, in case you didn't know. Your grandmother, and mine—they're both gone. I'm sorry.'

'I see.' He sank slowly back into his chair, speaking very softly. 'Thank you for telling me.'

'Dad says they got Grandfather out, but he was in the house when it happened, not the shelter. He's in hospital now—very ill—but he's still alive.'

Trevor's voice was a lifeless whisper. 'I'm sure he is. He would be, wouldn't he? I'm sure Uncle Marcus will be all right... But not my Gran.'

Lil yearned to go to him, to throw her arms round him, to soften the blow and take away the pain, but that was impossible. All she could do was to repeat helplessly, 'I really am very sorry.'

Then the door opened again and Bertie came in. He nodded to Lil and mumbled, 'Ah, hello there, they told me you were here. Good morning, Trevor.'

'A good morning?' Trevor looked at him with distaste. 'Is that what you call it?'

Bertie shifted uncomfortably from one foot to the other. 'So you've heard, then. Shocking thing to happen. I was going to come and tell you myself, but—at least Grandfather's been saved.'

'Glory Hallelujah,' said Trevor, in the same dead tone. 'Three cheers for good old Grandpapa.'

Bertie looked uncertainly at Lil, then back to Trevor, his double chins wobbling. 'I suppose we'll have to make the usual arrangements—funeral, and all that. Very regrettable... Are you going to deal with it, or shall I?'

'Oh, I think I'll leave it to you, Bertie.' With a sudden effort, Trevor seemed to pull himself together, and continued briskly, 'I've got plenty of other things to deal with, you know.'

He turned to Lil. 'Haven't you heard? These days we've got ships nipping in and out every five minutes, loading and unloading all round the clock. We're working ourselves into the ground, aren't we, Bertie? Making a quick turn-round—and a quick turnover at the same time.'

His smile was back in place now, and his eyes gleamed as he rattled on cheerfully: 'To tell you the truth, the jolly old Jubilee has never done so well, and if we keep on like this, we're going to do even better! So Bertie can make the funeral arrangements, while I make us all a bloody fortune. Because after all, when you come right down to it—what else is there to do?'

The war news was almost uniformly depressing.

Within a few months, the successes in North Africa had been halted by a German counter-attack, and the Allies were forced to retreat. German paratroops invaded Crete, and there too the British had to carry out a swift evacuation of the island. At home, jam, cheese, coal and clothes were added to the growing list of rationed goods, yet it was hard to feel totally despondent, because of the weather. It turned out to be a glorious summer, and on one day, London had nearly sixteen hours of sunshine. According to the records, Sunday 6 July, 1941 was the sunniest day of the century.

For Lil, it was a very special day.

Soon after she and Ruth got home from church on Sunday morning, the telephone rang in the little office behind the saloon bar. Connor answered it, then called Lil out of the kitchen, saying shortly, 'It's for you. Trevor Judge.'

Her heart leaped, and she went quickly to the phone. 'Hello, Trevor. This is a surprise.'

'You should know by now, I'm a very surprising sort of chap.' Though his voice was tinny and distorted, she could hear that he was smiling. 'Listen—I know you're not on duty today, so what are you doing this afternoon?'

'Nothing special.' Then she realised what he had said. 'How did you know I was off duty?'

He chuckled. 'Simple. I rang the Fire Station and asked.'

Her pulse was racing, but she tried to sound disapproving. 'You shouldn't have done that. I'm surprised they told you.'

'I spoke to a very obliging girl on the

switchboard, and explained I was your long-lost cousin by marriage. I can be very persuasive when I try, didn't you know that?'

Ignoring his question, she put another one to him: 'Anyway, why did you want to know?'

'I was hoping you might have some free time this afternoon. It's a perfect day; there isn't a cloud in the sky. Why don't I come and pick you up in the car, then we could go for a spin?'

'Oh.' Her heart was beating so loudly, she was afraid he might hear it as she said, 'No, I don't think so, Trevor. It's very nice of you, but I'd better not.'

'Why not?'

She tried to think of a plausible excuse, but could only come up with: 'I promised Dad I'd help out behind the bar tonight.'

'Pubs don't open till seven on Sundays; I'll bring you back long before that. We can drive out somewhere like Kew Gardens, and find a place to have tea. You'll only be gone a couple of hours.'

'No, I'm sorry. Some other time, perhaps.'

'We might never get another day like this.' He followed this up by asking, 'You said I'd saved your life, didn't you?'

'Yes, but—'

'One good turn deserves another—and now it's your turn to come and save mine, because I'm dying of boredom.'

She swallowed. When he put it like that, it seemed ungrateful to refuse him. Besides, more than anything in the world, she really wanted to go.

'All right, then. What time will you pick me up?'

Over lunch, she explained to the family: 'Trevor's at a loose end, and so am I. He's going to take me to Kew Gardens, and out to tea. I'll be back by the end of the afternoon.'

'I'm surprised he has enough petrol to go joy-riding,' growled Connor. 'What's wrong with the feller at all? Does he have no friends of his own, the way he's forever coming round here, pestering you?'

'That's not fair!' retorted Lil. 'It's only the second time in three months—what's so terrible about that?'

Ruth defended her nephew. 'I think it's very kind of Trevor to invite her out. A walk in the fresh air will do her all the good in the world.'

Mary O'Dell said gloomily, 'I dare say it's better than taking her to them terrible night-club places.'

Kaff said quietly, 'You promised yesterday you and me were going to the flicks this afternoon...'

'Oh Kaff, I'm sorry. I completely forgot!' Lil was contrite. 'We'll go to the pictures on my next day off, I promise!'

Kaff lowered her eyes. 'It doesn't matter,' she said.

Trevor arrived on the stroke of three. Lil hurried out of the pub, waved goodbye to her mother and climbed into the two-seater. They shot up Manchester Road and headed for the Blackwall Tunnel; Trevor gave Lil an approving sidelong glance.

'This kind of weather suits you,' he told her. 'You're looking very summery.'

'So are you.' He was wearing an open-necked tennis shirt with short sleeves, and smart grey flannels, and he was the most handsome man she had ever seen... But she mustn't stare at him. Concentrating on the road ahead, she said suddenly: 'This is the road to Greenwich. I thought we were going to Kew?'

'I said we were going somewhere *like* Kew,' said Trevor. 'There's a perfectly good garden at Sally's house; we can sit outside.'

'You did say something about having tea.'

'The tea's all ready. I've only got to put the kettle on,' he told her firmly. 'I suddenly realised—everybody in London will be rushing out to Kew on a day like this, or Hyde Park, or Kensington Gardens. We'd get trampled to death in the rush. Sally's garden may be slightly overgrown, but there are some magnificent roses—you really should see them.'

They roared up Crooms Hill and turned right into Acacia Grove.

'Do you really think this is a good idea?' said Lil in a small voice, as the brakes squealed. 'Sally might not like it.'

'Why should she mind? At this moment she's thousands of miles away in Egypt—probably sitting in a beautiful garden herself, surrounded by jasmine and palm-trees, or doing her song-and-dance routine in the shadow of the Sphinx. I'm quite sure she'd be only too pleased to know you're here to keep an eye on me, and make sure I don't get up to any mischief.'

301

He opened the front door and they walked through the house. She had expected to find a typical bachelor establishment—dust and disorder, unwashed crockery in the sink, half-empty tins of baked beans on the kitchen table—but everything was neat, tidy and spotlessly clean.

'You keep it very spick and span,' she said. 'How do you manage it? You're not here very often.'

'Well, that helps, actually,' he replied. 'And I'm quite house-trained. I can't stand living in a clutter.' Then he grinned. 'But I have to admit, there's a dear old lady from Shooters Hill who comes in once a week to clear up... Now, why don't you go through into the garden? You'll find a couple of deckchairs. Make yourself comfortable, and I'll bring out the tea-tray.'

He was quite right; it was a beautiful garden. Even though the lawn had gone to hay, and there were daisies and dandelions everywhere, the roses were running riot—drifts of pink and red blossom curved and twisted through the leaves. Lil sat on a deckchair and took a deep breath; their perfume was heavy on the warm air. After this, she would always associate roses with Trevor.

'What's this? Dozing off already?'

She opened her eyes, and he put the tea-tray on the garden table.

'I wasn't asleep—I was enjoying the scent of the roses.'

'Lovely, isn't it? Rich and scrumptious, like chocolate creams.' He began to pour the tea.

'Talking of cream, I hope you've got a sweet tooth.' He indicated a plate of scones, with strawberry jam and clotted cream. 'Genuine Cornish cream.' He winked. 'I've got a couple of friends in Penzance; they're very good to me.'

Once again he had worked some special magic; the tea—the garden—the weather—all a million miles away from drab, war-time austerity.

After tea they stayed where they were, enjoying the sunshine, enjoying the easy, effortless conversation. At one moment she remembered her cousin and felt a twinge of guilt.

'How is Sally? Have you heard from her lately?'

'She sent me a picture postcard with a camel on it. I gather she's having a high old time, being wined and dined in the Officers' Mess every night of the week.'

'I'm sure you miss her a lot.'

'Sometimes I do.' He smiled at Lil under long, dark lashes. 'Though not very much, at this particular moment.'

She tried to laugh, as if he had made a small, not very successful joke, and said, 'Well, I miss Mike—very much.'

'He still writes to you every week?'

'Sometimes the mail gets held up, and I don't hear for a while, then three or four letters come at once. He's expecting some leave soon—he certainly deserves it. His ship was one of the ones that chased the *Bismarck*. Their aircraft bombed her, before she was finally sunk.'

'Really...and you're looking forward to seeing him?'

'Of course I am. Like I said, I miss him a lot.'

'Even at this particular moment?'

Turning to look at him, she saw that although his voice was light and teasing, his face was quite serious. For a long moment, there was no sound but the twitter of birds and the hum of bees among the flowers. At last she answered reluctantly: 'Well, perhaps not at this particular moment.'

He began to say; 'Lil,' and then broke off. 'Damn it, I can't call you that!'

'What do you mean? It's my name.'

'It's not your name!' He sounded angry. 'You weren't christened Lil—it's ugly and cheap, and it doesn't suit you.'

'Lilian, then.'

'That's not right, either—it makes you sound old. I shall call you Lily, that's much more appropriate. Lilies and roses go together... Do you mind if I call you Lily?'

'If you want to—no, I don't mind.'

'Then, Lily—there's something I want to tell you. It won't be easy, but somehow I feel I could say anything to you, and you'd understand.'

She caught her breath, knowing a moment of pure joy. 'That's how I feel too,' she said. 'As if we'd known one another all our lives... And I suppose we have, since we were children together.'

'We didn't understand one another then. I thought you were just Danny's kid sister; I didn't take any notice of you. And since those days, a lot of things have happened to both of us...bad things.'

She felt suddenly afraid, wondering what he was going to say.

'After I left the Island, I heard about something that happened to you. One night—at a party, wasn't it—on the Wharf. You and Jimmy Judge.'

It was as if a bolt of lightning had fallen from that pure blue sky.

'You *know?*' She felt sick with horror. 'Bertie told you...'

'It wasn't Bertie. Someone else—it doesn't matter who told me. I want you to know you'll never have to be afraid of me, in that way. And that's why Sally need never be jealous. Whatever happens, I'd never do anything to hurt you—and you can always trust me. You do trust me, Lily, don't you?'

He remained in his chair, making no move towards her. Separated by a little patch of overgrown grass, they might have been a hundred mile apart and yet, looking into his eyes, she had never felt so close to any man.

'Yes,' she whispered. 'I trust you.'

Then a petal dropped from a dark red rose, brushing against the back of her hand, and it broke the spell. Looking up at the sky, she saw that the sun had gone behind the trees, and asked: 'What's the time?'

He glanced at his watch. 'Nearly six o'clock. Time for me to take you home.'

They hardly spoke at all as they drove back

to the Watermen; there were so many things to say—there was nothing they could say. Lil was aware of a powerful magnetism between them, like an electric current, though he never touched her.

When they reached the pub, Lil said, 'Come in for a minute. Mum and Dad will be pleased to see you.'

Connor and Ruth were in the saloon, getting ready for opening-time, and there was someone else with them—a sunburned man in a navy-blue uniform.

'Hello, Lil,' he said. 'I'm back.'

She stared at him in disbelief, then ran forward and hugged him. 'Oh, Mike! Why didn't you let us know?'

'Didn't you get my last letter? It'll probably turn up tomorrow. I tried to ring you when I got to Waterloo, and your Mum said you'd gone out for the afternoon.'

'Yes.' Remembering Trevor, she stepped back. 'Oh, this is Trevor Judge. My husband—Mike.'

The two men shook hands, and Mike said, 'I can't tell you how grateful I am. We never met, but you must be my best friend, because Lil told me you saved her life. It's good to know she's got someone like you to look after her while I'm away... I understand you're Mrs O'Dell's nephew? So that makes you a sort of cousin.'

'A cousin by marriage,' Ruth explained. 'Now then, why don't we all go into the kitchen, and I'll make you some tea.'

'Not for me, thanks,' said Trevor regretfully,

moving to the door. 'I couldn't eat a thing. We've just had tea, haven't we, Lily? Besides, I've got to drive back to town. But I hope we'll meet again while you're here, Mike... Bye-bye, Auntie Ruth—Mr O'Dell. Be seeing you, Lily.'

And he made a smooth, unhurried exit. Lil felt as if a part of her had gone with him, but she pushed this thought from her, concentrating on Mike.

'Oh, it's good to see you! You're looking so well and—' then she noticed the insignia on his sleeve. 'You've been promoted again!'

'Yes, I've been made up to Petty Officer.' He laughed. 'At this rate I'll be a Rear-Admiral by the time the war's over. I'd say this calls for a celebration, wouldn't you? So I'm taking you out to supper tonight, my girl. Let's go home, then you can put on your glad rags.'

'Oh, but—' Lil glanced at her father. 'I promised I'd help out behind the bar tonight.'

Connor threw her one of his rare, crooked smiles. 'I reckon your Mam and I can manage without you for once, eh, Ruth?'

'I think we might.' Ruth was smiling too. 'I don't suppose we'll be seeing much of you for the next few days.'

'No, I suppose not.' Lil took a deep breath. 'Right. I'm ready when you are, Mike. Let's go!'

As they strolled back towards Coldharbour, the western sky behind them was ablaze with gold, reflected in all the upper windows, and Mike said: 'Your Mum tells me Trevor took

307

you out to Kew Gardens this afternoon. You
certainly picked the right day for it.'

Lil was about to correct him, but she changed
her mind at the last moment and said, 'Yes, it
was lovely.'

'I'm glad. He seems a nice chap, but I noticed
he calls you Lily—why's that?'

'Oh, no particular reason,' she said lamely.

Lil had not set foot in their little flat for
months, and it all looked dusty and neglected.
As soon as they walked in through the front door
she began to apologise. 'If only I'd known, I'd
have come and given it a proper spring-clean.'

Undismayed, he retorted carefully, 'We'll
tackle it in the morning—leave it like it is
for now.' Then, as he entered the bedroom, he
added: 'But perhaps we should make the bed!'

At the sight of the bare mattress and the
pillows in their striped ticking, she felt ashamed.
'I should have got everything ready.'

She found clean sheets and pillowcases, and
they made the bed together. Mike said, 'Don't
bother about blankets. We won't need any, this
weather.'

The job was soon done; then Mike wanted to
wash and change, and Lil said if they were going
out, she must put on her best frock. As they
undressed, they went on talking. Mike asked
her for the latest news of her grandfather.

'I did tell you he's come out of his coma
now?' Lil said. 'Of course he's still very weak,
but he's able to sit up and take nourishment;
the nurses don't have to feed him any more.
Mum goes to visit him, but he can't talk much.

He gets tired so quickly. She's not sure if he knows where he is, or what's happened...she says he seems to be quite dazed, most of the time.'

Mike said nothing. In the mirror over the dressing-table, she saw him staring at her, as if he too were in a kind of daze. She turned to him and asked, 'What's the matter?'

'Nothing's the matter...' He spoke slowly; his mouth was dry, and he moistened his lips. He was standing by the bed, dressed in nothing but his singlet and underpants. Lil had taken off her dress, and was in her slip, but from the way he stared at her, she felt as if she were naked.

Her first instinct was to back away from him—and he seemed to read her thoughts, because he mumbled, 'I'm sorry, Lil. I can't help it... I'm just a bit—well, you know how it is. It's been a hell of a long time.'

'Yes, it has.' With an effort of will, she made herself walk slowly towards him. 'You want me, don't you? Here—and now.'

He looked at her as if he could not believe what he heard. 'Are you sure?' Glancing down at the smooth clean sheets, he added sheepishly, 'We've only just made the bed.'

'Then we can unmake it again, can't we?'

She held out her arms, and they moved together, tumbling on to the bed. He had never known her so responsive. As they made love, he exclaimed in ecstasy, 'You're wonderful—the most wonderful—God, I love you so much.'

She gripped him tightly, letting him take possession of her. Her eyes were closed, and there was a smile of triumph upon her lips. For the first time, she found it easy—amazingly easy—but Mike would never know that she was not thinking of him. In her imagination she was seeing another man's laughing mouth, feeling another man's body against her own...joyfully, she gave herself up to Trevor.

When Mike's leave ended, and he had gone back to rejoin his ship, Ruth confided to Connor one afternoon, 'I'm so thankful Mike and Lil had these few days together; it really seems to have brought them closer. I've never seen them so happy.'

'You're right.' Connor nodded, taking down a bottle of scotch from the shelves behind the bar. 'And I'm glad of it. Oh, I dare say your nephew's a decent enough feller in his way—and I've no doubt Lil was glad to have his company—but it was grand to see her with her husband again.'

Watching him, Ruth asked, 'What are you doing with that bottle? Is there something wrong with it?'

'Not at all—I'm just putting it away. Whisky's going to be in short supply soon; we'll keep this under the counter, for regular customers only.'

'I see.' Ruth glanced at the mirror and said, 'Oh dear, I look a sight, but I don't suppose Father will notice. I'm off to the Infirmary. Shall I tell him you send your best wishes?'

'If he believes that, he'll believe anything,' grunted Connor.

'I'll tell him anyway, though I'm not sure he

knows who you are. Sometimes I'm not even sure if he knows me!'

When she reached the Infirmary, a nurse stopped her as she was about to enter the ward. 'Mrs O'Dell, excuse me. Sister would like a word with you.'

'Very well.' A little alarmed, Ruth asked, 'He's not had a relapse?'

'Oh no, nothing like that. He's doing very well, really.'

At the end of the afternoon, Ruth returned to the pub. Connor met her at the side door, demanding: 'Where the devil have you been? You're generally back before this.'

'I had to see the Ward Sister.' Wearily, she took off her hat and coat. 'It took longer than I expected. Come into the kitchen—and you'd better sit down. This may come as rather a shock.'

Connor followed her in. 'The old feller's taken a turn for the worse?'

'No, they say he's doing well—as well as he'll ever be. That's the whole point.' She sat down at the table, facing him, and continued: 'There's nothing more they can do for him, and they need the bed. That's why they called me in. They want to send him home.'

Connor blinked, uncomprehending. 'Are they off their heads? Don't they know his house is nothing but a shell? How could he go back there?'

'They didn't mean his home... He'll have to come to ours.'

'Your father? *Here?*' Connor drew back his

head. 'Oh no, that's impossible. He'd never agree to it; you know how he feels about public-houses. He'd die, sooner.'

'He hasn't got much choice, and neither have we. I'm his next-of-kin; it's my duty to look after him. The Sister made that perfectly clear.'

'It's not up to some total stranger to tell you what your duty is. We can't have him here, and that's that. You know how it is between me and him; we'd be at each other's throats from morn to night.'

Ruth sighed. 'You haven't seen him lately, Con. He's not the same man he used to be. Don't forget—he is eighty-one years old, and he has nowhere else to go. I couldn't say no, could I?'

'I'm not having you wear yourself out, running up and down stairs, waiting on him.' Another thought struck him. 'Anyhow, where the devil could we put him? We've no spare rooms. Kaff and Lil are sharing already.'

'I've been thinking about that. He'll have to go into Daniel's room.'

'You can't turn the boy out of his own bedroom!'

'Dan's in North Africa; we don't know when we'll see him next. And when he does get leave, we can make him comfortable downstairs. The raids seem to be over, so he'll have the cellar all to himself.'

'It's not right! The boy's out there fighting for his King and country; he deserves to have his own bed when he comes home. I'm not kicking my son out to make room for Marcus Judge!'

Ruth got up and came over to him. Kneeling beside his chair, she took his hands in hers and looked up into his face.

'Con...I've had more fights with Father than you have, and I don't like it either. But I know what Mum would have wanted me to do; we'll just have to make the best of it.'

He studied her in silence, then leaned forward and kissed her. 'You're a good girl, and I don't know what I've done to deserve you. Very well, he can come here, and may God help us all... But if he starts preaching one of his hellfire sermons and disturbing the customers, I'm warning you here and now—I'll break his wicked old neck, so I will!'

A week later, an ambulance brought Marcus judge to the Watermen, and they carried him upstairs to Dan's room. Ruth put him to bed, and he drifted off to sleep almost at once.

Even Connor had to admit that it didn't turn out too badly. Marcus stayed in bed all the time; his meals were taken up to him, and he had to be washed and nursed, but apart from that he gave them very little trouble. Sometimes he read his Bible, at other times he dozed. He rarely spoke, though he would sometimes answer a direct question with a hoarse monosyllable. As Ruth said, it was hard to be sure if he knew where he was. Once or twice Connor looked in on the old man, and Marcus cocked a bleary eye at him, without any sign of recognition. As one day followed another, there was no change in the old man; he grew no better, and no worse.

Outside, the golden summer darkened, burnishing

313

the leaves with copper as autumn set in.

There had been no more bombs. By a cruel twist of fate, the attack that destroyed most of the Rope Walk, killing Emily and Louisa, seemed to have been the last major raid upon London. In August, the local authorities, preparing for the possibility of another blitz next winter, began to put up static water-tanks in the streets; the Fire Service would not be caught off-guard again.

But the evenings drew in without any air-raids. All over Occupied Europe, a new campaign had begun: *V for Victory* was scrawled on walls and doors—the dot-dot-dot-dash rhythm was repeated again and again, broadcast to clandestine radios, acclaimed in concert-halls at the start of Beethoven's Fifth Symphony. Optimism was in the air; people everywhere responded to the defiant message, and looked hopefully for a new dawn.

Then, in the middle of November, the news came through.

Lil had been on night duty at the Fire Station. It was a quiet shift, with no incidents, and she had managed to cat-nap from time to time, so when she got back to the pub she was feeling quite fresh and ready to face the day—but the moment she walked into the kitchen, she knew something was wrong.

Ruth was washing up the breakfast-things; as she wiped her hands, Lil saw that she had been crying.

'What's wrong?' she asked urgently. 'It's not Danny?'

Ruth spoke slowly, choosing her words. 'We don't know anything for certain yet, but there was a news-bulletin on the wireless, about half an hour ago, about Mike's ship... They say the *Ark Royal* has been torpedoed—by an Italian U-boat.'

Lil said firmly, 'Oh no, that's nothing. The Germans and the Eye-ties are always claiming they've sunk the *Ark Royal*—it doesn't mean a thing.'

'I'm afraid this time it's different.' Ruth's voice was very gentle. 'The Admiralty announced that she was sunk on her way to Gibraltar... Some of the crew were picked up, but—eighteen of them are missing.'

Still she refused to accept it. Mike would be one of the lucky ones—he would come home soon. He would be safe...

Three days later, the telegram arrived. Lil's hands shook so badly, the flimsy paper danced before her eyes, but a few words stood out clearly:

'*PO Michael Burns... Missing... Believed to be drowned...*'

10

It was not a white Christmas, but a black one. A year ago, the holidays had been unexpectedly happy for the O'Dell family; Christmas 1941 was in stark contrast.

Long after she had wiped away her tears, Lil went on living through each day in a fog of misery—longing for the celebrations to be over, yet knowing there could be no end to her unhappiness, for she would never see Mike again.

She got up and went off to work as usual; she came home, she shared the family's Christmas dinner, she opened her presents, she pretended to take an interest in the festivities—and it was all completely meaningless. Somehow she managed to get through the ritual with a tight, empty smile, hating every minute of it. Trivial details annoyed her. She felt a sudden, irrational rage at the sight of cheery Christmas cards, and when the others listened to the King's message on the wireless, with its good wishes for better times in the future, she had to go up to her bedroom, because she could see no future at all.

Everyone had been very sympathetic. When Dan came home on leave, he hugged her tightly, and said nothing; that was more comforting than any words. Coming from the Middle East, he had brought a kit-bag full of gifts—silk scarves for the womenfolk, woven in vivid, barbaric colours. Lil said politely that hers was very pretty, then put it away, unworn. He had two presents for Kaff; one was a toy camel, made of leather, but in case she considered it too babyish, he gave her a silk scarf as well.

She loved the camel, giving it pride of place on her bedside table, but when she tried on the scarf, her eyes glowed with pleasure, and from that day on she wore it every time she went out.

Although Lil was fond of Kaff, she felt she must get away from their shared bedroom. She had a desperate need for privacy now—a place of her own, where she could give way to her grief—and she told her mother she would move back to the little flat at Coldharbour. However briefly, it had been her home with Mike; she would feel closer to him there.

Ruth was concerned for her, and tried to persuade her to stay on at the pub, saying, 'It's not good for you to be alone. You mustn't let yourself brood over it.'

But Connor sided with Lil, telling Ruth, 'We must let the girl do as she wants. It may be better so.'

The little top-floor flat was cold and cheerless, but Lil went back to it gladly. She had been overwhelmed by too much warmth, too much sympathy. Even Matt Judge, dropping into the pub during his Christmas leave, had mumbled a few embarrassed words. She was touched by the attempt, but preferred the short letter written by Abram, which offered her his condolences, concluding:

'I don't suppose you feel like seeing people or talking about it for the moment, but if you do, you know where to find me. And if you should ever need any help, just send for me and I'll come at once.'

She had cried again when she read those words—and that in itself had helped a little.

The one person who did not offer her any

consolation was Trevor. He must have heard the news—everyone knew about Mike—but he did not write, or telephone, or send Lil any message. At first she was mystified, then she was indignant—but she finally decided that perhaps it was for the best. In her present mood, she was not sure that she could have coped with Trevor.

Lil was not alone in her unhappiness. It had been a bad year all round, and though most people tried to celebrate the festive season, it was not easy.

Since they first visited Silmour Street together, Gloria and Huw had been invited back by Rosie and Ernest every few weeks, and the two couples had become close friends. As food-rationing tightened, the meals had become less ambitious; nowadays it was generally sandwiches and bottled beer, followed by a game of cards. They had tried Solo Whist, but Glory complained that she could never remember all the cards that had gone down, so they settled for Rummy, which was less taxing.

However, when they sat down to supper on Boxing Day, Rosie produced a small joint of salt beef, with carrots and dumplings. The guests were very impressed, and Glory exclaimed. 'I haven't seen boiled beef for ages! Wherever did you get it?'

Rosie smiled knowingly. 'Ask no questions and you'll be told no lies!'

Clearing his throat, Ernest took off his spectacles and began to polish them, saying,

'Frankly, I prefer not to know. I have to say I disapprove of the black market—but under these circumstances, I suppose we must turn a blind eye.'

'Certainly we must! Oh, I've no doubt it's all very wicked, but it's a poor look-out if we can't bend the rules a little at Christmas!' said Rosie firmly. 'We've got to make this a special occasion, haven't we?'

Glory's smile dimmed a little as she said, 'It's always a special occasion for me, anyhow. I can't help thinking back to another Boxing Day.'

'I beg your pardon?' Replacing his spectacles, Ernest peered at her. 'Another Boxing Day?'

Rosie threw him a reproachful look. 'You know very well—it's the day Saul was killed. Now why don't you make yourself useful and carve the meat, while I serve the vegetables?'

'Sorry. We're here to enjoy ourselves, aren't we?' Under the table, Glory pressed her foot against Huw's and gave him a secret, apologetic look. 'I shouldn't have said anything.'

'What a pity Matt couldn't have joined us,' said Rosie, ladling out mashed potato. 'I suppose he's out celebrating with some of his friends?'

'Yes. He sent you his best wishes, though.' Glory improvised rapidly. 'He said he'd have loved to come, only he'd already promised to see some of his pals—you know how it is.'

Rosie sighed, 'Of course. Abram couldn't be here, either. He's on his rounds tonight with the ambulance, but he said he'd try and look in later.'

'They don't know what they're missing!' said Huw appreciatively, as Rosie put a plate in front of him. 'Anyhow, all the more for us.'

It was an excellent meal, but nobody seemed to have much of an appetite. However hard they tried, the conversation kept taking a gloomy turn. It was impossible to keep the war from creeping in—the bulletins from the desert, the sunken ships, the casualty lists. And there was some uncomfortable news, closer to home.

Ernest turned to Huw, saying, 'You know I was on duty at the Post last night? I heard there was some trouble at one of the pubs in Manchester Road, so I thought I'd look in to see what was going on.'

'You'll get into trouble yourself one of these days,' Rosie scolded him. 'You're an Air Raid Warden, not a policeman. I wish you wouldn't poke your nose in.'

'I'm glad I did,' said Ernest. 'Somebody had been handing out leaflets—stupid, poisonous messages. Here, you can see for yourselves.' He dug into his breast pocket and pulled out a small sheet of yellow paper, very crudely printed, which he passed round the table.

'I don't know why you kept it,' said Rosie. 'I told. you to throw it away.'

The leaflet was brief and barely literate, but the message came through clearly enough.

'Down with the Yids! Why are we suffering? Hitler, he had the right idea, wiping out the Jews in Germany. Now he's doing the same for us and good luck to him clearing out the slums and sweatshops. This is your chance to

320

build a new Britain. Don't let them stuff you full with Government propaganda—throw out the dirty Sheeny millionaires and vote for racial purity and vote for peace!'

Glory handed back the paper, wrinkling her nose. 'It's disgraceful!' she said. 'Where did it come from? Who'd want to print rubbish like that?'

'It's probably being passed round by Nazi spies,' suggested Huw. 'Or else it's the British Fascist Party up to their tricks again.'

'I thought they'd all been locked up?' said Rosie.

'Mosley and a few of his cronies have been put inside, but most of them are still out and about,' Huw told her. 'They've just gone into hiding, that's all.'

'Well, whoever's responsible, it nearly started a riot in Manchester Road. There was a free fight going on by the time I got there,' said Ernest. 'It reminded me of the bad times we went through in the last war.'

'That's quite enough of that!' Rosie did not like to think of those days, when Ernest's parents had been the victims of mob violence. 'Can we please talk about something else?'

When the meal was over, they cleared the table. Rosie made some coffee and Huw presented his contribution to the feast—a half-bottle of brandy. They moved into the sitting-room and began to relax a little. Seeing her reflection in the mirror above the mantelpiece, Rosie patted a curl into place and said, 'My hair's such a mess. It's time you gave me another perm, Glory. When can you manage it?'

'Well, I'm not sure...' Glory hesitated, looking at Huw. 'The trouble is, I might not be doing perms very much longer.'

Huw frowned. 'Don't let's start all that again, for goodness sake!'

Rosie looked from one to the other. 'Is something wrong?'

'We've been having a bit of a disagreement,' began Glory. 'You see, I can't help feeling I'm being completely useless. I mean, here we are in the middle of a terrible war, and what am I doing? Ladies' hairdressing—I ask you!'

Huw tried to interrupt. 'Someone's got to do it...'

'That's no excuse!' Once Glory had started, there was no stopping her. 'This is my war too, you know. Hitler killed poor old Ma, didn't he? I'd like to have a go at him myself, one way or another. There's plenty of women registering for war-work, so why not me? That Ernie Bevin was on the wireless the other day, asking for volunteers!'

'Yes—women up to forty. That's different.'

'Oh, ta very much!' Glory turned on Huw indignantly. 'Are you trying to tell me I'm too old, is that it?'

'I didn't say that!' He began to feel he was fighting a losing battle, and turned to the Kleibers for support. 'This is all because she saw something in the paper about them needing women to work at Woolwich Arsenal, making munitions. I've tried to tell her, it's very hard work—and it's dangerous—but she won't listen.'

'If a forty-year-old woman can do it, I'm damn sure I can,' snorted Glory. 'You never know, I might be the one who fills the shell that finally knocks Adolf's block off—what's wrong with that?'

They all began to argue at once, making so much noise that they did not hear Abram coming in through the shop and up the stairs. When he entered the sitting-room, Rosie broke off, staring at him in horror. Instinctively, she reverted to her Catholic upbringing as she gasped: 'Mother of God—whatever's happened?'

Abram was a sorry sight. His clothes were smeared with whitewash and one sleeve was almost torn from his jacket. His face was covered in blood, and an ugly bruise threatened to close his left eye.

'I got in a fight,' he said thickly.

'I can see that!' Rosie rushed to his side. 'What in heaven's name has been going on?'

Ernest rose to his feet, saying, 'I think perhaps I can guess. Come to the bathroom; we must clean up those cuts. I have some arnica in the cabinet, for the bruises.'

The story Abram told them was simple. Driving round in the ambulance with one of his colleagues—who also happened to be Jewish—he had noticed a gang of hooligans with a bucket of whitewash, daubing a slogan on a wall which read: *This is a Jewish war—down with the Yids!*

Slamming the brakes on, they jumped out to

protest, and a pitched battle ensued.

'Unfortunately, there were five of them and only two of us,' Abram explained ruefully. 'Still, we did our best. I knocked one of 'em for six—he hit his head on a lamp-post as he went down—and another one finished up with the bucket on top of him!'

Rosie made her son a fresh pot of coffee, and offered some more to her guests, but it was getting late and Huw and Glory said it was time to make their way home. They thanked the Kleibers for an enjoyable and interesting evening, and set off into the black-out.

When they had gone, Abram sipped his coffee and said quietly, 'I didn't like to tell the whole story while Mrs Judge was here. I thought it would be better not to.'

'What do you mean by that?' asked his father.

'One of the gang we found painting the wall—the one who crashed into the lamp-post—that was her son,' said Abram. 'Matt Judge—I recognised him at once, and I'm pretty sure he knew me as well. I wonder what she'll say when he gets home covered in whitewash, with a lump on the back of his head.'

'Are you certain about that?' began Ernest—then broke off.

Rosie had slumped into a chair, and tears were running down her face. 'Oh no,' she sobbed. 'Not Matt. Dear God—not Matt!'

Bewildered, Ernest patted her shoulder helplessly. 'My dear, you mustn't let it upset you. What difference does it make who it was?'

She shook her head, unable to reply; it was a long time before she stopped crying.

Christmas had been bad enough, but Lil was afraid New Year's Eve would be worse still. On the last day of December, she woke up with a dull feeling of dread, even before she realised what the date was. Then she remembered: tonight there would be a big party at the Watermen, and she was expected to be there.

She had tried to tell her parents that she didn't want to be part of a jolly, noisy crowd, but Ruth said she couldn't possibly see the New Year in all by herself, alone in her flat.

Con put his arm round his daughter's shoulders, saying, 'We know how you feel—and if it gets too much for you, you can always slip away to the kitchen for some peace and quiet, or go up to bed in Kaff's room. But we'd feel a lot happier if you were here with us, under our roof.'

Since it meant so much to them, she had agreed, but this morning she regretted her decision, as a cold fear clutched her. She pictured the scene: half-drunken revellers persuading her to dance—she imagined herself in their arms as they pawed her, breathing beery fumes into her face and possibly trying to kiss her—while they all sang *Auld Lang Syne* and swore undying maudlin love for each other... The prospect appalled her, but she could not get out of it now.

After a hasty breakfast of tea and toast, she

went off to work. She was on the day-shift at the Fire Station, and rather wished she had volunteered for night duty instead—although that would probably have been just as bad. There was bound to be some kind of celebration among the night crew, and she would have been trapped there, unable to escape.

Well, there was nothing for it but to try and get through the next twenty-four hours as best she could; she looked forward to her return to solitude when it was all over.

The day passed uneventfully; someone had the bright idea of decorating the duty-room, and she helped to blow up balloons and hang paper-chains. Although alcohol was normally forbidden on the premises, the rules had been slightly relaxed on this occasion, and as she was leaving, she saw some crates of beer being carried in. She hurried out of the building, glad to get away.

A car was parked on the other side of the street; this was unusual, for private cars were a rarity in the Island nowadays, and she gave it a closer look. Even in the black-out, she recognised the outline of the smart two-seater, and her heart beat a little faster.

She heard the driver's door open, and a shadowy figure strolled across the road to meet her.

'Hello, Lily,' said Trevor. 'Can I give you a lift?'

She did not know what to say. She had not seen him or talked to him for months, but he spoke so casually, it was as if he had picked up a conversation that had only been broken off a few moments ago.

'Well, yes. I suppose so, thanks,' she stammered. 'Which way are you going?'

'Wherever you like,' he replied easily. 'Come on, in you get.'

Like someone in a dream, she obeyed. The motor sprang into life, and the little car slid away.

'How did you know where to find me?' she asked.

'I called in at the pub and asked Auntie Ruth; she told me what time you finish work. She also mentioned that there's some sort of party there tonight, and asked if I'd like to come along. It was very kind of her, but I explained I don't really enjoy crowds.'

'Nor do I, but she's determined that I shouldn't see the New Year in all on my own.'

'That's all right—I explained that you won't be on your own. You're coming to have supper with me instead.'

'What?' His calm assurance took her breath away. 'But what did she say?'

'She said if that's what you wanted to do, it was up to you.'

'I see.' Again she was aware of that indefinable electric charge passing between them. 'How did you know I'd want to?'

'I had a hunch you might not be in a party mood... So—where are we going next?'

She tried to think, but her head was whirling. 'I don't know. But I can't go anywhere like

327

this—I'm still in uniform.'

'That's easily solved. I gather you've moved back to your own flat now? Then I'll take you there, and wait while you change.'

For an instant, she felt a shiver of uncertainty, but he seemed to be able to read her thoughts and elaborated immediately: 'I'll wait in the car, while you get changed.'

As she was wondering what she should wear, he continued, 'I'm afraid most of the decent restaurants will be jam-packed tonight, that's why I thought you might prefer supper at Acacia Grove... Nothing very special, but at least it will be quiet and comfortable.'

'That sounds very nice. Thank you.'

When they got to Coldharbour, she changed into her best dress, did her hair, and put on some lipstick—then, as an afterthought, splashed on a few drops of perfume. Her pulses were racing; she told herself that she was behaving like an excited schoolgirl. It was so long since she had felt anything at all, she could hardly recognise this unfamiliar sensation—but then she realised it was happiness.

They drove back to Greenwich. The house was warm and welcoming, with a log-fire in the hearth. Trevor turned on the gramophone and she watched with surprise as it began to play a stack of records that dropped neatly into place one after another, to provide a background of music as they talked.

At first they kept to frivolous, unimportant subjects; they compared notes about their favourite food—Trevor said he was particularly fond of cold roast duck, which was waiting for them on the table, beside a bowl of lettuce and a potato salad. He opened a bottle of white wine and as he filled their glasses, Lil told him: 'I never used to drink alcohol, until the night you took me to the Café de Paris.'

'And you a publican's daughter?' he asked quizzically. 'You mean to say you'd never tried it before?'

'Only once—when I was still quite young. That put me off.' As a rule the mere thought of that experience sickened her, but tonight it seemed like something that had happened to someone else, long ago. She tasted the wine and said, 'This is very good—lovely and cool.'

'It's been chilling all the afternoon in a bath full of ice, along with two bottles of champagne. We can't see in the New Year without a glass of bubbly.'

After supper Lil settled into a big armchair, curled up among the cushions, and he told her she looked like a contented cat.

'I can practically hear you purring. That's meant as a compliment, by the way—I approve of cats.'

She smiled. 'Do you know, this is the first time I've felt like purring since—' Then she stopped. 'I don't remember when... A long time.'

He said nothing; the room was very quiet, except for the crackle of flames in the grate and the sound of Glenn Miller's orchestra playing faintly on the gramophone. Gazing into the flames, Lil broke the silence. 'You've never once mentioned Mike...'

'Did you want me to?'

'I don't know. Most people feel they have to.'

'Perhaps I wasn't sure what to say. You miss him, I realise that—it must have been a terrible shock for you. But "I'm sorry" seems rather inadequate.'

'That's true.' She felt confused; her pain was touched with pleasure that he understood her so well. 'Thank you, anyway.'

'You had a happy marriage.' He did not phrase it like a question, yet she knew that it was.

'Oh yes. Mike was the gentlest man in the world—the kindest. There'll never be anyone like him.'

'And you needed a man who was kind and gentle, more than anything.' Trevor's voice was soft. 'You needed a special kind of lover.'

So he understood that, too.

'Yes. Mike was—very patient with me.'

There was a tiny click, as one record ended and another fell into place; a slow, wistful tune, driven by a persistent underlying beat.

'This is nice,' she said. 'What's it called?'

'*Moonlight Serenade,*' he told her. 'I've played it a lot lately.' They listened to the music for a few minutes, then he said thoughtfully: 'In a way, I envy you.'

'Me?' She stared at him. 'What do you mean?'

'Oh, I know you're going through a bad time now, but that will pass. And you'll always have

330

happy memories of Mike. He loved you very much. I only met him once, but that was obvious in every look, every word he spoke... Not everyone is lucky enough to be loved like that.'

Lil started to say, 'You've got Sally. She worships you!'

His smile was a little rueful. 'She was mad about me at first, but then she realised I could be useful to her, and that changed everything. Don't get me wrong—we've had some good times together, and we've enjoyed ourselves, but that wasn't love. It was something we shared—a kind of hunger.'

Lil felt uncomfortable, as if she had opened the wrong door and trespassed on their privacy, yet she didn't want him to stop talking.

'Sometimes I wonder if it's a lack in me,' he went on. 'Perhaps there's something about me that no one can really love.'

'That's not true.' She broke off, afraid she was starting to blush, and finished, 'I mean, I'm sure Aunt Emily loved you.'

'Dear old Gangan. Yes, I suppose she did, in her own funny way. But she was the only one, and now she's gone... There was never anyone else.'

The last record in the stack came to an end, and the gramophone switched itself off. Trevor's voice was not much more than a whisper now.

'It's always been the same. My Dad was killed in the last war, soon after I was born, so I never knew him. I used to think I did. When I grew up, I could just remember some man taking me

331

on his knee, giving me chocolate and making a fuss of me—but later on I realised he couldn't have been my father. I suppose I was about three years old by then, so it must have been one of my mother's boy-friends. I expect he used to bring me sweeties as a way of getting round her... I've even got a hazy recollection of seeing them in bed together.'

'Oh, no!' Lil was horrified. 'Don't say that.'

'Why not? That's what she was like—you must have heard about my dear mother, surely? She'd go with anyone. After my Dad was killed, she married my Uncle Josh—when she got bored with Josh, she ran off with her American fancy-man, and no one's ever heard from her since. Oh yes, she acquired quite a collection of lovers along the way—all shapes and sizes—but she never gave a damn about me.'

One of the logs settled into the embers with a sudden crunch, jerking him out of his reverie. He glanced over at Lil and said wryly, 'Sorry about that. Story of my life—very boring. You should have stopped me.'

'No, I'm glad you told me.' Lil sat up, looking at him earnestly. 'Only I don't believe you've got it quite right—not all of it.'

'Every word, I promise you. My darling mama did have a taste for men, she did run off with a Yankee—'

'I don't mean that, I meant the part about you—about nobody being able to—' She could not go on. His eyes seemed to look right through her, into her heart and soul, and again she felt sure that he was reading her thoughts.

Then the telephone rang.

Cursing under his breath, he stood up and crossed the room to pick up the phone.

'Hello—speaking.' Then, heavily: 'Yes, Bertie, I recognised your voice. What sort of trouble? Where? I see. Right—I'll meet you at the warehouse in about fifteen minutes.'

When he put down the receiver, he was a different man. His movements were purposeful, his tone brisk and business-like.

'Do you feel like a jaunt in the car? I've got to go out. You're welcome to stay here or come with me—whichever you like—but I warn you I don't know how long it's going to take. Bertie says we've had a break-in at the Wharf. Thieves got into one of the warehouses, and turned it over. What do you want to do?'

'I'll come with you.' She did not have to think about it. Of course she would go with him—anywhere, any time.

The rest of the evening was a confused jumble of incidents. When she finally got to bed, she lay awake, trying to piece them together. Isolated moments came back to her: driving very fast through the black-out, with Trevor's voice saying, 'If they've broken into the Wharf, I might as well break something myself—even if it's only the speed limit'; going through the gates and along the harbour wall, with a line of huge freighters towering above the little roadster; pulling up outside a blank windowless building, and then stepping into an echoing cavern, with policemen searching for clues and warehousemen checking the stock against typed bills of lading; Bertie Judge, quivering and apprehensive, talking rapidly to a grey-faced nightwatchman, who kept repeating: 'I never saw nuffink, as God's my witness. I never saw hair nor hide of 'em.'

Lil hung about for what seemed a very long time, and watched Trevor asking questions, listening to the answers and taking notes. He had a long talk to the police officers and a muttered discussion with Bertie, then he pulled a fiver from his wallet and pushed it into the nightwatchman's hand, saying, 'It wasn't your fault, nobody's blaming you.'

At last, when Lil was aching with cold and boredom and having nowhere to sit down, he came back and took her out to the car, explaining: 'There's nothing to be done tonight. It was a very neat operation; they must have known what time our watchman does his rounds, and picked the right time to break in. They picked the ideal night for it, too—the dock was practically deserted. The ship's crews were all ashore celebrating, and I don't suppose we'd have known about it until the morning—only one of the lascar seamen had a nasty toothache. He didn't feel like going out with his pals, and he couldn't get to sleep either, so he happened to be up on deck when he saw some suspicious-looking characters flitting in and out of the shadows, and raised the alarm. By the time the police arrived, the thieves had got away and taken a lot of stuff with them: tea, coffee, sugar—tinned meat from America—it will all turn up on the black market, of course. At least we're covered by insurance, that's some consolation.'

As they got into the car, Lil tried to stifle a yawn. Contrite, he exclaimed: 'God, I'm sorry. I should never have brought you out, you must be exhausted... Come on, I'm taking you home. It's past your bedtime.'

'What time is it?' she asked, fighting off sleep.

He looked at the luminous dial of his watch and groaned, 'Ten past one. Midnight's been and gone, and we never even noticed. Happy New Year, Lily.' For a moment she thought he was going to kiss her. Instead, he took her hand and brushed it with his lips, then said: 'Better still—a happier New Year.'

Then he took her back to Coldharbour; they said good-night, and he drove away.

It wasn't until she was lying in bed, on the edge of sleep, that she remembered those two bottles of champagne, still unopened, in their bath of ice.

After that, the weeks went by without any word from Trevor. It had been such an extraordinary evening, she began to wonder if she had imagined the whole thing—but the memory of that strange rapport between them remained; that had been real, and unforgettable.

The dreary winter dragged on, and halfway through February Lil decided to cheer herself up by going to the pictures. By this time, so many people had told her how much they'd enjoyed *Gone With the Wind* that she was sick of hearing about it, and decided she must see it for herself. It was still running in Leicester Square, so when she had an evening off, she took Kaff with her, as a special treat.

It was an amazing experience for both of them. For one thing, they had never seen any film that lasted so long, with an interval in the middle. It was beautifully acted, right down to the smallest roles (though Kaff said Ashley Wilkes was soppy, and Rhett Butler was worth ten of him) and the costumes and settings were gorgeous—but it was the story that gripped them, holding them mesmerised until the final fade-out.

Above all, it was Scarlett herself who enthralled them.

On the way home in the Underground, they couldn't stop talking about her, recalling every moment, and Kaff said; 'Don't laugh, but I kept thinking that was *me* up there, doing all that. I know she was sort of a bad lot, but that's how I'd like to be...' A little shamefaced she added, 'Daft, innit? I mean her being white and me being—you know—like I am.'

Lil looked at the girl beside her; only fourteen years old, and small for her age. But she was wearing her silk scarf, and the brilliant colours set off her copper skin and dark, liquid eyes with their soft black lashes.

'I'll tell you something,' said Lil. 'You're going to be a knock-out. In a year or two the men will be falling over themselves for you, you wait and see.'

'Think so?' Kaff's lips curved faintly, as she gazed into the future, trying to imagine it.

Lil realised guiltily that Kaff wasn't the only one to picture herself up there on the screen with Scarlett O'Hara. She had felt very close to her—especially in the scene at the Charity Ball, when the young widow, lovelier than ever in her black mourning gown, danced with Rhett and scandalised the good ladies of Atlanta... Shamefully hugging her secret, she remembered dancing with Trevor—nearly a year ago, at the Café de Paris—and suddenly realised that it would soon be his birthday again. It wouldn't do any harm to send him a card and wish him many happy returns, would it?

While the tube train rattled eastward along the District Line, Ruth was sitting upstairs at the Watermen, wondering when Lil and Kaff would come home. She hoped they wouldn't stay out too late; she didn't like the thought of two girls travelling through London on their own, after dark.

When the Japanese attacked Pearl Harbor, before Christmas, the United States had been flung into the war, and although everyone was glad to have them as allies, opinions were divided about the arrival of American troops in Britain. Ruth couldn't help worrying; there were a lot of nasty stories going round, about sex-starved GIs and impressionable young women...

She sighed, trying to concentrate on the sock she was darning. When Connor didn't need her to serve in the bar, she often sat upstairs in her father's room, getting on with the mending, and perhaps keeping the old man company.

It was hard to tell if he was aware of her. He rarely spoke as he lay there, propped up against the pillows. Sometimes he dozed, sometimes he peered short-sightedly at his Bible, sometimes he did nothing but stare into space with vacant, red-rimmed eyes under shaggy brows.

Ruth went on plying her darning-needle. It was a never-ending job—Con was on his feet all day, and that was hard on his socks. Then, as she worked, she heard a voice say quietly: 'Ruth...is that you?'

Startled, she pricked her finger and let the half-mended sock slip to the floor. She turned to the figure in the bed, hardly able to believe her ears—his voice was so different, a frail thread of sound—but he was looking directly at her as he repeated: 'Ruth—my girl. That is you, isn't it?'

He held out one gnarled hand, and she went to him at once, saying, 'Yes, Father—it's me.'

'I thought so.' He squeezed her hand. 'You're a good girl.'

She could not understand him, and asked helplessly, 'Is there something you want?'

'Nothing. You look after me very well... I was wondering,' he lifted his head, his eyes roaming over the room, 'where am I?'

Not knowing what to say, she replied awkwardly, 'You're in my house. Mine and Connor's.'

'Yes, I thought so. Did something happen—to my house?'

She thought of the wreckage at the Rope Walk—the broken walls, the devastation—and

338

she took a deep breath. 'Yes, Father. Your house was damaged, during an air-raid.'

He pondered this for a moment, then asked, 'Badly damaged?'

'I'm afraid so. But you're safe now, with us.'

'God is very good.' His head trembled, and then she realised that he was nodding agreement, as he said, 'Yes. Safe—with you.' He squeezed her hand again, and his face took on an unaccustomed expression. It was the first time in her life that Ruth had seen her father smile. 'Thank you,' he murmured, then closed his eyes. 'I think I shall rest now... I feel a little tired.'

And he fell asleep, still smiling.

When the girls came home, Ruth met them in the kitchen. She sent Kaff upstairs to get ready for bed, saying: 'I'll bring you up a cup of cocoa in ten minutes.'

As soon as the door shut, she told Lil what had happened. 'I've never seen him like that before. He was so—I don't know how to describe it—different, that's all. He asked about his house, and I had to tell him it had been bombed, but he took it very well.'

'Did he say anything about Grandma?'

'No. I was afraid he was going to—he's bound to ask about her when he wakes up.'

'Perhaps he knows already; that's why he didn't mention her.'

'Perhaps. I hope he does—I don't know how I'd break it to him. Oh, I know he treated her badly sometimes, but deep down I think he

339

loved her.' She began to measure out cocoa into the mugs, adding, 'Anyway, he seems to be a lot better, that's the main thing.' Then, remembering where Lil had been: 'How was the cinema?'

'Marvellous. We really enjoyed it—you ought to get Dad to take you.'

'Ha!' Ruth made a face. 'Chance'd be a fine thing. Who was in it?'

'Vivien Leigh and Clark Gable. He was ever so good. He reminded me of Trevor a bit.'

'How do you mean? Trevor hasn't got a moustache.'

'No, well—apart from the moustache, there was just something about him.' Lil went on quickly, 'Matter of fact, I was thinking I must send him a card. It'll be his birthday soon.'

Ruth stopped pouring boiling water into the mugs, and looked puzzled. 'Whatever gave you that idea? Trevor's birthday's in the summer—June, I think.'

'No, Mum, you've got it wrong. His birthday's March the eighth. That's why he took me out last year, to celebrate.'

Ruth shook her head. 'He must have been pulling your leg. I remember the year he was born. It was somewhere around midsummer—there was a heatwave.'

She gave Lil her cocoa, then took another mug upstairs to Kaff. Alone, Lil sat and stared into the brown liquid, circling round the spoon as she stirred it. Why had Trevor told her a lie?

When Ruth entered Kaff's room, she found

her sitting up in bed with a writing-pad on her lap, and exclaimed: 'Good gracious, do you know what the time is, young lady? You're supposed to be settling down for the night!'

'Yeah, in a minute. I'm just writing a letter.'

'Oh? Who are you writing to?'

'Dan,' Kaff answered casually. 'I want to tell him about tonight, going to the flicks and all that. He won't mind, will he?'

'I'm sure he'll be very pleased. He likes to get news from home... Well, give him my love, but don't sit up too long or you'll strain your eyes. Five more minutes, and no more!' Ruth kissed her goodnight and left the room, while Kaff resumed her letter.

Dear Dan,

I hope you won't think I've got a nerve writing to you like this. Only I thought I would and your Mum said as how you wouldn't mind. I often think about you and wonder how you're getting on so I thought perhaps you'd like to know how we're getting on here. Tonight me and Lil went up West to see Gone With the Wind *and it was lovely. You would have enjoyed it too and I wished you'd been there...*

Over the next week, the question came back to Lil again and again: why had Trevor lied to her? She had tried to tell herself it wasn't worth bothering about, it was probably just a silly joke on his part, but she couldn't put it out of her mind, and the mystery tormented her.

At last she could not stand the uncertainty

any longer, and resolved to ask him for an explanation. She had been working a day-shift, and when she left the Station at the end of the afternoon, she made her way to the nearest public phone-box, and looked up the number of the Jubilee Wharf offices in the A-to-K directory. Then she put two pennies in the slot and dialled the number.

The kiosk was stuffy, smelling of stale scent and cigarette-smoke. She felt tense and nervous—when an unknown voice answered, she almost rang off, but then realised it must be one of the clerks, and asked to speak to Mr Trevor Judge. The voice told her Mr Trevor Judge was not in.

'Oh, I see.' She hadn't thought of that; perhaps he was at his office in the West End. 'You mean he isn't working with you today?'

'He's been here, but he's left. You only just missed him.'

Despair crept over her. How stupid, to have nerved herself up to it, all for nothing. Making a last effort, she asked: 'Will he be there tomorrow?'

'Yes, I think so. Can I give him a message?'

'No, it doesn't matter. I'll try again.' She was about to ring off, when another thought struck her. 'Just a minute. Before you go, do you know if he's staying over at Greenwich tonight?'

'I dare say. He generally does, when he's working here.'

'That's what I thought, so I could probably reach him there, couldn't I? The trouble is, I haven't got the number. Could you give it to

342

me, so I can phone him?'

The voice became chilly and unhelpful. 'I'm sorry, we're not allowed to give that information to callers.'

'But I'm a personal friend!'

'I'm sorry. You'd better try again tomorrow.' And then there was the dialling-tone.

So that was that. Defeated, Lil left the kiosk. She thought about ringing the Kleibers—they must have a phone-number for Acacia Grove—but she felt too shy to ask them. When she got back to Coldharbour, she made herself some tinned sardines on toast, feeling angry with Trevor for having left the office too soon and angry with herself for ringing him too late.

She imagined him in that warm, comfortable house—and suddenly had a brainwave. She could walk there, couldn't she? And it would be much easier to talk to him face to face, instead of on the phone.

It was a cold, damp evening. Earlier, it had been drizzling, so she put on her mackintosh and pixie-hood, in case it should start again, then set out on the long walk down Manchester Road.

Before she reached the Island Gardens, it began to rain, and this time it was more than a drizzle; she was glad to get under cover, beneath the domed pavilion at the entrance to the pedestrian tunnel. There weren't many people about on such a miserable night, and she was alone as she hurried down the iron staircase, setting up a noisy clatter that reverberated round the stairwell.

Down below, the tunnel seemed to stretch on for ever, lit at intervals by overhead lamps between patches of dark shadow. She heard footsteps echoing behind her—or were they in front of her?—and then, as the tunnel dropped to its lowest point, she saw two men approaching; lurching figures in khaki, supporting one another—both obviously drunk.

Sheer terror paralysed her. She stood still, pressed against the curved, white-tiled wall, unable to move as they came towards her—two infantrymen on leave, looking for a good time, but unable to find it.

When they came up to her, they staggered to a halt, and one of them said, 'Hello, darlin'. All on your lonesome, are you?'

'Same as us,' said the other. 'Come an' have a drink wiv' us, eh?'

He put his hand out, about to take her arm, and she said in a frozen whisper, *Don't you touch me...*'

Pushing past him, she fled, leaving them shouting after her, telling her to stop, assuring her they didn't mean any harm—but she did not stop running until she reached the other end of the tunnel.

When she emerged on the south bank of the river, it was raining harder than ever. She might have stayed under cover, hoping for a break in the weather, but she did not dare wait there and set off once more through the driving rain, up the long ascent of Crooms Hill.

It was bucketing down now; her mackintosh was a cheap one, and it could not protect her against such a downpour. Within minutes she was soaked to the skin, and when she finally rang the bell at the house in Acacia Grove, and Trevor opened the front door, she stumbled in, feeling like a drowned rat.

'Lily, my dear. What on earth?'

He took her inside—wringing wet, her hair plastered to her head, cold and wretched and feeling that she had made a complete fool of herself. She tried to speak—to explain—but instead she burst into tears.

Trevor took charge of the situation. 'Explanations can wait—we'll talk presently. The first thing is for you to get out of those wet clothes before you catch your death. I'll run a bath; there's plenty of hot water.'

The flat at Coldharbour had no bathroom. Now she was living there, Lil went back to the pub whenever she wanted a bath—and that was hardly luxurious. Although the O'Dells had not taken official warnings about saving fuel very seriously ('Keep below the plimsoll line—only five inches of water in the tub') the old-fashioned boiler at the Watermen was unreliable at the best of times.

Trevor's bathroom was very different. The room itself was beautifully warm, and there seemed to be an unlimited supply of steaming-hot water; he had added some bath-essence, which gave it a soft, creamy lather and a heavenly perfume. Lil took a deep breath and identified it... Roses, of course. Trevor and roses went together.

For a long time she lay in the water, basking.

When she got out, there were fluffy towels warming on the heated towel-rail, and a silk dressing-gown hanging on the back of the door.

She knotted the belt round her waist and made herself a towel turban to help dry her hair. Then, barefoot, she went down to the living-room.

Trevor heard her coming, and when she walked in he was already pouring two glasses of champagne.

'I've been saving this for you, ever since New Year,' he said. 'I'm sorry it's not very cold, but you've taken me rather by surprise.'

'I'm sorry,' she began, but he pressed a glass into her hand.

'Don't apologise. I like surprises, as long as they're pleasant ones—and this is one of the pleasantest I can think of. Cheers.' He led her to the big armchair, then took his place on the sofa at the other side of the fireplace, putting his feet up.

She tried again. 'I know I shouldn't have come here like this, but I—'

Again, he stopped her. 'Relax first—talk later.'

She sipped her champagne; it seemed to spread through her, unfolding like a flower, leaving no room for doubts or fears or anxieties.

'Better now?' he asked.

'Much better...I tried to phone you at your office, but you'd just gone, so I decided to come and see you instead. It was stupid of me.'

'Not at all, it was a wonderful idea.' He

gestured towards the gramophone. 'How about a little music?'

'No, thank you. If you don't mind, I'd rather talk. That's why I'm here—there's something I want to know.' After another mouthful of champagne, she felt brave enough to go on. 'Last year, you told me your birthday was on March the eighth.'

He looked at her enquiringly. 'Yes, what about it?'

'I was going to send you a card next week—only Mum told me I'd made a mistake. She says your birthday's in June; she remembers when you were born.'

'Ah.' He was still smiling. 'Careless of me—I might have guessed she'd know.'

'So it wasn't true. Why did you lie about it?'

'Let me put a question instead. Would you have come out with me that night, if it hadn't been my birthday?'

'Of course I—' She stopped and thought about it. 'I'm not sure.'

'If I'd told you honestly that Sally had gone away, and I felt like a night on the town without her—would you have accepted the invitation?'

'No, I suppose not.'

'Exactly. It was a white lie, but it did the trick, didn't it? I felt very guilty afterwards, when I realised you could have been killed.'

'But why ask me at all? Why didn't you take some other girl?'

He wasn't smiling any longer as he said, 'I didn't want any other girl. I've been in love with you since the day I walked into the Watermen and saw you again, after all those years—and realised how beautiful you are. Didn't you know that?'

She looked away, unable to meet his direct, steady gaze. Burying her face in her glass, she tried to understand what was happening; the wild excitement that swept through her—the longing—and at the same time that old, numbing fear, dragging her down. He had told her something she wanted to hear—and something she dreaded to hear.

At last she murmured, 'I don't know what to say.'

'You don't have to say anything. Perhaps I shouldn't have told you, but now we can be honest with one another. You understand that I'll never make any demands on you, don't you? You and I share something very special, something important to both of us. I'd never do anything to spoil that.'

'Oh, Trevor...' Choked with mixed emotions, she could hardly speak.

'I just want to be near you—to see you sometimes. I'll never ask for more than that, except, perhaps...'

He paused for a long moment, and she had to tell him to go on.

'This is a difficult thing to say, but... That night, when I brought you here after the raid, I had to look after you—to undress you. I saw your body, and ever since then I've never been able to put that picture out of my mind. I'd give anything to see you again—naked. I wouldn't touch you—I wouldn't come near you. I just want to see you, complete and perfect... Can you understand that?'

'Yes.' She was breathing faster. 'I do understand, but I don't think I—'

'No, of course not. I realise it's too much to ask.'

He looked so downcast, her heart went out to him. Slowly, she rose to her feet; she was a little dizzy and had to hold on to the chair to steady herself. With careful unhurried movements, she untied the belt of the dressing-gown, letting it slip from her shoulders to the carpet, and stood there, her skin catching the glow of the firelight. He lay on the sofa, quite still, watching intently, as if he were trying to memorise every detail of her body.

She lifted her arms above her head, in a kind of exaltation. She was giving herself to him in a way she could never have imagined—completely reckless, yet trusting him completely. Stretching her arms high and wide, she felt as if she were soaring into space—a free spirit...

'My lovely, slender Lily...' he said at last. 'Thank you.'

And then it was over. When she had put on the dressing-gown, he stood up and came towards her; even then, she was not afraid—all he did was refill her glass. For the rest of the evening, they stayed as they were, at opposite sides of the room. Before they had finished the second bottle of champagne, she was fast asleep.

She woke next morning to find herself alone

in his bed. He brought her breakfast on a tray—her clothes, which had been in the airing-cupboard all night, were ready to put on. Without having to be told, she knew that he had spent the night in the spare bedroom.

'Thank you,' she said.

'It was nothing,' he said.

11

'Hello, stranger. Fancy meeting you!'

When Gloria and Rosie came face to face in the Emmanuel Hall, they greeted one another like long-lost friends. The hall was filled with tables for a Spring Bazaar and Jumble Sale in aid of 'Warships' Week', and they had both come in, hoping to pick up a bargain.

'We should have been here as soon as they opened,' Glory added regretfully. 'All the good stuff's gone already—there's only the rubbish left.'

'That's not a very nice thing to say, is it?' broke in an indignant voice. Florrie Judge was presiding over a small table, within earshot. 'Some of us have gone to a lot of trouble getting things together for this Bazaar.'

'Hello, Florrie,' said Glory, without enthusiasm. 'What have you got there, then?'

'Needle-books—and I made them all myself, by hand,' said Florrie, showing off her wares. 'Only a shilling each.'

Rosie picked one up. It was heart-shaped, and opened up like a book. Covered in scraps of coloured material and stuffed with cotton-wool, with a few pins and needles stuck inside, it couldn't have been very difficult to put together, but Rosie felt she had to make some contribution to a good cause and said: 'Yes, lovely. I'll have this one.'

'You must be barmy,' Glory told her, as she paid for it. 'A shilling for that?'

'It's for the War Effort!' Florrie informed her, outraged. 'But perhaps you're not interested in doing your bit to beat the Germans?'

'I'm already doing my bit, ta very much,' retorted Glory. 'Didn't you hear? I'm working at Woolwich Arsenal now, on munitions. I'd say making bullets was a darn sight more useful than making needle-books.'

'Oh, yes, of course!' sniffed Florrie. 'We know all about the sort of women who go to work in factories—picking up good wages and taking jobs away from men... I should have thought you could spare a shilling, the money you're earning.'

'Just a minute...' Furiously Glory dug into her purse. 'There—take your bloody shilling and buy yourself a battleship—and you can stick your needle-book where the monkey put the nuts!'

Florrie's crabbed little face contorted with rage, but she snatched up the shilling before spitting out, 'Of course, you would have to descend to vulgarity. They say some women at that place are no better than they ought to be!'

351

'How about a nice cuppa?' interrupted Rosie, grabbing Glory's arm and steering her away. 'Let's go and take the weight off our feet, shall we?'

There was an improvised cafeteria at the end of the hall; they purchased cups of tea and found themselves a table for two. When they were settled, Glory apologised. 'I'm sorry. I didn't mean to let rip, but that old cow really gets on my wick...'

'You have to make allowances,' Rosie reminded her. 'It can't be much fun, living the way she does. How would you feel, being housekeeper to Bertie Judge?'

'He's welcome to her!' snorted Glory. 'You know, at one time I actually felt sorry for her. When she was married to Ebenezer, I'm sure he used to knock her about, but after he died she just seemed to get worse and worse.'

'Well, it's not surprising, is it? What with her son Tommy running off to America like he did.'

'It was her precious Tommy that did for my Saul...and do you know, she never spoke to me or said she was sorry? She was so taken up with her own troubles, she never even sent a wreath. No, you can't expect me to shed any tears over Florrie Judge.'

'Perhaps not.' Rosie changed the subject. 'Anyhow, I'm glad I ran into you like this; it's been a long time. I haven't seen you since you started the new job.'

'I know. Huw never stops grumbling, saying he never sees me nowadays. I'm on twelve-hour shifts—seven in the morning to seven at night.'

'That's awful! You must be worn out.'

'Oh lor', does it show?' Glory rolled her eyes. 'It's not too bad really, once you get into the swing of it. Of course it's hard work, but the money's good. I'm taking home ten quid a week, including danger money.'

'Danger?' Rosie was horrified. 'What do you have to do?'

'I'm putting caps on detonators. The cordite goes everywhere—it flies up in your face sometimes. We have to wear special overalls, and cover up our hair—and we're not allowed to wear any jewellery, except for wedding-rings. But it's the boredom that gets you down; working on an assembly-line, doing the same thing over and over again. They let us have *Music While You Work* on the loudspeakers and we all join in and sing—that helps. And they give us a day off every week—like today.'

'Well, next time you have a spare evening, you must bring Huw round. Ernest was only saying the other day, we miss our games of Rummy!'

'Oh yes, we haven't been to see you since—when was it? That night Abram came home in such a state.' Seeing Rosie's expression as she put down her cup, Glory added: 'What's up? Tea not sweet enough for you?'

'No, it's not that. I was just thinking—about Matt. I'm sorry I never got a chance to see him while he was home on leave. I think you said he was out with his friends that evening?'

'So he was. Mind you, I hardly saw him myself, come to that—he never came home

353

at all that night! He turned up a couple of days later with a rotten hangover, looking like something the cat dragged in. Gawd only knows what he'd been up to!'

Carefully, Rosie ran her finger round the rim of her cup, saying, 'These friends of his—who are they? Do you know?'

'Couldn't tell you, I'm sure. Some girl or other, I suppose. You're only young once, eh? Why, what makes you ask?'

'Oh, no special reason. I was just wondering what sort of people he goes round with. It would be a pity if he got mixed up with—you know—the wrong sort.'

Glory's face changed, and her voice hardened. 'So that's it. You don't like the idea he might be enjoying himself with a girl—having a good time. I hoped you'd got over all that.'

Rosie's cheeks were crimson. 'I don't know what you mean!'

'I mean you're jealous—that's your trouble! For heaven's sake, Rosie, when are you going to wake up and be your age? He's not interested!'

'Don't say that. It's—it's ridiculous! As if I'd dream of such—' Rosie pushed back her chair so suddenly, it nearly fell over. 'I don't want to talk about it. Excuse me, I must go. I've got a lot to do today.'

And she walked away quickly, between the long rows of tables and out of the hall. Glory watched her go. She was sorry if Rosie was upset, but it was time somebody told her a few home-truths. She caught sight of Florrie, still guarding her array of needle-books, staring

354

at her. Florrie turned away sharply, unwilling to meet her eye. Glory sighed. Why was everybody so touchy all of a sudden? She finished her tea, then, noticing that Rosie had left most of hers, she drank that as well. It would be a pity to waste it.

By the time Rosie got back to Silmour Street, she was feeling a little calmer. She walked into the photographic shop, expecting to see Ernest behind the counter but instead, she was startled to find an unexpected visitor.

'Sally! What a surprise!'

'Sorry to spring it on you like this, but you know how things are. Nobody knew which day we'd be flying home, it all depended on when the Air Force would lay on a plane for us.' Sally kissed her mother. 'How are you, darling? You're looking well, I must say—all pink and pretty.'

'You look wonderful—such a beautiful sun-tan. The weather must have been glorious.'

'The weather was the best thing about it. North Africa's terribly dreary—nothing but miles and miles of sand, though I must admit some of the officers were very sweet. One of them told me I was the most gorgeous women to hit Egypt since Cleopatra!'

Rosie looked round. 'Have you seen your father? I thought he'd be here.'

'Yes, he was, but when I told him I hadn't had a bite to eat since Cairo and I was starving to death, he went out to get some food in. He said he wouldn't be long. I hope you don't mind me landing on you out of the blue like this.'

'Mind? As if we'd mind—what a thing to say!' Rosie studied the stack of luggage piled up against the counter. 'It's so good to see you—how long are you staying?'

'Oh, I'm not staying here. I went to Charing Cross Road first, but Trevor wasn't there—I mean, there was nobody there—so I decided to come here instead and dump all my stuff. I've brought you both some presents from foreign parts—and rather a lot of dirty washing as well, I'm afraid. I knew you wouldn't mind. As soon as I've eaten, I'll call a cab and go across to Acacia Grove. Do you happen to know if Trevor's living there at the moment? Have you seen him lately?'

'No, we haven't, but then he's always so busy. You could ask Lil—she might know.'

'Lil?' Sally's smile switched off sharply. 'What's it got to do with Lil?'

'Oh, Ruth was telling me Lil's been in touch with Trevor a few times since —' She stopped short. 'You do know about poor Mike, don't you? I'm sure I wrote to you about that. Such a terrible thing to happen.'

'Yes, terrible. But do you mean that Trevor's been seeing Lil?'

'Well, I believe he's taken her out once or twice. I suppose, being her cousin, he felt sort of responsible. I thought it was very kind of him.'

'Very,' said Sally, shortly.

One week in three, Lil was on the night-shift at the Fire Station, but she was generally able to snatch some sleep in the duty-room, for emergency calls were very rare at the moment. The enemy were concentrating on other parts of the country now—Canterbury, Exeter, Bath and York had all been heavily attacked—while Londoners enjoyed an uneasy respite, and wondered when it would be their turn again.

When she got home at breakfast-time, Lil went to bed for a few hours, but by midday she was up and about, and often went round to the Watermen to help her parents with the lunch-time trade.

When the phone rang in the office behind the saloon, she answered it. By the time Connor came through from the public bar, she had already rung off.

'Who was it?' he asked. 'A wrong number?'

'Funnily enough, it was for me. Sally's home from Africa—she's coming round to see me.'

'Sally? Oh, you mean Sharon.' Like Ernest, Connor had never quite adjusted to his niece's stage-name.

'Yes, she's on her way over. It'll be nice to see her again.'

Ruth came into the bar and joined them, looking rather troubled. 'Con, I've just been upstairs, giving Father his dinner.'

'What's wrong? Is he off his food?'

'No, he's got a good appetite. But he said he wants to speak to you.'

'Me?' Connor frowned. 'What's he up to now?'

Although Marcus Judge's condition was still

357

improving, and Ruth had told everyone that he was a changed man, Connor could not quite trust this amazing transformation, and rarely visited his father-in-law's room.

'Him and me will never see eye to eye,' he growled. 'It's best I should steer clear of him. Wolves don't change their ways, just because they're in sheep's clothing... Didn't you tell him this is a busy time of day?'

'Please, Con. I'll take over the public while you go up. He seemed quite set on it—as if it was something important.'

Connor shrugged and went upstairs, still grumbling.

Marcus had changed in appearance too. His hair and beard were now quite white, and his face had filled out a little; those piercing, steel-grey eyes had softened, and he peered short-sightedly as Connor entered the room.

'Who's that? Ah, Connor. I hoped you'd come. I know you're a busy man; so I won't keep you long. Just shut the door, will you?'

Warily, Connor obeyed, but he was still suspicious. In the old days he had fought hard enough against the Brotherhood, under the rule of Marcus Judge—and he would not forget that easily.

'Well?' he asked. 'What is it?'

'Bring a chair and sit close by; I don't want to raise my voice.'

Connor remembered when that voice used to boom like a great bell, but again he did as he was told. 'Well?' he repeated.

'I had to send for you. This is a personal

matter—I don't care to discuss it with Ruth. You see, it's about her mother—about my wife.'

Connor caught his breath. This was the last thing he had expected, and he felt a cold chill of apprehension. 'What about her?' he asked cautiously.

'You understand, don't you, that I can't remember things so clearly nowadays? I know I've been here for some time, and Ruth told me my house was bombed, but she has never mentioned her mother—so I must ask you: has Louisa been injured in the bombing? I wondered if perhaps she was in hospital somewhere. Either that, or else she must be dead. Will you please tell me the truth?'

Connor lowered his head, saying quietly, 'I'm very sorry. Yes, your wife is dead.'

As he said these words he crossed himself automatically—and instantly blamed himself for reminding the old man that he was living in a Catholic household, since that had opened up such a chasm between them. But either Marcus did not notice the gesture or he chose to ignore it, because he said simply: 'I thought that must be it. I felt sure that if Louisa were alive, she would be here, helping to look after me. Thank you for telling me. I didn't like to speak to Ruth about it; I was afraid it might upset her.' He clasped his gnarled hands together and closed his eyes, and Connor realised that he was praying. Silently, he got up and left the room.

Downstairs, he found Ruth in the saloon and told her what had happened, finishing: 'I'd never have believed it. You were right—he's a changed man.'

'Do you think I should go to him?' she asked.

'Presently. I fancy he'd sooner be alone for a while.' Connor glanced round the crowded bar. 'Where's Lil gone?'

'She's in the kitchen, talking to Sally. Wait till you see that girl—she's so brown, she looks as if she's been away on holiday.'

The two girls had so much to catch up on, they were both chattering at once. Sally tossed back her blonde curls, perching on the edge of the kitchen table and saying, 'I've brought you back a little bottle of perfume. Don't tell a soul, I smuggled it through the Customs! You'll have to wait for it though, 'cos I haven't even unpacked yet. I felt I must come and see you right away.'

'I'm so glad. I'm dying to hear all about your travels.'

'And I want to hear your news as well,' Sally told her, reaching out to squeeze Lil's hand. 'Mumsie wrote and told me about Mike... Poor old you—I suppose I should have sent a card or something, but I never know what to say about things like that.'

'I know. It was—a shock. But I'm beginning to get over it now.'

'Yes, that's what Mumsie said. I'm so glad. And she tells me Trevor's been a big help, as well?' Sally was still smiling sympathetically, but the temperature in the kitchen had dropped a few degrees.

Lil tried to speak casually. 'Yes, Trevor was

very kind—everybody's been very kind.'

'That's nice. I gather Trevor's been trying to take your mind off it—asking you out—that kind of thing.'

'I've been to see him a few times, if that's what you mean.'

Still wearing that fixed, professional smile, Sally gave her a searching look. 'What I really mean is—are you having an affair with him, by any chance? I'm simply dying to know.'

Lil felt as if her stomach had turned to lead, but she managed to reply calmly enough, 'Of course not! Whatever gave you that idea? I've been over to Acacia Grove twice—and we talked about Mike—things like that...'

'Are you sure he didn't make a pass at you? You swear it?'

'I swear it,' answered Lil. 'He'd never do such a thing.'

'He didn't even try to kiss you?'

'No, he didn't. Sally, he's not like that. You know he isn't.'

Sally laughed. 'That's what you think! He's as sexy as a snake—but I suppose you're just not his type. Anyway, I thought I'd better make sure what's been going on.'

She left a few minutes later, with further protestations of love and friendship, and Lil breathed a sigh of relief. She had told Sally nothing but the truth, yet she had not told her the whole truth. A feeling of guilt, which had never been very far away, swept over her in a flood.

After her last visit to Acacia Grove, she was

afraid she had committed a mortal sin, and had gone to confession at St Anthony's. Kneeling in the semi-darkness of the confessional, seeing the blurred outline of the old priest through the grille, she had tried to list her misdeeds, ending: 'And I let a man see me undressed. I mean—naked.'

'Did you let this man touch you?'

'No, Father. It was only for a moment, and then I got dressed again. Nothing else happened.' She tried to hurry on to the end. 'For these and all other sins I cannot now remember, I ask forgiveness, Father.'

But he broke in: 'Had you been drinking?'

'Yes, Father, but I wouldn't say I was drunk.'

'Drunk enough to forget yourself, by the sound of it. Very well—avoid the occasion of sin another time, and for your penance, say ten Hail Marys.'

And he gave her absolution. Since then, she had not heard from Trevor, and she was determined not to see him again, unless other people were present. But sometimes—when she was lying in bed at night, just before she floated off to sleep—she couldn't help thinking about him.

When Sally left the Watermen, she was thinking about him, too.

Ignoring the gatekeeper, she walked straight through to the Guild administration building at the Jubilee Wharf, much to the amazement of the clerks in the front office.

'I've come to see Trevor Judge,' she said. 'Is he here?'

'Yes, but he's with Mr Bertie. They're waiting for a visitor.'

'That's all right, I'm a visitor,' she said brightly, and sailed on before anyone could stop her, throwing open the door to the inner room.

Astonished, Bertie and Trevor looked up from their desks, and Bertie began to bleat: 'I say, you can't come in here,' but Trevor interrupted him.

'Sally! Welcome home! You've brightened my day.' He turned to Bertie. 'By the way, do you know Sally King?'

Gobbling like a turkey-cock, Bertie managed to say, 'We have met. I believe you were a friend of my brother Jimmy.'

'Such a lovely man—I'll always miss him.' Sally clasped his hand with a sweet, brave smile. 'Divine to see you again.' She turned back to Trevor. 'Darling, I've left all my luggage at Silmour Street. Could you be an angel and help me take it over to Greenwich?'

Bertie chimed in: 'I'm afraid you've caught us at a very busy time, Miss King. We're waiting for the Police Inspector to arrive.'

'Oh dear, have you been naughty?' she asked roguishly.

Unamused, he reproached her. 'It's a very serious matter. One of the warehouses was broken into last night—not for the first time, either. The thieves got away with a lot of imported goods from America—tinned ham, corned beef, chocolates, cosmetics, nylons.'

Smoothly, Trevor managed to stem the flow.

'Perhaps you should go out and wait for the Inspector, Bertie? Then I can have a quiet word with Sally, before he gets here.'

'Oh yes, very well.'

Bertie heaved himself from his swivel chair and toddled out of the office. As soon as the door shut behind him, Sally giggled, 'He's put on so much weight, he looks like a barrage balloon! Give me a kiss, darling—quick.'

Trevor came to meet her. They embraced passionately, but then he broke free, saying, 'Not now—later. You know you're not supposed to come here. We don't encourage visitors.'

'Oh, really? But you do encourage visitors at Acacia Grove, don't you? Lil told me.'

He eyed her speculatively. 'You've already seen Lil?'

'Well, darling, she is my cousin! I called in at the pub to say hello—and she said you've been terribly kind to her.'

He smiled mischievously. 'Are we a tiny bit jealous, perhaps?'

She laughed—a full-throated laugh. 'Of course not! Mind you, if it had been any other girl, I'd be livid—but she told me you never even kissed her. Let's face it, the poor dear's not exactly your style, is she, darling?'

He slapped her bottom. 'You ought to be ashamed of yourself... Now run along—I'll see you tonight.'

'Oh, yes. Tonight you're taking me out to dinner, somewhere very grand and very expensive.'

'Tonight?' He made a helpless gesture at the

piles of paper on his desk. 'Tonight I'm working late. Perhaps tomorrow night.'

'Of all the cheek! Here I am, having flown all the way from the ends of the earth, into your loving arms, and you try and put me off! The work can look after itself; tonight we're going to celebrate.'

'I wish I could, but I do have an appointment tonight. I've arranged to meet somebody.'

'What's her name?'

He chuckled. 'His name's Henry, and he's a solid, respectable estate agent, who's trying to help me find some new warehouse premises and storage space. I've got to meet him—I can't get out of it now.'

'Fine. I'll come with you, and when you've seen your beastly warehouses, we'll go on to the West End and have dinner—all right?'

'Well...'

As he hesitated, she went on, 'Because if you don't I shall go straight to Piccadilly Circus and get picked up by one of those glamorous American officers I've heard so much about. They say there's a wonderful place called Rainbow Corner—and I've always wanted to go over the rainbow. But it's entirely up to you, darling.'

'All right,' he said at last. 'You win.'

That evening, after he had transported Sally and her luggage to Acacia Grove, and she had bathed and changed, they set out again. He told her he had arranged to meet the estate agent at a possible site in Stepney.

'Not a very pleasant neighbourhood. There's

365

some unsavoury characters around these days, so I think you'd better stay in the car, but I shouldn't be more than ten minutes or so.'

As they drove through the East End in the fading light of an April evening, Sally said, 'When I got into London this morning, I went straight to Charing Cross Road, but the people on the second floor said they hardly ever see you these days. You must have been spending an awful lot of time at Greenwich.'

'I have. We're working flat out at the Wharf. I've really got my work cut out to keep up with it.'

'But what about your own business? Why aren't you putting on shows? Everybody says the theatres are packing them in these days.'

'Sweetheart, for every hit there are half a dozen flops. Show business has always been risky, and the way things are now, it's more of a gamble than ever. But at Jubilee Wharf we're making money hand over fist. The theatre can wait —I'm on to a sure thing now.'

She pouted. 'That's all very well, but what about me? What about my career?'

'ENSA's still keeping you busy, isn't it?'

'Well, yes, they're sending me out on another tour very soon, but—'

'That's fine; let's leave things as they are for the moment. Believe me, I know what I'm doing.'

She sighed. Her dreams of a starring role in a West End revue seemed to be as far away as ever, and when Trevor stopped the car by a huge bomb-site, her heart sank still further. Across a wasteland of bricks and rubble and churned-up mud, a railway viaduct had somehow survived, undamaged. Huddling beneath its shadow was a fenced-off yard with a notice painted on a board: *Second-hand Cars Our Speciality—Best Prices—Also Scrap Metal.*

'This is where you're meeting the man?' she asked. 'There aren't any warehouses here.'

'There's plenty of storage space underneath those arches—and beggars can't be choosers,' he said, getting out of the car. 'Now you stay put. I'll be as quick as I can.'

She sat and waited. The sun had gone down—soon it would be getting dark. She didn't like the look of this place at all. Trevor must be mad to think he could store anything in a dump like this... She became more and more impatient; it seemed to be a very long ten minutes. At last she couldn't stand it any longer, and got out of the car.

Stumbling through the twilight, she picked her way over broken bricks and twisted girders, past the scrapyard, until the railway arches towered above her. She heard a low murmur of voices, and saw a tiny glimmer of light between the planks of the tall wooden doors. Putting her eye to the crack, she looked inside.

Trevor and a rough-looking individual in greasy dungarees were talking about money; the stranger didn't look like a respectable estate agent—he had a ragged moustache and a broken nose, and was counting off notes from a thick wad of fivers. Trevor took the money and tucked it into his wallet—and then Sally realised that the two men were surrounded by boxes and packing-cases. Some of them had been opened, and some had their contents printed on the sides—tinned ham and corned beef from the USA, chocolates, cosmetics, nylons...

Quietly and carefully, she retreated, crossing the wasteland again and getting back into the car. Trevor did not return for some time, but she didn't care about that now—she had too much to think about.

At last he rejoined her, slamming the car door and saying cheerfully, 'Well, that's that! Away we go.' The car backed, turned, and headed for the West End.

'Was it any good?' asked Sally innocently.

'Was what any good?'

'The warehouse. Will you be able to use it?'

'Oh, I shouldn't think so—not enough space. By the way,' he dug into an inside pocket and produced a cellophane-wrapped package which he dropped into her lap. 'A coming-home present for a good girl.'

She knew immediately what it was. 'Nylons! Where did you get them?'

'I just ran into an American officer who'd come all the way from Rainbow Corner, looking for you. He asked me to give you these—as a surprise present.'

'Oh, Trevor.' She snuggled closer to him. 'You're just full of surprises.'

Throughout the summer, Sally lived with Trevor at Acacia Grove. From time to time she went off on her travels, as ENSA sent her on a tour of military bases around Britain, but between trips she came back to Greenwich, where she shared a bedroom with Trevor, to their mutual satisfaction.

One Sunday afternoon in October they were lying on the bed, recovering after a long and deliciously exhausting bout, when the doorbell rang.

'Who the hell's that?' asked Sally. 'You're not expecting anyone, are you?'

'Certainly not.' He picked up his watch from the bedside table. 'Half-past three... Funny time for callers.'

'Take no notice, and they'll go away.' Sally rolled over, draping one leg across his body. 'Probably somebody selling something.'

'Not very likely, on a Sunday.'

'Forget it,' she whispered, and began to caress his thigh, but after a moment the doorbell rang again.

Trevor wriggled free, swinging his legs off the bed. 'I'd better find out who it is.'

'Trevor!' she protested. 'Don't be silly. Come back here.'

But he was already pulling on his dressing-gown and tying the belt. 'It could be something to do with the Wharf. I ought to make sure.' Smoothing his hair, he ran downstairs and opened the front door.

'Oh, good afternoon.' Rosie Kleiber looked very embarrassed. 'I'm so sorry—did I wake you?'

'Oh no, not at all. I was just changing,' Trevor told her glibly. 'I'm going out presently, so I

369

decided I must put a suit on. You know what it's like on a Sunday—slopping around the house in your oldest clothes.' He stood back. 'Do come in, won't you?'

'Well, if you're sure I'm not being a nuisance. I just looked in on the off-chance Sally might be here. I haven't seen her lately.'

'Yes, she's upstairs. I think she's been—um—having a bath. I'll just call her.'

Trevor went up to the half-landing and called out, 'Sally, it's your mother. I told her you were in the bath. You won't be long, will you?'

There was a frozen pause, then Sally's startled voice replied, 'No—I'm out of the bath, actually. I'll be down in two ticks.'

Trevor led Rosie into the living-room. 'Do sit down. Can I get you a drink? Or would you prefer a cup of tea?'

'Nothing for me, thanks, I'm not stopping. But Ernest's on duty at the Warden Post, and it was such a lovely afternoon I decided to go for a walk—so I came across to Greenwich Park, and as I was passing the end of the road I thought—why not come in and say hello?'

'I'm glad you did. As a matter of fact, I've had you on my conscience. I'm afraid I've fallen behind with the rent. I know we agreed I should pay you monthly, but I believe the last cheque I sent was in August.'

'Oh, I hope you don't think that's why I...I wasn't at all worried about the rent. Goodness me, we know you won't do a moonlight flit!'

'All the same, it's wrong of me to keep you

waiting for it. Hang on, while I go and find my chequebook.'

Halfway up the stairs he met Sally on her way down, still buttoning her dress, and she mouthed at him frantically, 'Do I look all right?' When he nodded, she continued down the last flight and hurried into the living-room, where she kissed her mother fondly.

Again, Rosie explained how she had just dropped in on the spur of the moment. 'We don't seem to have seen you for ages, and to be honest, I was rather curious to see how the house is looking these days. I haven't seen it since Trevor moved in.'

Sally took her mother on a guided tour of the ground floor, but did not suggest going upstairs. Rosie admired everything, saying: 'Such a change from the way it was when my poor mother was alive; everything's so nice and new-looking.' When Trevor rejoined them, a little breathless in a smart grey suit, she congratulated him. 'You've both done wonders with this place, you have really. I do like your furniture; you've got some lovely pieces.'

'Hadn't you seen it before?' He smote his forehead. 'That's terrible. You and Mr Kleiber must come over to dinner one evening, mustn't they, Sally?'

'That's right.' Eager to demonstrate that they had nothing to hide, Sally rattled on, 'Come any time you like—come this evening.'

'That's very good of you, dear, but we couldn't manage tonight. We've got Gloria and Huw coming round to supper... I'd invite you

371

both to come and join us, but there's only the one fish pie, and it's on the small side, so...'

Trevor hastened to reassure her. 'In any case, I'm not free myself this evening.' He turned to Sally. 'Didn't I tell you? I'm going out later on—I've promised to meet Bertie at the office. We've got the auditors coming in tomorrow so I have to make sure the books are up to date.'

'Oh Trevor, you might have said!' Sally began indignantly, but her mother broke in.

'Well, if you're going to be on your own, Sally, why don't you come over? I'm sure I can stretch the fish pie to one more helping... And if you finish work early, Trevor, you could join us later, perhaps? I know your Auntie Gloria would be pleased to see you.'

Half an hour later, when Rosie left them —still refusing all offers of tea or any other refreshments—Sally flopped on to the sofa, groaning, 'At last...I thought she'd never go.'

Trevor wagged a reproving finger. 'You're a bad, ungrateful child. You don't deserve to have such a lovely mother.'

'Oh, Mumsie's all right really—but having to be bright and sociable was such a strain. I kept wondering how I'd head her off if she decided to go and inspect the bedrooms!'

'I think she probably has a shrewd idea of the situation, don't you? She's very understanding.'

'Hypocrite!' Sally lay back along the sofa and held out her arms. 'You know very well you were just dying for her to go. Come here and do some unspeakable things to me.'

He shook his head. 'I haven't got time. I told

you, I'm going out soon.'

'What?' Sally sat up indignantly. 'I thought you were just saying that to get rid of her.'

'Certainly not. I really do have to go to the office—I must make sure the paperwork's all up to date. If they find any mistakes, the auditors will say we've been cooking the books.'

'Will they indeed? Yes—I suppose you do have to be careful,' cooed Sally. 'Not to get found out, I mean.'

Walking to the mirror above the drinks cabinet, Trevor knotted his tie a little more carefully, asking, 'What do you mean exactly?'

'Well, they might get suspicious if they knew just how much money you've really been making. You must be simply rolling in it by now. I bet you could buy me a beautiful diamond ring, and never even notice it.'

'The Wharf's doing very well at the moment, but that doesn't mean I've got money to throw away on diamonds,' he told her. 'The Company don't pay me that kind of salary.'

Looking in the mirror, his eyes met hers. She smiled back, teasing him. 'I'm not talking about your salary—I was thinking of what you make on the side,' she said.

When he had finished retying his tie, he turned to face her. 'I haven't the remotest idea what you're talking about.'

'Oh, darling—I wasn't born yesterday. What about all those boxes you had hidden under the railway arches? All the stuff that was supposed to have been stolen from your warehouse? How much did you make on that little deal?'

He crossed the room and stood over her, looking down with a faint smile. 'Are you suggesting I've been robbing my own firm?'

'Of course not—you didn't steal it yourself. I expect you arranged things so the crooks could break in, then they cut you in on the deal afterwards. And like you said, the Company was covered by the insurance, so everything in the garden's lovely, isn't it?'

He put his hand under her chin, tilting her face up and studying it. 'What a clever girl you are—and so observant. I wondered at the time how you knew right away there were nylons in that packet, when it was too dark to see in the car. So what do you intend to do about it?'

'Don't be silly—I'm not going to do a thing. If I'd felt like that about it, I'd have gone to the police ages ago. Besides, it's only the black market—everybody does a bit of that nowadays. Don't worry, angel, your secret is safe with me.' Then she caught his hand in hers, turning it over and tickling his palm. 'Actually, I would rather like a diamond ring...just a teeny one?'

On the other side of the Thames, the O'Dells were having a family celebration. Although the pub was shut for its afternoon break, a home-made banner hung from the upper windows, bearing the message: *Welcome Home, Sergeant!*

In the kitchen, Connor slapped Dan on the back, his mother kissed him and his grandmother wiped away a few proud tears, as they all congratulated Sergeant O'Dell on his well-earned promotion.

374

Kaff grabbed Dan's hand and said, 'Lil helped me make the banner. You didn't mind, did you?'

'Of course not, though maybe you should take it down before opening-time,' Dan grinned. 'When the customers come rolling in, they might think I'd won the war single-handed.'

Lil touched the three stripes on the sleeve. 'What's it like, being a Sergeant?'

'A big improvement. I've got a room of my own, and proper cooked meals in the Mess, and we've got our own bar and our own dartboard!' he told her.

'They must be very pleased with you,' Ruth said, hugging her son again. 'You got promoted so quickly.'

'What do you mean, quickly? I've been in the Army three years, Mum—it feels like a lifetime to me!'

'We think of it as an honour, son,' said Con. 'Not every man gets three stripes on his arm.'

'Well, I suppose that's true. Poor old Matt's a bit sick about it. He's still only a Lancejack, and to make things worse, he didn't get leave this time either.' Dan looked round the family group. 'I must say it's good to be home again. How's Grandfather, still making progress?'

Lil said, 'I just took him up some tea. I told him we were expecting you, and I'm sure he'd like to see you—why don't you go up?'

'Right you are...' Dan hesitated, then asked his sister, 'Will you come with me? I haven't got used to the old man being here. I still feel a bit awkward with him.'

So they went upstairs together, and Lil opened the door, saying, 'Look who's come to see you!'

'Who's that?' Marcus poked his head forward like an old tortoise. 'Is it Daniel?'

'You have to call him Sergeant Daniel now—he's had a promotion.'

Marcus shook Dan's hand and told him he was a good boy. 'You'll go far—I always thought so. I remember once, you came to my house and told me you were going to join the Brotherhood. That was you, wasn't it? Or am I mixing you up with somebody else?'

'No, that was me—though I don't think you were too pleased about it at the time.'

'Wasn't I?' Baffled, the old man shook his head. 'I'm sure I can't think why. But it was a long time ago. You were a good worker, I know that much. Who's in charge of the Brotherhood now, Daniel? Can you tell me?'

'It's Uncle Bertie, Grandfather.'

'*Bertie?*' Marcus' face changed, as if a shadow had passed across it, and they saw a brief glimpse of the Old Testament patriarch. 'That shouldn't be. The boy's a numskull... Why isn't his brother James in charge? And what's happened to their father? What's become of Joshua?'

'Joshua's gone, Grandfather—and so has Jimmy. They were both killed,' said Dan gently.

'Ah. So they were, so they were... So many of my boys are gone now, I keep forgetting.' Then he gave Dan a sidelong glance. 'I hope, when this war's over, you'll come back to us and take Bertie's place—*my* place—at the head of the Guild, eh?'

Dan could not tell him he had already left the Guild, sickened by its ruthless methods, even before the war had begun. Releasing his grandfather's hand, he said, 'I must go down and have my tea. I'll come and talk to you again, another time.'

When they left the room, Lil said, 'That was nice of you. I'm sure you must be dying for something to eat.'

She started to go ahead of him, down the stairs, but he stopped her. 'Just a minute. Before we go back to the others, I wanted a word with you on your own.'

'Oh? What's the matter?'

'It's Kaff. I'm a bit worried. Did you know she's been writing to me?'

'Yes, of course—she hasn't made a secret of it. And you write back to her, don't you? She's always so thrilled when she gets one of your letters.'

Dan sighed. 'I never know what to say when I write. I try and find things to tell her—things I've seen and done—ordinary, everyday sort of things... But her letters are different. She writes about the way she feels—and about me. They're almost like—I know this sounds silly, because she's only fourteen, but—they're like love-letters.'

Lil smiled. 'She's nearly fifteen. And you should be very flattered.'

'But what am I supposed to do about it? It's embarrassing.'

'Just carry on the way you are. Write back nice, friendly letters—that's all she wants. It's just a part of growing up—a phase she's going through. She'll soon grow out of it.'

Florrie Judge was making sandwiches in the kitchen at Denmark Place when she heard a faint rattling noise. She stopped smearing the bread with margarine and listened—what was that? Hearing nothing more, she decided it must have been a gust of wind shaking the letter-box, and continued to slice the loaf. She didn't know for sure what time Bertie would be coming home, but she prided herself on having a meal ready for him whenever he came in—even if it was only potted meat-paste sandwiches.

Then she heard the noise again, and realised that someone was clattering the door-knocker, very softly. Angrily, she put down the bread-knife and went along the passage. If this was some boy's idea of a joke, she'd give him a piece of her mind.

By now it was quite dark outside, and when she opened the door, a burly figure seemed to fill the frame, startling her. She gasped. 'Who's that? What do you want?'

A voice with a marked American accent said quietly, 'It's me—Tommy. Is it OK if I come in?'

Feeling stunned, and powerless to stop him, she shrank back against the hall-stand. He walked in, carrying a large cardboard box, and went straight through to the kitchen. She followed him, complaining in a whisper: 'What do you mean by it? You've no business walking in like this—you're not welcome here.'

'I guess not—but I had to see you, Mum.' Putting the box down on the kitchen table, he turned to face her, and she gasped again. She had not expected that he would be in uniform—the tailored, olive-green jacket and beige slacks of an American Army officer.

He took off his peaked cap and dropped that on the table as well. Still dazed from the shock of seeing him, she could think of nothing to say except: 'You had a beard last time... Your hair's going grey...'

'It happens to the best of us! Didn't you know I was forty, last birthday?'

'I hadn't forgotten,' she said bitterly. 'So you're a soldier now—an officer.'

'Colonel Timothy Jackson—that's the name on my records. Tommy Judge to you.'

Despite herself, she couldn't help feeling a glow of pride, but she went on grumbling, 'Gave me the fright of my life, pushing in like that. Rattling the knocker in that sneaky way put the wind up me...'

'I remember what the neighbours are like around here,' he said, with the hint of a smile. 'If I'd hammered on the door, there'd have been half the street peeping out through their lace curtains. I don't want anyone to see me.'

'No, well, I'm not surprised, after what happened... How you've got the nerve to show your face at all, I don't know.'

'You mean Maudie? We've done nothing to be ashamed of. She's Mrs Maudie Jackson now—I married her as soon as we got settled over there. I suppose in your eyes that makes her a criminal too—a bigamist.'

'Not any more,' Florrie admitted reluctantly. 'Joshua died, not so long after, but that don't excuse what you did. You're still a wanted man—wanted for murder!'

'It wasn't murder, it was self-defence,' he said wearily. 'I never meant to kill Saul Judge. He was trying to throttle me and I—'

'You should have said all that in court, if you're innocent,' she cut in. 'By rights I ought to hand you over to the law. I dare say there's still a warrant out for you.'

'After twenty-three years? I thought I'd risk that. Well, I had to come and find out how you were getting on. We've heard so much about London on the radio—the bombing and all. I wasn't even sure you'd still be here. And they say food's in short supply as well, that's why I brought you a parcel from the PX—tinned meat and eggs, butter—all kinds of stuff.'

Florrie's eyes widened, fixed upon the cardboard box. 'You brought all that—for me?'

'Sure. I reckoned you might be needing it.'

'Yes, we do.' Her tone softened. 'You'd better sit down. There's been a lot happening since you was here last... Do you fancy a cup of tea?'

Over the tea-cups, she told him the family news. They were so absorbed in their conversation, they did not hear the front door open again. When Bertie walked in, followed by Trevor, they both stopped and stared at Florrie's visitor.

She scrambled to her feet. 'Oh, Bertie. I don't know if you remember Colonel Jackson...'

Bertie's plump mouth sagged. 'Yes,' he said. 'I remember.'

'He's brought us a present—a food parcel. Very good of him, wasn't it?' Florrie went on quickly, 'Perhaps we'd better open it right away. I've only made you sandwiches, Bertie—you never said you'd be bringing Trevor back with you.'

Slowly, Tommy stood up. Ignoring Bertie, he stared at Trevor like a man in a dream. 'You... you're Trevor?' he asked.

Trevor realised that something very strange was going on, but could not understand it. The others seemed to have some secret knowledge that excluded him, and he didn't like that at all.

'Colonel Jackson?' he repeated. 'I don't think I've had the pleasure.'

'That's not his real name,' said Bertie, and turned back to Tommy. 'Last time you were here, you had a beard.'

'Right! I had to shave it off when I enlisted,' explained Tommy. 'Army regulations.'

'That's why I didn't know you then—but I recognise you now, Tommy.'

'Tommy?' Trevor stiffened. He had begun to hold out his hand, but now he stopped, frozen. 'You're—Tommy Judge?'

'I used to be,' said Tommy, taking Trevor's outstretched hand. 'You've grown up to be a fine young man, Trev. Your mother will be very glad when I tell her. Of course, you won't

381

remember me, but I knew you when you were just a little kid.'

'But I do remember you,' said Trevor, as they shook hands. 'You used to give me chocolates... You're the man who ran off with my mother.'

'I'm sure that's quite enough of that.' Florrie tried to break in. 'Why don't we all sit down? There's plenty of tea in the pot. It won't take me a minute to put out some more cups.'

But the men weren't listening. Tommy was saying: 'I married her, Trevor. Do you want to see her picture? I carry it everywhere I go.'

He pulled a snapshot from his wallet and showed it to Trevor; a small woman, with greying curls and big, dark eyes. After a moment, Trevor handed it back, saying politely, 'Yes—I remember her very well. Thank you for showing me. I just wish she'd sent me a photo as well.'

Realising he was hurt, Tommy hastened to say, 'She would have done—if we'd known where you were. Don't forget, you'd already left home, Trev. It took her a long while to get over that.'

'Still, she got over it in the end, didn't she? I hope you'll give her my best wishes, next time you write.'

Florrie was fussing round the table, pulling out chairs and setting knives and forks, saying, 'Tommy, I'll let you open the parcel, then we can all have something to eat.'

The moment of awkwardness passed; the three men settled down and began talking to each other in a friendlier manner. Even Trevor was looking more cheerful. Now he knew what the situation was, he felt a lot better. The pieces of the jigsaw were coming together—soon he would be in control again.

He glanced at his wristwatch, remarking, 'I mustn't stay long. I said I'd call in at the Kleibers on my way back, to pick up Sally.'

'The Kleibers?' Florrie looked anxious. 'You won't say anything to them about Tommy being here? If it ever got back to that Gloria... Well, you know what I mean.'

'Don't worry, I won't breathe a word to the Kleibers.'

Suddenly Trevor smiled—a brilliant smile, as the last piece of the jigsaw clicked into place. Gloria—of course! He clasped his hands together, like a gambler who has just seen his horse come in at twenty to one, then turned to Tommy and said: 'But their daughter Sally is a very good friend of mine—and she's been dying to meet an American officer. I promise I won't tell them who you are—why don't you come with me?'

12

As Trevor drove across the Island on the way to Silmour Street, Tommy Judge peered out of the car windows. The hooded headlamps did not give out much light, and it was hard to see very far in the darkness, but he managed to identify one or two landmarks.

'There's the gateway to the Wharf—I remember that all right,' he said. 'And we used to go down that road on Sunday mornings, on our way to Chapel. Is the old Emmanuel still surviving?'

'Yes, it's still there,' said Trevor.

'I guess the Almighty kept an eye on His own, huh?'

'He hasn't always been so protective about His property. Remember St Cuthbert's, in West Ferry Road? That went in the very first raid, back in 1940.'

'Wow...' Tommy screwed up his eyes, trying to penetrate the blackness. 'I couldn't believe it when I was walking to Denmark Place—so many buildings gone, I could hardly find my way. And Mum tells me the Rope Walk was pretty well wiped out. It's even worse than I'd imagined, and it's not just the damage, either. The thing I remember best is the people—there were always people on the streets, no matter what time of day. Now there's hardly a soul around.'

'Some of them are dead, some have been evacuated—and some of them just cut and run,' Trevor told him. 'In the last two years, the population's gone down by almost half.'

'It's like a ghost town—that's what they'd call it, out West.' Tommy shook his head, trying to come to terms with this. He remained silent for a few moments, but as they approached Cubitt Town he asked, 'This place you're taking me—did you say the folks are called Kleiber? Would they be any kin to Israel Kleiber?'

'Izzy Kleiber was Ernest's brother.' Trevor glanced curiously at his passenger. 'Why, do you know them?'

'I know of them. That's to say, I knew a little about them, no more than that.'

In the sitting-room above the photographic shop, the conversation had also touched upon the declining population of the Island. Ernest was saying: 'And there's no money about, either. If things don't get any better, I shall have to think about closing the shop.'

'Oh, surely not!' exclaimed Glory. 'You've always done so well here.'

Ernest shrugged, spreading his hands wide. 'How can you argue with the facts and figures? Each month when I make up the accounts, the profits are smaller. Soon I'll be running the shop at a loss.'

'What's the reason for that?' asked Huw. 'Don't people want to take pictures any more?'

'There's a shortage of film-stock; most of it goes straight to the Air Force, to take photographs over enemy territory. And anyway, the people who still live around these parts aren't often in the mood for taking snapshots! No, the sensible thing would be for me to cut my losses, shut up shop, and concentrate on taking wedding-groups and bar mitzvahs, by appointment.'

'You could take some more publicity shots for me, Poppa,' suggested Sally, who was sitting on a cushion by the fireplace, as close to the one-bar electric fire as possible. 'I don't care what Trevor says—it's time I sent some photos round the managements again. I'm getting sick and tired of doing troop concerts.'

The clock on the mantelpiece began to chime and Rosie said, 'There now, nine o'clock already! If we're going to have a game of Rummy, we'd better get the cards out or it'll be too late. Sally, how about you? Would you like to play?'

She yawned. 'No, I hate cards. You go ahead if you want to. I expect Trevor will come for me soon.'

So they pulled their chairs up to the table, and Ernest began to deal. Before they had played the first hand, Sally heard a car draw up outside.

'There he is now. Don't let me break up the party; I'll go down.'

'Oh, don't run away!' said Rosie. 'Perhaps Trevor would like to come up and say hello. You can make some coffee for us all, can't you?'

'I don't know if he'll want to.' Sally hovered in the doorway. 'He'll probably be tired.'

'It won't hurt him to look in for two ticks. I'm sure you'd like to see your nephew, wouldn't you, Glory?'

'I don't mind,' said Glory, still sorting the cards she held. 'It's up to him, isn't it?'

'We'd all like to see him—very much,' Rosie concluded firmly. 'You tell him that.'

They carried on playing while Sally went downstairs. There was a mutter of voices from below then she returned, looking rather puzzled.

'He's brought a friend with him. Do come in, Colonel—oh, I'm sorry, I've forgotten your name already.'

They all looked up in surprise as an American officer followed Sally into the room and Trevor, beside him, began to say: 'Good evening, Mrs Kleiber—Mr Kleiber. I'm sorry, I didn't realise you had company. May I introduce—'

But he was interrupted. Gloria drew a shuddering breath, then said hoarsely, 'Oh, my God. It can't be...'

The colour drained from her face, and Rosie went to her at once, asking, 'What's the matter? Are you ill?'

'No.' Glory never took her eyes from the newcomer, forcing the words out as if she were in physical pain. 'You don't have to introduce him. I know who he is...'

For a moment no one moved. Tommy stood quite still, looking at her, then said: 'I've been running away from this moment for more than twenty-three years... I guess it's time to stop running.'

At his shoulder, Trevor began apologising profusely. 'I had no idea. What can I say?'

'You weren't to know.' Tommy took a step toward the card-players, who stared at him, dumbfounded. 'I don't suppose it means anything after all this time, Glory, but I'd still like to tell you...I'm sorry.'

Looking from one to the other, Sally broke in: 'What is all this? What's going on?'

'Don't you know? Don't any of you know?' Gloria was beginning to get her breath back, but her face was still as white as death. 'This is Tommy Judge... The man who killed my husband.'

Rosie gave a little moan, and Sally turned to Trevor, asking, 'What does she mean? I don't understand.'

'I think it's time I took you home,' Trevor said quickly. 'It's nothing to do with us—better leave them to sort it out.'

'But I want to know what's happening...'

He gripped her arm, leading her out on to the landing. 'I'll explain later—come on.'

In the sitting-room, they all began to talk at once, but Glory's voice rose above the others. 'Isn't anyone going to send for the police? Or do I have to do it? Huw—don't let him get away!'

Uncertainly, Huw moved towards Tommy, who said in a tired voice, 'You don't have to worry, I'm not going anywhere. Call the cops if you want.'

Rosie turned to Ernest automatically. 'You'd better phone the police, dear.' She spoke to the others reassuringly. 'Don't worry—Ernest will do what's right.'

But Ernest was still gazing into Tommy's face. 'All in good time,' he said. 'Before we do anything else, I want to hear what he has to say.'

'What is there to say?' exclaimed Glory impatiently. 'We know what he did! I was there when the police found Saul—with the blood soaking through his shirt and that steel claw sticking into his heart!'

'I know.' Ernest put his hand on Gloria's shoulder, trying to soothe her. 'It was terrible for you—but we should listen to his side of the story.' He indicated the empty chair, vacated by Huw, and invited Tommy to sit down. 'Please...'

Slowly, Tommy obeyed. 'It all started a long time before that night,' he began, 'five years earlier, when another man died...Israel Kleiber.'

'So that's it.' Ernest sighed. 'Of course—it all goes back to the Brotherhood, doesn't it?'

Listening, Huw's face darkened, but he said nothing as Tommy continued.

'Israel Kleiber was punished because he talked too much, but the punishment went wrong—he was drowned. My father and my Uncle Josh were involved; they had to make it look like an accident, and so they called in Saul Judge to hide the body. He had to pretend to find it a few weeks later. By that time there would be no marks on it to point to foul play. They gave Saul some money to keep his mouth shut, and so he did for a while but eventually, when he was strapped for cash, he put the bite on my dad again.'

Gloria put her hand to her mouth, and Tommy said to her, 'Maybe you didn't know about that?'

She shook her head, unable to speak, and he nodded. 'Yeah—well, that's how it was. Saul threatened to go to the police with the truth unless Dad paid up. He went on blackmailing him. By then Dad was a sick man, and short of money himself. I found out what was going on, so I went to Saul that night—it was Boxing Day, and you'd taken young Matt to tea with

Aunt Emily and Maudie, at Millwall Road... I thought I could persuade Saul to lay off, to go easy on my dad, but he wouldn't listen. He lost his temper and grabbed hold of me—I was only sixteen, and he had his hands round my windpipe—I thought I was a goner. I pulled the steel claw out of my pocket—'

'Claw?' Rosie looked blank. 'What's that?'

Huw said quietly, 'The tool of the docker's trade—we all had one.'

'It was in my hand. I was trying to defend myself—that's how it happened.' Tommy stopped, remembering the scene; he had relived that moment in his mind a thousand times. Pulling himself together, he went on: 'I know I should have gone to the police right then, but how could I tell them my story without dragging Dad and Josh into it? That's why I ran away. I got taken on by a merchant ship sailing to America that same night, and—well, you know the rest... OK—make your phone-call. Maybe it's for the best. Dad and Josh are both gone; it can't hurt them any longer. Go ahead.'

There was a very long silence. Then Ernest turned to Gloria. 'Well?' he said. 'What do you want me to do?'

She shook her head. The make-up on her white face looked like a clown's mask; a tear trickled down her cheek, leaving a trail of mascara. Shock and grief had betrayed her, exposing her real age.

'Don't do anything,' she said. 'Just leave it... Take me home, Huw.'

He helped her from her chair, putting his arm

around her. In the doorway, she turned to say goodnight to Ernest and Rosie, then addressed Tommy for the last time.

'No, I didn't know about it—and I wish you'd never told me. But when you go back to America, give Maudie my love.'

Ernest followed them downstairs, to see them out. When he came back to the sitting-room, he found Rosie pouring out three small tots of brandy. She told Tommy, 'We keep a little by us, for emergencies. I think we could all do with a drop.'

Ernest raised his glass to Tommy. 'I always suspected that the Brotherhood were responsible for Izzy's death—and now I know it. Thank you for that.'

When he had tasted the brandy, Tommy asked, 'Are the Brotherhood still as powerful around here?'

'I think not. Times have changed. The docks are busier than ever, but that evil influence they used to have—no, that's all in the past. Such wickedness does not happen these days, and I thank God for it.'

'I'll drink to that,' said Tommy.

At Acacia Grove, Trevor and Sally were already in bed. He pulled her towards him, drawing his hands over her body, but she tried to draw away.

'No, not tonight—I don't feel in the mood. And I don't know how you can, either, after what happened. It's upset me, just hearing about it.'

'You're such a sensitive soul,' he teased

her, and continued to explore her with his fingertips. 'And especially sensitive, just about *there.*'

'Oh, don't—I said *no,* Trevor! It was so dreadful, Gloria Judge being there like that, coming face to face with the man who murdered her husband. And what made it even worse, he seemed rather nice—didn't you think so? Quite good-looking, really.'

'I might have guessed you'd find him attractive. You just can't resist that American uniform, can you? I suppose he's more attractive than I am?'

He was still caressing her, and she began to melt a little. 'You're attractive too, in a different way. You're wicked, that's what you are.' Then another thought occurred to her, and she said in a different tone, 'One thing I don't understand. You said you didn't know they'd got company tonight, but Mumsie told us Gloria would be there—don't you remember?'

Laughing, he threw himself upon her, but she persisted. 'You did know, didn't you? You knew all along—I believe you brought him there deliberately!'

'Yes, it all worked out very well, didn't it?' Trevor was exultant. 'And I sincerely hope he gets what's coming to him. With any luck, he'll be at the police station right now. It's going to come as a big surprise for my mother, when they write and tell her he's been arrested.'

'Oh, that's an awful thing to say. Your own mother! Like I said, you can be really wicked sometimes.' Then she gasped: 'No, Trevor, not like that—not so fast! Oh, Trevor! You're always so impatient...'

In another bedroom, far less luxurious, Gloria lay in Huw's arms. They were not making love; he was trying to comfort her, but she sobbed uncontrollably.

'I can't bear it. I thought it was all over, yet tonight, seeing him like that, it brought it all back as if it was only yesterday.'

'I know. It's the shock—you're bound to feel like this at first. It was just bad luck, him walking in with Trevor Judge when you happened to be there—a one-in-a-million chance. But you'll soon get over it, I promise you will.'

'It's not only the shock.' She tried to explain. 'It was finding out all the things that had been going on—about Ernest's brother, about Eb and Josh—things I never knew. And the worst thing of all was that I couldn't have believed Saul would do such a thing...blackmailing Eb like that.'

'It might not have been that bad. If he was really hard up, he probably turned to his cousin to help him out. It might not have been blackmail.'

'It was—I know it was. Oh yes, we were stony broke—no question about that. We didn't know where our next meal was coming from, and I had Matt to feed as well—he was only a baby then... But I remember the night Saul brought home all the food, and the money. He said he'd had a bit of luck, and I can still see the look on his face when he slapped

393

a handful of notes down on the table and said: *"There's much more where that came from, much more"*. Triumphant—that's how he looked. He was lying to me, Huw. He was ashamed to tell me the truth.'

He stroked her hair, saying softly, 'Try not to think about it. It is all over now, over and done with.'

'How do I know it's over?' She raised herself up on one elbow, gazing into the darkness of the room as if she were trying to see a long way back in time. 'How do I know what else he was ashamed to tell me? How many more secrets was he hiding?'

During his week's leave, Dan was perfectly friendly towards Kaff, but took care to avoid any situations where he might find himself alone with her. She tried several times to get him on his own, until she realised he was dodging her; after that she kept out of his way.

On his last day, Dan packed his bag and went around the pub, saying goodbye to everyone.

He began in his grandfather's room. Marcus had been dozing. When Dan sat beside the bed, he opened his eyes and looked at him, mistily confused.

'Who's that? Joshua?'

'No, Grandfather, it's me—Daniel.'

'Oh yes, now I remember. I think I must have been dreaming... It's good to see you, my boy. Are you home on leave again?'

Gently, Daniel corrected him. 'I've been home for a week; I'm going back today. I just came to say goodbye to you.'

'Of course. You must excuse me, my memory isn't what it was.' Marcus touched the rough khaki material of Dan's tunic, tracing the outline of the three stripes on his sleeve. 'Now I remember—they've made you a sergeant. But I expect you're looking forward to the end of the war, when you can come back to your old job, eh? Leaving the Army, to rejoin the Brotherhood?'

Dan tried to ease away from him, saying, 'I really haven't got time to talk about it now but I'll see you again, next time I get some leave.'

The old man clung to his arm, his bony fingers surprisingly strong. 'Don't forget what I told you: I expect you to be running the Guild some day. Bertie's not the right man for the job. I shan't be happy till you take his place.'

Realising he could not evade the truth for ever, Dan said quietly, 'I'm sorry, Grandfather, but that's impossible. I'd already left the Brotherhood before the war started. I got a job as an apprentice Dock Engineer at the Royal Vic and when I'm demobbed, I'll be going back there.'

Dismayed, Marcus loosened his hold, and as Dan stood up he asked: 'You left the Brotherhood? Why wasn't I told? You could have had a golden future if you'd stayed with us. What made you do such a thing?'

Dan hesitated, but there was no point in raking up the past. Instead he said simply, 'I felt I needed a change. Look, I really have to go now. I've got to be at Waterloo by midday.'

'Yes. Very well. Goodbye, my boy—and God bless you.' Confused and disappointed, the old man watched him leave the room, then fell back into an uneasy sleep.

Downstairs, Dan continued his round of farewells; he found Lil in the saloon bar, stacking the shelves with bottled beer, and hugged her as they said goodbye.

'I'll miss you,' she said. 'Come back soon.'

He studied her face for a moment. 'We haven't had much chance to talk this week. Half the time you're on duty at the Fire Station, and when you're here you're always working. But I suppose it's how you like it; maybe you don't have time to feel lonely.'

Smiling a little sadly, she said, 'Don't I?'

'Sorry, that was stupid of me. Of course you're lonely, bound to be.'

'Yes,' she said. 'I do get a bit lonely, sometimes.'

'Mike was a good bloke. You must miss him a hell of a lot.'

'Yes,' she said again, and turned away, arranging the beer-bottles. How could she tell him it wasn't always Mike she missed and wanted? Sometimes the temptation to pick up the phone and call Trevor was almost unbearable—but she was determined not to give in to it.

Down in the cellar, Connor and Huw were shifting a new delivery of barrels. When Dan joined them he tried to make himself useful.

'Here, let me give you a hand,' he began, but

they spurned his offer.

'D'you think we can't move a few barrels without your help?' his father scoffed. 'We're still fighting fit, the pair of us—isn't that right, Huw?'

'Course we are!' grinned Huw. 'Away with you, lad—back to your cushy Sergeant's Mess, where you get waited on hand and foot. Leave the real work to your elders and betters!'

'Well, I'm certainly not going to waste time arguing with you—I've got a train to catch.'

Connor followed Dan up the cellar steps, as Mary O'Dell and Ruth came out of the kitchen to see him off. He kissed them both, while they made him promise faithfully to take care of himself, and not to do anything dangerous—then he looked round.

'I haven't seen Kaff this morning,' he said. 'I must say goodbye to her. Where is she?'

They searched the pub, but she was nowhere to be found. Then Lil noticed that her coat was missing from the hall-stand pegs, along with the silk scarf Dan had given her for Christmas, and they realised she must have gone out without telling anyone.

'I don't understand it—she knew you were leaving this morning,' said Mary. 'We were talking about it when she was wiping up the breakfast things. I expect she'll be back any moment.'

Dan looked at his watch and said, 'I mustn't miss that train—I'll have to be going. Tell her I'm sorry I couldn't wait.'

Shouldering his kit-bag, he left the pub—and

five minutes later Kaff walked through the side door.

'So there you are!' exclaimed Mary. 'You've missed Danny. You can't have forgotten he was going, surely? Where have you been?'

'Nowhere special,' she said carelessly. 'I felt like going for a walk, that's all. I don't suppose he even noticed I wasn't here.'

'That's where you're wrong—he was looking everywhere. He said to tell you he was sorry he couldn't wait, he particularly wanted to say goodbye.'

'Did he really?' Kaff's face changed, as she made her mind up suddenly. 'How long ago was that?'

'Only a matter of minutes. He had to get a train, you see.'

'Which way did he go? I might catch him if I hurry.' With that, she rushed out of the house and away up the street, running on and on without stopping, past the bomb-sites and the derelict houses. A stray dog ran after her, yapping at her heels, but she ignored it—she was determined to see Dan before he went away.

She found him beside the bus-stop in Poplar High Street. He looked at her in astonishment as she blurted out breathlessly: 'Sorry I missed you. Didn't mean to—wanted to say goodbye...'

He laughed. 'Hey, take it easy. I did try to find you.'

'Yes, your Gran said. I went out—I didn't think you'd want to see me. You took care to keep out of my way, all the week.'

'Oh, come on. That's not true!'

398

'Yes, it is. I suppose you know how I feel about you, don'cher? But you think I'm just a kid. Well, I'm sorry if it embarrasses you, but I can't help the way I feel, can I?'

He put his hands on her shoulders, saying, 'Kaff, I do understand how you feel, but you're still very young, and I'm much too old for you. One of these days you'll meet some chap your own age, and then—'

'I won't!' she retorted fiercely. 'I know I won't. There'll never be anybody like you—never!' She was trying hard to be grown-up, and not to break down and cry, but he saw the tears in her eyes and pulled her closer to him.

'You're a lovely girl, and I'm very fond of you,' he said. 'And I want us to go on being friends—all right?'

'All right.' She sniffed unhappily. 'Is it OK if I go on writing to you?'

'Of course it is.' At the far end of the street, a red double-decker came into view. 'Here comes my bus. We'll talk some more, next time I come home.' Looking into her eyes, he recognised the same desperate loneliness he had seen in Lil, and he added impulsively: 'Tell you what—the next time, I'll take you out somewhere, just the two of us. That's a promise.'

She stared at him incredulously, then a smile spread over her face like the sun breaking through clouds, as she said: 'Oh yeah. I'd like that. I'll look forward to it.'

'So shall I.'

Then the bus drew up, and he climbed aboard. Kaff stayed at the pavement's edge, watching as it moved away, waving until it was out of sight.

By the end of October, Dan was back in the desert with the Eighth Army. When Montgomery took command, three months earlier, he had promised his men that they would knock the Afrika Korps for six—and now they saw to it that the promise was kept. The battle for El Alamein had begun, and within a few days they broke through Rommel's front line. By 4 November, nine thousand German prisoners had been taken, and the remnants of the Axis armies were in full retreat.

On Sunday, 15 November, Britain held a day of rejoicing.

For the first time since the invasion scare of 1940, the bells were rung from chapels, churches and cathedrals throughout the land, celebrating this major victory. At last, it seemed, the tide of war had turned.

In London, the King and Queen attended a service of thanksgiving at St Paul's, and watched a march-past by Civil Defence workers. A thousand firemen, policemen and wardens from all over the country turned out.

When Ernest was asked to send someone from his district, he nominated Connor. At first Con had refused, saying that this sort of thing wasn't his style at all, and suggesting Huw should go in his place—but Huw pointed out that he might look a little conspicuous, limping along and trying to keep in step with the others, and Ruth finally persuaded Con that it was an

400

honour to be asked to take part. When the Brewery Company heard that one of their tenants would be among the marchers, they invited Ruth to watch the parade from their office windows, overlooking Ludgate Hill.

She took Kaff along with her, and though they both felt a little shy among so many strangers—Head Office staff and their families—they forgot to be nervous when the wardens came past, saluting the King and Queen on the steps of St Paul's.

'There he is—there's Mr O'Dell!' shrieked Kaff, waving and cheering.

Ruth tried to cheer too, but there was a lump in her throat. She could not help thinking of all those who had died during the past three years—servicemen and civilians alike—and she wondered how much longer the war would drag on, and how many more would lose their lives before it was over.

But her doubts and fears were drowned out by the sheer volume of noise; the bells pealing, the brass bands playing, and the great waves of cheering from the crowds that lined the pavements.

Back at the pub, Mary O'Dell and Huw had been left in charge, and when they closed for the afternoon, Mary made a pot of tea and poured out three cups, saying, 'The old feller above will be wanting to wet his whistle. Would you take this up to him, there's a dear.'

Huw was tempted to make some excuse. Since Marcus Judge had come to live at the Watermen, he had had nothing to do with the old man. That had not been difficult, for Marcus never left his bed, and Huw never went upstairs—but he could hardly refuse to do as Mrs O'Dell asked without giving her his reasons, and he had no wish to go into that. But anyhow, it had all happened a long while ago, and by now the old man would probably have forgotten him altogether.

'Very well,' he said, and took the cup of tea upstairs. He knocked and went in, murmuring, 'Here's your tea,' and was making for the door again when a voice from the bed stopped him.

'One moment. Who are you? Haven't I seen you before?'

'I work downstairs, in the bar,' Huw replied gruffly. 'Mrs O'Dell asked me to bring your tea—the others are out for the day.'

'Don't run away—come here. Let me have a look at you.'

Reluctantly, Huw obeyed, and Marcus made an effort to focus upon him. At last he said: 'I have seen you somewhere... I feel sure I know that face. Were you employed at the Jubilee Wharf?'

Huw nodded, uncomfortably. 'For a time, I was.'

'What's your name?'

'Pritchard. Huw Pritchard.'

'Ah yes, from Wales, I believe? To the best of my recollection, you used to be a good worker, Pritchard—but you held very strong opinions. Is that why you left us?'

'You might put it like that.' Huw shifted his weight from one foot to the other; his game leg was playing up again. 'If you'll excuse me, I have to be getting back.'

But the old man would not let him off so easily, and said, 'Before you go, just tell me something. I was talking to my grandson the other day—at least, I think it was the other day. My grandson Daniel—I expect you know him?'

'Yes, sir. I've known Dan since he was a boy.'

'He was another good worker, and he left the Brotherhood too... Why do so many of our best men leave us? Had you been filling his head with your radical nonsense?'

'I wouldn't say so.' The pain in Huw's leg was becoming intolerable, and before he could stop himself he blurted out, 'Dan left because he was disgusted by the Brotherhood—and I left after they dropped a load of timber on top of me. I could have been killed outright, but I got off lightly. I was only crippled for life.'

Marcus shook his head in disbelief. 'That's not true. You're lying to me. It can't be true!'

'Watch me walk to the door, and you'll see if it's true or not...' Huw hobbled across the room, then turned back for a parting shot. 'I'm still alive, but Izzy Kleiber wasn't so lucky. When your Punishment Squad finished with him, they left him to drown in the river... Your precious Brotherhood was a gang of thugs, ruled by a tyrant—decent people like your grandson got out of it!'

Marcus' face crumpled, his mouth working, his whole body shuddering. 'No—don't say such things! It was never like that. I don't remember anything like that.'

'No?' Huw threw the words at him. 'Perhaps you don't want to remember.' And he left the room, slamming the door behind him.

Some time later, the rest of the family returned from St Paul's; they were in high spirits, and couldn't wait to tell Mary all about it.

'You should have seen it, Mam,' said Ruth. 'You'd have enjoyed it.'

'We had a good view, didn't we? We could see everything,' Kaff told her. 'We saw the King and Queen!'

'It was quite an experience. I'm glad I went,' Connor agreed. He turned to Huw. 'It's a pity you missed it. I told you, you should have gone instead of me.'

'It might have been better if I had,' said Huw grimly. He looked from Connor to Ruth. 'Could I have a word with you both—in the saloon?'

Realising that something was wrong, they followed him. As soon as they were alone, he began: 'Mrs O'Dell asked me to take a cup of tea to Mr Judge. I couldn't say no—I just hoped he wouldn't recognise me. But he knew me right enough, and he started asking why I left the Brotherhood, and why Dan left, as well. After that, I'm sorry to say I lost my temper and told him a thing or two.'

'What d'you mean?' Connor frowned. 'What kind of things?'

'It suddenly came over me: how could he ask me such a question, after the way he used

404

to run his bloody Guild? Begging your pardon, Ruth... He pretends he doesn't remember the Punishment Squad—the cruelty of it—the way Izzy Kleiber died... Perhaps I should have kept my mouth shut, but I couldn't stop myself. I think I may have upset him.'

'I'd better go up,' said Ruth.

When she entered her father's room, she was shocked to find him sprawled awkwardly across the bed, as if he had tried to get up and fallen back, unable to move. His cheeks were wet, and she realised he had been crying... Somehow the idea of her father in tears was unthinkable.

She settled him in a more comfortable position, plumping up his pillows and soothing him as if he were a child.

'You're all right now, Father—don't worry. You tried to get out of bed, and you couldn't quite manage it. You'll feel better after you've had a rest.'

'He—he said things to me. Terrible things.' Marcus dragged out the confession with a great effort, then looked up into Ruth's face, pleading with her. 'Was he telling the truth? Was I a cruel man? Tell me honestly, Ruth—was I really such a tyrant?'

Holding him gently, she whispered, 'Mum always said you were a fine husband to her, a good father to us children. That's all I can tell you.' Then she did something she had never done before; she put her lips to the old, wrinkled face, and kissed him.

He breathed a sigh of relief, his eyelids drooping. 'I thank God for you, every night and morning,' he said faintly. 'You're all I have left in this world.'

She stayed with him until he was asleep. When she went downstairs, Huw was waiting for her.

'How is he?' he asked. 'Is he very bad?'

'He'll be fine,' she told him. 'His memory comes and goes—he'll probably have forgotten about it by the time he wakes up.'

'But how could he forget things like that?' Huw wanted to know. 'Men lost their lives on account of the Brotherhood. If he doesn't remember that, he must be crazy.'

'I believe there was always a kind of madness in him,' said Ruth. 'And now he's sane, he can't bear to remember the time when he was mad.'

'You really think it's possible—that he's in his right mind again?'

'I think so. Do you know what one of the nurses at the Relief Centre told me? During the Blitz there were fewer mentally disturbed people than before—fewer nervous breakdowns, fewer suicides. She said they were afraid the bombing would drive people mad, but it seems it kept some of them sane. That's her theory, anyhow.'

'Well...' Huw scratched his head doubtfully. 'Let's hope it lasts.'

To a casual passer-by, Sidney Otley might have seemed an exception to that theory. He had a wild look in his eye, and his lips moved constantly as he talked to himself.

On a raw afternoon at the turn of the year, while daylight seeped out of a sodden sky, the old man left his house in that labyrinth of narrow streets, and looked up at the stormy clouds.

It would soon be dark, and he didn't like going out after dark. His sight wasn't too good at the best of times, and in the black-out he could easily trip over a broken paving-stone or into a bomb crater. Once he fell down, he'd have his work cut out getting back on to his feet, and if he were stuck there all night, waiting for someone to help him up, he might have to wait for ever.

Death came so swiftly nowadays, and Sid Otley was terrified of dying. That was another reason he hated going out of the house at night; there had been too many deaths in these streets, and too many of the buildings were standing empty. They gave him the shakes, just walking past them.

'All the same, can't stay indoors all the time, can you?' he muttered under his breath. 'Got to get your vittles, Sidney. Got to get a drink inside you now and then, to keep the cold out. And a packet of fags, an' all. Dying for a smoke, I am.'

He coughed—a hacking cough, hawking and spitting into the gutter. As soon as he could speak again, he went on: 'Besides, you got to have a bit of company sometimes. You got to talk to people, or you'd never get to hear what's going on.'

Sid liked to know what was going on; he

always kept his ears open when he went into his local for a pint, and he was the first to pick up any gossip that might be going round. He may have looked a little deranged, but Sidney Otley was still shrewd enough to store away these scraps of information, like a squirrel hoarding nuts.

'Never know when they might come in handy,' he told himself, as he tottered towards the main road.

It had begun to rain again, and he felt a clammy chill through his threadbare jacket. He stopped at the corner and looked both ways; peering into the gloom, he began to cross the road.

'Treat yourself to a quarter of rum, Sid,' he advised himself. 'Warm your blood, that will—do you a power of good.'

Suddenly, out of nowhere, a smart two-seater roadster roared past; he hadn't seen the dimmed headlamps. In the nick of time, he staggered back as the wheels ripped through a puddle, throwing up an icy wave that drenched his trousers and soaked his boots.

'Bloody driver!' he snarled, and suddenly realised where he had seen that car before. Of course—it belonged to Trevor Judge.

'Too high-and-mighty to stop and speak to the likes of me these days, aincher?' he wheezed resentfully. 'Too busy making money—you don't bother with your old pals no more.'

Then he remembered the rumours he had heard recently about Trevor Judge, and in spite of the cold and damp, he felt a kind of glow

408

inside him—almost as warming and comforting as a tot of rum.

'I fancy it's time we had a little talk, young Trevor,' he said to himself. 'Yeah—high time we did a little business together, you and me...'

By the time he reached the pub, he was feeling positively cheerful.

13

He soon found out that it wasn't going to be as simple as that.

Sid began by hanging around various places where he thought he might find Trevor; he knew he had been to call on his Auntie Ruth at the Watermen sometimes, so he made a point of visiting the O'Dells' pub, but Trevor never seemed to be there. From a scrap of overheard conversation between Mr and Mrs O'Dell, he gathered that Trevor was living somewhere across the water, in Greenwich, but they didn't mention the address. In any case, a trip to Greenwich would have been like a journey to the moon for Sid. He couldn't possibly walk that far, and he certainly wasn't going to throw money away on public transport, either.

In the end he took to hanging around the dockgates, hoping to see Trevor when he arrived for work at the Jubilee each morning. Unfortunately, Trevor never seemed to turn up at the same time two days running, and whenever he arrived, the gatekeeper always let him in very promptly, shutting the gates again as soon as the roadster went through.

The weeks passed, and Sidney Otley was still no nearer to that 'little talk' with his old friend Trevor Judge.

Then one February morning, he had a stroke of luck. He had been waiting outside the wharf for nearly an hour, and was just thinking about giving it up as a bad job, when the two-seater appeared.

For once, the gatekeeper was not at his post; he had been called away to be given long and complicated instructions about some long-distance lorry-drivers from Bradford who would be arriving shortly to pick up a cargo of wool from overseas. Impatiently, Trevor prodded the car-horn, announcing his arrival, but nothing happened.

This was Sid's chance; he lurched across to the car and tapped on the side window. Trevor glanced at him irritably, and was about to wind down the window when he recognised the decrepit old scarecrow and changed his mind. Through the glass, he said coldly, 'What the hell do you want?'

'Little talk... Ain't seen you for a long while,' wheezed Sid.

'Sorry, I'm much too busy. And I thought I'd made it clear I didn't want you to pester me any more? We've got nothing to say to each other.'

'Ah, but listen. I got to see you, Trev. I got things to tell you—important things.'

Before he could get any further, the gatekeeper arrived at a jog-trot, sweating and apologetic, calling out: 'Sorry to keep you waiting, sir!'

He unfastened the huge gates and swung them open, while Sid tried to detain Trevor. 'No, wait. Stop a minute—'

But Trevor drove on without another word or look, and once again the gates clanged shut. Defeated, Sid turned away, his shoulders drooping.

'Sorry about that, Mr Judge, sir. I got called away urgent-like,' mumbled the gatekeeper, as Trevor parked his car and climbed out.

'Yes, well, try to make sure it doesn't happen again, please,' he snapped, and went into the office.

Trevor was in a black mood already. Sid Otley was the last person he wanted to see. To make things worse, Sid had the brass cheek to call him Trev. The only other person who ever called him that was Tommy Judge, and Trevor had no wish to be reminded of their last meeting.

As he sat down at his desk, he found himself thinking of Gloria, and a deadly depression crept over him. That silly, painted bitch—he had been so positive she would take her revenge on Tommy that night, and hand him over to the police. Sally had reported what happened at Silmour Street after they left. Apparently a tear-stained Glory had agreed to let sleeping dogs lie; he had relied on the stupid cow, and she had let him down. Well, it had been a salutary lesson never to trust a woman.

As he sat there, gazing bleakly at the files laid

out upon his desk, all awaiting his attention, he remembered one woman he felt sure he could trust, just as she trusted him. Trust was, after all, at the very heart of their relationship.

His face relaxed into a half-smile as he picked up the telephone and began to dial the number of the Watermen.

When Lil arrived for her midday stint behind the bar, she smothered a yawn, and Ruth greeted her with a motherly scolding. 'You're not getting enough sleep, my girl!'

'I'm fine,' said Lil. 'It's just that I haven't been up very long. You know I'm on nights this week.'

'Well, you need your beauty sleep—you've got dark rings under your eyes,' Ruth told her. 'Oh, by the way, there was a phone-call for you this morning. Trevor rang up and said would you call him back when it's convenient? He's at the Wharf. I've written the number down somewhere.'

'It's all right,' Lil said. 'I know the number.'

She went into the little office behind the bar, wondering what he wanted to say—and wondering what she should say to him. Suppose he were to ask her to go over to Greenwich again? If he did, she must be very firm and tell him she couldn't go. It made things easier, being on nights this week. That gave her a good excuse.

When she got through, Trevor came to the point at once. 'Sally was just saying this morning that we hadn't seen you for ages. We'd like you to come have have supper with us one night this week. How does Thursday suit you?'

Of course, Sally would be there too. Well, that was a different matter. In a way, she was almost disappointed. It would feel very strange, being in that room with both of them—the room where she had behaved so recklessly—but she put that thought from her mind. It would be nice to see him; it would be nice to see them both.

'Thank you,' she said. 'I'd love to.'

'You're not on night-duty this week? I was afraid you might be.'

'Well, I am actually, but I can easily do a swap with one of the other girls. Thursday will be fine.'

When she went into the kitchen, Ruth asked, 'What did Trevor want?'

'Oh, nothing special. I said I'd go over and see him and Sally one evening soon, that's all.' She did not feel it was necessary to tell her mother she was going on Thursday, and that she would have to change the duty-roster. Mum would only go on about 'burning the candle at both ends'.

She managed to swap shifts without any difficulty, and on Thursday she put on a new dress that her parents had given her for Christmas. As she set off, she felt a tingle of excitement. She had decided to hang the expense and take a taxi—and that was just as well, because the weather was terrible. It had been raining on and off all day, and a storm seemed to be coming up. Occasional claps of thunder boomed across the Thames, and a sudden violent zigzag of lightning made Lil

413

blink. By the time she reached Acacia Grove, it was pouring cats and dogs, and she scurried up the garden path, huddling under her umbrella.

When Trevor opened the front door, she exclaimed: 'February Fill-Dyke—it's living up to its name!'

'You're not lucky with weather, are you?' he said, taking the umbrella and shaking it out. Then he ushered her in, adding, 'This reminds me of the last time you were here.'

She threw him a warning look, in case Sally did not know about her previous visit, but he merely smiled as he hung up her raincoat and ushered her into the living-room.

There was nobody there, just the log-fire burning comfortably in the grate, the shaded lamps and the music playing softly on the gramophone. She looked round, then said: 'I suppose Sally's busy getting the supper?'

'No, it's all ready. We're having my favourite— cold duck and salad. As a matter of fact, Sally isn't here.'

She stared at him. 'Not here? I don't understand.'

'Shame, isn't it? Those wretched people at ENSA are so disorganised, they rang up at the last minute and said they needed her to make up a party they were sending off to Aberystwyth—so she's on her way to Wales now. She sends her love, and asked me to make her excuses.'

'Oh, I see.' Lil sank into the armchair. She wasn't absolutely certain that he was telling the truth, and wondered whether she should leave the house and go home. But she couldn't possibly walk back in her new dress. If she rang for a taxi it might be ages before she got one on a night like this, and she didn't want Trevor to think she was making a fuss.

'I see,' she repeated. 'Yes, it's a shame she isn't here.'

He put a glass into her hand; an ice-cold cocktail. 'I think this was to your liking, last time,' he told her. 'That was such a perfect evening—I wanted everything to be exactly the same tonight.'

Slowly, she lifted her head, looking up into his face, wondering what she would find there—but he was still smiling, the same charming, gentle smile, and she found herself smiling back at him.

The supper was exactly the same too, and every bit as delicious. She was determined not to drink too much, but somehow her wine-glass seemed to refill itself magically when she wasn't looking. Afterwards they took cups of coffee back to the fireside—Lil in the armchair, Trevor stretched out on the sofa and *Moonlight Serenade* in the background.

When the last record had finished, Trevor said in a quiet, contrite voice: 'I can't go on pretending. Sally didn't go to Wales today, she went last weekend. I was lying to you again.'

Carefully, she put down her coffee-cup and said, 'Yes, I thought perhaps you were.'

'And you didn't mind? Oh, Lily—beautiful, adorable Lily—you understand me so well.'

'I think you understand me—too well. I really ought to go.'

'But you won't, will you? If I've wrecked the evening, I'll never forgive myself. I've thought about that other evening so many times, and I've missed you so much. I wanted it all to happen, all over again.'

She did not speak, but in her heart she answered him silently. 'I want it too...I want it so much.'

'Let me run the bath for you,' he said. 'I'll leave my dressing-gown ready for you, on the towel-rail.'

After the bath, his dressing-gown felt wonderfully soft and warm; she pulled it around her, knotting the belt, then went downstairs. When she walked into the living-room, she stopped. For a moment, she thought she was going to feel afraid of him after all.

While she was upstairs, he had undressed; he was almost naked, except for a pair of white undershorts, but he lay on the sofa with his hands behind his head, as if he were sunbathing on a beach—and somehow that made it seem quite natural, and she found that she wasn't afraid at all.

'You don't mind, do you?' he said, without moving. 'I suddenly had this idea we should both take our clothes off... I wanted to feel free—like you.'

By now he had put another stack of records on the turntable, and for a time neither of them spoke; they enjoyed the music that floated on the air, surrounding them, caressing them. Then he said quietly, 'Do you think you might come a little closer?'

She turned her head to look at him; a long, questioning look.

'There are things I must say to you,' he said. 'Things about you and me—things I can't shout across the room.'

Slowly she stood up; moving like a sleepwalker, she crossed the floor.

As the evening wore on, the storm intensified. Thunder-clouds gathered, exploding in stark white flares that slashed through the night sky, while the noise echoed and re-echoed through the Island streets.

At the Watermen, Connor received a phone-call from Ernest, asking for help. The Wardens' Post was in the basement beneath the local Food Office, and as the storm-water collected in the street faster than the choked drains and gutters could carry it away, the Post was being flooded.

Con told Ruth, 'I'll have to go—Ernest can't manage on his own. I'd better take Huw with me. You and Mam can hold the fort till we get back, can't you?'

'You know we can,' she said. 'Mind you wrap up well, and don't forget your rubber boots!'

When they got to the Post, it was difficult to see the extent of the damage. Ernest explained that the water had got into the fuse-box, and they had no lights—but Con had brought a torch with him. Standing at the top of the stairs, he played its beam over the jumble of incongruous objects floating beneath them.

The Post had been well-equipped, for the

sake of the men who spent the night in it: a primus-stove, a small store of food and a couple of camp-beds with pillows and blankets were provided. Now they saw the saucepans and a frying-pan bobbing about on the black, oily ripples, together with tins of spam and baked beans, a first-aid box that had burst open, casting bandages and sticking-plasters upon the water, an anti-gas cape, sodden maps and log-books, a wooden gas-rattle and a cat's-cradle of rope.

'Mother of God, what a mess!' exclaimed Connor. 'The first thing to do is unblock the drains; if we can get the water out, that'll be a start.'

His rubber boots were the first things to be discarded, then he began to pull off his jersey, stripping down to his underclothes. 'This reminds me of the time the river burst its banks, fifteen years back, when our cellars were flooded.' He stepped into the freezing water, grimacing. 'Seems like it's time for another cold bath.'

Huw followed his example, while Ernest commented: 'I hope there won't be a raid tonight. If we get called out to an incident, we'll be in real trouble.'

Back at the pub, Ruth and Mary were having a comparatively easy time. Not many of the regulars had ventured out in the storm, so the two bars were not very busy. Then, without warning, the whole place was shaken by a terrifying thud, rocking the building to its foundations.

'What was that?' gasped Ruth, but no one answered her.

The customers in the saloon looked blankly at one another. Mary O'Dell hurried in from the adjoining public bar, asking, 'Was it a bomb?'

'It didn't seem to be an explosion,' Ruth began.

One of the regulars suggested: 'Could have been a land-mine that didn't go off—it happens sometimes. Come on, let's get out of here.'

Several men scrambled for the door, ignoring the black-out. Outside somebody yelled: 'Christ—look at that. The roof's on fire!'

They rushed out; the street was illuminated from end to end by an unnatural yellow glow. Crossing the road, Ruth turned, looked up and saw with horror what had happened.

A barrage-balloon, struck by lightning, had burst into flames and fallen out of the sky. Dragging its cable, it had dropped on to the roof of the pub, where it was blazing fiercely.

Standing in the doorway, Mary called out, 'What's happened? Where's the fire?'

Ruth pushed past her. 'Don't just stand there, Mam. Go and ring the Fire Station—tell them to send an engine right away. Kaff and Father are both asleep upstairs; I've got to bring them down.' She called to one of the more reliable customers, 'My father's an invalid. I'm going to need your help to carry him down the stairs.'

Waking Kaff was simple; dragging Marcus out of bed took considerably longer, but Kaff helped as well, and between them they managed to wrap the bewildered old man in a blanket and steer him across the landing.

They were halfway down when Mary appeared at the foot of the stairs, shouting: 'I can't get through to the Fire Station; the phone's not working.'

'Damn...' Too late, Ruth realised that she had seen the trailing cable of the balloon entangled with the telephone wires outside. 'Of course—the lines are down. We'll have to send someone round there.'

'I'll go,' volunteered Kaff. 'It's not far—I'll run all the way.' Throwing a raincoat over her nightdress, she pulled on a pair of wellingtons and raced off on her errand.

'You shouldn't have let her, she's only a child,' Mary reproved Ruth, as she helped to manhandle old Mr Judge through to the saloon.

'There wasn't time to argue about it,' said Ruth. 'The important thing is to get help before the whole place burns down. Besides, she can probably run faster than anyone else.'

Kaff must have broken all records, because the fire-engine arrived in ten minutes; but by then the emergency was almost over, for the heavy rain had extinguished most of the flames, leaving nothing but charred balloon-fabric, a few smouldering beams, and a lot of hissing steam.

The fire crew dealt with the situation briskly, and half an hour later Marcus was back in bed, without the faintest idea what all the fuss was about, while Mary, Ruth and Kaff rewarded the firemen with drinks and sandwiches in the kitchen.

'You just need to get a tarpaulin up there tomorrow, till the roof's repaired, and you'll be sitting pretty,' said the Fire Chief. 'You were lucky it was no worse.'

'We're very grateful to you,' said Ruth. 'I was half expecting my daughter to turn up with a fire-pump. I expect you know her—Lil Burns? I know she's on night-duty this week.'

'She should be, only she did a swap with one of her mates tonight.' The Chief laughed. 'She'll be sorry she missed all the excitement!'

Only a few miles away, Lil was unaware of this crisis; she was in a strange dream-world that had nothing to do with ordinary, everyday life.

Still in the dressing-gown, she sat curled up on the carpet, next to the sofa, her eyes fixed upon Trevor. Although they were very close, he never tried to touch her.

'I love you,' he whispered. 'I love you—and I know we can be honest with one another. We need never be afraid or ashamed. Your naked body is so beautiful... I'll never do anything to upset you, but I want us both to be naked—together.' He glanced down at his undershorts. 'I want to get out of these silly things. Will you take them off for me?'

He left the decision to her; she could have refused, but something within her—something stronger than shame or embarrassment—was guiding her hands. Without any conscious thought, she let her fingers move across his smooth skin, on to the white shorts. Touching them, she realised they were made of silk. When he raised his hips, they slid down easily; he kicked them off and lay back, looking up at her with that same deep, understanding smile, as if he were sharing a secret with her. He was rigid with excitement and desire, and he said frankly: 'I can't help finding you attractive. I hope you're not shocked.'

She found it hard to speak. Her mouth was dry, but she managed to say, 'No, I'm not shocked.'

'I promise I won't do anything you don't like but, could you unfasten the belt of your dressing-gown?' Still in a dream, she did so, letting the gown fall open, exposing her own body to him. 'You're so glorious—it's a sort of agony for me... But in case you're afraid I might lose control, you could tie my hands together. Then you'll know there's nothing to be afraid of.' He crossed his wrists and held them out to her.

For a moment, she was tempted to do as he asked—then she shook her head. 'No,' she said. 'I trust you.'

If he was disappointed, he did not show it. Instead he said gently, 'My darling Lily—let's lie down together, by the fire. We won't do anything but kiss. I want us to kiss each other, again and again—all over.'

Moving slowly and easily, without any urgency, they stretched out side by side upon the carpet. He began to teach her another kind of love, and soon she found that her mouth was no longer dry but soft and moist, like his.

When Jimmy Judge had attacked her, she

422

was sixteen years old, and at that moment her natural sexuality had been arrested—frozen within an icy tomb. Now the ice melted; at the age of twenty-three she found herself being swept away on a rising tide of pleasures, of joys, of sensations, of physical passions she had never known before.

It was difficult to come down to earth again, next morning.

Trevor drove her back to Coldharbour; she went upstairs to the chilly, unwelcoming flat and changed out of her best dress. Putting on a plain blouse and skirt, she looked at herself in the mirror over the wash-stand, trying to understand what had happened to her.

Last night, in the space of a few hours, she had become another person; a girl with a different name, giving herself completely to the man she loved, sharing another kind of life with him.

And this morning she was Lil Burns—widow, part-time barmaid, volunteer driver in the AFS—back in the real world.

Later, when she went round to the pub and saw the state of the roof, where Civil Defence workers were removing the last traces of the burned-out balloon and covering the blackened beams with a tarpaulin, a feeling of guilt overwhelmed her, like a blow to the heart.

While she had been committing a mortal sin, a thunderbolt had come down from heaven, as if to punish her for her wickedness.

Ruth made her a cup of coffee, explaining

423

what had happened, finishing: 'We got off lightly, all things considered. Everyone's safe and well; nothing else matters.'

Connor came in from the backyard, where the clothes he was wearing last night were hanging on the line. He said: 'They're still soaking—this isn't drying weather. Looks like we're in for more rain.'

Ruth sighed. 'I'd put them over the clothes-horse by the fire, but we're nearly out of coal. If we don't keep a fire going in the saloon, the customers will grumble.'

'And I don't blame them, this place is like a morgue.' Con shivered. 'I'm going up to get another pullover. I can't seem to get warm this morning—the cold got right into my bones last night.'

When he left the kitchen, Ruth said suddenly, 'Talking of last night, where were you? One of the men told me you'd taken the evening off.'

'Yes, I went over to Greenwich.' With an effort, Lil managed to sound off-hand. 'You know Trevor rang up the other day? He asked me round to supper—I told you.'

'Oh, that was last night? I didn't realise... How's Sally? I haven't seen her lately.'

'She wasn't there. ENSA sent her off at the last minute, to do some concerts in Wales.'

'Oh, I see. So it was just you and Trevor?'

'Yes.' Lil finished her coffee quickly. 'I'd better go and start checking the bar-stock.' Unable to look at her mother, she left the room, dragging her guilt with her like a ball and chain. Ruth watched her go, her face clouded.

Confessions were heard at St Anthony's once a week, so on Saturday morning Lil knelt in front of the grille and tried to lay her sins before God.

'This man you spent the night with. How long have you known him?'

'Oh, a long time, Father, since we were both at school. But I didn't get to know him well until a couple of years ago.'

'And what are his intentions? Are you both contemplating marriage?'

The question took her by surprise. 'We've never even talked about that.'

'Hmmm...but you see him frequently? At your place of work, perhaps?'

'No, Father, we don't work together. I don't see him very often.'

'Good—it will make it easier for you to stop meeting him altogether.' She said nothing, and after a moment the priest went on: 'You do realise that's what you must do?'

'Yes, Father, but I can't promise... We're distantly related. I might meet him accidentally sometimes—'

'That's a different matter. You must not attempt to see this man—and if he asks you to, you must be strong and say no. Unless you promise me you won't try to see him again, I can't give you absolution.'

She took a deep breath, then said, 'Very well, Father—I promise.'

Nevertheless, when she left the church, she still felt troubled. The burden had been partially lifted, but she was not altogether free of guilt.

It was one thing to promise she wouldn't try to meet Trevor again; it was impossible to stop wanting him.

February dragged on, a dank, miserable month. There were a lot of coughs and colds going around and Connor, who prided himself on never having had a day's illness in his life, developed a chesty cold and a raw cough that kept him awake at night.

It kept Ruth awake too, and as she lay beside him, listening to him trying to choke back the paroxysms, every breath rasping painfully, she longed to help him. Once or twice she had offered to go down and make him a hot drink, but he told her sharply to stop fussing.

He would not admit that there was anything wrong with him, and when she tried to persuade him to spend a day in bed and sweat it out, he became quite indignant.

'It's nothing but a bit of a cold, for God's sake! D'you expect me to stop work on account of that? Next thing I suppose you'll be telling me to go to the doctor—well, you can save your breath. By the end of the week I'll be as right as rain, just you wait and see.'

But the rain went on, day after day, and there was nothing right about it; and by the end of the week Connor was still refusing to see a doctor.

Huw sympathised with Ruth; he'd had a similar problem when he tried to persuade Glory to seek medical advice. She too had refused at first, but unlike Connor, she had finally given in.

426

In her case, it was not a cold or cough. She had some sort of rash on her face—a few red blotches, which soon spread and came up in ugly lumps, like bee-stings. When she woke up one morning, the swelling round her eyes was so bad she could hardly see, and Huw insisted that she must take the day off and go to the doctor.

When he came home from the pub for his afternoon break, he found her sitting on a kitchen chair, looking very sorry for herself.

'What did the quack have to say?' he asked. 'Did he give you something for it?'

Miserably, Gloria said, 'He's given me some ointment to rub in, only he says it'll be difficult, on account of it's so close to my eyes.'

'But did he tell you what the trouble is?'

'Oh, yes. It's a sort of impetigo,' she replied. 'It's the cordite at work that's done it. He says as long as I go on doing this job, it'll keep coming back—and it's going to get worse.'

'Well, that settles it, doesn't it? You've got to give in your notice. It's lucky you're not one of the women who got drafted in to work there; you can leave any time you like—and a good job too, in my opinion.'

'I didn't ask for your opinion, Huw Pritchard!' she snapped. 'And if you say "I told you so" I'll crown you!'

'I wouldn't dream of it,' he said, trying not to smile. 'You'll just have to find another job, that's all.'

Unable to sit still, Glory got up and began to march up and down. 'At my age? There's no work going for women of fifty-five—what am I supposed to do with myself all day long?'

Huw stopped her restless pacing, taking her in his arms. 'You could marry me, that's what,' he said.

She tried to push him away. 'Don't talk so daft,' she told him. 'And don't keep smirking at me like that. I know I look a sight—'

'You look grand—even if you have got blotches round your eyes—and I'm asking you to be my wife.'

'*No!*' She broke away, turning on him angrily. 'Don't you dare feel sorry for me, offering to marry me out of pity. I won't have it, d'you hear?'

'Will you shut up and listen?' When Huw became indignant, his Welsh accent was more pronounced than ever. 'If you think I'm offering to marry you out of pity, you're a bigger fool than I took you for... You know damn well what you mean to me—we've been living as man and wife for long enough, haven't we? So why don't we make it legal, and have done with it?'

'Oh, ta very much. That's what I call a real romantic proposal, that is!' she snorted. 'All right, so you've asked me, and I've said no—let's hear no more about it. I want a job, don't you understand? I won't accept charity. I want to earn my own living and pay my own way—so what the hell am I going to do?'

When Huw spoke again, his tone was quietly reasonable. 'You used to be a pretty good hairdresser—why not go back to that?'

But she shook her head. 'I'm getting too old

to go traipsing round the streets, knocking on doors. If I still had the shop, that might be another story, but the way things are now...'

He interrupted her: 'Well, why not? It wouldn't take me long to get the shop smartened up again. New wallpaper, new lino, a lick of paint here and there...'

'And new wash-basins, new plumbing, new hair-dryers—and all the rest of it? Where's the money coming from?' she asked. 'It doesn't grow on trees, you know!'

On the last day of the month, the Kleibers asked them round for one of their Sunday get-togethers. When the meal was over, Glory helped Rosie clear the supper-table, while Ernest got out the cards. He said, 'By the by, I've finally decided I am definitely going to close the shop—until the war's over, anyhow.'

'Funny you should say that,' Huw told him. 'Glory's thinking of doing the opposite! She'd like to start up again as a hairdresser, if she could afford the furniture and fittings.'

Thoughtfully, Ernest placed the cards in the centre of the table, with a note-pad to keep the scores, then took off his spectacles and polished them, as he asked: 'And how much is that likely to cost?'

By the time the women joined them, he was jotting down figures on the score-pad, and Huw said eagerly: 'Wait till you hear this, Glory. Ernest's had an idea... How d'you feel about taking on a business partner?'

She looked at them blankly, and Ernest explained. 'When we opened this shop, we could never have done it without the help of Rosie's mother. She put up the capital we needed, and now I feel it's our turn to give someone else a helping hand. We could draw up an agreement—everything legal and above-board, you understand. I am prepared to lend you the money, and you can repay me at current interest rates—shall we say, over the next three years? It strikes me as a sound business proposition; people may not be taking photographs nowadays, but whatever happens, women will always want to have their hair done!'

The game of cards was forgotten; they spent the rest of the evening making plans. Glory became very enthusiastic, saying: 'I saw an advert in the paper the other day. There's a hairdresser in Cambridge Heath Road who's decided to give up his business and move to the country. He's selling off his equipment at very low prices... That might be just what we're looking for!'

She still had to work out one more week at the Arsenal, but Wednesday was her day off. Huw would be busy at the pub, so Ernest offered to go with her to Cambridge Heath Road, saying, 'If you like the look of what you see there, we could make him an offer for the whole lot. What do you say to that?'

Glory held out her hand. 'You're not just a partner,' she said. 'You're a pal!'

Sidney Otley had not quite given up hope, and since the weather was fine on Wednesday morning, he took his place outside the Jubilee Wharf once again. When he looked through the closed gates he saw with dismay that the little two-seater was already parked beside the Guild offices; today, Trevor had beaten him to it.

After that, there didn't seem to be much point in waiting, and he was about to go home when an enormous lorry drew up in the street, blowing a fanfare on the horn. The gatekeeper came out, unlocking the gates. Sid watched as the driver asked if this was Canary Wharf and the gatekeeper informed him that he'd come to the wrong place. The driver, who hailed from Glasgow, asked for directions to Canary Wharf, and the gatekeeper tried to tell him how to find it. This took some time, since both men had strong local accents and might as well have been speaking in different languages.

While they were talking, Sidney saw his chance and took it; he hobbled through the gates and straight into the Guild offices. When he said he wanted to speak to Mr Trevor Judge on private business, one of the clerks, looking him up and down, told him that was out of the question.

'Mr Judge only sees people by appointment. I suggest you should write a letter in the first place—'

Having got so far, Sid was not going to be put off, and stood his ground. The clerk lost his temper and told him to push off. Sid shouted hoarsely that he wasn't going to leave without seeing Mr Judge, and the inner door burst open as Trevor emerged, saying irritably: 'What the hell's all the noise about? Oh, it's you.'

'Morning, Trev. I come to see you on business,' said Sidney, giving him a toothless smile. 'Private and personal business, it is. I'm sure you wouldn't turn away an old friend, would you?'

Trevor was tempted to call the police, but he saw that the clerk was eyeing him curiously and changed his mind.

'You'd better come in—I'll give you five minutes,' he told Sidney. Then to the clerk, 'What are you staring at? Get on with your work.'

Within the privacy of his own office, he sat behind his desk but did not offer Sid a chair.

'Well, what's the idea?' he asked. 'Do you realise I could have you arrested for creating a disturbance?'

'Ah, you'd never do that. You'n me, we know each other too well, eh?' Without waiting for an invitation, he took the visitor's chair and made himself comfortable, looking round the office with approval. 'Nice place you got here. Doing all right for yourself these days, aincher?'

'Come on, get to the point,' said Trevor impatiently. 'I suppose it's money you're after? Trying to touch me for a fiver? Well, you've had a wasted journey. I told you before—that's all over and done with. I don't owe you anything.'

'Don't be like that.' Sid leered craftily. 'We go back a long way, Trev—a very long way. And we know a lot about one another. I've always took a great interest in you, sonny, ever since you was so high. I know more about you than anybody in the wide world. I dare say I know things as you'd prefer to keep secret.'

'So that's it.' Trevor smiled; it was a smile without warmth. 'You bloody fool, do you really think you can blackmail me? All right, I made a few mistakes in days gone by, but I've owned up to them and paid my debts. I've wiped the slate clean, and now I've got nothing to hide.'

'Nuffink?' Sidney cackled gleefully. 'I heard different! I ain't talking about days gone by—I'm talking about here and now... I don't suppose you'd want the Jubilee company knowing about your little deals on the side, would you, Trev?'

Trevor did not stop smiling, but his voice took on a certain edge as he asked: 'What are you talking about?'

'The black market, sonny-boy. Tipping off the gang when there's some special cargoes going through—bribing the nightwatchman—taking a rake-off on the deal...'

'You're out of your mind.'

'Pardon me, I happen to know one of the blokes what's been in on the fiddle with you. An old pal of mine he is. I won't mention no names, 'cos I wouldn't want to get him into trouble—and I wouldn't want *you* to get into trouble, neither...'

Then he broke off as the door opened again and Bertie entered the room, saying pompously, 'What's going on? Is this man making himself a nuisance?'

At once Sidney staggered to his feet, backing away towards the door and whining: 'No, sir, nothing of the kind. We been having a little chat over old times, ain't we, Trev? But I mustn't keep you from your work. Just think on what I said, and I'll see you again, very soon.'

In the doorway, he threw Trevor a last, knowing grin. 'I'm sure we can come to some arrangement. Ta-ta for now.'

He shuffled out, and Bertie shut the door firmly. Turning to Trevor, he demanded, 'What was all that about?'

Trevor thought for a moment, then replied, 'I think you'd better sit down. I'm afraid this may come as rather a shock. The man's a blackmailer.'

'I thought as much—disgraceful!' Bertie plumped into his swivel chair. 'I advise you to report him to the police. If he's trying to threaten you because of certain incidents in your past...'

But Trevor interrupted him. 'No, Bertie, you don't understand,' he said coolly. 'It's not my past he's interested in... It's yours.'

On Wednesday afternoon, Ernest and Gloria took a bus to Whitechapel, then continued their journey on foot along Cambridge Heath Road, looking for the hairdressing shop.

They had to walk about half a mile before they found it, but after that everything was plain sailing. The shop had already closed down but the hairdresser, who lived upstairs with his wife, was very glad to see them. Not many people were interested in setting up new businesses, and he was only too keen to meet them halfway.

434

'The wife and me have had our bellyful of London,' he said. 'She's got a married sister down in Taunton, and that's where we'd like to settle... Well, we're not as young as we used to be, and we want to take life easy—know what I mean?'

As he spoke, they heard an air-raid siren start to wail, and he jerked a thumb towards the shop window. 'We'll be glad to get away from that as well, I can tell you! Oh, I know the raids aren't like they was a couple of years back, but the wife says her knees turn to water every time that old moaner starts up. If you'll excuse me, I think I'll just pop up and make sure she's all right. Perhaps you'd like to take a look at the stuff in here? It's all got to go, you understand.'

When he came back a few minutes later, Glory told him she'd be glad to take everything off his hands, and they began to talk money. A bargain was struck, and Ernest said he would borrow a van to move the equipment across to Millwall Road during the next few days. They set out on the return journey, well pleased with their afternoon's work.

Although there had been no concentrated bombing for some time, isolated raiders occasionally broke through the coastal defences and got as far as London. The anti-aircraft batteries had recently been armed with powerful rocket-firers, and this afternoon they went into action for the first time.

Someone in the street had sighted a German plane overhead, and people were already running for shelter. Not knowing the area very well,

Ernest and Glory felt rather lost, and followed the crowd. Ahead of them, they saw the reassuring sign of the London Underground, and Ernest took Glory's arm.

'Come on,' he said. 'We'll be safer down below.'

That was when the guns opened up. One of the new rocket-firers had been stationed in nearby Victoria Park, and the noise was deafening—louder than anything they had ever heard. Terrified by the unearthly din, a girl began to scream, and the crowd panicked. Running for their lives, they surged into the building, fighting to get to safety; halfway down the stairs, a middle-aged woman carrying a baby tripped and fell, and an older man fell on top of her.

Within a few seconds, one hundred and seventy-eight people in the tube station at Bethnal Green were crushed to death.

14

'Ugh...this tea tastes worse than ever.'

With a grimace, Trevor put his cup back on its saucer. Since the milk ration had been cut to two and a half pints a week, the Guild Office had taken to dried milk as a substitute, and Trevor disliked it intensely. He turned to Bertie.

'You'll have to bring some proper milk from

home. I'm sure Florrie will let you have some if you ask her nicely, won't she?'

Bertie wasn't listening. Sunk into his swivel-chair, still brooding unhappily upon Otley's visit earlier in the day, he burst out, 'What I can't understand is, why did he come to you about it? Are you sure it's me he's getting at? Perhaps you misunderstood. Perhaps he didn't mean me at all.'

Trevor sighed. 'Who else in the Guild used to be members of the Fascist Party, except you and Jimmy? And now Jimmy's no longer with us, that only leaves you, doesn't it?'

'I suppose so, but why didn't he come straight to me?'

'He doesn't know you. I'm the one he knows.' Trevor corrected himself quickly. 'A long while ago, of course. When I was a kid, I used to run errands for him—take messages, things like that. That's why he's using me now, to pass the message to you—pay up, or else!'

'Oh, my God.' Bertie shuddered, his fat face quivering like a jelly. 'If this ever gets out, it'll ruin me!'

'I told you—forget it. Put it out of your mind. The old sod's barmy anyway. Even if he did talk, who's going to take him seriously?'

'I suppose you're right.' Bertie picked up his teacup, but when it was halfway to his lips, he began again. 'You don't think I ought to say something to the police, just in case? Get my story in first?'

'You mean the local cop-shop? The ones who took you in for questioning last time? That would be asking for trouble. Much better to ignore it. After all, he hasn't got a shred of proof, has he? He was probably lying about the photographs anyhow.'

The cup in Bertie's hand shook so violently, he slopped some tea on to his desk. Mopping it up with his handkerchief, he stammered: 'Photographs? What photographs? You never said anything about photographs!'

'Oh, no. I'm sorry, Bertie, I wasn't going to mention it. I didn't want to worry you about the photographs.'

'What photographs?'

'He claims he's got some photos taken at one of Mosley's rallies, showing you and Jimmy in uniform, with all the other Blackshirts, giving the Fascist salute... But I'm sure he's lying. I mean, how could he have got hold of anything like that?'

Bertie's face took on a greenish hue as he said, 'We daren't take any chances. We must ask him to bring the pictures—buy them from him...'

'He's too sly for that; he'd keep copies. If you give in to blackmail, there's no end to it.'

Bertie looked as if he were going to cry. 'Well then, what do you think I ought to do?'

Slowly and thoughtfully, Trevor appeared to be considering the possibilities. At last he said: 'There is one way we could shut him up. We could call an extraordinary meeting of the Brotherhood. After all, he's not just threatening you, he's threatening all of us. This could mean the end of the Guild. Why don't we instruct the Punishment Squad to deal with him? He wouldn't dare to try anything after that.'

'Yes, I see what you mean...' Although the idea appealed to Bertie, he was still trying to think straight. 'But how could we explain to the Guild members what it was all about? We can't tell them about—you know—the Blackshirts. The photographs...'

'Don't you worry.' Trevor was quietly confident. 'I've already thought of that. As Chairman, all you have to do is call a meeting of the Guild—and leave the rest to me.'

'Where do you want to store these gas-masks?' asked Huw.

'Oh, shove 'em under the stairs, out of the way,' Connor told him. 'They've never been used since the day they were issued, but I suppose we'd better keep them handy, just in case.'

As the basement underneath the Food Office was no longer habitable, the Wardens' Post had been temporarily housed in the Watermen cellars, and during their afternoon break, the two men were busy sorting out the hundred and one items they had salvaged from the flood.

Upstairs in the saloon, Ruth was putting out clean ashtrays, ready for opening-time, when she heard a car draw up outside the pub. A moment later there was a loud knocking at the door, and she drew back the bolts.

Pale and distraught, Rosie almost fell into her arms. At the pavement's edge, Ruth saw a taxi waiting, its engine still ticking over.

'Whatever's the matter?' she asked.

'It's Ernest and Glory. There's been an accident.' Rosie tried to explain, but her lips were trembling and she found it hard to speak clearly. 'I had a phone-call from the hospital at Bethnal Green... Where's Huw?'

'Down in the cellar. I'll call him.'

When Huw and Connor appeared at the top of the cellar steps, Rosie began again. 'They say there's been a terrible accident—I don't really understand it. Glory and Ernest have been taken to hospital; we've got to go there at once!'

'What sort of accident?' said Huw sharply. 'What's happened?'

'I don't know.' Helpless and afraid, Rosie burst into tears.

Putting her arms round her, Ruth said, 'Yes, all right. 'We'll come with you right away, won't we, Huw?'

Within a few minutes they were on their way to the hospital. The taxi-driver had picked up a garbled account of the disaster at the tube station, and he began to tell them about it, over his shoulder.

'All fell down on top of one another, they did. I heard as how there was hundreds of 'em, dead and dying.'

Rosie looked as if she were about to faint, and Ruth shut the man up firmly. 'We shan't know anything for certain till we get there. Let's just wait and see.'

When they reached the hospital, everything was in a state of confusion; ambulances were still coming in, unloading stretcher-cases, while

440

harassed women in white overalls were checking names on the ever-lengthening lists.

'Judge, Gloria—yes, she's in Women's Casualty. First floor, turn left when you come out of the lift. Kleiber, Ernest—Men's Casualty. That's on the ground floor. Straight through this corridor, second on your right.'

Huw was already halfway to the lift. Ruth called after him, 'We'll see you presently!' then she shepherded Rosie along the dark, echoing passage.

The Men's Casualty ward was crowded; the overworked nursing-staff were trying to cope with the sudden influx of patients and deal with anxious relatives at the same time.

Ruth and Rosie walked the length of the ward without seeing Ernest, then they retraced their steps, looking more closely at various motionless figures, partly hidden in bandages—but they could not find him.

'Excuse me,' Ruth stopped the Ward Sister who was hurrying past. 'We were told Mr Kleiber was here—Ernest Kleiber?'

'Are you a close relative?' asked the Sister, consulting her clipboard.

'No, I'm just a friend, but this lady is Mrs—'

The Sister interrupted crossly, 'Didn't they pass on the message? Only next-of-kin allowed in the wards! We can't have everybody crowding in...' She was about to move on, when a name on her list caught her eye. 'Here it is. Kleiber—I remember now, I only crossed it out half an hour ago... I'm very sorry, I'm afraid you're too late.'

Clutching at straws, Rosie asked, 'You mean—they've sent him home already?'

Before the Sister could reply, Ruth cut in quickly: 'This is Mrs Kleiber—his wife.'

The Sister's face changed, then she said in a completely different voice, 'I see, thank you. Would you both come into the office for a moment?'

She made them sit down, then told them as tactfully as she could that Ernest's injuries had been extremely severe. He was still in a coma when the ambulance brought him in, and he had died soon after being admitted without ever regaining consciousness.

On the first floor, Huw sat on a wooden stool beside a narrow bed covered in a white counterpane. Glory's left arm was rigid, encased in splints and bandages; her head was bandaged too, and her face was drained of colour—but he held her right hand in his, and took comfort from the fact that it was warm to his touch.

After some time she stirred slightly and began to cough—a pathetic little cough, like a child—and her face creased with pain. Her eyelids fluttered, and she looked at him in a dazed way.

'Huw?' she whispered.

'Yes, I'm here. Everything's all right,' he told her. It was a meaningless remark, but he could not think what else to say.

She winced again. 'My chest—it hurts. There's a pain when I breathe.'

'It's bound to hurt a bit; you've cracked some ribs.'

'What?' She tried to move her left hand, and found that she could not. 'What's wrong with my arm? I can't lift my arm!'

'Sssh—take it easy, girl. Your arm's broken too, but it'll soon mend. Nurse told me you've been very lucky. You're going to be fine.'

Her eyes slid away from him, trying to take in the long, echoing room. 'Where is this place? Where have you brought me?'

'It's a hospital, at Bethnal Green. I didn't bring you; I came as soon as I heard where you were.'

'Sorry. Sorry to be a nuisance.' She looked lost and unhappy. 'I don't understand—my head aches so, I'm a proper old crock, aren't I? What happened to me, Huw?'

'You've been in—in an accident,' he told her cautiously. 'Don't you remember anything about it?'

'No. I don't know how I got here... Was I knocked down in the street? Did I get run over?'

'Not exactly, but don't you bother about that now. The main thing is, you're going to get well again—very soon.'

'I just wish I could remember... Did you say Bethnal Green? What was I doing in Bethnal Green?'

'You'd come over to look at some equipment you wanted for the salon; you'd been to see some chap with a hairdressing shop.'

'Oh, yes—I know. Ernest came with me, didn't he? Where is Ernest?'

'He's in the men's ward; he was in the

accident as well. Rosie's with him now, and Ruth. I expect they'll come and see you, presently.'

Glory shut her eyes. 'I don't know as I feel like seeing anyone else just now, I'm so tired... But I'm glad you came. That was good of you.'

'Don't be daft—I had to come, didn't I? When I heard you were in hospital, I had to see you. We came in a taxi, and all the way here, I—'

'Taxi?' She opened her eyes at that. 'Shocking waste. Fancy throwing money away on taxis.'

'Shut up, will you? Let me finish. All the way, I could only think of one thing. When you get out of here, you and me are going to be married, girl. No arguments this time. I don't care what you say, I'm not letting you go, ever again.'

As the men filed in one by one and took their places round the great semi-circular table, Bertie found himself thinking: 'It's not the same. This isn't how Brotherhood meetings used to be.'

He remembered the old room, with green blinds over the windows, pulled down so that no stranger could look in—and the sound of the yellow gas-lamps hissing in the wall-brackets. When he had been taken to meetings of the Inner Circle by his brother, as a lad, he had been so frightened, he was afraid he would be sick.

Now it was different; the old buildings had been pulled down long ago, and they sat in the comparative comfort of the Jubilee Company boardroom; the windows were blacked-out, and a bright overhead light beat down on the table. Only the table itself was unchanged; curved like a shallow horseshoe, with chairs set at intervals along one side. He remembered when Marcus Judge used to sit where he was sitting now, a stern, granite presence; he remembered the expression on the faces around the table, when someone was hauled up before the Inner Circle for breaking their rules. The miscreant would stand before them, his hands tied behind him, his head shrouded in a black velvet hood... Marcus used to pass judgement on the prisoner, then leave the room; that was the signal for the Punishment Squad to set to work, closing in on the helpless figure—a dozen or more of them against one man, attacking him with fists, with clubs, with steel-toed boots—until he lay motionless at their feet, bruised, bleeding and half-dead...

Now, looking round the table, Bertie could not imagine his colleagues carrying out such a punishment; most of them were in their forties and fifties—family men, with wives and children—together with a handful of youngsters not long out of school, waiting for their call-up papers. There was no sense of danger here, no menace—and no victim.

How could he expect to rouse this ill-assorted group to punish an outsider, a man most of them had never even seen?

Trevor had never been a docker, so was not a member of the Inner Circle, but he sat in a position of honour at Bertie's right hand, and some of the members were eyeing him suspiciously. Sensing this, Trevor murmured in Bertie's ear: 'Hadn't you better explain why I'm here?'

Bertie wished he had not let Trevor talk him into this, but it was too late to change the plan now. He rapped on the table, and silence fell. Clearing his throat, he began:

'Before we open this meeting, brothers, I would like to explain why I have asked Mr Trevor Judge to join us tonight. Most of you will know him already—he is my stepbrother, my partner in the administration, and he acts as General Secretary to the Company. He has recently uncovered some very disturbing information, which he would like to lay before you. Does anyone present have any objection to this departure from customary procedure?'

They looked at one another, but nobody spoke. Bertie went on quickly, 'Very well. I shall now open the meeting in the usual manner, with a short prayer. Let us pray.'

The words had first been spoken by Marcus, some forty years ago; they were an appeal to the Almighty for guidance, invoking His protection for the Guild, and calling upon Him to open the vessel of wrath and destroy their enemies. Marcus' God was a God of vengeance, and as he repeated these awesome phrases, Bertie could not help recalling the rolling thunder of Marcus's oratory—and he was aware that his own voice sounded thin and ineffectual by comparison.

The men ranged to left and right of him watched and listened, and appeared to be unmoved. Bertie licked his lips, concluding: 'I will now ask Mr Trevor Judge to address you.'

Rising to his feet, Trevor began. 'First of all, let me say that I am honoured to be here with you. I would never have asked to intrude upon your meeting, except under these very special circumstances.'

Bertie saw their blank, impassive faces and thought: 'This was a mistake—they don't want to hear what he's got to say.'

Suddenly, without any warning, they were thrown into pitch darkness. The men gasped and exclaimed—Bertie rapped the table again—and Trevor's voice cut through the hubbub as he went on: 'Please, keep your seats. I expect it's just another power failure. Hang on, there should be some candles somewhere, in case of emergencies...'

Bertie heard him slide open the table drawer and rummage about; then there was the rattle of a matchbox, and a small bead of flame as he lit a candle.

'I'm sorry, it seems there's only the one. Well, this will have to do.'

He stood holding the candle in front of him, the soft glow shining upwards on his face, leaving his eyes black pools, like the sockets of a skull. As they all watched him, hypnotised, he began again.

'As I said, these are special circumstances, difficult and dangerous circumstances. I might almost say it's a matter of life and death.'

Slowly, giving full weight to every phrase, he

began to tell them about Sidney Otley.

'Some of you may have heard that he forced his way into these premises the other day, making threats—not against me or my brother—threats against the Brotherhood... Against all of you.'

He began to sketch in a few details about Otley's past; how he had been in trouble many years earlier, suspected of disgusting crimes against children, and how he had been a member of the British Union of Fascists.

Bertie opened his mouth to say something, then thought better of it. Trevor went on, lowering his voice, 'We found out recently that the Fascists have not been silenced; they simply went to ground, but we know they're still working hard. You probably saw the messages daubed on the walls recently, the painted swastikas. These men have started a whispering campaign, saying that Jews should be destroyed, and that the Nazis are the new leaders of the world. They're like Quisling in Norway, or Laval in France—Fifth Columnists, on the side of the enemy.'

There was total silence now; no-one in the room moved.

'Sidney Otley is one of these men. He has turned against Britain. I've heard it said that he comes originally from a German family—some people even say Otley is actually an English form of the name Hitler, though of course I can't say whether that's true... But we do know he's been poking and prying into the business of the Jubilee Wharf, hanging round the dockgates, taking note of the different cargoes going in and out, picking up our secrets... And why is he doing all this?'

Again he paused; the candle guttered, and his shadow danced triumphantly across the ceiling.

'I will tell you. This man is not just a Nazi sympathiser: I believe he is an informer. I am certain he is passing back information through a spy network to the enemy. Didn't it seem odd, when we were living through the Blitz, that the German pilots always knew exactly where to find the most inflammable targets? That the most valuable cargoes were always the first ones to be blown to hell?'

His voice was almost a whisper now.

'Sidney Otley is working for the Nazis—and he must be stopped. That is why I am calling on the Brotherhood to act, to defend our homes, our wives and families—to put an end to this treason. I am asking for volunteers to make up a Punishment Squad, to teach him a lesson he will never forget. Will all those in favour say aye?'

Their faces were no longer expressionless; the men were leaning forward, hanging on every word, their mouths open and their eyes gleaming, hungry for revenge. As one man, they joined the full-throated cry of approval: '*Aye!*'

The plans were simple enough, and quickly drawn up; instructions were given, and the meeting was officially closed. As the members of the Inner Circle streamed out into the night, the overhead lights came on again, and Trevor was able to blow out the candle.

He and Bertie were the last to leave the building; when they crossed the yard, the nightwatchman waited to see them out and lock the gates after them.

'Night, sir,' he said to Bertie, touching his cap, then he added to Trevor, 'I hope that was all right, sir? I turned off the mains for fifteen minutes, like you said. Did you find out where the fault was?'

'Yes. Like I thought, it was a short circuit, just a loose connection. I soon put it right,' said Trevor. Seeing the astonishment on Bertie's face, he took his leave of the man, saying with a smile, 'Anyway, thanks very much. I couldn't have done it without your help. Good night.'

At Silmour Street, time stood still. It was as though the clocks had stopped on Wednesday, 3 March 1943; from that date, life had ceased to have any point or purpose.

Everything was hushed. The Kleibers had never been a noisy family. Rosie used to flare up in a spasm of Irish temper sometimes, and Sally had thrown a dramatic tantrum when things didn't go right for her, but Ernest and Abram had always been quiet and reflective.

Now, no one talked very much at all. Stunned by the loss of husband and father, they could not bring themselves to speak of him.·

Rosie went through the motions of shopping, of cleaning the flat, of cooking meals which nobody felt like eating. They made conversation now and then, when they couldn't avoid it; they said hello and goodbye when they went in or out—they told one another it was raining, or it was getting warmer, or that the daffodils were out in the Gardens... But it all meant nothing, and they soon fell back into that all-embracing silence.

Abram and Sally had been very good to Rosie; they rallied round, trying to persuade her she was not alone, that they were still a loving family. But they were all afraid of giving in to their grief, as if, by ignoring it, they could put it away and forget it.

And every evening, they went their different ways.

Sally said, 'I have to go back to Greenwich at night, Mumsie. You do understand, don't you? I really need Trevor now; he's been so kind—so wonderful.' Perhaps she was trying to find a substitute for her father's love; certainly she had never depended on Trevor so much. She welcomed the physical expression of his passion, trying to lose herself in sheer sensuality. And perhaps she was afraid that if she slept at Silmour Street, she and her mother might hear one another crying in the night.

Abram did everything he could to take the burden of responsibility from his mother; Ernest had already closed the shop, and now Abram cleared out the photographic equipment, the remaining films, cameras and lenses, selling them off to other dealers at trade rates. He left the shop neat, silent, and empty of everything except echoes.

He would willingly have moved back to the flat upstairs, to keep his mother company, but he was not allowed to do so. Under the terms of his war-service, he had to remain billeted with the other non-combatants at the hospital. So, every evening, he hugged his mother, said goodnight and went away, leaving her all alone.

Rosie could not take any real comfort from Abram's love; she could only think of Ernest's kisses, the warmth of his embrace, the love she would never know again.

When there was no one there to see her, she used to open a bottle of gin and sit beside the electric fire, hoping to blur the unbearable pain, hoping she would fall asleep at last, and be able to forget... She had never felt so lonely, or so frightened.

Not very far away, another solitary figure passed his evenings in silence and loneliness.

Sid Otley had polished off the remains of some cold sausage and the heel of a loaf, spread with dripping. He put the greasy plate with the other unwashed pots and pans in the scullery sink, and returned to his front room.

By the light of a reeking oil-lamp, he took a tattered magazine from a pile under the armchair, and settled down to enjoy himself. This was the best moment of the day; a little treat he gave himself when he was feeling low.

Turning the dog-eared pages, he began to indulge in fantasies of a life he had never known. He looked at the blurred photos of athletic youths in various heroic poses—all of them naked—and let his imagination roam, picturing himself as young and handsome as they were, joining in their thrilling adventures.

He was recalled to reality by a faint tapping noise. Someone was knocking at the front door.

Hastily concealing the magazine under a cushion, he turned down the lamp, then shambled across the room and pulled the curtains slightly open, peering out—but he could see nothing in the darkness.

'Who's there?' he asked. 'Who is it?'

'Come outside, Sidney,' whispered a man's voice.

'Who are you? What d'you want?'

'I'm an old pal...I got a little surprise for you,' said the voice.

Sid scratched his wispy beard; perhaps it was someone wanting to sell him another magazine. It would be worthwhile to have a look at it, in case it was one he hadn't got.

'Hang on a tick,' he said. 'I'll open the door.' He went along the hall, which smelled of dry rot and cabbage water, and unlocked the front door. There was nobody on the step; he went out to investigate, and—

'*Gotcher!*'

The voice in his ear made him jump, but before he could turn around, four pairs of hands grabbed him; strong hands, that dragged him bodily down the street, hauling him along so that his feet scarcely touched the pavement.

'Here, what's the idea?' he panted. 'You let go of me!' He struggled, but old and frail as he was, he didn't stand a chance.

'Let me go,' he repeated. 'If this is some sort of joke, skylarking about, let me tell you—'

'It's no joke,' said the voice in his ear. 'You'll find that out soon enough, Mr Otley—or should that be Mr Hitler?'

'What are you on about? If you don't let go, I'll shout for help. I'll have the law on you, I will. *Help! Police!*'

'Shut your face!' snarled the ringleader. 'If you won't shut your gob, we'll make you!'

A handful of oily cotton-waste was stuffed into his mouth, and a thick, evil-smelling bag was pulled over his head. He could see nothing, and he could not cry out.

'You're going to be shown the error of your ways, you dirty Hun,' said another voice. 'You're a lousy German traitor!'

It was a nightmare; he did not recognise these voices, and he could not understand what they were saying. Worst of all, he did not know where they were taking him. Then, as abruptly as it had begun, the journey ended. They stopped, but they did not let him go.

'You old bag of filth, it's time you took a bath,' said the first voice. 'All right, lads. Up with him—up and over!'

He felt himself being lifted high into the air; he was suddenly afraid they were going to throw him into the river, and tried to tell them that he could not swim, but he could only mumble wordlessly through the gag. Kicking out, his boot struck something hard and metallic, making a hollow sound, and he realised what it was. They had brought him to the static-water tank at the end of the street. They were going to duck him in it...

454

At the same instant they let go and dropped him into ice-cold water. He tried to scream, but could not, as the water soaked through the bag, filling his ears, his eyes, his nostrils...

Then he felt the water fall away as he broke the surface once more, coming up for air. Hands grabbed him again, and he thought they would haul him out. Instead, they dragged the sodden bag from his head and pulled the gag out of his mouth. He gasped with relief, thinking the worst was over—but to his horror, they pushed him back, plunging him into the water, holding him under... Then there was nothing in the world but water, inside his mouth, his throat, his windpipe. He felt his lungs bursting. Soon—soon, for God's sake!—they must let him go...

'Keep his head under for a minute or two, that'll learn him,' said one of the gang.

He was still threshing about wildly, kicking up sheets of water that splashed over the four men, and they cursed him for wetting them.

'OK, that's enough—leave him,' said the oldest man. 'Leave him to climb out and find his way home. Come on, let's scarper.'

They took to their heels. If they had stayed a little longer, they would have seen that he was no longer fighting for his life. The old man had stopped struggling and was floating, motionless, face down in the water tank.

The following day, when Trevor and Bertie were working in their office, the junior clerk brought in a tray with two cups of coffee.

'Thanks.' Trevor did not look up. 'Put it

down there, will you?'

The clerk did as he was told, but instead of leaving the room, he lingered for a moment, saying: 'Excuse me, sir—I thought you'd like to know. That old tramp who came in last week, kicking up a fuss. He won't be round here bothering you any more.'

They looked up—first at him, then at one another. 'What do you mean?' asked Bertie.

'The gatekeeper just told me; he had a word with a copper he knows. He said they found him first thing this morning, in a water-tank near where he lived—drowned dead, he was.'

'Dead?' repeated Bertie, in a strangled voice.

'That's right. He must have been on his way home from the boozer, half-cut; they reckon he tripped and fell in somehow. Those water-tanks are proper death-traps. They say every month someone or other falls in. Dangerous, I call it.'

'But if he fell in,' Bertie stammered, the words tumbling over one another, 'Why didn't he climb out again?'

'Must have passed out with the shock. Seemingly he had a weak heart. I just thought you'd like to know.' Smugly pleased at the minor sensation he had created, the clerk left the room, and Bertie turned a stricken face to Trevor.

'Dead. Would that be manslaughter, do you think? Or murder?'

'Don't be a fool. You heard what he said—it was accidental death,' said Trevor easily. 'Anyhow, how the hell were we to know the old bastard had a weak heart?'

It had been a bad winter for everyone, and even though spring was breaking through, the warmer weather did little to raise their spirits. In backyards and window-boxes, blossom brightened the grey streets with splashes of colour. Even on bomb-sites, wild flowers had survived, and the graceful spires of willow-herb flourished everywhere; nicknamed 'fire-weed', it spread like wildfire.

But these cheerful torches were not enough to lift the dark clouds that hung over the Island.

At the Watermen, they had been looking forward to Dan's next leave, but on the day he was due to arrive he telephoned at breakfast-time, to say there had been a change of plan. Unexpectedly, he was being posted on a special training-course; it might be some time before he next came home.

Connor, who had taken the call, returned to the kitchen and passed on the message. The three women round the table reacted in different ways.

Mary burst out indignantly, 'It's not fair, promising the lad some time off, then stopping it at the last minute! They shouldn't be allowed to treat people like that!'

Ruth said quietly, 'I suppose it must be necessary, or they wouldn't do it... We'll just have to be patient, and wait a little longer.'

Kaff pushed away her plate. 'I don't want any more. I think I'll go upstairs now.'

'But you haven't finished your breakfast,' began Mary.

'Didn't you hear what I said? I've had enough!' she exclaimed fiercely, and ran out of the room.

Connor made a move to follow, saying, 'I'll not have her speak to Mam like that!' but a burst of coughing cut him short, and Ruth put her hand on his arm.

'Leave her, Con. I'll go and have a word with her presently. She didn't mean it. I know she's been looking forward to seeing Dan.'

Thumping himself angrily on the chest, Connor sank into his chair, grumbling, 'We're all disappointed—that's no excuse. What's got into the child at all?' He was still gasping for breath, and Ruth got up and fetched a bottle of cough-mixture from the sideboard, setting it in front of him.

'And I don't need any of that muck!' he growled. 'I told you before, my cough's practically gone now. I swallowed a bit of toast the wrong way, and got a crumb stuck in my gullet. Leave off fussing me, can't you?'

Ruth said nothing; she knew his chest was still troubling him, but he would never admit it and it was hopeless to argue.

That evening, when she was serving in the public bar, a young man in khaki walked in with a kitbag over his shoulder. For a moment she thought Dan had come home after all, and her heart leaped—then she saw it was Matt Judge, and tried to hide her disappointment.

'Hello, Matt,' she said, reaching across the bar to shake hands. 'They didn't send you on the training-course then, like Dan?'

'Not me. It was Sergeants and above,' said Matt cheerfully. 'I told him he was welcome to it... Give us a pint of best, would you?'

'On the house,' she told him. 'I'm sure your mother will be glad to have you home again; have you seen her yet?'

'I'm on my way there now.' He dumped his kitbag on the floor, and took the beer from her. 'Bottoms up!'

As he drank, Ruth remembered suddenly, 'Oh, you might not find Gloria at home. It's Huw's night off—they were going out together.'

'He's still hanging round, is he?' Matt wiped his mouth with the back of his hand. 'Damn...I haven't got a key to let myself in.'

'I believe he said something about going over to see Rosie Kleiber at Silmour Street. You might find them there.'

'Right. Can I leave my kit here? Save lugging it round the Island.'

'Of course.' A thought struck her. 'You heard about Rosie's husband, I suppose?'

'Yeah—bit of a shock, that was. Ma was one of the lucky ones.' Matt took another swig, then asked, 'By the way, is young Kaff Hobbs about?'

Surprised, Ruth said, 'Yes, she's in the kitchen—why?'

'Dan gave me a letter for her, just before I left. Could I have a word with her?'

'Not in here, she's still under age. But you're welcome to go through—you know the way, don't you?'

He ducked under the bar-flap, then went along to the kitchen and found Kaff reading a book. She had recently joined the Public Library, and the first book she looked for was *Gone With the Wind*. She was already halfway through it, re-running the film in her memory, scene by scene.

She was startled when Matt walked in; he explained his errand and produced the letter from the pocket of his battledress tunic.

'Dan told me he'd promised to take you out while he was here. He said he was sorry to let you down, but it couldn't be helped.'

'I know.' Her eyes shone as she saw the writing on the envelope; she couldn't wait to open it. 'Thanks ever so.'

'That's OK.' Matt was in no hurry to leave; he looked her over with approval. 'I was surprised when Mrs O'Dell said you was too young to go in the bar. How old are you, then?'

'Fifteen, but I'll be sixteen quite soon.'

'Is that so?' Matt perched on the edge of the table and grinned at her. 'Pity about Dan. I bet you were looking forward to a night out, eh? Where was he going to take you?'

'I don't know. He didn't say anywhere particular—just out.'

'Tell you what, seeing we're both at a loose end—why don't I take you out instead?' He glanced at the cover of the book in her hands. 'You like going to the flicks, do you? How about us going together?'

'No, thanks. I'd rather not.' She stood up. 'And thanks for bringing the letter.'

She walked out of the room. He watched her go—her slim waist, the curve of her hips, her long slender legs—and called after her sourly: 'Suit yourself, kid!'

She couldn't wait to read Dan's letter. It wasn't very long, and it didn't say much except for his apologies and a promise to make it up to her next time he came home, but she read it again and again, and that night she slept with it under her pillow.

At Coldharbour, Lil stretched out on her bed, staring at the ceiling. She had just come home from a long day on duty, and she was tired; too tired to make herself any supper, but not ready to go to sleep. If she slept now, she'd lie awake half the night, tossing and turning—and thinking of Trevor.

He had not been in touch with her again, and she had not tried to phone him. She was thankful she could not afford to have a telephone in the flat; if she had, she knew she would not have been able to resist dialling his number, at moments like this. She allowed herself occasional daydreams; she imagined him coming to collect her in the car—climbing the stairs, knocking on the door of the flat, sweeping her off her feet...

As these thoughts were running through her head, she heard the sound of footsteps on the stairs; she held her breath, and a moment later there was a knock at the door. No longer tired, she jumped up and hurried to the door, patting her hair into place as she passed a mirror.

461

Out on the landing, Abram said shyly, 'I wasn't sure if you'd be here. Can I come in?'

She pulled herself together. 'Yes, do come in. How are you?'

He thrust a bunch of roses into her hands, murmuring, 'I thought you might like these.'

'Oh, they're lovely. You shouldn't have...'

No, he shouldn't have. All she could think of was Trevor—why did Abram have to bring roses, when roses were Trevor's flower? She busied herself with a vase, putting them in water, while he sat watching her. Then she put them on the table, saying, 'I'm sorry I can't offer you a drink—unless you'd like a cup of tea?'

'Tea will be fine, thank you.'

He hadn't been to her flat before, and he looked around as she fetched cups and saucers. It was a bare, unfriendly room, without personality. He wondered how she could have lived here so long without impressing herself upon it in any way, but all he said was, 'You've got a nice place. I expect you get a good view of the river?'

'Yes, you can see a long way.'

They drank tea and talked about nothing for ten minutes; after that there was a silence. Then Abram said, 'I hope you don't mind me coming round without being invited?'

'I'm glad you did. It's nice to have company sometimes.' She added awkwardly, 'I never wrote and thanked you for the letter you sent me. You know, after Mike...'

'You didn't have to reply. But I meant what

I said—if there's ever anything I can do...'

'There's nothing, honestly. But it was good of you to offer.'

After another pause, he began, 'I just thought it must be very lonely for you now. I know what that's like. I get lonely myself, sometimes.' He could not look at her, but examined the pattern on the tablecloth, following it with the tip of his finger, as if he were putting it under strict professional scrutiny. She did not know what to say to him, and he went on: 'Of course I know it's nothing like you and Mike, but since my Pop was killed, I've got a rough idea what you must be going through. Momma seems to be lost without him. I try to help her any way I can, but I can't get through to her, somehow. It's like she's the only person left in the world—the rest of us don't exist any more. Is that how you feel—about Mike?'

'No, not really,' she replied. 'Not quite like that.'

'Good. Because it's not true; you're not alone. There are people who care about you—you know that, don't you? So if you ever need a friend—?'

He dared to look at her at last, and she smiled at him—a polite, conventional smile. Immediately, he knew that he had made a mistake. He should never have come here—he shouldn't have started this. Changing his tone swiftly, he smiled back.

'Well, I'm always around, if you want any help. I've been trying to help Momma as much as I can, winding up Pop's business—and Sally's

463

been very good too, though of course she doesn't get over to Cubitt Town that often. Well, the house at Greenwich keeps her busy.'

'Yes, how is Sally?' Lil asked. 'I haven't seen her lately.'

'She's a lot better now. It hit her very hard to begin with—she was lucky she had Trevor to look after her. He must have realised how much she needed him, because he's given her so much time, and love. I don't know what she'd have done if it hadn't been for Trevor... He's been really wonderful.'

'Wonderful...' repeated Lil.

Abram heard the catch in her voice, and glanced at her again; he saw the tears in her eyes and cursed himself for his stupidity. How could he have been so selfish, talking about Momma and Sally, reminding her of her own bereavement all over again? Abruptly, he stood up and said, 'I'd better be on my way. I've got to report at the hospital at eight—I'm on nights this week. Anyhow, thanks for the tea. See you soon.'

When he had gone, there was nothing in the room but the scent of roses. Lil bowed her head, resting it upon her arms, and began to cry.

'I'm so happy for you both.' Rosie managed to sound cheerful as she raised her glass of wine in a toast. 'Here's to you, Glory—and Huw—and here's to the new salon. I'm sure it's going to be a great success.'

They all drank to that, then Glory said, 'But are you sure you really want to go ahead with it? I mean, you mustn't feel under any obligation.'

Rosie cut in: 'Ernest gave his word, and I'm not going back on that. Besides, it's a good investment. I've told the solicitors to draw up the agreement. Now the shop's packed up, I'll be glad to know our money's doing some good, somewhere else. It's what he would have wanted.' She broke off as the shop doorbell pealed, saying, 'Blessed kids—they're always doing that, ringing the bell and running away. Take no notice, they'll soon get fed up.'

'It might be somebody wanting Huw,' Glory suggested. 'You told them at the pub where to find you, didn't you?'

'Perhaps I should make sure.' Huw began to get up, but Rosie stopped him. 'You stay there, I'll go. I know where the light switches are.' She went through the empty shop, turning out the light before she opened the street door.

On the pavement, a man in battledress said: 'Evening. Is Ma here, by any chance?'

'Matt!' For the first time in months, Rosie was surprised by a sudden rush of joy. 'Come inside! Yes, she's here—and Huw. Oh Matt, it's so good to see you.' She took him upstairs, announcing: 'Look who's here!'

Glory embraced her son, scolding him at the same time. 'You're a devil, you are. Why couldn't you let me know? How long are you here for?'

Rosie poured him some wine. 'It's nothing but celebrations tonight!'

Matt laughed. 'Seems like I came at the right

time. What are we celebrating?'

'Lots of things!' Rosie handed him the glass. 'Your leave—the new hairdressing salon—the engagement...' Then she saw the laughter die in Matt's eyes, and turned guiltily to Glory. 'Oh, I'm sorry. Perhaps I shouldn't have said that?'

Glory felt for Huw's hand and held it, as she said: 'That's OK. I was just going to tell him myself. Your old Ma's getting married again, my son—how about that?'

Matt emptied his wine glass at one gulp, and put it back on the table. 'Congratulations,' he said. 'Don't let me spoil the party—I'll leave you lovebirds together. Expect me when you see me, all right?' Then he turned and ran down the stairs.

Glory exclaimed: 'What's wrong with him? He's been on the booze, by the sound of it.'

'It was my fault, springing it on him like that,' said Rosie. 'I'll go and fetch him back. I'll explain.'

'I shouldn't bother!' called Glory, but Rosie was already on her way.

He was halfway along the street when she caught up with him, saying breathlessly: 'Matt, come back. I didn't explain properly. Come back and...'

He rounded on her sullenly. 'You don't have to explain. I might have guessed she'd have got her hooks in that little Welsh cripple by now.'

'That's a dreadful thing to say! Huw's a good man—he thinks the world of your mother. I'm sure they'll be very happy together. Come and have a drink with them—wish them luck.'

'They can do what the hell they like—I don't give a toss one way or the other. I'm going to have a drink all right—but not with them. I'm going to get blind, stinking drunk tonight, all by myself... Good night.'

He turned away, and she clutched his arm. 'No, Matt—don't. If you want to go drinking, let me come with you, please?'

He looked into her face, and began to laugh. 'Yeah, I heard you'd lost your old man. You don't waste any time, do you? Sorry—merry widows aren't my style!' He shook her off roughly, and walked away.

She stood there until the darkness swallowed him up; then, slowly, she went back into the empty shop, and climbed the stairs.

Huw and Glory looked at her enquiringly as she entered the sitting-room.

'Well?' asked Huw. 'What did he say?'

'Nothing. I wasn't quick enough... I must have lost him, somehow.'

15

Matt's reaction to the engagement upset Gloria very much. She hardly saw him at all during that leave; he stayed out almost every night, and when he did come in, he was either half-drunk, or recovering from a hangover.

Huw was keen to get married as soon as possible, but she told him she thought it might be better to have a long engagement. After all, they weren't a couple of lovesick youngsters, impatient for wedding bells, were they? They should wait for a while—till after Christmas, say. By that time, perhaps Matt would have calmed down and got used to the idea.

Huw agreed, reluctantly, and the wedding was put off until the following year—though he told the O'Dells privately that he thought Matt Judge was behaving like a spoiled kid, and needed a good clip round the ear.

Whether Matt was getting used to the idea or not, there was no way of knowing, for he never wrote to his mother now, and he did not come home on another weekend pass.

Early in 1944, they heard that all military leave had been cancelled anyway; it was said that there were plans afoot for a big attack on Europe, and people began to talk hopefully about a possible invasion.

In the light of these stirring events, Matt's disapproval seemed less important, and Glory finally agreed to name the wedding day. She decided upon Saturday, 1 April, because as she said to Huw: 'All Fools Day seems to be about right for us. Well, you've got to be a fool for wanting to marry me in the first place, and everyone knows I've been a fool all my life!'

It was not a glamorous wedding; it could hardly be that, when they were living through a time of stern austerity. Even the presents were practical rather than romantic. Most of their friends and relatives were generous with their own rations, and Glory and Huw were grateful for such precious gifts as a box of scented soap, a pound of sugar, a jar of marmalade, a caddy full of tea and—most highly prized of all—a tin of chocolate biscuits.

The ceremony took place at the Poplar Registrar's Office, just before noon, with Connor, Ruth and Rosie as witnesses. Afterwards, they returned to the Watermen, and when the pub closed its doors to customers in the afternoon, they set up a trestle table in the bar and invited their guests to make merry.

Ruth, Mary and Kaff had done wonders with the cold buffet; a tin of Spam went a long way when it was minced up in sandwiches and washed down with a fizzy white wine, which Con assured them was every bit as good as champagne.

At the centre of the table was the wedding-cake; an imposing, three-tiered creation, with fluted columns, silver bells, and garlands of orange-blossom. When it was time to cut the cake, its secret was revealed, for the entire edifice lifted off, revealing a plain fruit cake underneath. Since iced cakes were now prohibited by law, the outer shell was made of cardboard and plaster, and had been hired for a small fee from the local pastrycook.

But nobody cared; by then the party was going with a swing, and most of the guests were having a high old time. Only a few of them found it hard to join in the fun.

Rosie had not really wanted to come back to the pub at all; Abram could not be there because he was on duty, and Sally had been touring the camp-sites all the week, though she sent a telegram of good wishes and promised to join the party later, if she got back from Catterick in time. But at first Rosie sat alone, and the memories of her own wedding—and especially the reception, which had also taken place here in the pub—were hard to bear.

Kaff too was feeling low. Although everyone had told her Dan couldn't possibly come to the wedding, she had still been hoping, right up to the last minute. She hadn't seen him for a long time, and lately he hadn't answered her letters, either. She was beginning to think he was fed up with her, or—worse still—he had met somebody else...

Lil sat in the corner of the room, with a brave, fixed smile, wishing she were a million miles away. Naturally, Glory had invited the rest of the Judge family. Bertie and Florrie were there—and so was Trevor. They had said 'Hullo' when he arrived, but after that she took care to keep as far away from him as possible; she was determined not to stare at him, but in spite of the noise, she could still hear the sound of his voice through the singing and the laughter. He was wearing a new suit she hadn't seen before—beautifully tailored, in a silky dove-grey material. He looked more handsome than ever, and she thought that her heart would break.

'You're very smart, I must say!' Gloria looked her nephew up and down. 'Is that a new outfit? It must have set you back a bit, by the look of it. Made to measure, I bet—that never came off the peg.'

'I happen to know a very good tailor,' Trevor smiled. 'Just off Savile Row—and half the price!'

'Yes, but it's not just the money now, is it? It's the coupons,' Glory protested. 'I don't know how people manage. I mean to say, look at me!'

'Oh, I'm looking, believe me—and you're lovelier than ever,' Trevor told her.

'Get away with you!' she laughed. 'Remember the old saying, "Something old, something new, something borrowed, something blue"? Well, I had to borrow practically every blessed stitch I've got on; I only had enough coupons left for a new pair of knickers—but I made sure they'd got blue lace trimmings, just for luck.'

'Well, here's wishing you all the luck in the world.' Trevor raised his glass. 'Where are you going on your honeymoon? Or is it a secret?'

'Oh, we'll have our honeymoon a bit later, when the weather bucks up. I thought we might take a few days off and go down to Brighton. I haven't been there for donkey's years, but you can always have some fun in Brighton. I think it's the sea air that bucks you up.'

'I'm sure you don't need bucking up,' Trevor said, with a wink. 'Your husband's a lucky man!'

Glory turned and called to Huw, who was talking to Connor: 'Did you hear that, lovey? You're a lucky man—Trevor said so!'

But Huw wasn't listening, he was protesting: 'How much longer are they going to keep messing us about? Why can't they make up their blasted minds?'

'It's not the Civil Defence—it's the Board of Trade or some such,' Connor told him. 'They want to go on using the place as a store-room; they've got thousands of new books stacked away in that basement, under lock and key.'

'What are you both on about?' Glory wanted to know. 'Something to do with the Library, is it?'

'Not that sort of book.' Huw turned to include her in the conversation. 'You know we were going to move the Wardens' Post back to our old premises, under the Food Office? Con's just told me the latest—the powers-that-be have decided we've got to make do here a bit longer. Now that basement's been rebuilt and redecorated, it's too good for us. They're using it to store a load of new ration-books instead!'

'Well, if it belongs to the Food Office, I suppose they've got first call on it.'

'Only they're not food ration-books,' growled Connor. 'They're the next lot of clothing-coupons, waiting to be issued—that's what gets my goat!'

Trevor, who had been listening to this, was about to ask a question, but at that moment Bertie pushed through the guests and tapped him on the shoulder. 'Trevor, can you spare a minute?'

Trevor sighed. 'Yes, Bertie, what is it now?'

The overcrowded saloon was very warm, and Bertie's face shone with sweat as he explained, 'Auntie Ruth says my grandfather wants to talk to me.'

'Old Marcus?' Trevor glanced round the room. 'Is he here?'

'Upstairs—he's pretty well bedridden now. She says he wants to ask me about the Brotherhood. So I thought, perhaps it would be a good idea if we both went up. You could probably explain things better than me.' He mopped his brow with his handkerchief, and Trevor realised it wasn't the heat of the room that made him sweat. Bertie was a frightened schoolboy again, summoned by the head of the family to give an account of himself.

'All right,' he said irritably. 'Come on—let's go and get it over.'

They found the old man sitting up in bed. Too short-sighted to see as far as the door, he narrowed his rheumy eyes suspiciously and asked, 'What do you want? Who's that?'

'It's me, Grandfather—Bertie.'

'Ah, Bertie—yes. Come here, boy.' Marcus pointed to the chair beside the bed then, as Trevor followed Bertie, he frowned. 'Who's that you've brought with you?'

'It's Trevor, Grandfather—Uncle Arnold's son. You remember Trevor, don't you?'

'Yes, I think I remember Trevor. What is he doing here? I didn't send for him.'

'He's my partner at the Guild Office. He helps me run the Brotherhood.'

'Does he indeed?' Marcus poked his head forward, trying to see Trevor more clearly. 'It's the first I've heard of it—why did nobody tell me?'

'I'm sure we told you, Grandfather. After

473

Jimmy was killed at Dunkirk, I couldn't manage it all by myself, so...'

'Nobody told me,' Marcus repeated resentfully. 'I should have been told.' He addressed Trevor directly. 'Come closer, young man—where I can see you.'

'Good afternoon, sir. I hope you're keeping well?' Trevor was about to shake hands, but Marcus' skeletal fingers fastened upon his wrist, dragging him forward.

'Ah, yes. I know you now. We've met before. Sit down.'

As Bertie began to lower himself into the bedside chair, Marcus snapped, 'No, no. Not you—him! I shan't need you now, Bertie. You may go.'

'Oh, but Auntie Ruth said you wanted to see me,' stammered Bertie.

'So I did, and now I've seen you, you can go. Shut the door properly; I can't abide draughts.'

Bewildered, but grateful for the reprieve, Bertie hurried out of the room, and Trevor took his place in the bedside chair as Marcus resumed: 'No use talking to Bertie. The boy's an idiot—always was and always will be. I'd been wondering how he managed to run the Brotherhood on his own. I should have realised he couldn't do it without someone to help him...but I never knew you were there.' He gripped Trevor's wrist tightly. 'Making a go of it, are you?'

'Yes, sir—I think so. The Jubilee Wharf is doing pretty well out of the present situation.'

'And I dare say you're doing pretty well out of the Jubilee Wharf, eh?' Marcus' ivory fingers moved up to Trevor's sleeve. 'Fine material—expensive material. You pay yourself a good wage, I expect?'

'I pay myself what I consider I'm worth.' Trevor did not often feel nervous, but as he met Marcus Judge's penetrating gaze, he felt a shiver of unease. Fixing the old man's eyes with his own, he went on: 'And I'm worth a good deal to the Jubilee. Ask the Wharfmaster, if you don't believe me.'

'You may be able to deceive the Wharfmaster, but you don't deceive me, Trevor Judge. You bear the family name, but there's no drop of my blood in your veins, and I thank God for that.' Marcus lowered his voice until it was only a thread of sound, yet every word cut like the edge of a razor. 'I see you for what you are—I see through to your black heart and your rotten soul... And I tell you solemnly, you will pay for your wickedness in hellfire through all eternity.'

Pulling away from him, Trevor stood up, backing off and saying, 'I've had enough of this. You don't know what you're saying!'

'I know what evil is,' whispered Marcus. 'And I know what you are...'

Trevor left the room without another word. He slammed the door behind him, forcing himself to breathe deeply, trying to master the unfamiliar sensation of fear.

Someone emerged from the shadows on the landing; Lil had been waiting for him. 'I saw

Bertie come down,' she began. 'I was hoping to see you.'

Before she could say any more, his arms were round her, pressing her to his body, and she felt his heart beating quickly.

'What is it?' she asked. 'What's wrong?'

'That old man's sick—raving.'

'Do you mean he's delirious? Should I call Mum?'

'Oh, no—it's nothing like that. He's just talking nonsense... He probably had a bad dream; he'll be all right when he's properly awake.' Then he held her at arms-length, looking at her with longing. 'God, I've missed you so much.'

'I missed you too. But I thought—you and Sally..'

'Forget Sally. You're the one I want. I always want you.'

Down in the saloon, Sally had just arrived in a taxi, making a splendid entrance and talking nineteen to the dozen. She told everyone within earshot that she was simply dead, the train had stopped a million times between Yorkshire and Kings Cross, and she had to have a drink there and then before she passed out on the spot. Then she embraced Glory, congratulated Huw, thrust a gift-wrapped parcel into their hands, hugged darling Auntie Ruth—and at last she fell upon her mother, kissing her again and again, and saying effusively: 'You look simply heavenly, Mumsie. Honestly, I'm so jealous, you look younger every day—doesn't she, Ruth? I don't know how you do it. Oh, I can't wait to have a really long talk, I've got masses to tell you. By the way, where's Trevor? Don't tell me he hasn't turned up. He promised faithfully he'd meet me here, I'm relying on him to give me a lift back to Greenwich, because of all my luggage...'

Ruth managed to get a word in at last, saying, 'He went upstairs to see my father. I expect he'll be down in a minute.'

But Sally couldn't wait. 'I'll go and find him. I'll say hello to the old gentleman as well, shall I? I expect he'll be pleased to see me—old people always enjoy visitors.'

She had been in and out of the pub ever since she was a child, and knew her way around; she remembered that Marcus Judge had taken over the bedroom that used to be Daniel's, and she was about to knock and enter when she heard a low murmur of voices from another room, where the door stood ajar. They were both voices she knew well.

Without a moment's hesitation, Sally flung open the door of Kaff's room; they were standing by the window, their arms around one another.

She walked straight in. As they broke away and turned to face her, she said to Lil in a matter-of-fact way, 'So that's it... I knew it all along—I knew you were lying.'

Then she turned to Trevor, saying in the same bright, hard tone: 'Take me home, please. I've got some exciting news for you, darling—I'm pregnant.'

In the car, on the way back to Greenwich, Trevor was very quiet and after a while Sally prompted him. 'Well, go on—say something.'

'What were you expecting?' he retorted. 'An apology?'

She turned to stare at him. 'What for?'

'I thought perhaps you were expecting me to grovel and say I'm sorry about Lily—go down on my knees, begging you to forgive me—is that it?'

'I'd never expect you to apologise for anything,' she said. 'I know you better than that. But now you mention it, you might as well tell me what's been going on. I was under the impression she'd gone right off sex, after her N.E.'

'Her what?'

'N.E.—her nasty experience. Or didn't you know about that?'

'Oh yes, she told me. I couldn't help feeling sorry for the girl—what with that, and then losing her husband and everything, she needed someone to comfort her. You didn't imagine it was anything serious, did you?'

'Not really. But you'd better not encourage her; she might start getting ideas. Anyhow, I wasn't thinking about Lil. I meant, what do you think about us? You and me—and the baby?'

He threw her a sidelong glance. 'So it's true? You weren't just saying that to put Lily off?'

'Of course it's true, you fool. I've worked it all out—the baby's due about the middle of November. Well, then—are you pleased, or not?'

He took his time, concentrating on steering round the narrow right-hand turn into Acacia Grove, then said carefully, 'How do you know I'm the father?'

'Ooh, you can be a real swine sometimes. Of course it's yours. You know I don't go with other men.'

He stopped the car outside the house and pulled on the hand-brake, as he said, 'I don't know what you get up to when you're on tour, do I?'

'You should see the rest of the company! The troops prefer girlie shows; we've only got a sixty-year-old baritone and a teenage conjuror who's a boy wonder at card tricks and nothing else.'

'But I take it you get to meet some of the gallant fighting men? Cosy chats in the Officers' Mess after the show?'

'ENSA are very strict about that. We have a Company Manager who behaves like a prison wardress—I might as well be a nun in a convent. Honestly! Fancy saying a thing like that. I've never been so insulted in all my life.'

'Well, I couldn't help wondering, since I'm always careful to take precautions.'

'Not always. I've been counting back; I think it must have been when we went to the Valentine Day Ball at the Lyceum, and we both got rather tiddly—remember? You were a bit careless that night.' She shivered. 'I'm getting cold. Are we going indoors or aren't we?'

'In a minute.' He seemed to be in no hurry, but sat behind the wheel, gazing through the windscreen at nothing. 'I'm just thinking.'

'What's the good of thinking?' She was growing impatient. 'What are you going to do about it?'

'What do you want me to do?'

'Well, I was rather hoping you'd make an honest woman of me, actually! That's the usual procedure, isn't it?'

'I see.' He climbed out of the car and began to unpack her luggage from the boot, carrying it up the garden path. 'We'll talk about it presently. You must be exhausted after travelling all day. Why don't you pop upstairs and run yourself a bath? I've got to make a phone-call; I'll come up and see you in a minute or two.'

In the living-room, he waited until he heard the bath-taps running, then dialled a number. A man's voice answered cautiously, and he said: 'Pete? It's Trevor. Listen, I picked up an interesting scrap of news this afternoon. I think we may have a rush job on our hands, in the next few days. How soon can you get the lads together? Three or four—and we'll need a small van with a souped-up engine, in case we have a nippy getaway. No, never mind about a driver, I'll take care of that myself.'

A few minutes later he ran lightly upstairs. The bathroom door was open, and he walked in; Sally lay back with her eyes shut, veiled in steam, luxuriating in the warm, perfumed water. Trevor sat on the edge of the bath, admiring her.

'God, you're beautiful,' he said. 'You've got the most gorgeous figure I ever saw—it's too good to risk spoiling it by having a baby.'

She opened her eyes. 'What d'you mean? I hope you're not suggesting—'

'Hear me out, precious. I think we should discuss this quietly and sensibly. You've got your career to think about, remember.'

'My career? Tatting round drill halls and aircraft hangars? That's a laugh!'

'You're not going to be in ENSA much longer. I've got plans for you—big plans. This lousy war's not going on for ever. My guess is, it'll be over by Christmas—and that's when I'm going to launch a big musical revue in the West End, when the lights go up in Piccadilly. It would be a tragedy if you were so busy nursing a month-old kid, you couldn't take your place as the star of the show.'

'You really mean that?' She was pink with excitement. 'Oh, Trevor...'

'After all, there'll be plenty of time to start a family later, if that's what you want. But I do know a brilliant chap in Harley Street. He operates in an exclusive private nursing-home—it's more like a luxury hotel really.'

'I see...but won't that be terribly expensive?' she asked.

'Where you're concerned, my darling, expense is no object. And any minute now, I'm going to be rolling in money, so don't bother your pretty little head about that.'

He stood up and began to take off his tie, unfastening his shirt, unbuttoning his trousers. She lay back and watched him, saying with a mischievous smile: 'Why, Mr Judge. Whatever

481

do you think you're doing?'

'I'm sure you can make room for me in the tub if you try. It's our patriotic duty, didn't you know? Share a bath with a friend, and save hot water.'

That night, as Glory and Huw were getting ready for bed, he switched on the wireless, and she complained: 'Oh, that's charming, that is! Our first night as a proper married couple, and all you can think about is the ruddy news bulletin! Can't you find some nice smoochy dance music on the Forces programme instead? I don't want to share my honeymoon with some la-di-da bloke from the BBC!'

'Ssh, hang on a minute! You never know, there might be some good news,' Huw told her, as he tuned in the Home Service.

The plummy tones of the announcer came through the loudspeaker: '...And this is Alvar Liddell reading it. A Government Communiqué, issued today, states that for reasons of security all visitors are to be banned from travelling within ten miles of southern coastal areas. These restrictions will cover a district stretching from the Wash to Lands End, and will come into force immediately...'

They stared at one another, and Glory wailed, 'Bang goes our weekend in Brighton!'

Huw said, 'Yes, but it's good news all the same. Don't you see what it means? They're getting ready to strike back across the Channel. It won't be long now!'

That was what people were saying all over

482

the country: *'It won't be long now...'*

At the beginning of the year, the German High Command had begun a series of renewed air-attacks on south-east England, in an attempt to sabotage preparations for the Allied invasion of Occupied Europe. This was known as the 'Little Blitz', but by 1944 London's defences were so much stronger, few raiders managed to get through, so damage and casualties were comparatively light.

Once again, the principal targets lay along the banks of the Thames, for it was there, in the great dockyards—Surrey, Tilbury and East India—that concrete caissons were being manufactured and assembled, as a first step toward the building of Mulberry Harbour.

Even the Jubilee Wharf was playing its part; although they did not have enough space to house the huge concrete barges, which were like floating blocks of flats, they were able to construct some of the components. This meant fewer berths available for cargo ships, and as a consequence some of the warehouses were temporarily empty, but the work continued day and night—sometimes all round the clock—keeping up a ceaseless clangour of pneumatic drilling, of hammering, welding and riveting.

Many people knew what was going on, but they did their best to keep quiet about it. In cafés and pubs, posters went up: *Careless Talk Costs Lives and Be Like Dad—Keep Mum!*

Soon now, the pieces of the puzzle would be fitted together, and the prefabricated sections of the floating harbour would be towed out to sea, ready for D-Day.

On the first Friday in April, at the end of the afternoon, Trevor took a phone-call at the Guild Office. He kept his side of the conversation short and to the point.

'Yes—what time? Fine—I'll be here. As arranged. Yes, everything's under control.'

When he replaced the phone, Bertie looked up from his desk and asked, 'What was all that about?'

'The Wharfmaster was just checking up about the night-shift. The men will be working right through till dawn again; he wanted to make sure somebody would be on duty here, to keep an eye on things.'

'Another all-night duty?' groaned Bertie. 'How much longer is this going on? What did you tell him?'

'I said I'll be here. Well, I've got plenty of work I can get on with. It's rather peaceful in the wee small hours, with no phone-calls and no interruptions—I don't really mind.'

'Are you sure? Wouldn't you rather we split the duty? I could manage the first half of the night, say, and hand over to you later.'

'No, I wouldn't dream of it. You take things easy for a change; I'll catch up on some sleep tomorrow morning—I probably shan't come in till midday.'

'Well, if you're quite sure you don't mind?'

'Absolutely. Run along, Bertie. You push off now and get some rest—you deserve it. I'll take charge of everything tonight, don't you worry.'

484

As a rule, Connor O'Dell never took a night off. When he wasn't serving behind the bar, he would be on duty in the temporary Wardens' Post, down in the cellars. But tonight was an exception to the rule.

For some time, Rosie had been asking Connor and Ruth to come and have supper at Silmour Street. Con wasn't keen to go, but Ruth said: 'We can't keep putting her off, it's so rude. Besides, I think she's still very lonely. I know if I were her, I'd hate to live in that flat. The children have gone, Ernest's gone, even the shop's gone—it must be terrible for her. Surely we can spare one evening to go and keep her company?'

So they accepted the invitation. It wasn't exactly a cheerful occasion, although Rosie tried to lighten the mood by plying them with drink—gin before supper, cheap red wine during the meal, and generous measures of brandy afterwards.

Ruth, who had never been much of a drinker, soon found herself putting her hand over her glass each time Rosie tried to refill it, and even Connor, who had a very good head, told his sister that he'd had enough.

'If I drink any more, I'll be footless—and then we'll never get home at all!'

Only Rosie herself carried on drinking. At first alcohol seemed to make her bright and gay—then she became a shade too bright, and her gaiety took on a note of desperation, and finally she slumped into melancholy.

The evening dragged on, and the O'Dells made several attempts to leave, but Rosie begged them not to go.

'Come on now—the night's still young, another half-hour won't hurt you! I don't often have visitors; it makes a nice change for me—you must stay a little longer.'

It was difficult to refuse, but when Connor looked at his watch and saw that it was nearly midnight, he stood and said firmly: 'Huw promised to wait till we get home. We shouldn't keep him so late, Rosie—we really have to make a move.'

'Oh, no. Not yet—just a little longer!' She became tearful, clinging to Con's arm, and Ruth tried to explain.

'It's not that we want to go, but it isn't fair to Glory. She'll be getting anxious all on her own, waiting for Huw to come home.'

'It won't do her any harm for once,' said Rosie bitterly. 'She's got her man, hasn't she? She doesn't know what loneliness is like.'

When they finally dragged themselves away, she swayed down the stairs to see them off, and stood in the doorway, calling after them: 'You will come again soon, won't you? Please—very soon. We must do this more often.'

As they walked away down the street, Con grunted, 'Not if I can help it! She couldn't talk about anything but how hard-done-by she is. It's not easy to feel sorry for her, when she's so damn sorry for herself.'

'Don't be unkind,' said Ruth, linking her arm through his. 'We can afford to be

486

generous—we're the lucky ones. Do you suppose she drinks as much as that every night?'

'I'm afraid so. I saw the empties shoved under the kitchen sink. She'll destroy herself if she carries on like that.'

'Perhaps we should have said something? We really ought to try and help her.'

Connor shook his head. 'She wouldn't listen. You can't help somebody who doesn't want to be helped.'

They continued to walk up Manchester Road, then took a short cut, turning off into a side-street. It was a street Connor knew very well; halfway along was the Food Office, where the Wardens' Post used to be.

'That's peculiar,' he said 'There's some sort of van parked outside. What's it doing there, this time of night?'

Inside the van, Trevor sat waiting impatiently. What was taking the lads so long, for God's sake? They should have cleared the last load by now...

Out of the shadows at the far end of the street he saw two figures moving towards him—and he froze. Probably just a courting couple, but it seemed late for them to be walking the streets. As they came nearer, his heart missed a beat. In spite of the darkness, he recognised them—Connor and Ruth O'Dell. If they spotted him now, he was done for. Swiftly, he slid down behind the steering wheel, hoping against hope that they'd pass on without looking in.

He held his breath, willing them to walk by,

then he heard the footsteps stop and Connor's voice saying: 'Just a minute. Somebody's left a window open, along the alley. I'd better take a look.'

He heard Ruth's voice, urgent and apprehensive. 'I'll come with you.'

'No! You stay where you are.'

There was a narrow alleyway down the side of the building, and Connor walked along it, quietly and carefully. He realised that the open window led into the ground-floor toilet, used by the Food Office staff. As he drew near, he saw a movement inside, and he stopped dead.

A man, wearing a scarf round the lower part of his face and a stocking cap pulled down over his head, scrambled out and turned back immediately, reaching up to the open window.

Connor didn't waste words; he hurled himself at the stranger, spinning him round and grabbing him by the collar. The man struggled to get free, but he was caught in an iron grip. In retaliation, he lifted his fist, aiming for Connor's face.

Con deflected the blow with his forearm, and repaid it with a right-hook to the solar-plexus.

Reeling back, the man crashed against the wall and fell. Connor followed up his advantage, throwing himself on top of him, pinning him down. They wrestled together, rolling over in the muddy rubbish of the alley. The stranger had youth on his side, and he was fighting for his freedom—but Connor had the strength and stamina acquired through years of training, and the outcome was not in any doubt—until he found himself outnumbered.

While they were struggling, three other men had jumped down into the alley, and now they all piled on Connor. Taken offguard, he never stood a chance. He managed to land a few powerful blows, but two fists could not long withstand four ruthless men, and he went down under a storm of punches and kicks. As he fell, he remembered the night he was set upon by the Punishment Squad, long ago. He spat out some broken teeth, and the taste of blood in his mouth was the taste of defeat... He could not see his attackers, for the darkness was closing in on him, but his fist connected with a man's jaw. It gave him a brief moment of satisfaction as he slid into oblivion.

At the end of the alley a woman screamed: *'Connor!'*

They looked round and saw Ruth watching them; at once they left Connor lying in the mud, and moved towards her. She turned and ran, faster than she had ever run in her life—and one of the gang laughed. 'That scared her off...'

Trevor got out of the van, saying, 'You bloody fool—she's gone to get help! Is that the last lot? OK, get them in the van—and hurry!'

Within sixty seconds, the last bundle had been stowed away. The men jumped in after it and slammed the back doors, and Trevor trod on the accelerator.

Someone said, 'Where we goin' now, boss?'

'Don't ask questions; keep your heads down and leave this to me.' He was driving without lights; it was risky, but they weren't likely to meet any other traffic at this hour of the morning. He had made sure that the dock-gates would be open, and now he drove straight through—along the harbour wall and into Number 3 warehouse, which was empty.

'Right. Out you get, and start unloading.'

When the task was completed, he paid them off; it was a good wage for two hours' work, and nobody grumbled. Trevor double-locked the warehouse doors, before seeing them safely off the premises; he had taken the precaution of rounding up all the duplicate keys, making sure no one else could get in and discover the unusual cargo in store. It would not be there long—a few days at most—until the heat was off and the cops gave up the search. By the middle of next week, the stolen coupons would be changing hands for large sums of money, and Trevor would be a rich man.

It was three o'clock in the morning before he got back to Acacia Grove. Sally stirred, roused from sleep, as he climbed into bed beside her.

'Where have you been?' she asked drowsily. 'What time is it?'

'Late. I told you I'd be working late at the office tonight. Go back to sleep.'

As she drifted off again, she murmured, 'Oh, I did what you said. I made an appointment with your Harley Street doctor. He's seeing me on Wednesday morning.'

'Good. You'll like him; he's quite a ladies' man.'

'Mmm, he sounded nice. But I'm sure it's going to cost the earth—I could tell from the way he talks.'

'I told you, money's no object. This time next week, I'll probably be able to buy Harley Street.'

'What's all this then?'

Resentfully, Connor eyed the tray Ruth put on the bedside table.

'Breakfast in bed—you deserve it.'

'I never have breakfast in bed. I'm getting up!' He tried to move, but the pain hit him like a sledgehammer; he thought the top of his skull was coming apart.

'Don't argue. Stay right there, and don't you dare move,' she told him sternly. 'Doctor's orders!'

'I don't want any breakfast. Just a cup of tea, perhaps.'

She handed him the cup; he had forgotten that his right hand was bandaged, and he nearly dropped it.

'Shall I hold it for you?' she suggested.

'Mother of God, anyone'd think I was an invalid. I can manage!' he told her crossly. 'I just got into a bit of a fight, that's all.'

'Last night you said you couldn't remember it too well. Is it starting to come back now?'

'Well, bits and pieces... Remind me what happened.'

'You were set on by four thugs, making their getaway after the robbery. When I got back with the police, I found you lying there in the alley. For a minute, I thought you were dead, but they'd only knocked you out.'

'Knocked out? *Me?*' Furiously, he put down

the cup. 'I've never been KO'ed in my life.'

'Do you want to hear, or don't you? You didn't come round till we got the doctor to you. He patched you up. You've lost a couple of teeth, but he said you got off lightly—you can think yourself lucky you've a thick skull.'

'I tell you, I'm right as rain.' Con thought for a moment, then added, 'Those fellers—did you say they made a getaway?'

'Yes, they'd driven off in the van by the time we got back. Remember the van that was parked outside the Food Office?'

'Sort of... Did you get the number?'

'They had no lights on—it was too dark to see.'

'What were they looking for in there anyhow?'

'They didn't waste any time in the Food Office; as soon as they broke in, they pulled up the floorboards in the lavatory, and climbed down into the basement. Apparently there were a whole lot of clothing coupons down there, waiting to be issued. It's a mystery how they knew where to find them.'

'Some eejut must have been talking. You know how it is—people don't think who might be listening.' Depressed, Connor sank back against the pillows. 'So they got away with it, did they? No one stopped them?'

'You tried to. You did your best.'

'And a fat lot of good that was.' He threw back the blankets impatiently, about to get out of bed. It's high time I was up and about. I can't stay here all day.'

Then the pain struck again; his bruised ribs

screamed in protest, and he began to cough—a shattering cough, that left him breathless and exhausted. Ruth tucked him in, saying: 'You never listen, do you? The doctor says you've to stay in bed for a day or two. You're not well.'

He seemed to shrink before her eyes; he was fifty-four years old, and for the first time she saw him looking his age.

'I'm useless, so I am. I should have stopped them. I let them get away.'

'There were four of them, Con. I couldn't see their faces, but they were four great hulking brutes. You were no match for them on your own.'

'I would have been—once,' he said. 'But I'm too old now, and that's the truth of it.'

'For heaven's sake.' She put her arm round his shoulders. 'It's not a crime to grow old, is it?'

'No, it's not a crime,' he answered quietly. 'More like a punishment.'

16

Sally woke up and looked round the room. For a moment she could not think where she was; the brocade curtains, the chintz covers, the creamy rug beside the bed all looked unfamiliar. Then she saw the flowers—the huge bouquet of white roses from Trevor—and she remembered. So that was it—a little operation, a little sleep, and it was all over.

She felt so happy, as if she were floating on a soft, fleecy cloud; of course she had been mildly drugged—perhaps the pain would come later—but at this moment, she hadn't a care in the world. She felt like a princess, cocooned in luxury, cradled in loving care.

When she heard the discreet tap at the door, she did not even raise her head from the pillow but called out lazily, 'You can come in, I am awake.'

The door opened, and the doctor walked in, although she must remember that he wasn't called a doctor, because he was a gynaecological surgeon. The Sister had warned her she should call him 'Mister'—but when she met him, he had put her at her ease immediately by saying: 'We don't have to stand on ceremony, Sally. Trevor and I are old friends—call me Simon.'

He came and sat on the side of the bed and asked. 'How are you feeling?'

'I feel marvellous. Very comfortable—a little bit dreamy.'

'That's the idea. Well, let's take a look at you, hm?' He turned back the bedclothes, then—delicately—raised her nightdress, gently easing her legs apart, humming a little tune under his breath as he examined his handiwork.

'Yes... Very good—excellent. Ex-cell-ent,' he repeated. 'You're a model patient, my dear.' He covered her up again, adding, 'In fact, it did cross my mind that you might be a professional model! You certainly have the figure for it—but I believe Trevor told me you're a singer and

494

dancer, is that right?'

'Yes, that's why this was so important,' she explained. 'For my career, you see.'

'Quite.' His hand remained on her thigh, as he continued smoothly, 'And I look forward to the pleasure of seeing you on stage in the near future. Although, of course'—he chose his words cautiously—'I look forward to seeing you sooner than that—privately.'

'You mean, when I come in for my check-up?'

'That too, but I hope we may meet under less clinical circumstances. If you should ever find yourself in this part of town with time to kill, I shall always be delighted to offer you a spot of lunch, hm?'

There was no doubt about it; Simon really was rather a pet, with his wavy silver hair and the cornflower in his buttonhole, matching the blue of his eyes... She'd always had a soft spot for older men.

'That would be lovely,' she said demurely.

Somebody else knocked on the door. Without hurrying, Simon replaced the bedclothes then said, 'Come in.'

Trevor entered the room, carrying another bunch of roses. The two men shook hands cordially, and Simon said: 'I'm extremely pleased with Sally—she's given us no trouble at all; everything went according to plan. Now I must leave you both in peace, but do look in at my office on your way out, old man—a word before you go, hm?'

As soon as the door closed, Trevor said,

'That's his tactful way of reminding me to settle up. Cash on the nail—no bills, no receipts, nothing in writing that might be used as evidence later.'

Sally puckered her lips. 'Don't I get a kiss?'

He leaned over and kissed her, saying, 'You must be thankful it's over.'

'Oh, yes. And I'm sure you must be thankful too.' She gave him a shrewd glance under her lashes. 'You don't have to marry me after all.'

'You needn't put it like that!' he protested, settling himself in the bedside chair.

'Why not? It's true, isn't it? Come on, own up. You never really wanted to marry me, admit it.'

He took her hands in his, saying quietly, 'I thought you understood—I can't marry you. I can never marry anyone.'

'What do you mean?'

'It's not something I talk about as a rule, but...remember how I was rejected on medical grounds, when I tried to join up? This damned bug I seem to have picked up—apparently I could pop off at any time. So the idea of making any long-term commitment—a wife, a family—well, it simply wouldn't be fair. I just live one day at a time, and look on every day that's left as a kind of bonus.'

'Oh, Trevor.' Her eyes filled with tears. 'I should have realised. But you're so brave. You always carry on as if, well, as if there was nothing wrong. Of course I understand.'

He squeezed her hand fondly. 'I knew you would,' he said.

During the first week of June, everyone on the Island knew the invasion was about to begin. Every day more troops were moved into the area, until there were six Army divisions at London's docks, awaiting embarkation.

When darkness fell on Monday, 5 June, few people had an undisturbed night; as the hours went by, hundreds of troop-carriers set off down the river, while overhead the sky was alive with aircraft, heading across the estuary for the south-east coast in an endless stream.

At breakfast-time on Tuesday, the BBC announcer mentioned that reports were coming in on the radio from a German news agency, saying that Allied landing-craft had arrived on the French coast, although these reports had not yet been confirmed by the British Ministry of Information. It was not until nine-thirty that the programmes were interrupted for a special bulletin; the unruffled, reliable voice of John Snagge, stating: 'D-Day has come. Early this morning the Allies began the assault on the northwestern face of Hitler's European fortress.'

The news sent a wave of jubilation sweeping across the whole country. The long years of defence and retreat were over, and Britain was taking the initiative at last, mounting an attack.

In the middle of so much excitement, some people heard the news with mixed feelings; wives and mothers whose men might at that moment be fighting for their lives, somewhere on a French beach.

Of course there was no way of knowing whether individual servicemen had got through safely. It would be a long time before D-Day could be measured in terms of success or failure, profit and loss, the living and the dead. So the families at home could do nothing but wait, and hope, and pray.

For others, the news was a tonic in itself, calling for a celebration; in the pub, customers raised their glasses to a speedy victory, drinking to Hitler's imminent collapse. Connor said nothing. Recovering slowly from his injuries, he was already back at his post behind the bar, pulling pints and refusing to acknowledge the aches and pains that still plagued him. His years in the boxing-ring had taught him never to take the result for granted until the bell sounded for the last time, and the fight was over.

Certainly, Hitler was not going to give in without a struggle.

Exactly one week after D-Day, the air-raid sirens sounded again in East London, and there were two major incidents that night. Connor picked up the report next day from the Civil Defence office in Poplar, and when Lil came in later, on her way home after a day on duty, he mentioned it to her.

'Two German planes shot down—one on Dagenham marshes, another at Bow; it must have had a load of bombs on board—they say it made a damn great crater in Grove Road.'

Lil shook her head. 'That wasn't a plane. HQ told our Chief this morning that it didn't even have a pilot on board.'

It was the first flying-bomb; the first of more than two thousand unmanned aircraft which were to explode in London during the next twelve months—Hitler's 'secret weapon': the V-1 flying-bomb. 'V' stood for *vergeltungswaffe*, from the German word for 'revenge'—and '1' because, as Goebbels was quick to announce, this was to be only the first in a whole series of such devices.

In England, they became known as the 'doodlebugs' or 'buzz-bombs', on account of the noise they made. The EastEnders tried to make light of them, but there was something sinister about those mindless, automatic missiles, and they were deeply feared and hated.

Rosie came round to the pub, seeking comfort and reassurance, telling the O'Dells: 'I heard two go right overhead this morning. The noise they make puts the fear of God in you, like an old sewing-machine, getting louder and louder—but waiting for it to stop is enough to drive you mad.'

That was the signal to take cover; when the motor cut out, it meant the flying-bomb would change course and glide to earth.

'You're right—it's unnatural, so it is,' agreed Mary. 'I found myself praying to Our Blessed Lady not to let the thing stop over our house—isn't that terrible? Praying it would go on and land elsewhere, to murder some other poor innocent souls.'

As always, Ruth prescribed a pot of tea as the best remedy, and put the kettle on. As she was setting out the cups and saucers, Rosie sprang up suddenly, exclaiming: 'Listen! There's one now—I can hear it!'

They held their breath; something that sounded like a decrepit motorbike was coming slowly nearer. Nobody moved. They looked at one another uncertainly then Ruth went to the door and called through to the bar: 'Do you hear that, Con?'

'Of course I hear it!' he retorted. 'D'you think I'm deaf? Or daft?'

They listened and waited—and the sound stopped abruptly.

'Right! Under the table—quick!' said Ruth. She helped her mother-in-law to get down on her knees, and the three women crawled beneath the sturdy kitchen table. Seconds passed with agonising slowness... Five, ten, fifteen...

The explosion made the whole building shudder. The cups and saucers rattled, followed by the crash of falling glass, and a fine shower of plaster-dust floated down from the ceiling. In the saloon, Con yelled furiously: 'That's our front windows gone again! The lousy bastards!'

'Language!' said Mary, as an automatic response, while Ruth helped her back to her chair.

Rosie was shaking uncontrollably. 'I can't bear it,' she said. 'I really can't bear it.'

'It's all right. You're perfectly safe—nobody's hurt,' Ruth told her. 'Sit down and get your breath back.'

'We're not hurt, but I dare say somebody is,' said Mary.

Later they heard that the bomb had landed

outside the Rest Centre in St Anthony's Church hall. It had left a wide hole in the road, and the blast had cut a swathe through the surrounding streets, but although several people were injured, including three Sisters from the Convent, nobody had been killed.

Seeing that Rosie was still suffering from shock, Ruth invited her to stay at the pub overnight. 'We haven't a spare room to give you, but there are beds in the Wardens' Post down below. You're very welcome to one of those, if you want?'

Rosie wouldn't hear of it. 'I'd never sleep a wink down in the cellars; I'd be afraid the whole place would come down on top of me. Anyway, the nights aren't so bad. These flying-bombs mostly land in daylight, out of a clear blue sky—that's what makes it so horrible.'

At the Jubilee Wharf, Bertie had taken shelter under his desk. He emerged, white and quivering, and gasped: 'The next one could land on top of us. We can't stay here—what are we going to do?'

Trevor, who hadn't bothered to take cover, went on totting up the accounts. He shrugged. 'We carry on with our jobs—what else can we do? Running away isn't much use. How do you know where the next bomb will land? You might be running smack into it!'

This so unnerved Bertie, he made a dive for the filing cabinet and after fumbling to open the bottle, poured himself a large scotch.

'We can't go on like this,' he said hoarsely.

'It must be stopped. Somebody ought to *do* something.'

The feeling of helplessness was the most frightening part. Rosie spent a miserable evening in her own flat, and got through half a bottle of gin, but for some reason it didn't seem to have much effect; the fear did not go away.

At about ten o'clock Abram arrived home unexpectedly. He still had a key, so he let himself in and ran upstairs, finding his mother curled up in her chair with the bottle beside her and an empty glass in her hand.

'That won't make things better,' he said, taking them from her.

'I know...' She looked up at him in despair. 'What am I going to do?'

'You're going to get undressed, and you're going to bed,' he told her. 'That's why I came round. I'll sit with you till you're asleep. I'm going to try and slip away from the hospital every evening, to make sure you're safe, and to say good-night.'

He made her some cocoa and sat beside the bed until she nodded off; then he let himself out quietly. Someone was covering for him while he was away, but he couldn't risk staying too long.

Some time after midnight Rosie woke up in the big double bed; she rolled over, expecting to find Ernest there—and then she remembered she was alone. She was grateful to Abram. He was a good boy and he had helped her to get some rest, but she knew he couldn't stay with her all the time—she wouldn't expect him to.

Now she was wide awake, and she stared up into the darkness, her thoughts chasing one another in circles. She considered the possibility of moving across to the house in Greenwich. Sally and Trevor couldn't object to that, could they? It was her house, after all... But she had heard that the bombs were even worse on the other side of the river, so that was no good.

She couldn't expect any more help from her family; they had their own lives to lead. But how could she possibly face up to this fear—this unbearable sense of guilt—all by herself?

Unable to get back to sleep, she waited for dawn, counting the hours. When the first glimmers of light streaked the sky, she got up, washed and dressed; she did not make herself any breakfast—perhaps she would be hungry later on. Then she unlocked and unbolted the street door.

It was quite cold outside. Though it was midsummer, there was a nipping breeze off the river, and she wrapped her coat more closely about her.

It was not a long walk. When she reached St Anthony's, she found the road cordoned off, closed to traffic, and the bomb-crater outside the Rest Centre was like an open wound, but a few men and women were picking their way across the rubble, going into the church next door.

St Anthony's always celebrated the first Mass of the day at seven, and though most of the windows were missing, and the chairs, broken and splintered, had been cleared into one of the side aisles, out of the way, a handful of worshippers were gathered in front of the chancel.

Rosie felt the broken glass crunch beneath her shoes; more broken glass lay on the altar steps. It was cold inside the church, with doors and windows open to the morning air, and the candle-flames guttered in the draught, but as the priest carried out the old, familiar ritual, the rhythm of the Latin phrases came back to her—so easily, she found herself joining in the responses: *'Benedictus qui venit in nomine Domini; hosanna in excelsis...'*

The consecration followed; the bread and wine were lifted high, and finally the little congregation went up and knelt at the altar rail to receive communion.

Rosie had not set foot in a church since she rejected her parents' faith, to join the man she loved. Now she stood apart from the others, in the shadows at the back; she was not in a state of grace, and she could do nothing but watch and listen, and join in the prayers—and ask for the mercy of God.

But she knew she could not be forgiven without making a full confession of her sins; and the sin that weighed her down was so terrible, she could never confess it to anyone.

A few days later, a young soldier in battledress—balancing a kitbag on his left shoulder, for his right arm was in a sling—walked up Millwall Road and entered the hairdressing salon.

There was no one in the shop; he looked around curiously, for it was the first time he had seen it since it re-opened for business. It all looked very smart, with its bright new paint and fancy wallpaper; there were two new wash-basins, and two new hair-driers—but there were no customers.

Alerted by the ping of the shop doorbell, Gloria came bustling through from the back kitchen, hastily pulling on her lilac smock and calling out: 'Morning, Mrs Morton, you're bright and early—' The words died on her lips. She swayed a little, and gripped the back of the nearest chair to steady herself. '*Matt*. Oh, thank Gawd for that. I've been worried sick...'

She threw her arms round him, laughing and crying, while he exclaimed: 'Hey, take it easy, will you? Give us a chance to breathe!'

'Sorry.' She released him at once. 'What have you done to your arm?'

'Got in the way of some shrapnel, didn't I? Tore my shoulder to pieces, it did. Those Jerry buggers were dive-bombing us, the minute we landed. Bloke next to me got his head blown off. I was pretty lucky, considering.'

Matt's part in the invasion was short-lived; strafed by enemy fire as he leaped out of the landing-craft and raced up the Normandy beach, he had been left for dead among the sand-dunes for several hours, until a patrol of medical orderlies, looking for survivors, had come across him. His wounds were too serious to be patched up at the field ambulance-station, so they pumped him full of pain-killers and sent him back to England in the next transport. He had spent a week in a military hospital, and

505

after an operation to remove all the fragments of shrapnel, he was now home on sick-leave.

'They'll have to conquer Europe without me this time,' he concluded. 'Well, I think I'll take my kit upstairs and get my head down for a couple of hours, providing your husband doesn't have any objections?'

'Of course not. Huw will be very glad to see you—we've kept your room all ready for you.'

'Much obliged, I'm sure. But of course he won't be using it any more, will he? He's got the best bedroom now, eh?'

'Matt, don't be like that,' she began, but the doorbell pinged again, interrupting her.

'Good morning. I'm not too early, am I?' Glory's next appointment had arrived; a chirpy little woman, smiling roguishly. 'Don't tell me—I think I can guess. You must be Mrs Pritchard's son! Am I right?'

He gave her a baleful look, then picked up his kitbag and lugged it into the kitchen without a word.

Glory and Huw did their best to make him feel welcome, but it wasn't easy. At first he did not want to go out much, and sat around the house, reading cowboy books or listening to the wireless—Tommy Handley in ITMA was a particular favourite. When Huw came home from work, Matt made himself scarce, shutting himself up in his room most of the time. He came down and joined them for meals, but even then he rarely took part in the conversation.

At the Watermen, Huw let off steam, telling the O'Dells: 'If he wasn't Glory's son—and if he hadn't got that bad shoulder—I'd give him a piece of my mind, I can tell you!'

'Why don't you ask him if he'd like to come over and see us one evening?' Ruth suggested. 'That would give you and Glory a break.'

'And what about us? We'll be stuck with him!' protested Connor. 'What the devil would we talk to him about? Besides, the evenings are our busiest time!'

Kaff, who was helping to peel potatoes in the scullery, called out eagerly: 'I'll talk to him if you like—I don't mind. He's not so bad when you get to know him.'

So Matt came round and had high tea with the family, and when the pub opened and the O'Dells went to work in the two bars, and Mary went upstairs to sit with Marcus, Kaff stayed in the kitchen to keep Matt company.

'I'm glad we're on our own,' she said. 'I've been wanting to talk to you.'

He cocked an eye at her. 'Sounds good. What d'you want to talk about, eh?'

'I wanted to ask you about Dan.'

'I should have known.' He pulled a comic face. 'Don't tell me you're still smitten with Sergeant O'Dell? Still think he's the answer to a maiden's prayer, do you?'

'I don't know what to think. He used to write to me, but he hasn't written for ages. He is all right, isn't he? I mean, he didn't get hurt like you, and sent to hospital?'

'Not so far as I know. But I ain't seen him for weeks. I got sent back home, didn't I? He's still out there in France—killing Jerries and

507

winning medals, I dare say. He always was a lucky so-and-so.'

She hesitated for a moment, then asked the question that was tormenting her. 'Before you went to France, do you know if he found himself a girl? Did he ever talk about anyone else?'

Matt was sitting in an armchair by the fireplace; Kaff sat on the rug beside him, her arms round her knees, gazing up at him with big, pleading eyes. Not for the first time, he thought what a tasty little piece she was.

'I wouldn't know. He don't muck in with us lower-orders. He's on his way up the ladder now he's got three stripes. We're not mates any more, him and me.' Looking into those dark, lustrous eyes, he added, 'But I shouldn't be surprised. He's very popular with the birds, our Danny-boy. Off out with a different bit of skirt every night, he is.'

Kaff turned away, so he could not see her face; even the way she hung her head was attractive. Tentatively, he put his hand on her shoulder. 'Cheer up,' he said softly. 'Don't go upsetting yourself, he ain't worth it. Better forget him, find yourself some other bloke.'

She looked up at him and tried to smile. 'Thanks,' she said. 'You're very kind.'

'It's easy, being kind to you,' he said. 'You're a lovely girl, d'you know that?'

She put her hand up to her shoulder; her fingers met his. 'You're just saying that,' she told him.

'I mean it. And I'll prove it, and all. How about you and me going out one night? There's

508

a dance on at the Blue Lagoon Ballroom, Saturday night. We could have a good time together... Why not?'

Impulsively, she squeezed his hand. 'Yes, why not?' she said.

Next day, when Kaff told the O'Dells that Matt had asked her to go dancing, it provoked a certain amount of argument. Connor, who had never liked Matt, felt they should not allow her to go. She wasn't much more than a child, after all.

'She's sixteen,' Ruth told him. 'Just a few months younger than I was, the first time you met me! And she doesn't have many friends round here. It can't be much fun for her, living in a house full of older people. I think she deserves a bit of a treat. She'll be so disappointed if we say no.'

Kind-hearted Mary agreed with Ruth. Provided Matt promised not to keep her out late, she'd come to no harm. Huw's instinct was to side with Connor, but at the same time he didn't want to do anything that might put an extra strain on his already difficult relationship with Matt, so he refused to be drawn into the debate.

When Lil called in at the pub and heard what was going on, she found herself in a dilemma. Like Ruth, she didn't want Kaff to be disappointed, but she couldn't help remembering that Matt was the first boy who ever made sexual advances to her, when she worked as a very junior assistant in Glory's salon. But she didn't want to stir up any more trouble by telling her parents about that; it was a long time ago, and Matt's fumbling attempts at intimacy had not been difficult to fend off.

In the end, she kept quiet about it, and even offered to help Kaff to smarten herself up for the great occasion, lending her a dance-dress and giving her a shampoo and set.

While Kaff sat in her bedroom with a towel round her shoulders, Lil took the opportunity for a gentle warning. 'You're going to look lovely tonight, Kaff—and very grown-up. In fact, Matt might get quite carried away.'

'Think so?' Kaff smiled. 'You mean he might try and kiss me or something?'

'Or something...' Lil met her eyes in the mirror above the wash-stand. 'He might try to go a bit further than that—you know what I mean. So you will be careful, won't you?'

'Course I will. I'm not a kid any more.'

Saturday was a warm night, and the Blue Lagoon was very crowded. When they walked in, Kaff's eyes widened; she gazed around her, dazzled. This was what she had always dreamed of—the band on stage in their smart dinner-jackets, the coloured lights hung in clusters between the pillars, the mirror-ball on the ceiling that sent glittering points of light cascading over the dancers—she had never seen anything so glamorous. At last she was Scarlett O'Hara in Atlanta, she was Cinderella at the palace—so what did it matter if Matt wasn't Prince Charming or Rhett Butler? He was her partner for the evening, and she loved him because he had brought her into this marvellous, magical world... And she wasn't even going to think about Dan O'Dell.

Besides, Matt wasn't bad-looking really. There was something rather romantic about him having one arm in a sling; all the other girls glanced at him curiously, and Kaff felt proud to be seen with him.

'Sorry about the war-wound,' he said, as they began to dance. 'I can't hold you the way I'd like to.'

It didn't seem to matter; although she couldn't hold his right hand, his left arm was firmly round her waist, and he managed to steer her through a waltz, a fox-trot and a rhumba without much difficulty. Only when the tempo speeded up and the dancers hurled themselves enthusiastically into the new jitterbug craze, he had to apologise.

'Better give this one a miss,' he told her. 'I wouldn't be much good, trying to swing you round! Let's go and have a drink—I'm thirsty.'

'Me too,' she said, and they pushed their way through to the bar.

Although she was under-age, Matt introduced her to gin and tonic, and they stayed in the bar for some time, listening to the thrilling rhythms of *Chattanooga Choo-Choo*. Matt bought several more drinks, and the world seemed more wonderful to Kaff than ever before; she had never been so happy.

'Phew, bit sticky, innit?' Matt asked, giving her a sidelong look. 'I can't hardly breathe in this crowd. Wotcher say we slip out for a breath of fresh air?'

'If you like.' Kaff was quite content to go wherever he wanted, only asking, 'But we're not going home yet, are we?'

'Home? I should say not!' he grinned. 'We'll just have a breather, then come back after.'

The doorman pressed a rubber stamp with the word 'Pass' on the backs of their hands, and let them out.

Above the rooftops, the midsummer sky shone with the faint afterglow of sunset; the air was still, and Kaff heard the distant hooting of a boat, somewhere on the river.

'It's a lovely evening,' she murmured.

'And it's gonna get better,' Matt told her, putting his good arm round her shoulders.

He knew where to go; there was a narrow alley behind the dance-hall, overshadowed by tall buildings on either side. It was very dark down there, but Kaff saw the red glow of a cigarette, and heard whispers among the shadows—they were not alone.

'Let's go back,' she said uneasily. 'I don't like it.'

'Don't you worry, you're gonna like it all right,' he assured her. Pulling her towards him, he began to kiss her.

She had been expecting that, and she didn't mind, though the smell of whisky on his breath was unpleasant, but she didn't object until his left hand started to explore her body.

'Hey, don't do that!' she exclaimed, and a few yards away she heard a girl sniggering.

'Shut up,' whispered Matt, unbuttoning her dress. 'This ain't easy for me. You've got to be nice—you've got to help me.'

Not wanting to make a scene, she let him go on, and felt his fingers groping her breasts. Perhaps he'd stop soon, and then they could go back inside the Blue Lagoon, back to the lights and the music... But he didn't stop. Instead, his hand slid down her body, pulling up her skirt.

'No, stop, please! You mustn't,' she begged him, trying to push his hand away.

'Go on—all you darkies are hot stuff.' His voice was husky with excitement. 'Let's have a feel. You can have a feel of me, if you want. Here, cop hold of this.'

Suddenly she remembered Dan, and a wave of shame swept through her.

'Let go of me!' She pulled away from him, not caring if she made a fool of herself. *You make me sick!*

He tried to hold on to her, but she slipped from his grasp and ran away along the alley, running blindly from him, and from herself...

Left alone, Matt cursed under his breath—and heard strangers in the darkness laughing at him. Stupid little cow, he was well rid of her. Furiously, he made his way back into the dance-hall, trying to ignore the doorman's inquisitive stare, and headed straight for the bar.

After a double whisky, he began to feel a lot better, and decided to look for someone else. Most of the girls already had partners, but he saw two women sitting together. They were no spring chickens, but he wasn't choosy. Strolling across to them, he addressed the prettier of the two, asking if she'd like to cut a rug?

She looked him up and down scornfully. 'You're pissed,' she said.

'Wotcher mean? I'm all right. C'mon, let's dance.' He tried to take her arm, but she slapped his hand away.

'You're pissed, and you're a bloody cripple,' she said. 'Now push off, will you?'

'Oh, all right then.' Swaying slightly, he turned to her companion. 'How about you, sweetheart?'

'Get knotted,' said the other one.

So he went back to the bar and had another drink. Bloody women—they were all the same. Suddenly it seemed vitally important to find himself a woman; somewhere, there must be someone who wanted him. Then, through a haze of alcohol, he had an idea.

Rosie was alone at Silmour Street as usual; there had been another flying-bomb explosion earlier in the day, just across the river in North Woolwich, not so near as the last one, but close enough to terrify her.

Though she had promised herself she wouldn't have a drink this evening, because she knew Abram hated it, she eventually decided she would give herself a tiny drop to steady her nerves. Now, looking at the level of the gin left in the bottle, she realised uncomfortably that she had got through rather more than a drop.

When the doorbell rang, she put the bottle out of sight and made her way downstairs. Abram must have forgotten his key. As soon as she opened the door, Matt pushed past her into the empty shop. After her initial amazement, she felt overjoyed, and followed him up the stairs, chattering:

'Well, this is a nice surprise. Glory told me you were home on leave—it's lovely to see you. How are you? And how's your poor shoulder?'

In the sitting-room, he threw himself on to the settee with a meaningless smile on his face, and she realised he was half-drunk.

'You bad boy—I do believe you've been on the razzle!' she said playfully. 'Well, I mustn't scold you. After what you've been through, I'm sure you deserve a bit of fun sometimes. How are you feeling?'

'Fine. I feel fine...' With a fixed smile still on his lips, he stared at her, glassy-eyed, then patted the empty space beside him. 'Come and sit down.'

'Would you like some coffee?' she asked. 'I expect we could both do with a cup. It won't take a minute.'

'I said sit down,' he repeated, thrusting out a hand. 'Come here.'

'Well, all right.' She sat next to him. 'I'll tell you a little secret; I was having a drink myself, before you came. Well, why shouldn't I? It helps to pass the time, doesn't it? It's not much fun, living all on your own, I can tell you.'

'That's right.' He spoke thickly, making an effort to articulate the words. 'Like you said—you gotta have a bit of fun sometimes.'

He put his left arm around her waist, pulling her close to him, and she tried to struggle free,

515

laughing politely, although she was beginning to feel frightened. 'Matt, don't be silly! I really think I ought to make that coffee.'

'Sod the coffee,' he told her, and brought his mouth down upon hers, kissing her hungrily. 'You know what I want—and you want it, too, I know you do.'

Panic exploded within her. She tried to push him away, but he forced himself on her, pinning her down, and she began to scream: *'Stop! For God's sake, you must stop!'*

He took no notice. He was tearing at her blouse with his free hand, ripping it apart, and she began to sob with fear.

Neither of them heard Abram coming upstairs. Taken by surprise, Matt could not defend himself when Abram grabbed him. Losing his balance, he rolled heavily off the settee.

Weeping, Rosie picked herself up and backed away, frantically trying to cover her breasts with the torn blouse.

'Go to bed, Momma,' Abram told her. 'Leave him to me.'

'Be careful, he's been drinking,' Rosie warned him.

'You've both been drinking,' he said quietly. 'Please—just go.'

She disappeared into her room and threw herself on the bed, abandoning herself to a flood of tears.

Under different circumstances, Abram might have found it difficult to get Matt out of the house, but there was no trial of strength tonight; one-armed, drunk and humiliated, Matt shuffled to his feet and made an undignified exit. Abram watched him stagger away down the street, then locked the front door and bolted it.

Rosie heard him coming upstairs again and tried to control herself; she wrapped the counterpane around her and was sitting up, blowing her nose and wiping her eyes when Abram came into the room.

'What happened?' she asked. 'What did he say?'

'Nothing happened; he didn't say anything. He just took himself off. Don't worry, he won't be coming here any more.'

For some reason that made the tears start to flow again, and he tried to comfort her. 'I'll stay here tonight, Momma,' he said. 'I don't care what they say at the Hospital—I won't leave you on your own. I understand what happened. You felt lonely and asked him round for a drink, and he got the wrong idea. You'll just have to be a bit more careful in your choice of friends another time.'

She could not stop crying, but managed to blurt out, 'It wasn't like that. It wasn't what you think. He'd only been here five or ten minutes. The doorbell rang, and I let him in; I thought you'd forgotten your key...'

'You mean he just barged in and started mauling you about?' Abram's face darkened. 'If I'd known that, I'd have broken his bloody neck.'

'No! You mustn't say that.' She was sobbing helplessly now. 'It wasn't really his fault. It's my fault—it's always been my fault.'

'I don't understand.'

'I've been so afraid lately—afraid of the bombs, afraid I might be killed. I don't want to go to hell with this sin on my conscience. I need to make a good confession.'

'What are you saying? You're not a Catholic, not since you married Poppa!'

'That doesn't make any difference; it never lets you go. I have to confess—I have to tell the truth. I owe it to you—and to him.'

At Coldharbour, Lil was already in bed when she heard the footsteps on the stairs. For a second she wondered if Abram had come to call on her again—but she realised he would never disturb her at this time of night. And then she knew, without any shadow of doubt, who it was.

Pulling on her old dressing-gown, she went through and opened the door.

'Lily.' Trevor stood and looked at her. 'I had to see you.'

She stepped back without a word and let him in. He sat at the table, in one of the upright kitchen chairs; she took the chair facing him, on the other side of the table.

'Is it about Sally?' she asked. 'The baby?'

He sighed, massaging his forehead; he looked very tired. 'I was forgetting, you don't know about that. I should have told you...we lost the baby. Sally had a miscarriage.'

'Dear God.' Lil crossed herself quickly. 'I'm so sorry, I had no idea.'

'No, well—we didn't spread the news around, as you can imagine.'

'How has she taken it?'

'Pretty well, considering. And I'm doing all I can to help her get over it. I'll make it up to her, she knows that. I'm going to get her a job in a show—a really good job.'

'That's not quite the same thing, though, is it?' said Lil. 'It's you she wants now, not a job. You, yourself.'

'I'm afraid that's impossible,' he said. 'I can't give her what isn't mine to give.'

Immediately she knew what he meant. She began to rise to her feet, saying, 'No, Trevor, don't say any more. Sally needs you!'

He stopped her with a slight movement of his hand. 'No, please. Sit down—we have to talk about this. We have to be honest with one another. I used to think I loved Sally, but that was all over long ago. That Christmas Day, when I saw you again at the pub, I fell in love with you at that moment—and I know you love me too.'

His eyes held hers, and she felt hypnotised; she could not look away as he continued, 'Nothing can change that. You're in my mind and my heart, every minute of the day. I can't live without you.'

'But, there's Sally...'

'I'll make Sally a big star—that's what she wants—but I can't live without you. I'm going to move back to my flat in town, and I want you to come with me.'

Time stood still. She could not speak—she could hardly breathe.

Then, for the last time that night, Lil heard

519

footsteps—light, running steps, hurrying up the stairs. Someone knocked at the door, and the spell was broken; Lil stood up and called, 'Who is it?'

'It's me, Kaff,' said a miserable little voice. 'Can I come in?'

At once Trevor moved silently towards the bedroom, whispering, 'Get rid of her. I'll wait in here.'

'No, Trevor, I can't do that.' She went and opened the door, and saw the girl's tear-stained face. 'Come in, Kaff.'

As she entered the room, Kaff saw Trevor and hesitated. 'You've got company.'

'Mr Judge is just leaving.' She brought Kaff in, and held the door for Trevor, saying to him, 'We'll talk another time.'

'Whenever you like.' As he passed, his hand touched hers briefly. 'Whenever—wherever. Just call me.'

She closed the door and heard him going away down the staircase, taking part of her life with him.

'I'm sorry to bother you,' sniffed Kaff unhappily. 'I didn't know where else to go. I couldn't face them at home. Not yet, not like this.'

Lil sat her down in Trevor's chair, and heard herself saying kindly: 'Well, now—what's the trouble? Tell me what happened.'

Next day was Sunday, so the hairdressing salon was closed. When Abram arrived at Millwall Road he had to ring the shop bell. At first nothing happened, and he began to think he'd had a wasted journey, but then the roller-blind inside the glass door rattled up, and he found himself face to face with Matt.

Seeing Abram, Matt scowled and said between his teeth, 'What do you want? Come to make more trouble, have you? Why the hell can't you leave me alone?'

He was about to pull the blind down, but Abram interrupted him. 'Wait—please. I've got to talk to you.'

Matt stared at him with puffy, bloodshot eyes, then reluctantly unbolted the door, spitting out hatred: 'I got nothing to say to you, you Jewish git. Except you can think yourself bloody lucky. I'm warning you, Kleiber—when I get my strength back in this arm, you're a dead man.'

Disregarding the threat, Abram took a step inside the salon and glanced around. 'Where's Gloria?'

'In bed. Her and her Taffy husband like a lie-in of a Sunday—what's that got to do with you?'

'Nothing, only I had to see you on your own. You've got to come with me—right away.'

'Here, what are you on about?' Matt drew back suspiciously. 'If this is some sort of a trick—'

'Please listen. My mother sent me; she says she's got to see you—it's very important. There's something she has to say. She told me she wants to put things right.'

Matt groaned, 'I don't know what you're

talking about. I don't feel so good this morning. I was up half the night, spewing my guts out. I wanna go back to bed.' He turned away, scratching himself. He looked as if he had slept in his clothes—unwashed and unshaven, suffering from the excesses of the night before—but Abram stood his ground.

'I promised her I'd bring you. I don't understand it either—she said something about a secret. I can only tell you she's nearly off her head with worry. She's very frightened and unhappy. You must come, for God's sake.'

Matt didn't feel strong enough to argue. He pulled on an old coat, and they set out together, heading down West Ferry Road in silence. After a few minutes, Matt said, 'This ain't the quick way to Silmour Street. We should've took the short cut.'

'We're not going to Silmour Street. I left her at Burrells Wharf; she's waiting for us there.'

Burrells Wharf was on the south-west shore of the Island; normally a busy, bustling place, it was deserted on a Sunday, and as the tide was out, there were only a few barges and lighters moored along the river wall, keeled over at odd angles on the mud. A few seagulls wheeled in the fresh morning air, screaming harshly.

'Where is she then?' asked Matt.

'I don't know. She was sitting here on the steps, when I...' Then Abram broke off and pointed.

A solitary figure was walking over the mudflats, wrapped in a black shawl, among the shallow puddles that shone like silver in the rising sun. They walked out to meet her, with the wet mud sucking beneath their feet, and she turned to face them.

'Thank you,' she said. 'I think I'd have died if you hadn't come.' She pulled the shawl more tightly around her shoulders, and they walked together along the water-line as she began to talk.

As simply as possible, she told them something about her girlhood; how she had left home, how she had moved in with Ernest Kleiber above the photographic shop. They had been very happy, and she wanted to marry him, but in 1914 they were overtaken by the outbreak of war. Ernest and his German parents were interned as aliens, and she thought she would never see him again.

That was when she discovered she was pregnant. She could not face her own family, and there was no one else she could turn to. When the baby was born, she thought of having it adopted, but she was afraid that with all the red tape and form-filling it entailed, her secret might somehow get back to her parents. In the end she took a cowardly way out; she planned to abandon the baby, hoping and praying it would be found, and given a good home.

Abram could not help breaking in. 'But what about Poppa? It was his baby too.'

'I told you, he was in the prison camp; I didn't know if he was alive or dead. And by the time the war was over and he came out, the baby had been adopted. I never had the courage to confess. How could I tell him that

523

I'd given his first-born son away?'

She resumed her story. One afternoon, when she was at the end of her tether, she had been walking by the river with the baby in her arms-right here at Burrells Wharf—when she met a man she knew slightly: Ruth's cousin, Saul Judge.

By that time Saul was married to Gloria; they could not have children of their own, and suddenly it seemed like an answer to prayer. They came to an agreement. Rosie gave away her baby son, making Saul swear never to tell anyone. He returned to Glory with the child, saying he had found it abandoned on the mudflats...and they brought him up as their own.

Slowly, Abram turned and looked at Matt as if he had never seen him before.

With his brain fuddled by alcohol and lack of sleep, Matt was a shade slower to understand, but at last he forced out the words: 'Your baby...that was—me?'

Above them, the seagulls cried out with a sound like mocking laughter.

Rosie nodded. 'You are my son—the son of Ernest Kleiber. Abram is your brother. And I'm asking you now—both of you—to forgive me.'

Abram put his arm round his mother, then looked at Matt. 'Well?' he said.

Matt's face was grey, as the full meaning hit him. He licked his lips, unable to speak. His head swam, his bowels churned, and he thought he was going to be sick. The thing he hated most in all the world had turned upon him, taunting and triumphant—life itself was nothing but a filthy joke. And the joke was on him—the son of a Jew! With a great effort, he managed to drag out a few halting words.

'I'll forgive you, if that's what you want, but don't you go telling Glory about this neither. She's been my mother all my life—this don't change nothing. We won't never talk about this again.'

He set off alone across the muddy puddles without looking back, returning to his own family; and Abram took his mother home.

17

Throughout the summer of 1944, Lil was kept very busy, as the V-1s continued to fall on London, often starting fires. She did not make any attempt to see Trevor or to get in touch with him, and she did not hear from him again until one evening in late October.

When she arrived home after work, she found a bunch of dark red roses on the doormat outside the top flat. There was no card with the flowers, but she knew at once who had left them there.

After supper, she sat at the kitchen table and began to write a letter.

Dearest Trevor,

Thank you for the roses. They are in front of me on the table, and their scent fills the room. It was very kind of you to send them, and very generous, since I have treated you so badly. I know I should have written to you, or telephoned, but life has been rather hectic lately.

No, that's a feeble excuse. The truth is, I didn't know what to say to you. Last time we met, you asked me to come and live with you, in your flat, and I have never given you an answer. I suppose I wasn't even sure what you were asking exactly; you never said anything about marriage, but perhaps you meant it as a proposal? If so, I am very, touched and very honoured, but you must understand I am not free to marry again. At present Mike is still officially 'missing'—I can't even think about re-marriage until his death is confirmed.

But I expect you already realise that. If you were inviting me to live with you, that is still difficult for me. You know I'm a Catholic—not a very good one, I'm sorry to say—but it would be hard for me to take such a step and go against all my instincts and upbringing, even though I love you.

There is something else that holds me back. For some time now, you have been living with Sally, and except for a tragic accident, by now she would have given you a child. I am sure she still loves you too, and I don't have the right to take you from her.

Now you see why I put off replying for so long. Although I love you, and the idea of sharing your life is very tempting, you must see that as things

*are now, it's really impossible. Perhaps we should
try and be patient, and wait. The news has been
so good lately; now that the Allies have got to Paris,
people seem to think the war can't last much longer.
When it's all over, things could have changed for
both of us. Until then, I can only ask you to forgive
me, and assure you of my deep love for you. I long
for peace, and—'*

As she wrote these words, the window-panes
rattled and she felt a faint vibration run through
the building. She knew what would follow, and
sure enough, several moments later she heard a
distant, double thunderclap, followed by deep
rumblings that died away into silence.

It was not the sound of a flying-bomb, and
there had been no air-raid warning, yet such
explosions were becoming more and more
frequent. They had begun in September, and
nobody knew what they were, though rumours
were circulating everywhere. There was no
official explanation. Lil's Station Officer referred
to them as 'flying gas-mains'. They only knew
that these mysterious bombs arrived without any
warning, making a deep crater and causing total
destruction wherever they landed, though they
did not send waves of blast over the surrounding
area like the V-1s.

In early November, the Government finally
admitted that these were Germany's latest
weapon—long-range rockets, or 'V-2s'.

Their very suddenness struck terror into
many hearts, but some people found them
less frightening than the slow, sinister approach

of the V-1s; if you didn't know when they were going to hit you, you didn't have time to worry about them.

To Bertie, who was in a highly nervous state already, they were the last straw.

One afternoon, he was on his way to meet his opposite number at the Royal Victoria Docks, to confer upon the latest Government regulations about the conveyance of ammunition through the docks, en route for Western Europe. Bertie suffered agonies of anxiety whenever any high-explosives had to pass through the Jubilee Wharf, and he was hoping fervently that all such cargo could be routed via the Royal Vic in future—but the planned conference never took place. He was riding on a bus, along Silvertown Way, when there was a blinding flash of white light, and a split second later a gigantic double bang—the loudest noise he had ever heard.

The driver jammed on his brakes, and the bus skidded to a halt, shuddering as the shock-waves hit it. Bertie clapped his hands over his ears; his skull felt as if it had been split wide open by the force of the sound, and he slumped on to the floor, paralysed with terror and convinced that it was the end of the world.

A couple of hours later, at the Guild Office on Jubilee Wharf, Trevor heard that a rocket had landed within a stone's-throw of the Royal Vic. He tried to telephone and enquire if Bertie was safe, but the lines were down and he could not get through. By the end of the afternoon, as there was still no sign of him, he decided he should go round to Bertie's house and break the news to Florrie Judge.

When he reached Denmark Place, he found Bertie, shaking and sweating, frantically cramming clothes into a suitcase. Florrie stood by, handing him items to go in, and keeping up a perpetual whining commentary.

'Oh, here's your spare pair of pyjamas. The others are still in the wash. They'll need ironing, but I can send them on to you... Here's your washbag, it's got your flannel and your razor in it—but what's going to become of me, Bertie? I don't want to stay here all on my own, do I? It's all very well for you, going off—oh, here's your pullover, you'll be wanting that now the weather's turned so much colder, and I found your woolly scarf as well—don't you think you ought to take me with you?'

Trevor interrupted: 'What the hell's going on?'

Florrie turned to him for support. 'Bertie's going away. I don't think it's right, him going like this, but he says he can't stay here no more.'

With trembling fingers, Bertie continued to fold shirts and vests, saying; 'I was damn near killed this afternoon. One of those rockets nearly got me—just a few hundred yards away, it was...I can't stand any more. I've got to get out of London.'

Trevor started to argue, 'Oh, come on. Look at you, not a scratch on you. You should thank your lucky stars, you've got a charmed life.'

Bertie brushed this aside and went on breathlessly, 'Some neighbours of ours moved down to the West Country during the Blitz. They've bought a house near Barnstaple, and they said if I ever decided to get away from London, I'd always be very welcome—so that's where I'm going.'

'But what about the Jubilee? What about the Guild?' Trevor asked.

'And what about *me?*' Florrie chimed in, but Bertie ignored her.

'Bugger the bloody Guild. I tell you, I've had enough.'

Florrie gave a little whinny of distress. 'You shouldn't say such dreadful things. Why won't you let me come too? I could make myself useful as a housekeeper.'

'I can't expect my friends to find room for two of us; it wouldn't be right to impose on them,' Bertie told her. 'Besides, you've got to stay here to look after the house. If you're worried about being on your own, perhaps Trevor would move back for a while, to keep you company.'

Florrie swung round, pleading with Trevor. 'Ooh, yes—will you do that? Will you move back here?'

'I'm sorry.' Trevor shook his head. 'Unfortunately, I've made other plans. I'd already decided, I'll be going back to my own flat in Charing Cross Road quite soon. It looks as if this is the parting of the ways for all of us.'

He left them still arguing, neither of them really listening to what the other was saying, and both getting more hysterical as the tension mounted—but instead of driving straight back to Greenwich, he made a short detour to the Watermen.

In the saloon bar, Connor greeted him with a non-committal grunt. Trevor enquired if Lil was on the premises, and Connor told him she was not.

'Never mind—it's really old Mr Judge I came to see. I hope he's well enough to receive visitors?'

'Yes, the old feller's pretty spry, all things considered. My wife's with him now; I'm sorry I can't take you up, but as you see—'

'Don't bother, I know the way.'

Trevor went straight to Marcus' room. Ruth had just been giving her father his supper, and she looked up in surprise.

'Trevor—hello! How nice of you to drop in; it's been a long time.'

'I'm afraid so, but we're all busy these days, aren't we? In fact that's why I'm here—on a business matter, about the Guild. I'd like a word with Mr Judge, if it's convenient.'

Ruth turned to Marcus. 'Do you hear that? Trevor's come to see you!'

Marcus' bushy brows were drawn down firmly. His face was set into lines of disapproval as he growled, 'I have nothing to say to him.'

'Excuse me, sir—I think you should hear me out. There are going to be some changes in the management and I felt it was right to tell you.'

Ruth tried to intervene. 'My father retired from the Guild years ago. He doesn't have anything to do with it now.'

'He's still respected by the membership—and the Wharfmaster—and the Harbour Road. He founded the Brotherhood; without Marcus Judge, it wouldn't exist today. He has a right to be kept informed.'

Marcus' mouth worked, as if he were chewing something distasteful. At last he said wearily, 'Very well. Come here, young man, and say what you have to say. Ruth, take the tray with you, my dear. I'll ring if I need anything.'

He indicated a brass cow-bell, brought from Benares at the turn of the century and purchased at a Sale of Work in aid of the Foreign Missions; it stood on the bedside table, and he rang it whenever he required attention.

'All right, Father.' Ruth picked up the tray. As Trevor took her place by the bed, she said softly, 'Don't stay too long—we mustn't tire him.'

When she had gone out, Marcus thrust his head forward, struggling to bring Trevor's features into sharper focus, and asked: 'Well? What is it you have to say?'

Trevor told him that Bertie had decided to throw up his job with the Guild and take himself off to Devonshire; he mentioned in passing that Bertie was suffering from nervous strain after his escape from annihilation, but did not express any great sympathy.

Marcus narrowed his eyes until they were red slits, and asked: 'Do you mean to tell me you will be in sole charge of the Guild Office?'

'For the moment, yes. But I must warn you, I can't give the work my undivided attention. I have my own affairs to attend to—I think you know I have an office in the West End, and since the war seems to be in its closing stages, I must make some preparations to start up in business again. I'll do what I can to keep an eye on the Guild; I'll look in to see that things are running smoothly, and check the accounts—but I can't guarantee to be at the Wharf regularly. I thought you should know that.'

If he expected gratitude, it was not forthcoming.

Marcus seemed to be having difficulty in drawing breath; his lungs rattled as he gasped, 'Traitors... Traitors and cowards, the pair of you. Get out of my sight, do you hear?'

'Don't try to bully me, old man,' said Trevor. 'I'm not like the others—I'm not afraid of you.'

'I don't ask you to fear *me*,' said Marcus.

As Trevor watched, the old man threw back his head and squared his shoulders. His eyes opened, no longer dimmed by time but sharp and shrewd; it was as if he had thrown off old age, recovering his power, as he intoned: 'You should fear the Almighty—fear the wrath of God, and everlasting punishment.' His eyes shone, and his cracked voice became a roar: *'Fear destruction. Fear damnation. Fear death...'*

Trevor tried to out-stare him, but could not meet that piercing, fanatic gaze. He scrambled to his feet, moving away from the bed and muttering, 'I'm sorry I came. I won't make that mistake again.'

And he fled from the room, leaving the door wide open. In a sudden frenzy of determination, Marcus seized the brass bell and swung it with all his might; the clanging metallic sound pursued Trevor down the stairs—it was still ringing in his ears as he left the pub.

Ruth hurried up to the old man's room. 'Yes, Father, what do you want?'

The effort had taken its toll of Marcus; his determination died, leaving him exhausted.

'I want to speak to that Welshman—what's his name? Pritchard. Tell him to come and see me at once.'

A few minutes later, Huw sat in the bedside chair, and Marcus tried to marshal the last remnants of his strength to explain the situation. Rambling, sometimes incoherent, frequently repeating himself, he concluded: '...Now I am ashamed of my family. I always knew Bertie was a broken reed—and the other one is wicked, through and through. There was a time in my life when I closed my eyes to such wickedness, but now I see it all too clearly. The Guild has been left in the wrong hands—that is why I ask for your help. I know you left the Brotherhood—I don't recollect the circumstances, but I have the impression that you were treated unjustly. If you are prepared to take charge of the Guild, I will speak on your behalf to the Wharfmaster and to the Board. My own family have proved themselves unworthy. I rely on you to set matters right. Will you do that?'

For a moment Huw said nothing. At last he murmured, 'I'm obliged to you, sir, and I'm glad to have your good opinion, but I have a job here already. I must discuss it with Connor O'Dell first.'

534

Marcus nodded. 'Very well. Speak to O'Dell, but tell him it is my wish that you should be the new leader of the Brotherhood.'

When Huw got home to Millwall Road, Glory was already in bed. As he undressed and climbed between the sheets, he told her of this unexpected turn of events.

'But do you think the Wharfmaster will agree?' asked Glory. 'Do you suppose he'd take you, just on old Marcus' say-so?'

'He might—if they've nobody else. Thanks to Con, I've learned a bit about office management—ordering, book-keeping—and I had years of practical experience at the Jubilee; I know how the Wharf operates.'

Glory hugged him. 'It's the chance of a lifetime. You'll be ten times better than that fool Bertie, or slimy Trevor. Oh, I'm so proud of you!'

He interrupted her. 'Wait a bit, I haven't finished yet. There's just one snag.'

'Oh? What's that?'

'I talked it over with Connor. He won't let me go.'

At the same moment, lying in bed above the pub, Con was holding Ruth in his arms as she exclaimed: 'You mean you stood in his way? How could you do such a thing?'

'What else could I do?' he asked unhappily. 'Your father should never have offered him the post without talking to me first. How could we manage without Huw? This place is a full-time job for the three of us—how could we run it without him?'

'We could find somebody to take his place. We'll advertise.'

With all the young lads away at the war? And where would we find anybody one tenth as good? We gave Huw a job when your father chucked him out of the Brotherhood—how dare they take him back, when we need him here?'

'Oh Con, we'll manage somehow. I'm sure your Mam would be pleased to do a little extra in the pub.'

'For God's sake, woman, Mam's over seventy! It's too much to expect of her...and it's too much to expect of me.' In the darkness, Ruth heard a catch in his voice, and she felt him tremble as he continued: 'I'm fifty-four years old—I'm not the man I used to be. Time's catching up with me, Ruth. I'm too old—and too tired.'

She said nothing, but held him to her breast—stroking him, consoling him. Connor O'Dell, the strongest and most courageous man she had ever known, was afraid at last.

During the weeks that followed, Trevor began to divide his time between the West End and the Jubilee. Having heard no more from any official source about his situation with the Guild, he continued to manage the office, though he left most of the daily routine to the clerks. This suited him well enough; he still retained control of the Wharf and could channel their finances, while he took steps to re-establish his place in the entertainment world.

One evening he came back to Acacia Grove

rather late, expecting Sally to greet him with a flood of reproaches and complaints, but she was surprisingly sweet and almost contrite as she greeted him.

'I'm so sorry—there isn't any supper for you. When you didn't turn up or telephone or anything, I thought you must have decided to stay at your flat tonight, so I didn't bother to cook; I just made myself some bread and cheese. I think there's a bit of mousetrap left, if you're hungry.'

'Don't bother—I had a snack in town, before I left.' Relieved to be spared an angry scene, he kissed her, adding, 'You'll be pleased to know I've been working hard on your behalf, trying to set up the new show.'

'Oh, you're so good to me,' she purred. 'How soon do we open?'

'Don't rush me! I don't want to bring it into the West End until the war's over, but I'm planning to open out of town—a pre-London tour in the spring will give us a chance to iron out any little problems. We'll start rehearsals soon after Christmas.'

'Another bloody tour?' She rolled her eyes in mock-anguish. 'Anyone would think you were trying to get rid of me... Well, I suppose it's all in a good cause—and I can stay in town with you while we're rehearsing, can't I?'

'Well, yes. We'll see...' His eye fell on a letter propped up on the mantelpiece; he recognised Lil's handwriting. 'Hello—when did this arrive?'

'Oh, it was nearly midday. The posts are all

over the place now. I suppose it's because of the doodlebugs and rockets and everything.'

He tore open the envelope and read the letter quickly, then he screwed it up and threw it into the fire, watching it curl up in flames.

'The writing looked sort of familiar,' Sally said. 'I thought it might have been from Lil, only I couldn't imagine why she'd be writing to you.'

'Yes, it was Lil,' he told her casually. 'Sending us the season's greetings, hoping we might drop in at the pub some time over the holiday. I don't think we'll bother, do you?'

When the last scrap of paper had turned to black ash, he said, 'I think I'll go and run a bath. Be an angel and bring up a brandy.'

As he left the room she called after him playfully, 'Shall I come and scrub your back as well?'

She was still smiling to herself as she poured the drink. It was a good thing Trevor didn't notice the envelope had been steamed open and re-sealed. Well, she had to find out what the little bitch was up to, didn't she?

Next morning she telephoned Auntie Ruth at the Watermen, and found out what time Lil finished work. When Lil returned to Coldharbour after a day-shift at the Fire Station, her cousin was waiting for her on the top landing.

'Darling, lovely to see you—and looking so smart in your lovely uniform!' Sally exclaimed. 'I've brought you a little something. I went Christmas shopping this afternoon, and I simply couldn't resist these.' She thrust a bunch of holly and mistletoe into Lil's arms, saying, 'I bought them in the market. I thought they'd give your flat a festive touch.'

Feeling at a loss, Lil said helplessly, 'That's very kind. Won't you come in? Can I make you a cup of tea or coffee?'

'No, nothing—I can't stop long.' Sally looked critically round the kitchen. 'Shall I help you put up the decorations? I do think it's nice to have it looking Christmassy, don't you?' Then she added in the same bright, cheery tone, 'By the way, if you're expecting Trevor to kiss you under the mistletoe, I'm afraid you're out of luck. He's already spoken for.' Lil's world turned upside-down; she felt dizzy, and sick to the stomach. 'What do you mean?' she asked, when she could speak.

'Exactly what I say. Oh, I know he can be very naughty sometimes—coming to see you like that, saying silly things, sending you roses—but he doesn't really mean any of it. I'm sorry you took it so seriously.'

'He—he showed you my letter?'

'Well, of course—we tell each other everything. Anyway, you couldn't possibly live in his flat, because I'll be moving there myself very soon. He's starring me in a new show, and since we'll be rehearsing in town, it'll be much more convenient.'

She was still moving around the room, sticking sprigs of holly behind the pictures and on the shelves of the dresser, talking all the time.

'In fact, I'll let you into a little secret. We

shall probably be getting married before long. So I wouldn't try to get in touch with him again, if I were you—it will only be an embarrassment all round. Because you were quite right—you can't take him away from me. I won't let you.'

She turned and surveyed her efforts. 'There, that will have to do for now. Still, I think it looks more cheerful, don't you? I must fly—Trevor will be waiting for me. Happy Christmas, darling.'

On Christmas Eve, three generations of the O'Dell family attended Midnight Mass together; Mary, Ruth and Lil set out after closing-time, on their way to St Anthony's. Only Connor stayed behind; he said he would look in at church in the morning—they couldn't leave old Marcus alone in the house. Besides, it had been a long day, and he wanted to get his head down.

As they walked through the darkened streets, Mary put into words the fear that was in Ruth's mind. 'I'm anxious about Connor. He's never once missed the Midnight, since he was a babe in arms. It's not like him to stay at home.'

Ruth tried to excuse her husband. 'We had a heavy evening in the pub—he's rather tired.'

'And that's not like him either. I can't help thinking of his father. Do you remember how Patrick seemed to lose heart when he was about Con's age? He got tired and old before his time, and took to his bed. I pray to God that Con won't go the same way.'

540

'I'm sure he won't,' said Ruth, with more confidence then she actually felt. 'He's never really thrown off that nasty cough he had, but when the good weather comes again, he'll be a new man. Don't you think so, Lil?'

'Perhaps,' said Lil. 'Perhaps we'll all feel happier then.'

The little church was still scarred with bomb-damage, and most of the windows were boarded up, but inside they found it packed with worshippers, and bright with candles.

Mary dipped a finger in the stoup by the door and crossed herself, then craned her neck, saying, 'There's still a few empty chairs down at the front. Let's go and see—I'm not standing at the back for an hour or more.'

As they pressed through the crowd, Ruth brushed against a woman in black, who turned to her—and they embraced one another.

'Rosie!' exclaimed Ruth. 'I never expected to see you here!'

'Well, old habits die hard—isn't that what they say?'

Mary kissed her. 'It's good to see you, my love—and looking so much better, too.'

'I'm feeling well.' It was true. Rosie had lost some weight, but her eyes shone in the candlelight and she had an air of confidence about her.

'We're going to find some chairs. Won't you sit with us?' said Mary.

'No, thanks. I might not stay to the end...I'll be fine here.'

'But you are coming to us tomorrow, aren't

541

you?' Ruth reminded her. 'For Christmas dinner?'

'I wouldn't miss it for worlds. Christmas with my family.'

The sacristy bell rang, and the priest appeared; there was no organ and no organist now, but with one voice the congregation began to sing:

'Oh, come, all ye faithful
Joyful and triumphant
Come ye, oh, come ye to Bethlehem...'

Although they were looking forward to the spring, they had to get through the winter first—and that year it was long and hard. Temperatures fell below freezing, and there were continual flurries of sleet and snow. When it went a few degrees higher, the weather turned to fog—thick, yellow fog, making eyes sting and choking the lungs. It brought back Connor's cough. Ruth begged him to go to bed and rest, but he insisted on carrying on.

At the Fire Station, the AFS went down with 'flu, one after another; Lil escaped the infection, and volunteered for extra duties. The Station Officer told her not to push herself too hard, but she said she'd rather work than sit at home doing nothing. It was only when she was working that she could put Trevor out of her mind, and forget the ache in her heart.

One evening towards the end of January, an emergency call came through; a V-2 had landed in Poplar, near the Ring o' Bells public-house, and extra pumps were needed urgently.

Lil had been about to go off-duty, after a full day-shift, but she said immediately, 'Let me do it, Chief. I'd like to.'

There was no one else he could send, so he let her go.

Lil attached the trailer-pump to the back of her old cab, and reversed out of the yard. She always boasted that she knew her way blindfold round the Island, and tonight she had to make good that claim, because in the freezing fog she could not see more than a couple of yards ahead. Driving as fast as she dared, she crept forward, occasionally putting on a burst of speed when the fog thinned; dropping back to a crawl as it closed in again.

The V-2 had landed at the junction of four roads; the Ring o' Bells was crowded, and under the force of the explosion the saloon floor had caved in, throwing customers into the cellar below. The upper stories tumbled in after them, and through the mixture of fog and brick-dust, Lil could see flames leaping up at the empty window-frames.

A fireman directed her to an emergency water-supply, and she ran the suction hose from her trailer into the tank. The fireman coupled up the branch and gave the signal to turn on—and nothing happened.

'What's wrong?' he yelled. 'Don't tell me the bloody tank's empty?'

They ran to investigate. He shone his torch into the blackness, and they saw that the suction strainer was lying uselessly on top of a thick layer of ice. It was only after he had attacked it with an axe that water flowed through the hose, and he was able to direct a powerful jet on to the building.

As Lil waited by her cab a spurt of flame caught her eye. Away to the side, she saw first one and then another tongue of fire licking through the rubble that had once been a pavement. A scrap of red-hot shrapnel had ignited a service gas-pipe; as she watched, the fire was becoming a blaze.

Everyone else was too busy to notice; Lil ran to the spot and began to stamp on the flames, kicking loose earth and debris over them, determined to put them out. At first it seemed hopeless—as fast as she got one patch under control, another would burst out, but she carried on, kicking and stamping, until she had put them all out.

At that moment a man picked her up in his arms, saying, 'Are you trying to kill yourself or what?'

It was Abram. He had been called to the emergency in his ambulance, and as he waited for the victims to be pulled from the wreckage, he had caught sight of Lil, doing her desperate fire-dance.

Without listening to her protests, he carried her to the ambulance and sat her down—pulling off her shoes and socks, rolling up the legs of her charred navy-blue trousers.

'You've scorched yourself badly—you're lucky it's no worse,' he told her, as he began to apply some soothing ointment.

She tried to argue that she was perfectly

all right, she didn't need any help, but he interrupted her sharply. 'Shut up, will you? This is my job—I know what I'm doing.'

When he had finished, she said in a small voice, 'Well, I suppose I ought to thank you.'

Then they looked at one another—and burst out laughing.

'Sorry I barked at you,' he said. 'You're OK now—how does it feel?'

'Much better,' she said. 'How are you? I haven't seen you for months.'

'I'm very well,' he said.

'You look well,' she told him. 'You've changed, somehow.'

'So have you...' Then, as someone shouted for him, he added; 'I've got to go—they'll be needing stretchers. When can I see you?'

'Next time we both have a night off, whenever that is. Call me at the Watermen.'

'I'll do that. So long for now.'

Trevor had promised Sally that rehearsals for the new revue would begin after Christmas, but January dragged on into February, without any news of a starting-date.

One evening, when he got home to Acacia Grove after a day at the Guild Office, there was a surprise waiting for him. Supper was laid for two on a low table by the fire; his favourite cold roast duck, with a bowl of salad, and a bottle of champagne in an ice-bucket.

'Good lord!' He turned to Sally, seeking some explanation. 'It's not my birthday, is it? What have I done to deserve this?'

'It's not for anything you've done, my sweet—it's what we're going to do. I wanted to celebrate our engagement.'

Seeing that she was smiling, he smiled back, assuming it was some sort of joke, but she said: 'I mean it, Trevor. I want you to marry me.' Before he could say anything, she continued, 'To be perfectly honest, I'm getting rather tired of being messed about. You told me I was going to star in your new show—but nothing ever happens.'

'Darling, you know what the theatre's like at the moment. This is no time to start anything. What with the fog and the frost and the damn rockets, nobody's doing any business. When the weather brightens up, we'll get going. I'm lining up dates already, I promise you.'

'Touring dates—and I'll be on the road for months, in third-rate digs, while you have a whale of a time in town. I'd rather be Mrs Trevor Judge. I'll feel much safer once we've tied the knot.'

He took her hands in his, saying gently and sincerely, 'My angel, we've been through all this. You know I love you—and you know why we can't be married. With my medical history, it wouldn't be—'

'Balls,' she said sweetly.

'I beg your pardon?'

'The last time you told me that, I fell for it, but I don't want to hear it all over again. I don't believe I told you this, but I had lunch with that divine doctor friend of yours once or twice...dear Simon.'

Trevor's smile hardened. 'He's a god-awful liar. You can't believe a word he says.'

'Oh, but I do. When I explained I was worried about you having that dreadful illness, he told me not to give it another thought. It was all a put-up job, he said, to keep you out of the Army. He did it *"For dear old Trevor, as a great favour—hm?"'*

With her talent for mimicry, she created a swift impression of the smooth gynaecologist. Despite himself Trevor snorted with laughter. 'That stupid bastard talks too much. So you had lunch together, did you? Are you sure that's all you had?'

She lowered her eyes demurely. 'I can't think what you mean!'

'I don't suppose he told you why he did me that "great favour"? Good old Simon happens to have a taste for naughty girls from the East End; I introduced him to quite a few obliging little tarts in the old days.'

'I don't want to hear any more about that, thank you. And I don't want to hear another word about your fatal illness, either. I know you, Trevor Judge—through and through. You're a liar and a letch, and a pimp into the bargain by the sound of it, but I happen to have taken a fancy to you, and I'm going to marry you, so that's that.'

He said sadly, 'You're a gorgeous girl, and I'd love to say yes, but it wouldn't do. Sorry—I'm not the marrying type.'

'Listen carefully. You don't seem to have cottoned on. I'm not asking you—I'm *telling*

547

you. You're going to marry me, or else!'

He raised an eyebrow. 'Or else what?'

'Think about it... I know more about you than anyone in the whole wide world. I know how you faked your medical, and I know who did it for you. I know how you've been cooking the books at the Jubilee—I know how you've been doing black-market deals on the side. I even know where you hid the loot... So you don't have any choice, do you, precious? You've got to marry me—to keep my mouth shut. Now then, shall we start on the champagne?'

He looked at her for a long moment, then laughed.

'I can see I've under-estimated you, darling.' He picked up the bottle and began to untwist the gold wires holding the cork in place. 'All right, I give in. I'll come quietly, guv... But I'd like to make one small suggestion. Let's keep our engagement to ourselves for the time being, shall we? Just one more little secret for us to share...'

Then the cork moved under his fingers, sliding out suddenly with an explosion—like a pistol-shot.

Lil was changing out of her uniform, and getting into her best dress. In accordance with the Government 'utility' label, it was very simple, with no extra frills or pleats, but it had been a Christmas present from Mum and Dad, and this was the first chance she had had to wear it since the AFS party on Boxing Day.

She looked at herself in the bedroom mirror,

over the chest of drawers; the deep burnt-orange colour suited her, lending an extra glow to her cheeks.

'You'll do,' she told herself.

The doorbell rang. Abram was on time—as she knew he would be.

On her way through the kitchen, she realised that she was looking forward to this evening. She had always liked Abram—he had been a good friend to her—but tonight she felt an extra tingle of excitement, as if that friendship were about to move in another direction. He was going to take her out to supper; he had heard good reports of a new Cantonese eating-house off Limehouse Causeway, and Lil had always enjoyed Chinese food, ever since she was a child.

When she opened the door, she knew that this was an important occasion for Abram, too. He was wearing a smart new overcoat and his face shone with happiness.

'You're very punctual,' she said. 'Do you want to go right away, or would you like to come in first?'

'If you're ready, we might as well go,' he replied.

'I've only got to put a coat on. Come in anyway—no need to stand about on the landing.'

As she held the door open for him, she was surprised to see someone following him up the stairs. It was little Miss Briggs, the old lady who lived in the ground-floor flat—alone, except for half a dozen stray cats she had taken in. Although they had been neighbours for years,

Lil didn't really know her well. Miss Briggs was lame, and climbing to the top floor was a great effort for her. Once, Lil had accepted an invitation to tea, and the old lady had been most hospitable, but the smell of cat was so overpowering, Lil had not stayed very long.

But now Miss Briggs was dragging herself up the stairs, hanging on to the banisters and apologising for her slowness.

'I should have come up sooner, dearie. The postman brought this while you were at work. He made me sign his book before he'd give it me.'

Lil took the letter—one look at the printed address on the back flap was enough—but she managed to say: 'Thank you so much. I'm sorry to have put you to all this trouble.'

'No trouble, dearie. I thought as how it might be important.' And she set off down the stairs again, one painful step at a time.

Her heart pounding, Lil took the letter and put it on the dresser. Abram looked at her and asked, 'Aren't you going to open it?'

Lil shook her head, trying to smile. 'Not now. I think I know what it is.' She took down her winter coat from the peg behind the door, and he helped her into it, but her fingers were shaking and she could not fasten the buttons.

'Hey! Sit down a minute, you're as white as a sheet,' Abram told her. 'Is it bad news?'

She nodded. 'I'm afraid so. It's the official confirmation from the Admiralty. Of course I've been expecting it, ever since Mike went missing, but now it's come...'

He helped her into a chair. 'I can't take you out like this. Look, we don't have to go anywhere, if you don't feel like it. I'll nip round the corner for some fish and chips. We can go to the Chinese place another time, can't we?'

'I suppose so.' She couldn't take her eyes off the envelope; it was like a time-bomb waiting to go off. 'I'll be all right in a minute. I'm so sorry, Abram.'

'You don't have to be sorry. I'm glad I was here. But don't you think you should read the letter? Get it over?'

'Yes, you're quite right. It's no use putting it off.'

He passed it to her; she found it difficult to tear open the envelope and unfold the letter—and then she had to read it twice before she could take in the meaning of the words. At last she looked up at Abram blankly.

'It isn't what I thought,' she said slowly. 'You'd better read it—I can't quite believe it. They say he's alive.'

She gave him the letter, and he scanned it quickly. It was couched in cool, impersonal phrases, but the meaning was clear enough. After the *Ark Royal* was torpedoed, eighteen of her crew were missing. Some of them had been picked up later by other vessels, but PO Burns had the bad luck to be rescued by an Italian destroyer. He was taken to Naples, where he was put ashore as a prisoner-of-war.

The letter went on to say that while PO Burns was being driven to a prison-camp, his transport came into collision with another vehicle in a narrow mountain pass. Some of the guards were killed, and in the confusion, Mike managed to escape. Seriously injured, he was picked up several days later by an Italian peasant, who took him to a farm where he was sheltered and nursed back to health. He stayed there, working as a labourer in return for his board and lodging, until the advancing Allied troops liberated this remote mountain district of northern Italy. The letter concluded by saying that PO Burns was now safe and in good health, and would be returning to England shortly.

Lil covered her face in her hands and prayed silently, 'Thank God. Oh, thank God.' These were the only words that would come to her. At first she felt nothing but astonishment—it was as if Mike had come back from the dead, and while her mind accepted the miracle, her heart was slower to comprehend it.

Then, gradually, the full meaning swept over her like a tidal wave, and she exclaimed joyfully: 'He's alive, Abram! *He's alive!*' She threw herself into his arms as her tears began to flow. 'Isn't it wonderful? Mike's coming home.'

The letter fell to the floor; Abram held her tightly, feeling the softness of her cheek against his face, tasting her salt tears on his lips, breathing in the smell of her skin, her hair, her body...

When he let her go, she was radiant; she had never looked so beautiful.

'I'm very happy for you,' he said.

'Thank you.' She squeezed his hand. 'Thank you so much—I'm glad you were here, too.'

But she wasn't really thinking of Abram at that moment. The thought of Mike filled her head and her heart and her soul, and she longed to see him again. Then she remembered Trevor; in this moment of joy she knew that he could never have taken Mike's place in her life. She saw her love for Trevor as an obsession; it was like a dream that had seemed overwhelming during the long night, but she was awake at last, and Mike would bring her back into the daylight.

She felt nothing for Trevor now except kindness. She wanted to wish him well—she hoped he and Sally would be as happy as she was.

When Abram spoke, she had to ask him, 'I'm sorry—what did you say?'

'I was asking about supper. Do you want me to bring something in. Or do you feel like going out to celebrate?' he asked.

'Celebrate, of course!' She was exultant. 'Come on, let's go out!'

They hurried down the staircase, hand in hand, and ran out of the building. At the end of the street, Lil saw the dim glow of a telephone kiosk, and she had an idea.

'Could you wait for a minute?' She scrabbled in her purse for coppers. 'I must make a phone-call.'

Suddenly it seemed very important to tell Sally and Trevor the news; she wanted them to know that there was no need for jealousy or rivalry. They could be good friends again, without any complications.

She dialled Sally's number at Acacia Grove, but the line was engaged. She waited for a few moments, then dialled again; it was still engaged. Oh well, Sally was a great talker—she'd try later. Instead, she called the Watermen, and Ruth answered the phone. Lil passed on the news, and her mother was overjoyed.

As they went on talking, Lil said, 'I tried to tell Sally and Trevor as well, but their number's engaged. Well, at least that means they're at home.' On the spur of the moment, she added: 'I think I'll run over to Greenwich and surprise them! Then I'll look in at the pub on my way back. I'll be there before closing-time.'

When she left the phone-box and saw Abram still waiting, she felt a pang of guilt. He was being so kind, and she was being so selfish. She put her arms round him and kissed him; he looked at her in surprise.

'What's that for?'

'Nothing. I'm just so happy—I hope you're happy for me.'

'You know I am.'

'Yes, I do know. But there are so many people I want to tell, other people I have to see—would you hate me very much if I put off our supper date to another night?'

'I could never hate you,' he said. 'Where do you want to go? Would you like me to come with you?'

'I think I'd sooner be on my own, do you mind? But we'll have our supper very soon, I promise.' Then she saw a taxi-cab approaching—and that was another miracle, because cabs were few and far between on the Island. She hailed it eagerly, then kissed Abram for the last time and climbed in, asking the driver to take her to Acacia Grove, off Crooms Hill, Greenwich Park.

Abram stood and watched the taxi disappear into the night; then he turned up his coat-collar and walked away.

She didn't ask the driver to wait, because she had no idea how long she would be—though when nobody answered the door, she began to think she had been rather stupid. She stooped to look through the letter-box; she could see a light in the living-room, and thought she could hear music playing, so she banged on the door-knocker again, very loudly.

At last she heard somebody coming. Then Trevor opened the door, wiping his hands on a towel. He stared at her in amazement.

'Lily? What on earth—'

She walked in, saying, 'I tried to ring, but your phone was engaged, so I hopped into a cab and here I am! I've got something wonderful to tell you—you and Sally.' She walked into the living-room. It was empty—the gramophone was playing softly to nobody. Trevor followed her in, and switched the music off. Glancing at the telephone, Lil saw that the receiver was lying beside it.

'Oh look, you must have left it off the hook,' she said. 'I thought Sally was having a long conversation.'

Trevor replaced the receiver, saying, 'Yes, she

was—but she's gone upstairs. She went to bed early.'

'Already? But it's only eight o'clock!'

'She was feeling rather sleepy... So what's this wonderful news of yours?'

Lil slipped off her coat and sat down. She told him about the official letter, and the news of Mike, and she told him how happy she was. He looked at her blankly, and she felt he didn't understand what she was saying.

'Don't you see?' she asked. 'Now we can all be friends again. It's a second chance for all of us. I had to come and tell you right away... And I want Sally to know, too.' She stood up. 'Do you think she's still awake?'

'Oh, I wouldn't disturb her, if I were you.'

'I'll just go up and see. If she's asleep I won't wake her.' Before he could stop her, Lil was out of the room and running upstairs.

She went straight to the big bedroom. The door was open and the lights were on, but the bed was made up; it had not been slept in. Bewildered, she was about to go downstairs again when she heard the faint dripping of water. She saw the bathroom door was ajar, and went to investigate.

'Sally? Are you there?' She pushed the door open—and stopped short.

The room was hot and steamy; the bath was three-quarters full, but water had splashed all over the floor. Sally lay in the bath. Her legs were hanging over the edge, near the taps, but her head and shoulders were submerged under several inches of water; her eyes were wide open and her blonde hair floated round her face like seaweed. The scent of rose bath-essence was sickly and overpowering.

Lil rushed to the bath and tried to drag her out. Behind her, Trevor said, 'It's no good doing that. She's dead.'

'We might be able to save her. You must ring for a doctor!'

'It's too late, I tell you.' He started to explain. 'I didn't want to upset you. I found her like that, just before you arrived. She must have fallen asleep and slipped down.'

Lil did not wait to hear any more. She ran past him, down to the living-room, and snatched up the telephone. She had dialled 999 when Trevor took the phone from her hands.

'Don't call the police,' he said, hanging up. 'It was an accident.'

'I was going to call an ambulance,' she began—then she stopped, and looked at him. 'If it was an accident—if she slipped down, like you said—why was there so much water on the floor? She must have been struggling to get out—'

He was still holding the towel; sitting on the sofa, he went on wiping his hands automatically as he said, 'We've got to talk about this. You've got to listen to me.'

'You...' Slowly, the realisation grew. 'You did it, didn't you?'

His face was concerned and sad. 'I had to. She was trying to blackmail me, you see. She knew things about me—things that happened a long time ago. Things I'd done... Well, you know yourself—I've been a bad boy sometimes.'

He smiled at her—a charming smile, inviting her to share in the conspiracy.

'She threatened to go to the police. Well, I couldn't let her do that, could I? So tonight—it was really very simple—she'd had too much to drink as usual, and I suggested she might like to have a bath before we went to bed. Then I went in and sat on the side of the tub, and got hold of her ankles—'

Seeing Lil's expression, he broke off. 'Oh, I know—it's all pretty beastly—only I didn't have any alternative. But it's going to be all right now, I promise you. Everything's going to be all right.'

She moistened her lips and asked, 'What are you going to do?'

'First I'll pull her out and get her dry, then I can put some clothes on her. It'll be quite easy to bundle her into the car—there's nobody about after midnight round here—then I'll drive down to the river...' Helplessly, Lil shook her head, and he added quickly, 'Oh, don't worry. I'm not asking you to help me. I can manage on my own.'

Slowly, Lil moved towards the telephone, and he stood up immediately.

'What are you doing?'

'We have to call the police,' she said.

'Don't be silly, darling—you mustn't do that.' He came towards her, still smiling. 'You love me—I know you do—that's why I'm telling you all this. I trust you, Lily. Once this is over, there'll be no more trouble. We can be together, just you and me.'

He had got between her and the telephone; she backed away from him, circling the room, edging towards the door. She tried not to panic. He mustn't see that she was afraid of him.

'Please don't go,' he said. 'Beautiful Lily, don't leave me. I want you to stay with me—always...'

She made a sudden dash for the hall, but he was too quick for her. Gripping her by the shoulders, he forced her back against the banisters, and the smile on his lips contorted into a rigid mask.

'You don't think I'm going to let you go now, do you?' he asked.

In one swift movement, the towel was round her neck, and he pulled it tight—tighter still. She clawed at his hands, struggling to get free.

And at that moment everything changed.

All the lights went out, and for an instant they were in total darkness. Then the darkness itself cracked apart. She caught a glimpse of the night sky, sprinkled with stars, and the outline of a tree bowing low, dragged down by some shattering force—and then everything started to fall away... Bricks, broken glass, timbers and roof-tiles—everything was slipping and sliding on top of her, dragging her down, down into blackness, down and down...

She never heard the deafening double thunderclap as the V-2 exploded.

18

They heard the sound of the rocket at the Watermen, two and a half miles away.

Like the tremors of a distant earthquake, the vibration made the pub lurch. Doors and windows rattled, and the glasses rang on the shelves as the last rumbles died away.

In the saloon, Ruth and Connor were behind the bar. They looked at one another and Ruth said, 'That was near, wasn't it?'

'Hard to tell,' said Connor. 'The shock waves travel a long way.'

Huw looked in through the arch from the public bar. 'That might be a job for us—it sounded near enough.' Although neither of the men were on call that evening, all air-raid wardens were expected to rally round in an emergency.

'You'd best ring up and ask,' Connor said.

So Huw went into the office and phoned the local Headquarters at Poplar; they told him they had heard the explosion, but had not as yet received any details of its location.

He put his hand over the phone and told Connor, 'The usual red tape! They're checking it now—I've got to hold on.'

Ruth said, 'I'll go and take over the public, in case Huw's called out.'

Connor nodded, and a few minutes later Huw

emerged from the office to report, 'It's OK. It wasn't even on the Island. Further off than I thought—across the river, in Greenwich.'

Connor looked at him sharply. 'Whereabouts in Greenwich—did they say?'

'Somewhere off Crooms Hill. I didn't catch the name of the road—I think it was something Grove.'

Without wasting time in explanations, Connor pushed past him, calling for Ruth. When she reappeared, he asked her, 'Where did you say Lil had gone this evening?'

'Over to Acacia Grove, to see Sally and Trevor.'

'That's what I thought. Ask Mam to help you in here. Huw and me are going out.'

Ruth did not ask questions; she knew from his face that Lil was in danger.

Grabbing their tin hats, the two men left the pub. As they turned into Manchester Road, they saw a lorry coming towards them, heading south. Immediately Connor stepped in front of it and flagged it down. The brakes screamed, and the driver wound down his window, shouting furiously, 'What the hell do you think you're playing at?'

Connor cut in: 'We need a lift to Island Gardens—as fast as you can make it.' Something in his tone made the man pause. Grudgingly, he opened the passenger door and they climbed aboard.

As they set off again, he asked, 'What's up, then? Matter of life and death, is it?'

'I didn't say that,' growled Connor, putting

an end to the conversation.

They scrambled out at the Gardens and raced down the stairs into the pedestrian tunnel, their hurrying footsteps echoing behind and before them. They did not speak; they needed to save their breath. Only when they had scaled the iron staircase at the far end, did Connor break the silence long enough to grunt: 'Mother of God, I'm getting too old for this.'

He had hoped that they might pick up a lift from another vehicle going in the right direction, but the roads were deserted, so they set off at a jogtrot on the long ascent of Crooms Hill.

Huw tried to keep up with Connor, but his game leg handicapped him. After a moment, Connor realised this and said: 'Hang on a second, will you? Bit of a stitch in my side.'

So they slowed down to a brisk walk, and Connor tried to control his impatience, wondering what lay in wait at their journey's end. Then they saw flickering lights and movement—half a dozen figures swarming round a police car at the end of Acacia Grove, and a sign that said No Entry.

Connor squared his shoulders and marched straight ahead, with Huw at his side. Someone in a boiler-suit had tried to stop them, but Connor shook the man off. 'ARP wardens—official business,' he snapped, and they walked on.

There was a thick haze of dust and smoke hanging in the air, and for a moment Connor could not make out what had happened. He saw a fire engine drawn up across the road, and uniformed men running out hoses—and he heard the crackle of flames from a ruined building.

'Would that be the house we're looking for?' Huw asked, trying to get his breath back.

Connor had to count the rooftops along the road—they looked different and unfamiliar—but then he shook his head.

'No, that's the one next door. This is Moira's house,' he broke off and corrected himself. 'I mean, this is where it used to be.'

The rocket had landed in the space between two houses, leaving a crater fifty feet wide and ten feet deep. The house on the right had two walls still standing; a staircase remained, leading nowhere, with fires blazing all round it. An ambulance stood waiting, and a Heavy Rescue team struggled to free survivors from the wreckage, as firemen prepared to tackle the blaze.

But the house on the left, which had once belonged to Moira Marriner, was no longer recognisable as a house. Everything had gone—walls, roof, doors, staircase—nothing remained but a hideous mound of rubble at the edge of the crater. There were no flames to be seen, and no sign of life; that was why the rescue services had concentrated on the neighbouring property.

'This is where they lived,' said Connor. Suddenly he felt very tired, hardly able to speak. 'This is where Lil was.'

Huw didn't know what to say. He put his hand on Connor's shoulder, then asked: 'What are you going to do now?'

Connor lifted his head and stared at him. 'Find her, of course,' he said.

Together, they began to shift the rubble with their hands. The job was not physically strenuous, but it was hard to keep at it, for with every load of lath and plaster and broken brick they removed, they dreaded what they might discover. Most of the objects they turned up had been smashed to pieces but some, amazingly, were intact; by the glare of the flames from the house next door, Connor recognised a photograph of Moira in a silver frame—the glass was still unbroken.

Slowly the night wore on; the two men beavered away at their hopeless task until Connor stopped short, his hand paralysed with fear. He had touched human flesh... Brushing away the dirt, he uncovered a foot—a leg—the naked body of a girl. Gently, the two men lifted her from the filthy wreckage; there was no scratch or bruise upon her. Two wide eyes stared up sightlessly at the night sky... It was Sally.

Connor slipped off his coat and covered her body; then they carried on with their search.

Presently they came upon the huge cross-beams that had supported the upper floor. Huw straightened up, and asked quietly: 'Do you think it's any use going on?'

Connor did not reply. Methodically, he was still pulling the debris away, piece by piece. After a moment Huw dropped to his knees, helping him.

Then they made a discovery. The whole weight of the first floor was being held up by what was left of the central staircase, and a huge piece of broken masonry balanced precariously on a sturdy oak chest. Connor remembered seeing that chest, years ago; it had always stood in the hall, at the foot of the stairs.

He looked at it—and looked again. Behind the wooden panels, grey with dust, he could just see an outstretched hand. He reached into the narrow gap, and grasped it—soft skin—a girl's hand—and it was still warm.

'Now we can start work,' he said. 'She's alive.'

But there was no way to get through that tiny space without pulling out the oak chest first—and if they did that, the whole weight of masonry and timber would collapse on top of her.

'Right,' said Connor. 'I'll hold it up while you get her out.'

He managed to squeeze his head and shoulders into the constricted space; he wasn't sure whether, once Huw eased the wooden chest out, he could hold up the weight above him, or whether it would crush him instantly, but he had to take that chance.

He waited—and braced himself as he heard Huw say: 'Look out—it's coming free!'

He heard the crunch as Huw dragged the chest through broken glass and brickdust and then...

For an instant, he thought he would die. He had never felt such pain; it weighed down upon him so hard, he could not move. It imprisoned his rib-cage, so he could scarcely breathe; he did

565

not know how long he could bear this agonising pressure.

He heard Huw's voice again, faintly. 'I'm being as quick as I can, but it's going to take a bit of time... I've got to go gently.'

Then he understood; any sudden movement could bring the whole lot down. He set his jaw and began to pray, letting the words run through his head, and trying to concentrate on their meaning. If he could just fix his mind upon them, he might be able to ignore the agony that was grinding him to pieces...

'*Our Father, Who art in heaven, hallowed be Thy name...*'

It was hard to cling on to that thought. He felt himself becoming weaker, and he was afraid that he would pass out—but he must not give in.

'You're not licked yet, O'Dell,' he told himself. 'You'll get through this somehow. You've always got through.'

As if in a nightmare, past and present were mingling together. He found himself remembering the night he was expelled from the Brotherhood, more than thirty years ago, when the Punishment Squad had set upon him. He had been blindfolded then, with his hands tied behind him, so he could not fight back; they had laid into him with their clubs and their steel toe-caps—but he had survived.

He thought of his early days as a prizefighter, under Solly Gold's management; he'd had many a beating then, and learned to take his medicine... And the toughest fight of his life was when he had been challenged by a visiting

American—a smiling negro from Galveston, who turned out to be the World Heavyweight Champion, Jack Johnson, travelling incognito and amusing himself. Connor had been lucky to live to tell that tale.

But he had lived to fight another day... Like the time he had gone into a blazing warehouse, blinded by searing smoke and flame, to rescue Joshua Judge and carry him out to safety. He could have died that night, but God had been on his side...

'...*For Thine is the kingdom, the power and the glory, for ever and ever...*'

Then, very far away, he heard Huw saying, 'She's all right. Let's get you out of there.'

With Huw's help, Connor burrowed his way out, and staggered to his feet. As they both stepped back, the entire upper floor collapsed in a choking, blinding fog of dust.

But they were safe, and Lil was alive.

Alive—but badly injured, with multiple fractures. The ambulance took her straight to hospital, and she was admitted to the Orthopaedic Ward. Her condition was serious, but not critical; the Ward Sister assured Ruth that her daughter would make a good recovery, but warned her that it would take several weeks.

Connor went to bed as well, but it was not a hospital bed. With a lifelong hatred of all institutions, as soon as he had been examined in Casualty, he insisted on Ruth ordering a taxi to take them home.

Once there, she had to undress him, because

567

he was too exhausted to take his clothes off. He asked for a cup of cocoa with a tot of brandy in it; by the time she brought it upstairs, he was already asleep.

He slept for twenty-four hours without a break, until Ruth became very anxious, and wondered if she should call a doctor—but at last he opened his eyes. He stared up at her for a moment, then winked, and gave her one of his rare, lop-sided grins.

'How are you feeling?' she asked.

'All the better for seeing you,' he said. 'How's Lil?'

She told him that Lil was making very good progress, and that he could visit her as soon as he was well enough.

'What's wrong with now?' he roared, throwing back the bedclothes. 'I've never felt better in me life!'

The rest of Ruth's news was less cheerful. Trevor's body had been recovered some time later, not far from Lil, but so horribly crushed and mutilated as to be almost unrecognisable. And Ruth had broken the news of Sally's death to Rosie.

'How did she take it?' Connor wanted to know.

'Of course she was terribly upset; that's only to be expected. But by the time I left she seemed to be a bit calmer. Abram has taken some time off work, on compassionate grounds—he'll be staying with her for a week or two.'

Life ceased to have any meaning for Rosie. She felt like a clockwork toy, wound up and set to repeat the same routine over and over again—dressing and undressing, cooking and eating and washing up—but none of it seemed real. If it hadn't been for Abram's reassuring presence, she did not know how she could have endured it.

One afternoon they were sitting together in the living-room, turning the pages of an album in which Rosie had lovingly pasted all her pictures of Sally, from childhood snapshots to photos in her stage costumes, taken by her father, along with newspaper clippings that gave glowing notices of her performances in shows all over the country.

'What a shame she never appeared in the West End,' said Rosie sadly. 'She would have enjoyed it so much.'

She was interrupted by the arrival of a visitor. Abram went down to answer the front door and returned with Matt. He looked sheepish and ill-at-ease, and carried a bunch of tulips which he thrust into Rosie's hands as if he were glad to be rid of them.

'Here...' he said gruffly. 'I thought as how you might like them. I only heard about Sally this morning, and—I thought I oughter come round, like, and say I'm sorry.'

She took his hand and thanked him, then asked if he could stay for a cup of tea? He was about to refuse, but Abram was already filling the kettle, saying, 'Sit down, Matt. It'll only take a minute.'

Rosie asked how his shoulder was, and he said it was mending nicely. He'd left off the sling—he'd be going back to Barracks in a week or two. An awkward silence fell; they did not know what to say to one another.

Matt finished his tea as quickly as possible, then wiped his mouth with the back of his hand and stood up. 'I gotta be going now,' he said. 'Ma will be expecting me.'

They shook hands again—stiffly, uncomfortably——and as an afterthought Matt said, 'Oh, I nearly forgot. When's her funeral?'

'Next Monday.' Hardly daring to suggest it, Rosie ventured: 'I don't suppose you'd come too?'

'That's why I asked. I think I might.'

Rosie and Abram looked at one another, and Abram added quietly, 'You do realise it will be at our Synagogue?'

Matt's face changed. For a moment he said nothing, then he blurted out: 'Yeah, that's OK. Well, she was my sister.'

It was delivery day at the pub; the brewery dray was outside, and Huw opened the trapdoor in the pavement so they could run the barrels straight into the cellar.

When he went down below to meet the barrels at the bottom of the chute and roll them into position, he found Connor already there.

'I'm doing this,' Connor told him.

'What d'you mean? I always do it,' said Huw. 'It's part of my job!'

'Not any more. From now on, I'll be in charge of the deliveries. You're not wanted down here—and while we're at it, you're not

570

wanted upstairs either. Ruth and me can take care of the bars. If we need any help, we've got Mam and young Kaff to lend a hand.'

Huw stared at him, thunderstruck. 'Do you mean you're giving me the sack?'

'That's one way of putting it.'

'But why? What's it all about?' Huw was beginning to feel indignant. 'If I've done something wrong, you might have the decency to tell me so.'

Connor roared with laughter. 'You great eejut—you've done nothing wrong. Don't you understand? I'm letting you go. Tell that old feller upstairs to put in a word for you with the Wharfmaster; you're free to go and manage the Guild Office—isn't that what you want?'

A slow smile broke over Huw's face. 'But I thought you said you couldn't spare me.'

'I changed my mind, didn't I?' Connor flexed his muscles. 'Ruth and me had a talk last night. I don't know what's been wrong with me at all, but I'm fit as a flea now, ready to tackle anything that comes my way. So you can shift for yourself. You're welcome to the bloody Brotherhood, and good luck to you!'

A shadow fell across them, as the first barrel appeared in the open trap above their heads.

'Look out below!' yelled the drayman, and Connor shouted back, 'Right! Let's be having you!'

Upstairs, Ruth was sweeping the saloon, getting ready for opening-time. When she heard someone knocking at the side door, she put aside her broom and went along the passage.

Outside on the step was a young man in strange, foreign-looking clothes. He was bare-headed, and his hair was unusually long, falling over the nape of his neck in glossy curls. He was lean and spare, his arms well-muscled and his back was broad; but the most remarkable thing about him was his complexion—burned by a fiercer sun, his skin was almost the colour of mahogany. When he smiled, his teeth were startlingly white.

'Don't you remember me, Mrs O'Dell?' he asked.

As soon as he spoke, she knew him. 'Mike!' she said, and held out her arms to him.

'They told you I was on my way home, didn't they?'

'Yes, Lil had a letter from the Admiralty, but they didn't say when.'

He let her go, looking around him. 'It's good to be back, though I've noticed a few changes on the way here. But never mind that—where's Lil? I went to Coldharbour first, but she wasn't there, and I lost my door-key years ago, along with everything else. I can't wait to see her—is she here?'

Ruth took him through to the kitchen and sat him down. Gently, she explained what had happened, finishing: 'But she's doing very well. The hospital say she'll be coming home quite soon now. I'll take you there this afternoon—you can visit her every day.'

As soon as visiting-hours began, Ruth showed Mike the way to the Orthopaedic Ward, but left him at the doorway.

'You go on in,' she said. 'I'll come and say hello presently. She'll want to have you all to herself for a while.'

It was a strange meeting. Lil had been looking forward to seeing him so much, yet when he sat by her bed and held her hand she could not stop crying.

'I'm sorry,' she sobbed. 'Silly of me—can't help it. Can't stop...'

'You cry all you want,' he told her. 'Tell you the truth, I feel a bit choked up myself.' He put his arms round her, and she rested her head on his shoulder, crying until she could cry no more. And then they held one another in silence, and he knew he was home at last.

When she had dried her eyes, she wanted to hear everything that had happened to him after he was rescued from the sea, and he said he had been very lucky. If it hadn't been for that collision in the mountains, he would certainly have finished up in a POW camp. Perhaps he would have been transferred to a German prison; he might never have been heard of again. He told her about the Italian farmer who sheltered him for nearly three and a half years.

'He didn't speak a word of English, so in the end I learned to speak Italian, and I finished up like one of the family. It was quite sad, saying goodbye to them, but I promised one day I'd come back for a visit—and next time I said I'd bring my wife.'

She smiled for the first time, and he smiled back. 'That's my girl. Now, I want to hear all about you. Your Mum told me how you were dug out of a bombed house. I reckon we've both been very lucky.'

Her smile faltered for a moment. 'Yes, luckier than I deserve. Trevor and Sally—they were both—'

She could not go on, and he said, 'I know—she told me that too. But you're here now, and I've found you again, that's all I care about. I love you very much.'

She looked into his eyes, and was able to tell him honestly, 'I love you, Mike. More than ever.'

By the middle of March, Huw was established as the manager in charge of the Guild office. He had no real qualifications for the job, except his knowledge and experience of the Wharf, but he was quick to learn—and by that time the Wharfmaster and the Board were so desperate, they were grateful to have him there.

With Trevor gone, and Bertie hundreds of miles away, conditions in the office had become chaotic, and for the first few weeks Huw put in very long hours, working until late every night, trying to get the accounts up to date and deal with the backlog of paperwork.

Glory, who had been thrilled by his appointment, began to complain that she never saw her husband at all, but he gradually knocked things into shape, establishing a new and more efficient routine, and came home to her every evening at a reasonable hour.

At least, almost every evening. One night at

the beginning of April Huw called in at the pub, carrying a bulky brown-paper parcel. He found Connor in the public bar, and said to him: 'Can you spare a few minutes? I've got something to tell you.'

So Connor called Kaff, and asked her if she would take over the bar; Mary was already minding the saloon, and Ruth was upstairs with her father.

Leading Huw into the back kitchen, Connor closed the door. 'Now, then—what's it all about?' he asked. 'Something confidential, by the sound of it.'

'I suppose it is. Official Guild business—private and confidential, as they say.'

'In that case it's nothing to do with me, that's for sure,' snorted Connor. 'I left the Guild soon after you were born.'

'All the same, I reckon you might be interested. Today I turned up all the old records—books and papers written by your father-in-law when he founded the Guild; rules and regulations, membership lists—and the Discipline Register...'

Connor frowned. 'I thought that stuff was destroyed entirely in the warehouse fire, years back?'

'That's what I understood too, but it's not so. Today I went through the whole lot, and when I'd finished I took it upon myself to do something that ought to have been done long ago. I wound up the Organisation known as the Brotherhood; I disbanded the existing membership, and re-established them as a union branch, to be affiliated to the National Union of Dockworkers, as they should always have been.'

He untied the string of his parcel and unpacked it on the table-top. 'Here you are. I brought it all away with me.'

Connor reached out, dipping into the yellowing pages, opening the covers of ancient, cloth-bound books, turning over the minutes of secret meetings long forgotten—and the records of punishments suffered by men long dead. At last he said: 'This should have gone up in flames... It's time we put that right.'

Though it was April, there was still a fire burning in the kitchen range. One by one, Connor dropped the documents on to the glowing red coals. Side by side, the two men watched them burn.

'So that's that,' said Huw. 'D'you think we should tell the old man upstairs?'

'That's a matter between you and your conscience,' said Connor. 'If you feel you owe him an explanation...'

At that moment the door opened, and Ruth entered the kitchen. Seeing Huw there, she forced a smile, saying he was quite a stranger—he must bring Glory round for supper one of these days... Then she broke off, and turned to Connor—and he realised something was wrong.

'Is it your father?' he asked. 'We were just this minute talking about him. How is the old teller?'

Huw broke in: 'I was wondering if I should go up and see him?'

Ruth shook her head. 'Not now,' she said. 'It's too late. I'd just been settling him down for the night; I sat with him for a few minutes, holding his hand. He'd said his prayers, and I waited until he dozed off. Then I noticed his hand seemed to grow heavy, and it slipped from mine—and that was when I realised he'd gone. So I said another little prayer, and I put his hands together, and I left him there. I suppose I'd better call the doctor; he'll know what has to be done.' She sighed. 'In two weeks' time it would have been his eighty-fifth birthday. He was looking forward to that.'

As she was about to leave the room, she noticed the remains of the books and papers, still burning in the grate.

'What's that?' she asked.

'It was the end of the Brotherhood,' Con told her. 'There's nothing left of it now.'

During the winter, the black-out restrictions had gradually been relaxed; since the only enemy attacks were from unmanned aircraft and rockets, there was no longer any real need for total darkness. First 'half-lighting' was permitted, then drivers were allowed to remove the headlamp masks from their cars, and churches could show lights inside stained-glass windows—if they still had windows.

At last, at the end of April, there was a Government announcement that the black-out would be totally abolished, except for coastal areas.

It was Lil's first day out of hospital; Mike

brought her home in a taxi and insisted on carrying her up three flights of stairs to the top-floor flat. He had done the shopping too, and proudly fried some sausages for their tea.

After they had washed up, Lil said, 'Let's go out. I'd love to have a walk, especially now the lights are on again.'

'Do you think you should? I mean, this is only your first day. Maybe you ought to take things easy...'

But she was determined. 'I've been lying in bed for ages. I want to get out. I'm sick of the smell of hospitals—I need some fresh air.' So they went for a short walk, with her arm tucked through his.

She had been looking forward to this moment, and she was enjoying her new freedom, but she noticed that Mike was very quiet. After a little while, he said, 'I think that's enough, don't you? Let's go home.'

'Honestly, I'm not a bit tired,' she told him. 'I'll tell you when I've had enough.'

'I'm sorry, Lil—I've had enough already,' he said. 'This has come as a bit of a shock to me. Oh, I knew there'd been a lot of raids on London—I was prepared for that, but I'd no idea it would be like this. I used to know my way round every inch of the Island, and now I hardly recognise it. There isn't a street without some sort of damage—and whole areas have been wiped out altogether. It's not the same place any more.'

'I know.' Lil squeezed his hand. 'I'd sort of got used to it, 'cos I was here while it was happening. I watched it change—but it must be different for you, I can see that. Dad was telling me the other day that before the war, there were twenty-one thousand people living on the Island. Now he says two-thirds of them are gone. A lot of them are dead, and some of the others will never come back.'

'There's not much for them to come back to.' Mike looked around him; under the unaccustomed glare of the street-lights, the open spaces, the bomb-sites and gaping craters made up a landscape of desolation, and he shivered. 'Come on, let's go home.'

When they got back to the flat, he asked, 'What do you say to an early night?'

She gave him a sidelong glance. 'But it's not nine o'clock yet.'

'I know, but we can talk for a while, in bed. It'll be cosy.'

She turned her head away; he could not see her face. 'All right.' Her voice was quiet and expressionless. 'If that's what you want.'

He put his hand under her chin, turning her towards him. 'Only talk,' he said. 'Nothing else. I know we've been away from each other a long time. I wasn't expecting...you know what I mean.'

'Yes, I know.' Again her eyes slid away; she could not look at him.

'If you want to get undressed first, I'll go in the other room,' he went on, but she stopped him, saying: 'It's all right. I don't mind about that.'

So they undressed together, but he kept his

back to her all the time, taking care to get into his pyjama trousers before pulling his shirt up over his head. When he turned round, she was already in bed. He switched out the light, and slipped in beside her; their bodies touched, and he edged away.

After a moment she said, 'Did you want to talk about anything special?'

'Well, I've been thinking.' He cleared his throat. 'I know you're very close to your Mum and Dad, and I'm fond of them too—they've always been good to me. And I know you've got friends here, on the Island—friends and relations...but I wondered if—well, what I was thinking—'

He hesitated so long, she had to ask: 'What are you trying to say?'

'I don't know how you'll feel about this, only I've been working on a farm these past few years—outdoors all day and every day—living right out in the wilds, miles from anywhere... And I sort of got to like it. So I wondered what you'd say if we were to move away from London.'

'Move? You mean—for good?'

'Well, yes. London's not the same any more. Besides, when the war's over, I don't want to go back to being a policeman; I've got out of the way of wearing a uniform. What I'd really like is to try and find a place of our own—a little market-garden, perhaps, where we can grow our own vegetables and sell them. I'll have a bit of cash when the war's over, from my gratuity. We could afford to buy a plot of land and a little cottage. I mean, London's no place to bring up kids, is it?'

Then he broke off, adding, 'But I don't know how you feel about that, either. Starting a family, I mean. I know it's a lot to ask.'

By way of reply, she turned towards him, putting her arms round him. 'I think it's a wonderful idea,' she said.

When he touched her, he found that she was not wearing a nightdress, and she began to unbutton his pyjamas.

'Lil, are you sure?' His excitement was mounting, but he tried to control himself. 'I mean, I wouldn't want you to think—just because it's our first night together, that you've got to—'

'I'm quite sure,' she whispered. 'I'm sure I want to, and I'm sure I love you.'

So they began to make love; her legs sliding against his, her hands exploring his strong, firm body, and her mouth upon his. Then she moved on—her lips, her tongue seemed to be everywhere, leading him from one delight to another—delights he had never known before... He met her passion and matched it, giving and receiving love.

At last they lay together, their limbs entwined, and he drew a long, breathless sigh.

'Never before...' he managed to say. 'The most wonderful—ever...'

'Yes,' she said. 'The most wonderful.' In the darkness, her voice took on a different tone as she continued, 'Mike, there's something I have to tell you. When I got the telegram, saying you were missing, I thought I'd never see you again. I thought you'd gone for ever... And after that, there was someone—'

He pulled her to him, stopping her mouth with his, silencing her. When they could speak again, he whispered: 'Three and a half years is a long time. In Italy—on the farm—there was a girl...but that's all over now, and we can begin our lives again. Starting here—starting tonight.'

By the beginning of May, it seemed obvious that peace was just around the corner. Hitler was dead in a Berlin bunker, German troops were surrendering everywhere, even the Board of Trade made a cautiously cheerful announcement: 'Until the end of May you may buy cotton bunting without coupons, provided it is red, white or blue.'

On Tuesday, 8 May, at three o'clock in the afternoon, Winston Churchill broadcast to the nation from Number 10, Downing Street:

'...*The German High Command signed the act of unconditional surrender. Hostilities will end officially at one minute after midnight tonight... Long live the cause of freedom—God save the King.*'

Connor switched off the wireless and said to Ruth, 'Better roll your sleeves up, my girl; looks like we're going to be busy.' Then he gave her a kiss. 'Cheer up! Didn't you hear what the man said? It's the end of the war!'

'Yes.' She tried to smile, explaining, 'I couldn't help thinking of all the people who won't be here to join the celebrations.'

It wasn't easy to remember them, in the middle of such a party. All over Britain, people had been waiting for this moment. Flags were brought down from attics and strung between lamp-posts, lengths of coupon-free cotton bunting decorated bomb-scarred buildings, and the sun shone down on crowds of merrymakers, singing and dancing in the streets.

'Roll out the barrel—we'll have a barrel of fun...'

The Watermen was packed with customers, and Connor and Ruth had their work cut out to serve them all. Huw and Glory managed to push their way into the crowded saloon, and offered to lend a hand. Glory was kept busy washing up glasses and making sandwiches, while Huw joined a group of amateur removal-men, trying to push the bar piano out into the street. Despite their efforts, it got jammed in the doorway, and Huw said: 'Hang on a tick. I'll go round through the public and find out what's stopping it.'

'That's all right,' called a familiar voice from outside. 'I'll give it a tug from this end. All together now—one, two, three, *heave!*'

The piano shot out suddenly, and the newcomer walked in through the door, saying cheerfully, 'Anything else you want shifted? Sergeant O'Dell reporting for duty.'

Ruth left her post behind the bar and hugged Danny. Connor followed, slapping his son on the back and exclaiming: 'What in the world are you doing here? We thought you'd be liberating Berlin by now!'

'I was one of the lucky ones. I managed to wangle a fortnight's leave. We dropped anchor at Dover at one o'clock this morning. There were no trains running, but I managed to hitch a lift most of the way, and walked the rest... Well, I wasn't going to miss a beano like this, was I?'

He greeted Huw and Glory, and kissed his grandmother, then he saw Kaff standing a little apart from the others, watching him.

'Hello, there,' he said. 'Remember me?'

'Just about,' she said. 'Welcome home.'

He was going to kiss her too, but something held him back. She had changed a lot since he saw her last; slim and lovely, she was a young woman now. Uncertainly, he shook hands with her instead, while outside a raucous gang of revellers were dancing round the pub piano, singing: *'Happy V-Day to you! Happy V-Day to you!'*

Dan looked at all the smiling faces that surrounded him, and asked: 'Where's Lil? Don't tell me she isn't here?'

Ruth explained that Lil and Mike were celebrating at the Fire Station; the AFS were having a party of their own, but they'd promised to come back to the pub later.

'I might not be here by then; I was thinking of going up West, to see the fun and games,' said Danny.

'What, all by yourself?' Smiling, Glory put her arm round Huw's waist and said, 'That's not much of a celebration!'

'Well, as a matter of fact,' Danny turned to

Kaff and added, 'I was hoping you might like to come and keep me company—unless you've made any other plans?'

Kaff's face lit up but then she looked round for Connor. 'I'm not sure. I might be wanted here, to help behind the bar.'

Glory gave her husband a nudge. 'Go on, do your stuff. You haven't forgotten how to pull a pint, have you?'

So Huw took over, and Kaff was free to go out with Dan O'Dell.

After the sun had gone down, the shadows gathered, but it was never really dark that night. All over London, lights were blazing, and the sky was crisscrossed with searchlight beams—some of them, in pairs, stabbing the darkness with gigantic V-signs.

In Piccadilly, high on a balcony outside the Criterion Theatre, a young singer raised a glass of champagne, leading the crowds in a chorus of the song that had brightened the black-out: *'I'm going to get lit up, when the lights go up in London...'*

Arm in arm, Dan and Kaff wandered through a joyful wonderland; at one point they were caught up in a triumphant conga-line, through Piccadilly and down the Mall, joining a tide that flowed toward Buckingham Palace.

As they approached the palace, the floodlights were switched on, and the whole façade was bathed in light. They walked on, and Dan put a protective arm round Kaff, but it wasn't really necessary. This was a happy crowd—they weren't going wild, they had come here to celebrate the end of a nightmare, and to give thanks.

Dan managed to find some space on the steps below Queen Victoria's statue, with a splendid view of the royal balcony, draped in crimson and fringed with gold. A few rockets exploded in the sky—no longer bringing death and destruction, but a bouquet of harmless, glittering stars. And then the King and Queen appeared, with the two Princesses; the crowd began to cheer—one continuous shout that went on and on as if it would never end, while the Royal Family smiled and waved.

Kaff turned to Dan with her eyes shining. 'They're waving at us,' she said, above the din. 'The King and Queen—they look like they're pleased to see us!'

'I dare say they're glad we're still here,' said Dan.

She said something else he couldn't quite catch, and he bent his head closer. She put her lips to his ear, and he heard her say softly, 'I'm glad you're still here...'

'I'm glad too,' he said—and then he kissed her.

It was the first time, but not the last.

When the Watermen closed its doors, it was nearly midnight.

Mary O'Dell was very happy, but she looked tired, and although she offered to stay and help clear up, they told her she must go to bed.

Lil and Mike made a start, collecting dirty glasses and washing up. Huw and Glory joined

586

them, but when Connor and Ruth were about to pitch in, Glory said, 'Don't be daft. It's time you two had a break. You've been on the go all day.'

As Connor started to argue, Huw said with a twinkle in his eye: 'You're not wanted here, Mr O'Dell. We don't need you tonight.'

'You cheeky devil,' roared Connor, but Lil broke in: 'He's quite right, Dad. You and Mum have been cooped up indoors all day. Take her out for a breath of air before bedtime.'

Mike agreed. 'There'll be street parties going on till all hours. Off you go and enjoy yourselves. We'll clear up while you're gone.'

Connor looked at Ruth. 'What d'you say? Do we take them at their word?'

'We don't have much choice,' said Ruth. 'We're out-numbered.' She threw a coat round her shoulders, and they went out together.

It was turning chilly now, but they did not notice it; the night air was fresh and sweet after the smoky fug of the saloon. Mike was right. There were still bands of revellers in the streets, and on some of the derelict sites, people were dancing round bonfires.

But they weren't in the mood for any more festivity, and they walked on towards the quiet, open spaces of the Jubilee Wharf, where the calm waters reflected the searchlights on the horizon, with an occasional splash of colour as a late firework blossomed in the sky.

'I wonder where Dan and Kaff are,' said Ruth. 'And what they're doing.'

'They'll be enjoying themselves, wherever

they are,' Connor told her. 'Why wouldn't they be?'

'I just hope Kaff doesn't get hurt. She's really serious about Dan—you know that, don't you?'

'From the way he looked at her this afternoon, I've a notion he's more than halfway serious himself,' said Connor. 'Would you mind, if they try to make a go of it?'

'Of course I wouldn't mind. Only I can't help being a little afraid, too. It won't be easy for them.'

'When has it ever been easy, for any of us?'

They stopped by the harbour wall, listening to the peaceful lapping of the waves against the brickwork. Very faintly, they could still hear the sound of merrymaking, but in the vast emptiness of the Island, it seemed insignificant. Ruth felt for Connor's hand, and held it tightly.

'Some people seem to think now the war's over, everything's going to be the same as it was before—but it won't, will it?' she asked.

'Nothing can ever be the same,' he said. 'People come and go—things are changing all the time.'

'That reminds me. I saw Florrie for a minute, this evening. She'll be leaving the Island as well, before long. Tom and Maudie have invited her to go and stay with them in America; they've sent her the money for her fare.'

'Good for them,' grunted Connor. 'Though I'd sooner stay here, myself'

'So would I,' said Ruth. 'If people keep going away like this, what's going to happen to the Island?'

Sounds carried a long way upon the water, and from very far off they could just hear the chimes of Big Ben, and the slow, deliberate strokes of midnight. As the last note died away, all the ships in the docks and on the river began to sound their hooters; three short blasts, followed by one long one—'V' in the morse code—'V' for Victory. The war was over.

Connor lifted his head and stood listening. When it was quiet again, he answered her question.

'I dare say the old place will go on changing, over the years,' he said. 'But whatever happens, there'll always be Islanders living here—people like us. And the Island will be here, for ever and ever...Amen.'

This Large Print Book for the Partially sighted, who cannot read normal print, is published under the auspices of

THE ULVERSCROFT FOUNDATION